The Forbidden Chapters

Part 1

AFTERLIFE SAGA

By
Stephanie Hudson

Copyright

This ebook is copyright material and must not be copied, reproduced, transferred, distributed, leased, licensed or publicly performed or used in any way except as specifically permitted in writing by the author, as allowed under terms and conditions under which it was purchased or as strictly permitted by applicable copyright law. Any unauthorised distribution or use of this text may be a direct infringement of the author's rights and those responsible may be liable in law accordingly.

Copyright © 2016 Stephanie Hudson
All rights reserved.
ISBN: 9781980313502

This book is a work of fiction. Names, characters, places and incidents are either a product of the author's imagination or are used fictitiously. Any resemblance to actual people living or dead, events or locales is entirely coincidental.

Cover design by: © Blake Hudson Designs

Warning!

This is not the next book in the saga!
It is simply an extra.
Also…

This book contains explicit sexual content, some graphic language and a highly additive Alpha Male.

This book has been written by an UK Author with a mad sense of humour. Which means the following story contains a mixture of Northern English slang, dialect, regional colloquialisms and other quirky spellings that have been intentionally included to make the story and dialogue more realistic for modern day characters.

Thanks for reading

Books by Stephanie Hudson

Afterlife Saga

Book 1 - Afterlife
Book 2 - The Two Kings
Book 3 - The Triple Goddess
Book 4 - The Quarter Moon
Book 5 - The Pentagram Child /Part 1
Book 5 - The Pentagram Child /Part 2
Book 6 - The Cult of the Hexad
Book 7 - Sacrifice of the Septimus /Part 1
Book 7 - Sacrifice of the Septimus /Part 2
Book 8 - Blood of the Infinity War

Afterlife Spin offs and Extras

Afterlife's the Forbidden Chapters - Part 1

Afterlife Chronicles:

The Glass Dagger – Book 1
(The first in an Afterlife Young Adult Series)

Children's Books:

Marching to a Royal Beat.

About the Author

Stephanie Hudson has dreamed of being a writer ever since her obsession with reading books at an early age. What first became a quest to overcome the boundaries set against her in the form of dyslexia has turned into a life's dream. She first started writing in the form of poetry and soon found a taste for horror and romance. Afterlife is her first book in the series of seven, with the story of Keira and Draven becoming ever more complicated in a world that sets them miles apart.

When not writing, Stephanie enjoys spending time with her loving family and friends, chatting for hours with her biggest fan, her sister Cathy who is utterly obsessed with one gorgeous Dominic Draven. And of course, spending as much time with her supportive partner and personal muse Blake who is there for me no matter what.

My Love and devotion is to all my wonderful fans that keep me going into the wee hours of the night but foremost to my wonderful daughter Ava...who yes, is named after a cool, kick ass, Demonic bird and my son Jack, who is a little hero.

Afterlife Saga is going to be 11 books in total with a spin off series soon to come, starting first with Vincent's story.

CHAPTERS BOOK
Intro.

First, I would like to thank all the Fans out there, who made this book possible. Without you asking to read these chapters they would still be stored away on my dusty old laptop, unseen and unread.

So, thank you for requesting their release into the world.

I can only hope that they don't disappoint.

I thought it best to start this book by explaining what it's all about and the concept behind it. When I first started writing this massive saga I had no idea it would be so big. I knew the story from start to finish, which I will call the spine but it's all the middle bits, the flesh, that I had no idea would become so huge. And although you can try and plan these things out, writing to me is what I like to call, an organic process. Sometimes, things just feel right and I end up riding the Afterlife wave and seeing where it takes me.

Other times however, it ends up leading me to a place I don't want to be or getting me there sooner than I would like. So, I ended up re-writing the chapter or sometimes cutting it out altogether. This breaks my heart a little as a lot of it was fun to write. Hence why I could never bring myself to cast it into the abyss I call 'Cyber Death' or better known as 'Delete World'.

No, instead I squirreled them away like a dirty secret I am now happy to release onto the world as a collection, hopefully for you to enjoy. In this Volume, you will find all the 'Secret Pages' from Afterlife, The Two kings and The Triple Goddess. The next Volume will contain all the ones from the rest of the saga, something that will be released after the last book is out for obvious reasons.

So just to explain how this book works, some of these chapters you will recognise parts of, as they were pieces used in the original books. I have added these in so that you know where in the story we are up to. But for those of you who don't want to go over old ground, I have created a break and added the word '**NEW**' so that they can be found easily.

But mainly this book is a collection of whole new chapters for you to enjoy that I have added **'Author's Insight'**, (that's me) to explain some of the craziness that was going through my head at the time and reasons for the Chapters being 'Cut'.

But don't worry if you want to skip right to the good bits, instead of reading me waffling on, I won't take it personally... ;)

Right well without further ado I give you...

THE LOST CHAPTERS OF AFTERLIFE...

AUTHOR INSIGHT.

BOOK 1
Afterlife

First, we start off where it all began…

Now you will find that a large portion of this book is taken up with 'Forbidden chapters' from book 1 and the reasons for this are most probably down to it being my first book. I was torn a lot of the time in which direction to go down as I knew part of the strength of the story was the anticipation in getting our two lovers together.

However, I would still find myself impatient enough to write this union sooner than I knew I should. In truth, there were many ways that I wanted the important factors of this story to happen, but with my imagination running wild, it was hard to choose. In the end, I presented the world with the version I felt was best and preferred personally.

To be perfectly honest the story came from a series of dreams (Very, very nice dreams, wink, wink, nudge, nudge.) But as I had no experience writing anything before, I did so as more of a personal venture than thinking it possible to ever be published one day.

Thankfully, I made the brave decision to put myself out there and what we have now is seven years on from this point and the end of the saga is near.

However, book 1 will always have a most special place in my heart as it was not only the start of Keira's epic journey but also the start of my own.

AUTHOR INSIGHT.

Chapter 20
Book I

In these next chapters, we see what life working in the VIP for Keira is really like, as my original plan was to have a few chapters that showed how Keira adapted to her new job. However, in the end I thought it took you from the flow of the story, so decided to have a rethink. That night I had a dream of Draven driving Keira back to her home after she hit her head in an accident. After this, it occurred to me that this would be the perfect opportunity for her to find the abandoned cabin.

This was done so that the reader could identify with a place where I always intended to have the big fight scene at the end. I think it worked better this way but this meant that the concern Draven first shows at Keira hurting herself would have been overshadowed by her hitting her head.

And really, just how many times can a girl hurt herself before she is classed as a hazard to be around ;)

So, this next chapter should have been chapter 20 in the book. Now the other reason I chose to cut this chapter is because of what Keira is asked to do in it. After only a week, she finds Sophia asking her to do what she thinks is an impossible task. This includes being close to Draven at the top table and meeting his council for the first time. I loved the way this chapter went but in the end, I also wanted to make a bigger deal of her being at his table for the first time. Along with this I also wanted it to be when they had finally got together as a couple and to be introduced to everyone for that reason.

But I think you will agree with me, it's a sweet few chapters showing Draven's softer side when Keira thought he didn't have one...not unless he was in her dreams anyway. So here is the first part for you to enjoy ...

Book 1

20
Not a Request.

NEW…

After my first shift in the VIP things strangely started to resemble normality. Yes okay, admittedly I was still working in a place that wasn't surround by the usual types you would have found in a VIP area of a nightclub. There were no businessmen toasting the success of a new business venture. There were no designer wearing celebrities or rich playboy types with scantily dressed beauties draped over them. There wasn't even a single group that seemed to be there of their own accord, like a party or anything. No, strangely everyone in the room seemed to be there for one purpose only and that was to see the man who owned the room…*literally.*

The whole room and everyone in it seemed to be centred around the man seated above the rest, and what a man at that. Draven wasn't exactly your typical 'centre of attention' type you would have expected from a man who owned all around him. He didn't move from his seat and 'work' the room, as most businessmen would be expected to do. In fact, in the whole week I had been working the VIP, I don't think I saw him even once approach another table, let alone speak to someone from it.

It was a bit confusing to be honest, as there wasn't even a hint of what he was doing there. He didn't exactly look as though he was living it up and having the time of his life every night, that was for damn sure. Nor did he look to be having a business meeting with the people sat at his table. But most importantly, well for me personally, I never saw him framed by a couple of beauties on each arm. Something I had to admit, I was most thankful for. And it wasn't as if the choices were lacking as there were enough females dotted around the room to take anyone's fancy.

No, the only people that I ever saw sitting next to him was his brother, Vincent and sister, the fabulous Sophia. And at least I had one person who seemed happy to see me whenever I turned up for my shift. Well, Karmun was always nice to me but he seemed like the type of guy that would have been nice even if my dragon of a Maths Teacher had turned up to wait tables. Speaking of which, this was something I was finally allowed to do after my first night.

Even though I was given the quietest section it was still a step up from collecting glasses. And even after I first approached the table as though they were going to eat me, they quickly put me at ease and seemed really friendly. They even asked my name and in return told me theirs. This was nice and welcoming but on the other hand I really hoped they weren't expecting me to repeat them back at any point as most I couldn't even say, let alone remember. One of them sounded like you needed a mouth full of water to even pronounce it, as I swear it was gargled.

But overall, it seemed quite normal, other than trying to condition myself not to keep looking longingly over at the living God that sat there like a king surrounded by his entourage. I tried, I really did but it was as though something in my head just snapped. I was drawn to him in a way that was bordering on the ridiculous and already beyond the realms of obsession. Each night I would watch the time ticking down far too quickly and the same thing would happen.

My palms would sweat and I found my heartbeat would kick up a notch because two things would happen. The first was that I would cruelly convince myself that tonight was the night like the first, he would approach me and we would actually have our first official conversation. And the second would be the only definite thing that I had to hold on to. Because there was only one way I could walk out of there and that was past his table. The second night I did so trying not to look but thanks to Sophia, it didn't play out this way. Thinking about it, it never turned out this way as every night I walked past she would shout my name.

My reaction was the same every time. I would blush, bite my lip and look up enough to give her a little wave allowing my eyes to meet Draven's for a split second. But the look of disdain I would receive back had me lowering my head quickly so that it could barely be classed as a look at all. I didn't know what his problem was with me, but he was making it perfectly clear, that was for damn sure!

Some nights at home in my bed, doing something mundane like brushing my hair, I would be free to daydream it went differently. At first it was just a simple smile or even a wink as I walked by, but then my imagination would get the better of me and that wink would morph into him pointing a finger my way. I would do the whole 'looking around dramatically and mouthing the words, 'who me?' back at him'. Then with a brief nod he would motion me to come to him with his finger, pointing it then to his side.

Of course, I would go to him and once there he would hand me a drink and ask me to join them. This was the part of the fantasy that usually turned slightly sexual as there was never a seat empty for me so it meant me sitting on his lap. Once there, his hand would wander but looking at his stern face you never would have suspected. I would gasp and wriggle against him, feeling the evidence for myself what he would rather be doing. Usually, it would just end there with him whispering a single word in my ear...*Mine.*

But then on a rare occasion he would tip my head back, pulling it slightly to the side so that he could look at me. His fingers would linger by my cheek before pushing them back through my hair, gripping it tightly in his hand before crushing his lips to mine. Then I would get lost in his kiss, uncaring about the room full of people watching us. I found myself asking how I knew his kiss would be dominating the way I always pictured it.

Actually, that wasn't completely true as the answer was blatantly obvious with just one look at the man. And tonight was no different. He wore a tailored navy, three-piece suit, white shirt and blue tie looking as though he was born to wear it. But he also had that old-world warrior look about him. You could just see him wielding a sword fitting better in his hand than that of a briefcase. Personally, I didn't know which side of him I found sexier.

I reached the bar, placed down my empty glasses, and released a sigh I didn't release I was holding on to until a voice spoke.

"Surely, it's not that bad, unless you're thinking about History class today that is." I smiled and turned to face Sophia.

"Well it was brutal, and that's just Reed with his assignments, not the French Revolution we were being lectured on." Sophia laughed and she could have brought men to their knees with just one wink, given the way she looked. She wore an A-line halter neck dress patterned in big black, lace flowers covered in shimmering sequins. Her hair was swept back to one side in a loose bun with a few curls escaping, and her makeup was classic sixties style, with large black eyeliner flicks over each eye.

Cute sandal heels completed the look. My look however, was as far from glamourous as you could get. No, tonight I was rocking the hired help look, with black trousers and a black top that had long, wide sleeves. It had a scooped neckline that showed only a hint of the ample breast size I was hiding beneath it. To be honest, other than a plain black shirt that tied at the back, it was the only other smart top I owned. However, wearing this meant a hot night for me as thanks to the bell sleeves I had no choice but to wear my fingerless gloves underneath for fear that someone would notice my scars.

As always, my long hair was tied back in a twist with the shorter bits framing my face, bits that I constantly would push behind my ears. Something that I found myself doing right now.

"Looks like a quiet night," Sophia said nodding to my half empty section.

"Yeah, it is, I guess that…Uh, Sophia?" My intended sentence trailed off and ended with a question thanks to the smirk she was giving me.

"We are a girl down at our table, so I was wondering if you wouldn't mind filling in," she said looking back over her shoulder at the top table, and the source of my main focus in life. I looked to Draven and it was as if he knew because he turned his head to us both at the bar. Then he knocked his drink back in one and turned his harsh stare elsewhere.

"Uh…I don't think that's such a good idea," I told her, keeping my response mellow, not the screaming and freaking out I felt myself doing inside.

"Sure it is," Sophia said smiling and I choked on a laugh.

"That look said anything but. Trust me on this one Sophia, I think the last person your brother wants to see working his table is me," I told her honestly and hated the wobble in my voice for how much the truth hurt.

"That couldn't be further from the truth, you can trust me on that," she told me and my look said it all, because now she was laughing. She nudged me and said,

"Come on, what's the worst that could happen?"

"I could get fired," I told her and this time she really laughed, as in the kind that just bursts from someone unexpectedly. To be honest I didn't see what she had found so funny.

"Besides, I really think one of the other girls would be better suited."

"Why?" she asked affronted, as though I was insulting myself or something.

"Well for starters, they have been here a lot longer than I have and your brother obviously doesn't hate them," I told her glancing a look at him to see him ordering a drink from the other waitress, Lauren. It looked like the bitchy one was missing for the night. Couldn't say I was disappointed as it made a change from getting scowled at every time our paths crossed.

"My brother doesn't hate you, come on, you will see. Karmun, Keira is working the top table tonight. Get her a bottle of bubbles on ice to carry over." Karmun gave her a look of disbelief, similar to my own, only his didn't last as long, as mine still hadn't left me yet.

"Sophia, I can't..." I started to say before she could walk away but she interrupted me by taking a step closer to me so that she could pat my cheek twice, whilst informing,

"Don't worry, he won't bite you." Then she laughed and walked away with a natural born swagger. I, on the other hand, was left looking about as graceful as a damn guppy. In fact, it was only Karmun clearing his throat that made me realise that I still had my mouth open in shock.

"Uh...did that really happen?" I asked to the bar resting both hands on its top so that I wouldn't crumble to the ground like I wanted to. Only we were on the top floor, so I doubted I had much chance of it swallowing me whole like I was hoping.

"Afraid so, honey…here you go," he added pushing something to me and I looked up to see an elaborate looking cut glass, black ice bucket with an expensive bottle of champagne sticking out from the folded white cloth. Then I looked up at Karmun and he said,

"Good luck." I swallowed hard and straightened my back and muttered,

"God help me" as I turned around and faced my worst nightmare yet…

Draven's Table.

BOOK I

21
Shattered Peace.

NEW...

'Okay so I can do this. I can do this...I can't do this!' I said to myself turning around once only to have to turn back to the table, knowing there was no way out of it. I loved Sophia, but right now I just wanted to dump the bottle, tap her on the back and shout, 'see you in class' as I legged it to the door. Yes, that would have been the smart thing to do. Not walking up to the table as I was currently doing, trying to stop myself from shaking like a leaf. You could hear the tapping of the ice water clinking against the glass cooler.

So, I did the unthinkable, wishing I was back in my room and daydreaming about acting this out cooler unlike the shrinking violet act I was currently playing out as I stepped nervously up onto the dais. There I was joined by Lauren who smiled warmly at me and thankfully it helped calm my nerves.

"Oh goodie, time for bubbles of my favourite kind, thank you Keira." Sophia said and Draven's head shot to where Lauren was stood with the extra addition... *me*. I bit my lip and looked away first as the look of disdain he gave me was crushing. It was so bad I almost felt like weeping like a little girl who had been caught stealing cookies.

Lauren touched my hand getting my attention and making me jump. I looked to her and she mouthed the word 'glasses' at me and then nodded back to the bar. Whilst this happened, Draven turned his attention back to the culprit and snapped,

"Explain yourself, Sophia." I saw Sophia roll her eyes and say,

"Oh relax, she is only serving us drinks and besides, I thought it would be a good opportunity for her to see you as something other than a grumpy asshole," she said and I nearly gasped out loud as I passed. I know that she was his sister but she definitely had balls bigger than most!

"End it!" he demanded.

"No and neither will you. For fuck sake Dom, she is near terrified of you, is that really what you want?" Sophia said and the heat of embarrassment flushed across my cheeks. I didn't hear his reply but instead almost ran to get their glasses, then I was so outta there. I would give them to Lauren and then make up some excuse about not feeling well.

"Here you go, honey, all ready for you," Karmun said and then saw my face which must have said a lot more than I wanted it to.

"Hey, are you alright?" I looked back to Draven when Karmun asked this to find him looking at me. It also didn't take a genius to know when Sophia hit him on the arm what she said to him, trying to prove her point.

"Yeah, I will be. Goodnight, Karmun." I told him, making him frown in confusion but I didn't elaborate. I just picked up the tray and tried to walk back over there with my back straight and this time my hands steady. I was too far gone to care what he thought of me anymore. Hell, it wasn't like he wasn't making it obvious he didn't like me, the only answer I wanted to know was why?

"Ah here she is, a glass would be lovely," Sophia said pretending nothing had happened and I placed the tray down on a small round table used for such things. Then I turned to face Sophia and just started to make my excuses,

"Sophia I'm sorry but I can't..." Just then Lauren popped the bottle, startling me. Then I watched as she was just about to pour the first drink when Draven's hand came up, stopping her.

"Go and help Karmun with orders..." Draven said and I thought he was talking to me but when he turned around to face us, he looked to Lauren and finished his sentence,

"Keira is going to serve us tonight."

"Yes, My L..." Lauren was about to call him something but with a slight shake of his head, she stopped and nodded instead. Then she walked past me, giving me a beaming grin and a wink to match.

"I'll take one also, sweetheart." Hearing this new voice, I looked almost dumbstruck to Draven's handsome brother who looked like some casually dressed angelic model. I swallowed down the hard lump of uncertainty and grabbed a glass off the tray. Then I picked up the bottle and tried to keep my hand steady as I tilted it to one side and filled it. I was about to pass it to Draven's brother first when he looked to his side, telling me I should always serve Draven first.

I gave him a small smile in thanks and like Lauren, he winked at me in return. So, I did the very last thing I thought I would be doing that night...

I served Draven his drink.

"Thank you, Keira." I almost choked when swallowing...did he really just thank me? I didn't allow myself too much time to think about it, instead I cleared my throat and whispered,

"You're welcome, Sir." Then I turned away from him and concentrated on pouring the rest of the drinks. I poured the next two for Sophia and Vincent, getting thanks from both. I then handed all the others theirs one by one, taking notice for the first time of everyone else sat

around his table. Two of the men I had seen before when Draven first entered the club, but the other two women I had only ever seen sat at this table.

Once I was done and everyone had a drink I moved back, about to walk to the bar until I was needed next. But one more step and Draven stopped me without turning in is seat. No, instead his hand went up like before, telling me not to move.

"You can wait here by the table. Lauren will know if you need anything."

"Oh...okay," I said feeling the need to answer him. Well at least this wasn't snapped out, so who knows, maybe we were making progress. Sophia looked side on, watching us with a slight smirk and before I could retreat further she spoke up.

"But how rude of me, let's introduce you to the table...brother?" Sophia said turning to face Draven rolling her hand out at him, expectantly. He turned to look at her and raised an eyebrow, a look she just rolled her eyes at before nudging him, urging him on. I didn't quite get what was going on between these two but something must have worked because Draven cleared his throat.

"Keira, this is my council, to my left you have Takeshi and Zagan." Each of them nodded to me and in return I gave them a shy little nod back. Zagan was the name of the Albino who, once he smiled at me, didn't look half as terrifying. The Japanese man however always looked kind and gracious.

"And to my right is Aurora and Celina," he said and I looked to see there wasn't an ounce of kindness coming from the blonde, Aurora, who simply looked bored. The redhead Celina at least smiled.

"This is my brother Vincent and of course my sister Sophia you know from school."

"Hello everyone," I said giving the group a little wave and feeling stupid whilst doing it.

"Well isn't this just precious, tell me Dom, will we be introducing ourselves for all the hired help or is she just a special case?" Aurora asked callously.

"Oh yes, that would be a problem for a stuck-up bitch like you, wouldn't it?" Sophia snapped and in that moment, I would have loved to have been stood by her side giving her a high five. But in reality, I just bit my lip and kept my mouth shut.

"May I remind you, she is serving us drinks for a reason, so I see no need to lower myself in..."

"Enough!" Draven suddenly shouted banging a hand down on the table, silencing the room.

"Keira is my sister's friend and you Aurora, will be respectful of that whether she is serving you drinks or here drinking with us...do you understand?" Draven demanded firmly and this time I actually did think that I was dreaming. Did Draven just stick up for me? And more importantly, did he just say that I might be drinking with them?

"Drinking with us?!" she said sounding outraged, and other than the outraged bit, I had been tempted to ask the same thing in the same stunned tone.

"I asked if you understood, not if you could repeat me," he said glaring at her.

"Yes, I understand," she snapped back finally relenting.

"Good, then I suggest you keep your thoughts to yourself in future," Draven added before swigging back the rest of his drink. Sophia's smirk reached new heights as she too sipped her drink, looking like the cat that got the cream. I, on the other hand, didn't know whether I was coming or going! Did this mean he liked me, hated me or just tolerated me for Sophia's sake?

I was still playing out this conundrum when the sound of someone clearing their throat brought me back to the room. I looked towards Vincent who was kindly alerting me to the fact that Draven's glass was empty.

Why, oh why, did he have to drink it so fast. I gave Vincent a nod of thanks before grabbing the bottle and stepping up to Draven's side. I wished I could stop myself from shaking the way I did and hated feeling like some kind of skittish doe in the sights of a hunter.

He saw me approach and held up his glass for me. I went to take it but he never let it go, obviously expecting me to fill it right next to him. I was sure the hard lump I swallowed could have been heard across the room as it certainly seemed to echo in my mind. He didn't look at me but instead looked to his side in a motion that indicated why I hadn't yet filled it. So, I bit my lip and started.

"Sorry," I muttered shamefully as I couldn't help the bottle rim clinking on the side of the glass as my hand continued to shake. At first, I wasn't sure he had even heard me but once it was filled he placed it down in front of him and then motioned for me to come closer. Confused, I took the last step I possibly could, putting myself flush with his side, but this didn't seem enough.

"Come here," he ordered retracting two fingers, telling me to lean closer, so that he could tell me something. I took a deep breath and held it tight in my lungs as I did as I was told. I had to place my hand on the table in front of him just to steady myself. He was so close now that I knew if I would only allow myself to breathe then I would take in his intoxicating scent. Then he placed a hand over mine and that breath I was holding came out in a whoosh before he said only one word,

"Relax." Then he squeezed my hand once before letting it go. This was my cue to leave and all without muttering a single word back. So, I straightened myself up, stepped back, grabbed the bottle and asked in a strained, high-pitched voice,

"Top up anyone?" Sophia burst out laughing and said,

"Always."

After this encouragement from Draven, I found myself doing as he had asked and managed to relax a little. So, because of this, the rest of the night continued down a smoother path. The next shocking thing that came from Draven happened about an hour later. I had just been handed a bottle of expensive looking whiskey. It had the name 'The Dalmore' under a golden stag's head and I nearly choked when I saw the age was 46 years. I dreaded to think how much this single bottle alone cost and decided it was too much of a risk for someone like me.

Draven must have sensed my hesitation, that or he was getting impatient.

"Is there a problem, Keira?" he queried, this time looking over his shoulder to see me looking down at the expensive bottle as if it would explode if I touched it. I first looked to him and then at the rest of the table, thankfully finding no-one but him looking. Although Vincent seemed to be listening.

"I...uh...it looks expensive," I said after clearing my throat but the panic was probably clear to hear.

"It is fine," Draven said, waving it off as if my fears were unfounded.

"But I..." I started to say what I thought he needed to know before he let me loose on something of this magnitude. I mean what if it was $200 a bottle or something?! So, I made the decision to step closer to him, which seemed to take him by surprise. Then I leaned in close and quietly told him the embarrassing truth.

"I don't mind serving you...Uh, I mean it...! The drink that is." Great start, Keira. I felt like taking a moment to slap my forehead and his smirk said that he knew it.

"But?" he enquired.

"Well I think you should know that I am clumsy and I would hate to drop it or something and when I say clumsy, I mean on like an epic scale...So maybe I should get Lauren to..." Draven cut off my rambling and said,

"Keira, you are overthinking this. It is not that expensive, so I am sure you will be fine." I bit my lip and nodded, deciding to take his word for it. So, I turned around but I swear when I did I was sure I heard him chuckle. I frowned at the table and just then Lauren turned up with a tray of cool iced glasses. Inside each one was a small cut glass frosted mountain. It not only looked cool once the whiskey was poured over it, but it helped to keep the drink cold without watering it down.

Once I had poured four, I handed them out to the men who wanted them, as the women preferred to continue with champagne. I handed Draven his first and then received a thank you from each but it was the one that I received from Draven that meant the most.

"Mmm, gotta love the good stuff, smooth as silk," Zagan said smirking at Sophia who he was sat next to. I had to say that being this close to the table, you could certainly tell they had a thing for each other. Flirting wasn't even the right word for it!

"Yes, well for $215,000 a bottle you should hope it tastes good." I heard Draven groan aloud just as my mouth dropped. Of course, being me, this wasn't the only thing that fell as the bottle slipped out of my hand and headed for the floor. My hands flew to my mouth just as Draven's seriously fast reactions saved the bottle. This before it could smash along the floor, scattering like diamonds, for how expensive it was.

"Oh, my god! I am so, so sorry, I didn't..." I said rambling and flinging my arm out, managing to fling his glass onto the floor instead, this time smashing it. I cringed, closing my eyes tight as if this would help with the shame. I counted to three and then with tight lips, looked at him to see that thankfully he didn't look angry.

"Now, I am really sorry!" I said quickly bending down to start picking up the pieces.

"Keira please, it is fine but leave it alone before you..."

"Oww..." Too late I thought as one of the pieces sliced into my palm, getting stuck there.

"Keira?" Draven said my name in question and suddenly my shame was mounting.

"Oh, it's nothing but let me just go and get something to clean this up with. I will be right back...just, uh...nobody move or the glass might...um yeah, I will be back..." I got up quickly and started to move away before anyone could see the blood dripping down my hand and onto the floor. Then I quickly rushed over to the bar, holding my hand in front of me, trying to contain the blood in my palm. Holy Hell, it stung like a wasp with a machete!

"What happened?" Karmun asked referring to the sound of broken glass, before seeing my hand, as I kept it from sight.

"I happened," I said with a sigh and then elaborated.

"I broke a glass. Do you have a cloth and a dustpan and brush?" I asked him.

"Yeah sure I..." A sight cut him off as his eyes moved over me to whatever was behind. I was just turning around when I heard Lauren say,

"Hey, what happened to your hand?" And then I came face to face with Draven. He first looked at my face, scowled, then looked down at my hand that was cupping an overflowing palm full of blood. I didn't think of what I was saying but just blurted out,

"It's just a scratch." His raised eyebrow said it all.

"Clean cloth," he ordered over my head to Karmun.

"Lauren, go down to the main club, they should have a first aid kit behind the bar. Bring it to my office."

"Yes sir." she said bending slightly that looked half nod, half bow. Then Draven stepped closer and caught the cloth in his hand without even looking. Wow, he had skills, it had to be said.

"Honestly it's really not that..." I started to speak, reassuring him when he growled down at me, stunning me into silence. Then he issued me a warning.

"If you're about to tell me that having you bleeding in front of me is 'fine' or 'not that bad' then I will stop you now before you find yourself really in trouble...now put that on your hand and come with me," he commanded and I found I couldn't disobey as he handed me the cloth to place over my hand. His voice sounded strained, as if he was fighting with himself on some level. In the end, I took his advice and remained silent as I followed him past the bar. But that was until I saw where we were headed.

"Umm...I was told not to go through there," I told him falling behind a step at the sight of the huge doors at the back of the room. Doors I had been specifically warned against. He was just within reach of the doors before he looked back over his shoulder at me.

"Is that right?" I nodded and finally that harsh frown disappeared and something new appeared in his eyes. A light flash of purple, that must have been a glint of the club's lights below and this combined with a playful crease appeared at the corners, as he grinned. Then he said something that had my heart rate kicking up a notch at just the thought of what it could mean...

"Time to break the rules then."

22

Draven's Domain.

NEW...

"Time to break the rules then," he said and then pushed the doors open for me to follow. I looked back to Karmun who looked shocked, along with others in the VIP. In fact, I think there was only two people that didn't looked shocked and that was Vincent and Sophia.

I walked through the doors and was faced by a long wide hallway that looked as if I was stepping right into a castle.

Who the Hell were these people anyway?

There was a door at the very end along with others along the way but for some reason it was the one at the end that was drawing me closer. So much so in fact, that it was only when Draven called my name that I realised I had walked further than I should.

"Keira?"

"Oh, right, sorry...I just...um yes." I mumbled in embarrassment and walked into the door that he held open. Into a room that was obviously his office and a very grand one at that. Expensive antique artwork adorned the walls. Solid carved wooden furniture dotted about the room, which included a massive desk that was big enough that two people could have spread out across it...now where did that thought come from I wonder?

I heard the door close behind us and I jumped, alerted to the fact that the two of us were in an enclosed room alone. I felt the heat invade my cheeks again and decided to look around the room, so that I could give my face time to calm down. At the far end of the room were marble arches that led onto an enclosed veranda and the cool night air certainly helped take the blush from my cheeks.

"It's a nice room," I commented after a long period of silence.

"Umm." He made a noise that could have meant many things. He agreed, he didn't, or he couldn't give a damn, so I turned around to face him. I never expected to find him leaning casually back against his desk with his hands gripping the edge by his sides. But it wasn't his position that took me by surprise but more the way he was looking at me…watching me…analysing every move I made.

"Let's take a look at that hand, shall we?" he said giving me a slight nod of his head, telling me to go to him. Personally, I was so nervous that I would have preferred to have remained where I was. But seeing that my whole reason for being in there in the first place was this damn cut, then I could see that I didn't have much choice.

So, I walked over to him keeping my eyes on the floor until I was about three feet away.

"Are you always this shy around people, Keira or is it just when you are around me?" Draven asked bluntly making me look up at him. I was stunned by the question, certainly too stunned to answer him anyway.

"I will take your silence as my answer. Now, give me your hand." I bit my lip and did as he asked, trying not to shake. He looked down at it, the once white cloth now crimson with my blood. Then he stepped to the side and issued another order nodding to the high desk,

"Sit down."

"Sorry?" I asked confused but he just answered my question with action as he suddenly gripped my waist with both hands and lifted me up and sat me on it.

"Oh...oh okay," I muttered making him smirk as he took over and pulled the cloth slowly off my palm.

"The glass is still in there?" he questioned, not if it was because he could see plainly that it was, but more as to *why* it was.

"I was going to pull it out, I was just working myself up to doing it." I told him sounding like a wimp.

"Then allow me," he said and I tensed up, waiting for the pain. He held my hand in his, making sure I wouldn't yank it back. Then he was just about to pull it out when a knock at the door made me scream.

"Easy," he said reassuring me before answering whoever stood the other side of the door, not once taking his eyes off me.

"Enter."

Lauren walked in carrying a green case, a bowl and a bottle of water. She silently placed the items down on the desk next to Draven, then turned to leave when I quickly blurted out,

"Thank you, Lauren," before she left. She looked back at me with shock that quickly morphed into a soft smile.

"You're very welcome, Keira." Then she left. Draven's lips looked to be fighting off a grin and I decided to be brave,

"What?"

"People like you." It wasn't so much a question but more like an observation.

"I...uh...I guess so," I said not knowing how to answer that at first.

"My sister thinks I scare you," he said shocking me. I looked up at him and the second our eyes locked he pulled the glass shard out of my palm, making me wince.

"Oww!" I grumbled making him chuckle.

"You did that on purpose," I said feeling cheated and with it forgetting that I was talking to my boss…*my very intimidating boss.*

"Baby," he teased, looking at my hand but then raised his eyes to mine for a second and my breath caught on a hitch. Hearing the way he said this, well then, I just knew it would end up starring in the next months' worth of fantasies about him. I bit my lip because of it, his gaze followed the action and the teasing look changed to another…*want.*

It only lasted a second but it was enough to confuse the hell out of me and ask myself if what I had seen had been right?

"Now let's see what the damage is," he said stepping closer into me and my natural reaction was to open my legs to allow him to do this. Wait, but was that him swallowing hard I just saw or only my imagination kicking in? I think he purposely tried to ignore the action and instead busied himself by opening up the green bag. He then ripped open a few pads of sterile gauze and placed the white squares onto my palm.

"We need to stop the bleeding. Hold these here and raise your arm above your head," he said raising my arm up as he spoke.

"Umm…you seem to know what you're doing.," I told him, once again questioning in my mind who this guy really was.

"Let's just say it's a skill I acquired." I laughed once.

"Have many clumsy waitresses working for you, do you?" I joked and he gave me a small grin as he continued to get out all the things he would need to 'fix me up'.

"Just the one," he added, this time making me smile.

"Well don't say I didn't warn you" I teased and for a moment I forgot all about how much he intimidated me. I forgot he was my boss. I forgot how insecure he made me feel and even how scared I had been around him.

"Keep it up," he told me looking side on and noticing my arm had dropped.

"Oh, yeah...sorry." And there it was, my shyness back. Well it was nice whilst it lasted. Once he had everything he needed he turned back to me and started rolling up his sleeves when he nodded to my arm.

"Do you find it cold in my club, Keira?" he asked and I frowned, not understanding the reason behind the question. Then I realised where he was looking and to my horror found my long fingerless glove on show, thanks to my wide sleeve that had gathered around my shoulder.

"I...uh...have bad circulation," I said, telling him the same excuse I told everyone else. He raised an eyebrow at me, telling me silently that he thought I was full of shit.

"Well if that is the case, I think taking it off now for a few minutes won't cause any lasting damage," he said now confirming with words that he didn't believe me.

"I...well, can we not do this with it on? I really like my gloves," I said trying for a new angle.

"Even blood-soaked ones?" he tested and I looked to see he was right, they were soaked with blood all the way up past my wrist. I started to look panicked and he could see it.

"Hey, it's fine okay. Relax, I just need to get to the palm," he said in a soothing voice before bringing my hand down again now that the bleeding seemed to have stopped. Then using both hands, one to hold me steady and the other he used to fold back the glove gently, slipping my thumb out of it.

"Please I..." I started to say as he folded it to my wrist, where I knew my first scar was.

"Look at me." I did as I was told and his features softened at the sight of my inner turmoil.

"Just to here, okay," he said leaving it exposing only my hand and nothing else. I nodded, swallowing down my stress and taking a deep breath.

"Now let's see how bad it is," he warned pulling the gauze away and I hissed with pain.

"This looks quite deep, you might need stitches," he said and I shook my head.

"No, no, I can't..." I tried to find a good excuse.

"What is it?" he asked as I shook my head again before looking up at him and told him the truth.

"I don't like hospitals." He gave me a small smile and said,

"I don't think anyone *likes* hospitals, Keira," he said missing the point. So, I gripped his arm, gave it a squeeze, and said in a more serious tone,

"I mean, I *really* don't like hospitals." Then I sadly nodded down at my concealed arm, hoping this time he would get it...*he did.*

"Ah, I see. Well in that case, let's wash it and see what we can do." I nodded hoping a trip to the ER wasn't on the cards.

Then he nodded to the bowl of water. So, I got off the desk, with his help and turned around to face the desk. I was just about to dunk my hand in when he stopped me.

"Here, allow me." I sucked in a jagged breath when I felt his arms come from behind me, hugging me to get closer to my hands. Thanks to his size and him being over a foot taller than me, he had no problem getting to my hands. I felt so torn in my senses because as he softly took my hand in his and began to wash it with the other, I felt the pain from the action start to melt into sexual intensity, sending my mind into sensory overload.

The feel of his hard, muscular body against my back. The soft feel of a pair of large, strong hands gently handling me. The knowledge of him being so close to me, that if I were to turn suddenly I would be in his embrace. I think I was close to panting by the time he had finished and even the sight of a crimson bowl in front of me stained with my blood, wasn't enough to dispel the hunger that was building. I wanted him like no other and after this I knew it would be too painful going back to the shadows where I had once resigned myself to staying. Looking at him from afar and memorising every detail of him, banking it away for when I was alone, safe to dream.

"Right lets...um...let's have a look, shall we?" he said having to clear his throat first and making me wonder if he had felt it too, the heat and the sexual tension between us? He turned me around and for a single moment I could believe it. His eyes gave me the slightest hint that what he was feeling mirrored my own thoughts and then in a single breath that window of opportunity was closed. Shut down as he lifted me back onto the desk and set himself back to the task of caring for me.

"Well, I think you're in luck."

"Um?" I asked thinking there was nothing lucky about not being kissed when I wanted it more than my next breath.

"Your hand," he reminded me softly as if he knew what I had been thinking.

"Really?" I asked hopeful.

"We could just put some butterfly stitches on this and it should heal nicely." I released a happy sigh and he smirked at me. Then he looked down at the first aid kit and I followed him.

"I don't suppose you have any in there handy for bleeding damsels in distress, do you?" I asked in a teasing tone.

"No, I am afraid not, my lady," he said teasing me back making me giggle.

"I just have to make a call. I will be back in a little while. Please make yourself comfortable," he added, once more helping me down. After this he walked to the door but stopped before walking through it. He looked back at me and said,

"Oh, and Keira, just for the record..." he paused for a second and strangely smiled to himself before continuing,

"You're my first bleeding damsel in distress." Then he winked at me and left. I sucked in a surprised breath and found myself mentally pinching myself to make sure I hadn't slipped into a Draven fantasy induced coma.

"Oh Jesus, Kazzy, you're in real trouble now," I said to myself deflating onto one of the sofas there. It looked like a velvet Chesterfield and I sank into it with a sigh.

"What am I gonna do now?" I asked myself, looking down at my hand, knowing that forever more this scar was going to remind me of Draven. The painful thought was that it was most likely going to be the only thing I would be left with once he left this place and me behind with it. Hell, that thought was more painful that the cut itself.

I let my head fall back against the sofa and then turned to look back at the desk where we had shared our moment…our one single moment that I knew he had felt too. But then I frowned and sat up as something on the desk caught my eye.

"That's weird," I said to no one, then got to my feet to check I was seeing it right. I walked over to the desk and picked up the antique receiver, hoping it was just there for show. I placed it to my ear and heard the dial tone as clear as day. I placed it back down slowly now asking myself one question…why did he need to leave the room to make a call if there was a phone right there on his desk?

"Do you need to make a call?" The sound of Draven's voice startled me and I dropped the receiver. It clattered to the desk with a thud and I jumped again. He calmly walked over to me, reached around me, and placed it back without taking his eyes off me.

"I told you I was clumsy," I blurted out again.

"That you did," he agreed and then nodded back to the phone, no doubt wanting an answer to his question.

"Uh, no, no, that's alright…I'm good." I told him awkwardly not wanting him to know that I had just been checking it, secretly questioning his reason for leaving the room. He raised an eyebrow at me telling me without words that he knew what I had been up to. I knew this when he pulled a mobile phone from his pocket and placed it down on the table. Of course, he had probably needed it to get a contact from his phone and I knew this when it rang.

"You have what I need?" he said answering it in a cool manner that spoke volumes of who was in charge.

"I do my L..."

"Good," he snapped quickly interrupting them mid flow. There was definitely something he was hiding as he had done the same thing with Lauren when she too had been about to call him something.

"Bring it to me," he demanded before hanging up. Hearing all this and seeing Draven back to his domineering ways I didn't know what to say. I looked down not wanting to be the next subject of his annoyance but as soon as I did this, his demeaner changed.

"How is the pain?" he asked me, gently lifting my hand for his examination.

"It's...it's okay," I muttered quietly.

"I think after all this you will deserve that drink after all," he told me, surprising me enough that my gaze shot to his just to check if he was serious or not.

"I...um..." I struggled for words and he smiled down at me.

"Come now Keira, surely you are not going to deny me the honour of buying you a drink, after all, you did shed blood in the line of duty serving me, it is the least I can do, don't you think?" he said in a teasing tone and in my mind I replied, 'A kiss would do better' but thankfully I didn't say this, even though his expression changed as though he had heard me.

"I would like that...thank you," I said shyly after first composing myself from the shock I felt. He wanted to buy me a drink! Holy shit, I felt like jumping off the desk and freaking out the only way a girl or gay diva knew how to do…silly dancing and foot stomping screeching Halleluiah!

"Come in," Draven commanded and I gave him a confused look before the door opened and in strolled Sophia.

"Oh dear, Keira!" she said running over to me and Draven took a step back to allow her to get to me without pushing him out the way.

"It's fine, just a silly accident, that's all," I told her making Draven frown.

"It looks deep," she said looking back to her brother and he nodded giving her a look I couldn't place. She gave him a slight 'no' in return and I watched on, frowning in confusion.

"Well lucky for you I brought some pain killers," she said holding up a little bottle that didn't look like any pills you would have bought from a pharmacy, not in the last fifty years at least I could imagine. It was a small brown glass bottle, with a tiny cork sticking out the top and she popped the lid and knocked a few into her hand. They were tiny and didn't look like any aspirin I had ever seen.

"Uh…that's okay, really the pain isn't that bad," I told her, not really trusting the sight of those pills. Sophia made a strange face and then looked to her brother, not doubt wanting him to intervene. He took the bottle from her and grabbed the rest of the water from the table, one I had been sure had been empty not long ago.

"The pain will hit once your adrenaline has all been spent. Trust me on this Keira, it is that or I could drive you to the hospital, it is your choice," Draven said after knocking out two more pills onto his hand. I swallowed hard and knew that even though this was blackmail, I would do anything if it meant I got out of going to hospital. So, I took the pills and the water and knocked them back in one gulp. He took the bottle and said,

"Good girl." Hearing this nearly made it all worth it and my blush told him so.

"Oh, and here is the Steri-Strips our friend brought us," Sofia said handing Draven a small package and once more conveying a look I couldn't decipher.

"Thank you. You may go back to the table now, we will be out shortly," Draven said dismissing her and she smirked when asking,

"The both of you?"

"Yes, Keira has kindly accepted my offer to buy her a drink," Draven said in return making Sophia's smug smile beam.

"I am sure she did," she replied making me turn crimson with embarrassment. She winked at me once and then left with a laugh she didn't even try to hide. I looked back to Draven and laughed nervously trying in vain to react as though her teasing about how I felt about him wasn't as obvious as she just made it.

"Now let's see what we can do with this hand of yours, shall we?" I nodded deciding it was best not to speak, this way there was less chance of further embarrassment on my part. So instead I watched as he opened a sterile package with strips of tape and find a vial of sterilizing fluid that was no doubt for cleaning my hand. He snapped the lid and poured half onto a piece of gauze, taking my hand back in his.

"This may sting," he warned before pouring the rest of the liquid onto my cut, making me hiss with pain. He ignored my reaction and instead went about wiping it clean with the gauze. For such large hands, I was once again amazed at how gentle he could be, which was made more so with the small comforting circles he was drawing on the back of my hand.

"There, all clean. Now let's get this stitched," he said giving me a look, no doubt trying to gauge how I was doing. I nodded for him to go ahead, torn between wanting to get this over with and never wanting it to end. Being here with Draven was like finally living out one of my many fantasies, minus the blood that was. But I had to admit that having Draven taking care of me this way was certainly worth the pain and I knew that the scar would be deeper on the inside that it was on the flesh.

So, I watched as he went to work in getting the stitches in the right place and for a moment I half expected him to say that it was no good and I did need to go to hospital for stitches as they were right, it did look quite deep. I was just about to ask if it was ok, when something started to happen.

"Keira, are you alright?" Draven asked me obviously noticing it for himself.

"Yeah...I think so, just...I'm starting to feel a bit funny," I told him trying to concentrate enough to get my words out in the right order. My vision started to blur slightly as I tried to focus on the man in front of me. I felt him lift my face up with a hand under my chin. Then I felt him open one eye as if trying to judge my pupil's responsiveness like a doctor would.

"Don't worry, you will be fine, sweetheart," he told me softly and I sucked in a startled breath when I could have sworn I just heard him call me 'sweetheart'. Then I felt myself falling forward into him without being able to help it.

"I'm sorry, I...I..." I tried to say as I lifted my other hand as though it was filled with lead. He took it in his and whispered down into my ear,

"Ssshh now and trust me," he said gently before moving his arms around me. It took me a good long moment to realise he was lifting me into his arms and the thought had me near panting. This time I didn't know if this was really happening or I had just passed out and was now dreaming. Well whether it was a dream or not, I felt myself being held against a strong chest with arms that secured me to him like he was protecting me against the world. I didn't know what was happening, but to me it seemed like for the longest time he didn't move but just remained still, holding me to him as if basking in the moment.

This is how I knew it had to be a dream.

"Now I can heal you the way I want to," he said cryptically and my fuzzy mind must have heard it wrong...that or it had been made up completely. I felt him place me down on what I could only assume was the sofa and he took my hand in his, sitting next to me.

"Heat," he said first and the second he said it the heat started to warm my hand as he drew a fingertip across the few stitches he had placed there. I couldn't help my reaction as my body bowed slightly as I released a moan. The heat he spoke of might have started in my hand but it quickly travelled down the rest of my body, warming my insides as if his hands were caressing my skin.

"Deep breaths for me, Keira," he told me, leaning down and whispering the command over my neck. It sent shivers down my spine and at the same time he added the next stage,

"Let's cool down that heat, shall we?" he said running another fingertip across the damaged skin on my palm. And he was right, the heat that warmed my blood soon cooled enough to send shivers down my spine for a different reason this time.

"That's enough I think." I don't know what he meant but the second he said it the cold chill that wracked my body started to subside and once more my body's core started to regulate itself.

"Wha...what's happening... to me?" I forced the words from my lips.

"A reaction to the drugs we gave you, but don't worry, nothing a little rest won't cure. Now it's time to sleep, my beauty," he told me and once again I found myself second guessing what I had just heard him call me.

"But I...can't," I told him.

"Why not?" he asked me curiously.

"Because you can't fall asleep in a dream and I am already dreaming," I told him honestly, the drugs making me say whatever came to my mind.

"Why do you think you are dreaming?" he asked and I opened my eyes and saw his purple eyes looking intensely back at me.

"Because in my dreams you are always nice to me, because in them you have purple eyes that look at me like you want to kiss me and because... *I always see you in my dreams,"* I told him and I tried to bite my lip but it slipped from my grasp as my head fell back and I fell quickly into a deep slumber. The last thing I heard before giving into the pull that I felt tugging at me, dragging me down to a place I was ready to go was Draven's voice,

Draven's confession...

"You are always in my dreams, Keira."

Book 1

23

Broken Offers.

NEW...

I woke up to find myself in a place I least expected. Now what I had expected to see was my foggy view of the national park in all its dark and moody glory. But this wasn't what I faced. No, what I faced now was the silky dark night in between the arched pillars of Draven's private office.

I sat up gingerly feeling my head as if I had some kind of hangover. What had happened? Had I really passed out and if so, what had happened to Draven? I looked down at my hand and saw that it was now bandaged up tightly and I definitely didn't remember him doing that.

I tried to swallow but it felt like the back of my throat had been replaced with sandpaper. I looked around to see if the bottle of water had any left which was when I found a fresh bottle on a small table next to the sofa. I could have sworn that it hadn't been there before when I had sat down, so had Draven put it there so I would find the water. Either way I was more than grateful for it as my hands shook trying to get the lid off quickly.

This was when I noticed the note...

Keira,

You fell asleep so I left you to get some rest but when you wake I would be pleased if you would be so kind and join me for a drink at my table.

D. Draven.

I read it again and again and then couldn't help finishing by lifting it to my nose, to see if I could get even a hint of his scent that he might have left on the simple page. There was something but it wasn't enough...*it would never be enough.*

I decided to get up and do as he had asked, joining him for a drink but then I stopped.

"What are you doing Keira?" I asked myself aloud as fear quickly seeped in. It was strange, as in here alone with Draven I had found it easier being around him. Being close to him. But out there...? Well that's wasn't a world I belonged in and I knew it. I didn't want to admit it, but out there he was someone different and that part of him terrified me. In fact, it could quite possibly crush the most perfect experience I had ever encountered with him and I didn't want to ruin it.

I think it would have been different if I had been walking back in there with him, as just having his presence around me was enough to get me to agree to anything he asked. But now my doubts had taken root and were quickly growing into full out panic. I couldn't go out there and sit with him at his table, pretending that I belonged, if only for a short time.

Because the simple matter was the most heart-breaking one. I wasn't a part of his world and nor would I ever be. I wasn't beautiful like those other women who sat beside him. I wasn't rich where I could afford $200,000 bottles of whiskey. And let's face it, I was always going to be the hired help who was never born to drink that whiskey but only ever serve it. Ha, and I could barely even manage that I might add.

So really, what would drinking at his table accomplish? Where would it get me other than cruelly giving me a taste of what it would be like to live in his world if only for an evening.

I just didn't know how Cinderella had done it. To want something like that, if only for one night, knowing what she would have to go back to and face for the rest of her life. Alright, so I had a pretty good life, with friends and family who loved me and Hell, it wasn't like I was planning on serving drinks for the rest of it but still, it was a hard decision to make. Because the soul of the matter remained...giving me a taste of Draven was a dangerous thing, one I knew I would never get over, the way I knew I would *have to.*

No, I would walk out there, go up to his table, thank him for helping me and the offer of a drink and then finish my shift the way I could only hope to accomplish...with a shred of dignity left. Yes, that was what I was going to do. I sucked in a deep breath, pulled down my top and took a last swig of water before walking out the door, looking back one last time as I doubted I would ever see it again.

The second I made it to the hallway I couldn't help but look down the other way that was opposite to the doors that led to the club. I don't know why or what was compelling me to seek out that door but it was as if something was calling me towards it. I looked back quickly at the main doors just to check and bit my lip, not knowing what choice to make. I knew I could possibly get into trouble by snooping around, which let's face it, there was no other way to put it. So, calling a spade a spade, or in this case a nosey cow a nosey cow, I decided to risk it.

So, keeping a close eye back on the door I knew I should be walking through, I was walking towards the one I knew I shouldn't. I quickly made it and paused a second before making that last step needed in satisfying my curiosity. What if someone was in there? What if there was something private inside? Oh God, what was I doing?!

"You're going inside, that's what you're doing Kazzy," I told myself as I took a deep breath and pushed down on the handle. I then opened the door and stepped inside.

"Oh, this is a bad idea," I said as I took in the splendour of the room around me. It was like stepping back in time to the private chamber of some Lord of the manor. It was definitely a man's room, the battle covered tapestry said as much. I looked at it more closely and saw that it depicted a war between Heaven and Hell displayed by hours of needlework in a vast array of colours.

I turned around and took in the rest of the room, eyes focusing on everything there was to see. Everything from the antique, carved furniture to the luxurious and elegant soft furnishings and all of it seemed so much bigger. Just like where I was headed now, towards the biggest bed I had ever seen! It was huge and I wasn't surprised to see that it stood alone on its own dais. It was covered in black silk that looked more expensive and opulent than cheesy. And this matched the heavy material that hung down the trunk like posts that held up an elaborately carved roof. In fact, the whole room and everything in it was as though it had been built for someone not only important but also someone large in stature...

"Oh god...could it be...?" I asked myself the question looking down at the bed and running my fingertips dangerously across the silk. That was when a voice behind me answered my question.

"My room, yes... yes, it is." In my utter shock at being caught I turned too quickly and tripped on the steps that surrounded the bed. I put my hands out behind me to try and steady myself, looking down for only a second and quickly found myself being saved not by my quick reactions but by someone else's…

Draven's.

I ended up half bent over the bed with Draven holding me to him, bracing his free hand on the closest wooden post. Neither of us spoke but seemed to be caught up in the moment and I swallowed hard. His eyes looked over me, following the motion along my neck with narrowed eyes. He reminded me of some jungle cat watching and waiting for the moment his prey made chase and the game really began. I bit my lip at the sight of those hungry eyes drinking me in and his eyes quickly snapped to my mouth.

Then as if something in him clicked he raised us both up off the bed slowly as if any sudden movements would frighten me. Then once straightened he raised his free hand to my lip, gently pulling it from my teeth, rubbing a thumb along it for a moment.

"You shouldn't bite your lip that way." I cleared my throat enough to whisper a single word,

"Why?" His first answer was a dark grin before he leant down towards my neck, first breathing deep as if taking advantage of the opportunity. Then he told me why,

"It's very distracting," he whispered seductively and I sucked in a startled breath.

"Now shouldn't you be elsewhere?" he said pulling back and granting me with a questioning look.

"I uh…oh I am so sorry. I wasn't snooping, I promise," I rambled on and he stood back, crossed his arms over his chest and raised an eyebrow at me. Jesus but the man nearly had me panting at how hot he looked!

"No?"

"No, I was…well I was…" Damn it, think Keira, think! I bit my lip out of habit again, trying to think of a believable excuse and his eyes moved to them and my second mistake. I think he was trying not to grin when I let go of my lip with a pop.

"You were saying?" he prompted.

"I uh...bathroom!" I suddenly shouted thinking it as good an excuse as any.

"And you thought to find it by my bed?" he challenged with a slight teasing glint in his eyes.

"Oh, well no...but I saw it and kinda got side tracked," I told him without thinking.

"Side tracked by my bed?" he asked making me go nuclear on the blushing front. Damn but it felt like my cheeks were close to sliding down my chin!

"Well...erm, when you say it like that it does sound a bit..." I stalled for the right word and without taking his eyes off me he lifted my injured hand and rubbed gently over the bandage.

"A bit?" he said, repeating the broken part of my sentence back to me in a question. Then he lowered his eyes to my hand, examining it this time more closely and all the while I was still trying to form words, finding this difficult with him touching me this way.

"Intrusive," I said making him burst into laughter. I don't know what he found so funny but I can't say that I hated the outcome. In fact, just hearing the evidence for myself that he found me funny, made me grin as he laughed. Then what he said next had me serious in a second, terrified that he could possibly know what I dreamed of most nights.

"Maybe I should turn up in your bedroom unannounced...tell me Keira, would you find that *intrusive?*" he asked almost purring the question, his eyes burning into mine and what did I do...cough, half choking when I tried to swallow the hard lump of sexual tension he had placed there.

He laughed again, dropped my hand and patted my back gently.

"Relax, I am teasing you, sweetheart. Come on, let get that drink," he said nodding towards the door and I could barely believe that not only had I seemed to have gotten away with sneaking in his room but also finding this easy-going side of Draven because of it. Talk about confused, this was a whole new word for it.

"After you," he said like a perfect gentleman and I couldn't help but grant him a smile back before making for the door. But just before I could get there I felt him hold me back, placing a gentle hand on my shoulder.

"Wait, I thought you needed to use the restroom?" His question completely caught me off guard and I found myself stumbling verbally once more for an answer.

"I uh...well yes but, well I guess it must have passed," I said lamely. However, no matter how crap of an excuse it sounded, it did make him lean closer into me from behind, pulling me back into his chest slightly. I must have tensed in his hold as he gave me a squeeze when he whispered in my ear once more,

"It's a sin to lie you know."

He must have heard me swallow hard as he then let me go with amusement lacing his words,

"I think you're ready for that drink now, let's go beautiful," he said and I was suddenly astounded. To the point I couldn't move, even when he walked past me and even stopped to see why I wasn't following him as he had probably expected.

I know it was silly but just hearing him call me that, I found I could think of nothing else. Did he really think me beautiful or was he just being nice? But then if it was just all for his sister's sake, then what was with all the flirting? All the touching? All the whispered words spoken like secret promises and delivered in such a way the hairs on the back of my neck still stood to attention.

Could it be possible...could Draven like me? But if that was the case then what had caused the ice-cold treatment only earlier tonight...what could have changed?

"Keira?" He said my name with concern and I looked around one last time just in case I would never see it again. Because I knew that now was not the time for this. I mean, there was never a good time for an internal meltdown because of how much you were falling in love with your boss. Not when he showed you the slightest bit of attention back. So, I shook it from my mind and nodded before joining him. But now Draven was looking at me as though he had heard my inner turmoil, or more embarrassingly, the part when I admitted to myself that I was falling in love with him. Now I could only pray to every God out there that I hadn't unknowingly said it aloud.

"Did I...?" I started to ask because seriously, the more I looked at his face, the more I convinced myself that I had said the unthinkable.

"I think it wise we get back to the club now." Was all he said in a stern voice and I felt the harsh tone of it crush me. So much for my theory I thought as I nodded and walked past him down the long hallway, tensing when I heard the door slam behind me.

We walked in silence and the second we made it through the doors at the end everything changed. It was as if we had stepped through a different portal and the second we did, we lost the magic that had started to connect us together. But now we were back in the real world and lines were clearly drawn. A switch had been flipped and the Draven I had encountered was long gone, I knew that with just a look. So, I wasn't surprised when he said,

"I think it best if we forgo that drink. Your shift ended fifteen minutes ago and Frank will be waiting for you." I closed my eyes and nodded without him seeing the pain cross my features. Then I plastered on my fake face for the first time since being here and presented him with a part of me I thought I had left at home...back in England...*back in my private Hell.*

"I think that is for the best. After all, we wouldn't want to give anyone any reason to gossip, your reputation if far too important to darken it by getting too personal with... *your staff.*" I said giving him a smile that never reached my eyes let alone the sound of my voice.

"Keira that is..."

"Good night Mr Draven... *Sir,*" I said interrupting him and then I turned my back on him. I walked into the small room to retrieve my bag and jacket before I walked out of there with more purpose than ever before. I briefly noticed that Draven was now back at the seat of his domain and poor Sophia looked so confused to see me storming out, she made a move to get up when Draven stopped her.

"Let her go," he snapped and then downed his next drink with just as much purpose as I had done in getting out of there. So, Sophia stayed put and I was glad for it. I wasn't exactly in the mood to hear any more excuses for her brother's favourite type of behaviour backlash. I mean Jesus, it was like walking on eggshells before getting on a rollercoaster named Afterlife...one being operated by Draven!

I stormed down the stairs and for the first time since I first walked through those doors to Afterlife I was desperate to get out of there. I practically ran through the busy club and hated myself even more when I looked back to the VIP. What I saw there just added to the confusion that was Draven as I saw him stood there in shadows, looking down and watching me flee from his club. I hated that he knew how much he had obviously upset me just through my sudden actions. I wished I didn't care. I wished I had it in me not to even look back at him but more than anything else, I wished I had it in me not to shed the tears that were now rolling down my cheeks.

I pushed my way out of the front doors in an unintended dramatic exit, ignoring Jo as he tried to ask me if I was alright. I was just glad that Frank was late and even though I had been warned by Mr Almighty himself not to be out here alone, right now Draven could shove his concern up his ass!

I ran out of sight and growled in frustration. Both angry with myself and the man who had played with my emotions this way. I just didn't get it. Why act that way and then change so suddenly? I thought back to what I could have done wrong. What I had said I couldn't remember, but it was only how I had felt inside that had slipped through the net. But that was something I was sure I had only thought, not said aloud. Although he had certainly acted as if it had been heard.

Well I had been a damn fool for thinking something in him had changed towards me. Maybe this had all just been a game to him and suddenly he realised he was the only one playing. Maybe then he decided to cut me some slack and make me realise it wasn't real. Just a brother being nice to some shy little waitress for Sophia's benefit...because she asked him to?

"Oh God, Kazzy, you're stupid, stupid!" I said to myself as the realisation just hit me. That must have been it! It was just too shameful to bear. Well, tomorrow at class Sophia would need a good speaking too, no matter how much she had thought she was doing me a favour. I would have to tell her that I could no longer work the VIP and that I thought it best to keep as much distance between me and her brother in the future. This was perhaps a good thing. After all, my obsession with Draven was getting out of hand. I mean I was falling in love with him for Christ sake! Dreaming of him every night, thinking about him every day and then having to see him as someone completely different in the evenings at Afterlife. It was messing with my head and I knew more than most how dangerous that was.

I grabbed my head with both hands in a ridiculous attempt at trying to grip on to reality when I felt someone watching me. I looked around and saw nobody...or should

I say, no-one with a body because what I did see was a great black bird sat high on the VIP's balcony balustrades. It was watching me in such a way it was either keeping watch over me or that it could actually be believed it felt my pain and knew of my struggles.

It was at this point that I heard a car coming through the green tunnel of trees. I looked that way to see Frank's car pulling up and when I looked back to the bird...

It was gone, like I was.

AUTHOR INSIGHT.

Chapter 24
Book I

These next few chapters follow on from the ones before and therefore I made another heart-breaking decision to cut them as I also couldn't add these to the original copy, as they wouldn't have made sense. Besides, I think in the end I decided it was too soon for our lovers to come together this way and knew that it would have made my plans for the story very difficult to write if I continued down this path.

It also felt wrong for Keira to see Draven in his true form for the first time in what she believes to be a dream. I knew that I wanted to make more of an impact with this crucial moment in their lives and felt that the beginning of this next chapter didn't cut it. Also, the first kiss they shared didn't feel right under such a volatile reaction from Draven, no matter how sexy Draven dominating the page can be. And as for the second, well, in the end it also didn't feel 'right'.

But none of that can still take away that in these next few chapters, we see a side to Draven that is almost human. Even vulnerable in a way, when he sees Keira again. And I liked that once more Sophia played a hand in getting them together.

So here it is…technically, their first date…

Book I

24
Dream Situations.

NEW…

I woke with a start early the next morning after once again dreaming of Draven. Seriously would I ever learn? It felt as though my mind was betraying my heart and stabbing it in the back every time I thought of him. And this time was even worse as it felt like he had come to me in my dreams out of guilt for his treatment of me. The darker element to the dream I couldn't account for though as it had been a first. I had dreamt that I had awakened to find him in my room, stroking back my hair and wiping away the invisible lines my tears had made but long ago dried up.

"I hate seeing you cry," he told me softly and I sighed before replying,

"I hate it when *you make* me cry." He winced and swallowed hard as I had done so many times when around him.

"I deserved that," he admitted.

"I don't understand why…why do I keep doing this to myself?" I told him knowing none of this was real and hating just how real it felt.

"Why you keep dreaming of me you mean?" He wanted to clarify, which I did with a nod.

"Only you can answer that," he told me softly and I tore my eyes from his, feeling ashamed of myself and not wanting him to see my disgust.

"Does it hurt you to dream of me?" he asked in such a way that he could do something about it and it wasn't my own sickness.

"It hurts that I enjoy it so much when in real life, it is nothing like how I picture being with you is in my mind," I told him, feeling like this was the weirdest form of therapy I had ever encountered. It was a twisted dream I believed in and I wanted to make the smoke and mirrors disappear. I was sick and tired of living in the shadows of his world and tonight I had finally got a glimpse of what it was like with his spotlight being shone my way. But then he had cut that light with no explanation and worst of all, no warning so that I could arm myself with my barriers. No, he had torn them down and made me trust in his soft words, his gentle teasing, and his tender touch.

He had made me vulnerable and then crushed me by taking advantage of my trust.

"I am sorry you feel this way," he told me and I shrugged my shoulders and gave him a small smile in return.

"It's not like you're real so what does it matter. The person who owes me that apology will never say it in real life, so it means nothing as it is coming from the subconscious part of my brain that is wishing her life away on a fantasy," I told him and hearing this my dream Draven seemed to get angry. He got up from the bed and walked over to the window, one that was open. It was always strange how my mind conjured up a plausible way for him to get in here, even though he was just a figment of my imagination...like a handsome ghost conjured up by my daily memories of him.

"And here I am wishing my life away trying to convince myself this is for the best. That I am saving you the physical hurt when all I end up doing is inflicting the emotional kind. I see that you are as tortured as I and keeping you at arm's length is almost as painful as keeping you close," he told me cryptically and with so much sincerity that I could almost believe that the man in front of me now was the real Draven.

"Then the answer is simple." He turned back to face me and I continued,

"You must choose which one hurts less for I know the answer to my own. Trust me when I say the emotional pain is far worse as I have already experienced my fair share of physical pain in my life but it is not my choice...it never was," I told him knowing that doing so was practically pointless but speaking the words aloud at least helped my mind to deal with the heartache.

He looked to my covered arms when I spoke about the pain I had experienced and it wasn't the type of attention that I wanted from him.

"What happened to you, Keira?" he asked me, making me frown and rub nervously at my arms out of awkward habit. But even if he was just a dream, it still wasn't a story I ever wanted to tell him.

"That's not something I share with anyone."

"Yes, but I am not just anyone," he told me, not with arrogance but more a certainty, as though it was his God-given right or something.

"No, you're right because last night you made it perfectly clear that I am just that...*a nobody to you.*" Hearing this made him angry and he turned away from me again just as I saw his eyes start to turn purple the same way that they had done last night.

"That could never be true...you don't know what you are saying," he told me and finally I snapped.

"No? I only have your treatment of me to go by Draven, so how do you think I get these notions of disdain...? I will tell you how, if it isn't your continued dismissal of me, or your blatant irritation or annoyance at having me around, it's when you pretend to be nice to me for the sake of your sister's demands!" I told him angrily. And this was when the dream took a different turn than I was used to.

He growled low in his throat as a purple darkness seeped into his eyes before spreading out, using his veins to travel around the rest of his body. He tensed as did I, when suddenly a massive shadow fell upon the room. A pair of great and mighty looking wings erupted from behind him like some dark Angel had just been set free from the cage of humanity he had kept it imprisoned in.

"Take that back, Keira!" he warned, grating out the demand in a demonic threat. I swallowed hard in fear for where my dreams had suddenly hit the realms of where nightmares were born. I scrambled back in my bed, as he came closer and I couldn't understand what I was seeing. Why would I be seeing him this way and if so did this mean I would have to cast him from my mind too, like all the others? That thought was almost as scary as the sight before me now.

"Keira, I will not ask again," he warned and I closed my eyes and shook my head, telling him no, I just couldn't. I couldn't take back how I felt. After all he had been the one to put those feelings there, driving that painful wedge into my heart so that only the one who inflicted the blow could take it back and save me.

I jumped when I felt his heated touch. I flinched back but he wouldn't allow this and I screamed when I felt a hand circle my throat. It didn't hurt but it was a serious enough move to make me open my eyes and look at him, which was what he wanted.

"Keira?! Are you alright?" I heard my sister's voice from behind the door and Draven looked towards it, growling like some far-gone beast, snarling demonically.

He snapped out his hand and suddenly the door started to morph into a metal door that belonged on some ancient fortress. Strong metal rivets drove themselves deeper into the bars that appeared across the door. The panicked screams of my sister and frantic shouts from Frank started to increase and I watched open mouthed at what I was witnessing. Then suddenly Draven's hand quickly made a fist and the fearful sounds of those I loved stopped and silence descended as the dark wave of power swept over them both.

"What did you do!" I demanded getting angry and hitting his chest in vain. He grabbed my wrists and pulled me towards him roughly.

"They sleep and will not be a part of your dreams any longer. Now you owe me something before I leave you for good." I sucked back a sob and hated the way I still felt about the idea of him leaving me, even looking like this...I still couldn't stand it!

"I will not take it back, not now, not ever!" I verbally spat at him trying to pull myself from his grasp on not just my arms but mainly on my heart.

"Then I will leave you," he threatened and I let out a cry of defeat. It was the last thing I wanted and my head fell forward onto his chest. He released me and put a hand to the back of my head to hold me there as I cried. Long quiet moments later he spoke.

"I hate it when you cry," he told me softly and I looked up at his purple gaze and said,

"And I hate it when you make me cry." And that was it. We had once again come full circle.

"Just take it back and the pain will leave you...I promise," he told me and I closed my eyes, releasing the last of my tears before saying quietly,

"You can't ever promise that."

"Just watch me," he said sternly before lifting my head up to his with both hands at my cheeks before he kissed me. I felt his lips touch mine and I suddenly became lost in the darkness he had cast upon the room, giving me a guiding light from deep within. So, I gave him what he wanted. I pulled back enough to whisper over his lips,

"Then I take it back."

After this his kiss grew in intensity and I realised that I was lost before and only now felt what it was like to be found in his arms…in his kiss…

In his heart.

I bolted upright and I was lost once again as his arms were no more.

His promise was gone.

And I was left cold and alone.

Book I

25

I Call Bullshit.

NEW...

After that explosive dream, I felt strange. It was almost as if there had been some cosmic shift in my world that I didn't yet know about. I just kept going back to that promise he had made and even though I knew it hadn't been real, I just couldn't seem to get past it. Even when I was getting ready for college and then again when in the car with RJ.

"Rough night?"

"Sorry?" I said jolting at the sound of another voice bringing me out of my inner turmoil. RJ laughed and said,

"I will take that as a yes."

"I cut myself at work." I told her holding up my hand and letting the cuff of my jacket fall back, showing her the bandage.

"Oh shit, so yeah, it must have been a rough night if you ended up in the ER," RJ said looking at it and seeing it through her eyes then yes, it must have looked that way given how professionally it had been bandaged. I looked at it again, taking in the obvious precision in which it had been wrapped and I frowned thinking back to just twelve hours before.

"Actually, Draven did..." I was cut off when some other driver beeped their horn at RJ as she had stopped at a red light that had quickly turned green. The old car struggled to pull forward and RJ stuck her head out of the window, one we had to keep open to stop the windscreen from fogging up.

"IT'S AN OLD CAR, ASSHOLE!" she screamed at the other driver who just flipped her the bird in reply.

"What a douchebag, can you believe that guy?!" she said turning back to me as we plodded along in her dying VW. I just shook my head in a way that agreed with someone when they didn't really have any feelings about it. After all, I was dealing with too much mental anguish to have anything left over for irate and impatient asshole drivers.

"So, you were saying...?" RJ asked and I looked out of the window with a sigh and said the truth,

"It doesn't matter, it wasn't that important."

Once at college, I thought getting my mind off him would be easier with droning lectures to listen to but I couldn't have been more wrong. All I found myself doing was clock watching and wondering what my next shift would bring. Half of me wanted to call in sick just so that I didn't have to face him, but then that thought alone had me wanting to kick myself. I was just so confused. Last night I had been dead set on quitting the VIP for good but now I wasn't so sure. Because the plain sad truth of the matter was as simple as it was sad...the thought of never seeing Draven again actually hurt.

I wanted so badly to be strong enough to walk away, but the more the day went on, the more I just wanted to get home so that I could get ready for work. I didn't know when my life had become so focused on one thing and it worried me, even if my obsessive dreaming had already become out of hand. It was unhealthy, I knew this and if I was ever going to get past it then I knew cold turkey was the only way and doing that required giving up that obsession...*Draven.*

Speaking of whom, my last class of the day was where I would find one of the culprits from last night. I knew that Sophia was only trying to help as she obviously had a bee in her bonnet about getting us both together, something I still found hard to understand. But it seemed to be doing more harm than good and was obviously just pissing off her brother, if last night was anything to go by.

"Hey," I said as I sat down next to her and the second I said it, she started,

"Okay before you say anything or try and tell me something silly like you are quitting, just let me explain."

"Sophia, it's okay really. I get what you're trying to do here but I think last night should be where it ends. I appreciate your effort in trying to set your brother up and you obviously just want to see him happy, but I really think we should both just take the hint." I told her and the second I finished for some odd reason she scowled at the guy behind her. I raised an eyebrow in question at the look they exchanged.

"I told you, I am not kicking the back of your chair!" The guy said forcefully before looking to me. I don't know why but the whole exchange was a weird one, like they knew each other or something. Sophia looked to me and saw my expression full of confusion so left it after first saying,

"Well see that you don't! You have done enough damage already!" Okay so that last bit was certainly a strange thing to say and when he rolled his eyes at her it was done more in the sense of someone spilling a secret and in exasperation than at having someone have a go at them for something they didn't do.

"Umm...are you okay?" I asked, leaning into her so the guy wouldn't hear.

"Yeah just stubborn, pig-headed males annoy me," she said which didn't really fit in with the description of someone accidently kicking her seat. The guy behind her released a sigh and then made it his mission to try and ignore her. I looked back at him when she wasn't looking and mouthed the word *'Sorry'.* To which he granted me a genuine smile and even winked at me, making me blush.

"So, getting back to working the VIP," I said trying to get the conversation back on track.

"Oh no, no, no, you're not doing that to me," she said getting worked up for some reason.

"Hey," I said softly placing my hand on hers.

"I was just about to say that it would be best if I just stuck to my own section and keep out of your brother's way. I will still work in the VIP," I told her, knowing I couldn't stand the idea of hurting her feelings by quitting as I had intended.

"You mean that?"

"Yeah, well that is if your brother doesn't fire me first." She made a disgusted face which just looked cute on her. Then she laughed once without humour.

"Well that isn't likely to happen any time soon!" She always seemed so sure and I was tempted to ask her why? Why had she gotten it in her head that I was the one she wanted to see with her brother? Because really, what did I have that a million other girls didn't have? It wasn't that I was belittling myself but really, a man like that with someone like me?! No, it just didn't seem plausible.

"Oh, really Keira, you need to take a good long hard look in the mirror sometime, then maybe you will see what the rest of us sees," she said as if she was responding to my thoughts. I gave her a strange look but never got the chance to ask her what her outburst was about as the dreaded Reed walked into the room.

After class, I walked out with Sophia, not missing the way the guy behind us looked at her before opening the door for me. It was as if he had silently been issuing a warning to Sophia and then turning his kindness on me.

"Is there something going on with you and that guy?" I asked as I watched him walk away and out of sight.

"Hell no!" she shouted, seeming affronted by the idea.

"He's just irritating that's all…so anyway, I wanted to ask you something," she said quickly turning on her sweet voice for me.

"Okay, shoot."

"I was wondering, as it's a while before your next shift, if you would like to have dinner with me?" I gave her a coy smile and she knew what I was about to say,

"No tricks, I promise. Just me and you having girl time." I smiled big this time and said,

"I would love that. Let me just text RJ to tell her I won't need a lift home and I am ready to go…unless I need to change first?" I said looking to Sophia and as always feeling like an utter scruff bag next to her. However, she just waved off the notion and said,

"Oh no, that won't be necessary, you look lovely as always. I have a car waiting and don't worry, I will make sure you get home in time for your shift," she said smiling as if it was all going to plan. All I could hope for was that this plan didn't include a certain, tall, dark and handsome, broody brother of hers.

I decided not to press the matter as I found it better to let her believe in what she was doing was the right thing rather than crush her ideas too early on. I mean who was I to get in the way of what she thought was best for her brother. But on the other hand, he had the right to and he had made it perfectly clear on what he *didn't* want and that unfortunately was me.

We both walked to the car just as I received a text from RJ telling me not to worry as she had to stay later anyway to try and get an assignment finished in the library. For all her fun and quirky ways, what surprised me was how academic RJ was and she was certainly driven to get good grades.

When we got to the big blacked out beast of an SUV I looked at the door with trepidation. Sophia laughed at me and said,

"Don't worry, he's not in there." She laughed again when I released a held breath in a big sigh. I went to open the door just as the driver got out to do that for us….yep, very cool moves Kazzy, I thought to myself. We both got in and were instantly surrounded by luxury and bless RJ and her little car but it was a far cry from how I arrived that morning.

"So, any ideas on where we should eat?" I asked, sitting back against the soft leather and sinking in to the comfort provided.

"Oh, I hope you don't mind but I already booked somewhere." I looked at her side on to see her looking sheepish and I smirked.

"Should I be worried at how predictable I am?" I asked jokingly.

"Nah, I just knew you could never say no to me," she teased back making us both laugh.

We arrived after about an hour's drive and to my horror it was much more than a simply jeans, T shirt and Doc Martin wearing kinda place. It was also in bloody Portland, not Evergreen Falls Mall food court as I had been hoping. Although thinking about it I doubted very much you would have needed to book to go there.

"Uh…Sophia, I don't think I am dressed for silver service, a la carte right now." She looked back at me still hovering in the car even though the driver was still holding the door open for me to follow Sophia out.

"Oh please, don't worry about it, I come here all the time and most of the time never dress for the occasion," she said and I sighed,

"Yeah right." I muttered under my breath, making her laugh anyway. Then I followed her up to the entrance, trying not to look like some beggar following her around for scraps of food or loose change. A doorman opened the door for her and I smiled my thanks at him for doing the same for me. Walking through the lobby of the hotel it was times like this that I knew I would never fit in Draven's world and maybe he knew it too, as that must have been a big turn off for a man like him.

The sheer expense of staying somewhere like this had me now panicking about paying my half of the bill…maybe soup was cheap enough, I thought mentally counting the notes I had in my wallet. I couldn't say I appreciated the snooty looks I was receiving as I followed behind the gorgeous and glamourous Sophia. But what was at least nice was to see that Sophia looked completely unaffected or more importantly unashamed to be seen with me. She even stopped and linked my arm as we were shown to our table. It was a nice quiet section in a cute booth big enough for four people at a squeeze. She nodded for me to sit down and did so herself opposite me.

"Wow, this place is incredible." And it was. I looked around the huge open space that looked like it was half restaurant, half art gallery. Massive metal sculptures hung from the high ceilings that were integrated with the lights. Even the bar looked as though it had first known life in some artist's studio before being converted into a piece of the restaurant.

"Thank you," she said and I gave her a questioning look.

"We own the hotel," she stated as if it was something someone said on a regular basis and I had to wonder if it was the equivalent of little Mrs Jenkins on our street who used to use her homegrown strawberries when she made her famous cheesecake. She used to say things like, 'oh you like them, I grow them in my garden'.

"Of course, you do." I said making her laugh.

"My brothers' often use it for meetings and such things," she said waving her hand around as if it was nothing. I didn't think much more about it as soon after this she was ordering some expensive bottle from the waiter. I, on the other hand, ordered a tap water making Sophia burst out laughing.

"I'm on duty later remember, speaking of which, we will have enough time to get me home won't we?" I asked getting worried about the time as I hadn't expected the hour's drive here on top of eating what I think Sophia was planning was a three-course meal. Well that was if her excitement over the starters was anything to go by.

"Oh, don't worry about such things, we will get you there in time...in fact, I will be surprised if my brother even lets you work, due your injury that is," she said smirking into her menu.

"What!? Oh no, surely not, I mean it was only a little cut and my hand is fine," I told her, silently panicking that he would use this as an excuse to not let me work. Maybe he needed a break from me...could that be it.

"I mean, did...did he say something?" I asked getting anxious and again making her laugh with my desperate tone, one I wished I could have taken back.

"Keira, really, you worry too much. I all I meant was that my brother would be concerned if you were to pull one of your stitches and I wouldn't let him hear you calling it a 'little cut'...not unless you want to intentionally piss him off," she said reading her menu.

"I think I do enough of that already without even trying," I said frowning and wondering why he would even care about my stitches. All right, so last night he had seemed to care, a lot in fact. But that was until I found out that it was most likely due to Sophia and me being friends.

"Really Keira, most of the time he is angry at himself, not you." I laughed without humour at that excuse.

"I don't think so but nice try, Sophia. Anyway, lucky for me he's not here so I..." this was when that sentence trailed off as right at that moment who should be walking down the centre of the restaurant, but the man himself...

Draven.

BOOK I

26
First Date.

NEW...

"*Sophia!*" I hissed her name in panic, sinking back into my seat trying my best to hide, but that was a bit difficult seeing as she had positioned me so he would have to walk right past me. Sophia looked round and saw her brother walking down the centre aisle with purpose and looking like...well, like he owned the damn hotel!

"Oh, would you look at that, they must have had a meeting here today, well how lucky." I growled at her knowing it was bullshit and she had once again orchestrated the whole thing.

"Okay, time for me to go," I muttered looking back at the exit and seeing if I could make it in time.

"Keira?" Draven said my name and I turned around to face him, knowing that there was no damn chance of my getaway now!

"Hey," I said in a quiet but high-pitched voice.

"Ah Dom, I didn't know you had a meeting here today."

"Yeah, right."

"Yeah, right." Draven and I both muttered this at the same time and then gave each other a look...but only one of us smiled and it wasn't me.

"Why don't you join us," Sophia offered with a smirk and Vincent, who I now just noticed behind him, sat quickly next to his sister and said,

"What good timing, we were just about to get a bite to eat before heading back, I am famished!" Draven shot him a look to silently call bullshit but he didn't say anything. No, instead, amazingly he unbuttoned his jacket and sat down next to me. I shifted over, pressing myself as far into the wall as I could so that we weren't touching. He looked down at what I was doing and then back up at me. Then he leant closer to me and said,

"Easy sweetheart, I don't bite." I think if I had been eating I would have spat my food out cartoon style, that or started choking! Did he seriously just start flirting with me again...after last night! So, I decided to give him a taste of his own medicine and say something completely out of character.

"I doubt that," I said referring to his changeable attitude rather than the sexual reference it could be taken as. Sophia burst out laughing and Vincent slowly followed.

"Well she has you there, brother," Vincent said in jest. Draven continued to look down at me and agreed with a simple noise,

"Umm." And a nod of his head. His staring was making me feel uncomfortable and I shifted again in my seat which Sophia took for another reason.

"If you're hot take your jacket off, it is quite warm in here isn't it...your cheeks are going red," Sophia added probably knowing full well my blush had nothing to do with the heat.

"Um...yeah," I muttered and unzipped my jacket wondering how I was going to do this without knocking my arm out against him...damn but these booths should really be bigger.

"Here, let me help you," Draven said taking hold of my shoulders and turning me away from him so that he could help in pulling it down my arms. His hands lingered for a moment before he slowly drew the thick material down and off me. Then he made a signal with his hand in the air getting someone's instant attention. He handed them the folded jacket as if it was some prized possession and whispered something to the waiter I couldn't hear.

"Thanks," I said quietly pulling down nervously at my sleeves, hiding my gloves and trying to hide my bandaged hand. Of course, he noticed. So, instead of asking me about it, he simply reached down to my lap and picked up my hand, bringing it closer to him as though it was the most natural thing in the world. He acted as if touching me was somehow his given right and I found I was too shocked to make it otherwise.

"How is it feeling today?" I gently tried to pull it back as I said,

"It's fine." But he wouldn't allow this and instead spent far longer than was necessary looking down at it. I mean what did he have, the Superman gene and X-ray vision? I coughed, clearing my throat hoping he would get the hint that I wanted my hand back but it was Vincent who got it for me by saying,

"I think she wants her hand back there, Dom." Sophia smirked when Draven shot him a scathing look, one that Vincent obviously ignored with a grin. He let go of my hand, looked back at me and said,

"I am glad it is feeling better."

"It is, thank you." I gave him a small smile and then looked back at the menu, trying to pretend that I wasn't freaking out that there wasn't even a pricelist printed. At least they had soup I thought wryly. The waiter turned up with Sophia's bottle and my tap water, which made Draven look at it as though it was poison. Vincent tried to swallow a laugh watching his brother's reaction.

"Did you order this?" he asked me and Sophia answered for me.

"She did." I blushed and then said,

"It's fine, I am not that thirsty and…"

"Waiter!" Draven quickly called him back before he could go too far, interrupting me.

"Yes sir?"

"What do you like to drink, Keira?" Draven asked me and I bit my lip trying to think of what to say.

"Well I…uh don't know, I usually just drink Corona but I guess I like white wine…"

"Bring us a bottle of Domaine Ramonet Montrachet Grand Cru," he said railroading me again and for a second I seemed to be lost in the sound of his voice as he spoke the foreign words as though he had been born speaking them.

"I uh…that won't be necessary, really just the water will be…" And once again, Draven took no notice and spoke over me,

"And you can take this back and bring the lady a real bottle of water." The waiter nodded and said,

"Yes Sir, right away Sir." Then took the glass and disappeared.

"Umm, so what looks good?" Sophia said, no doubt trying to move the conversation along but I was determined to say what I had been trying to say all along.

"That was kind of you but you might want to change that order." I told Draven trying not to let myself become intimidated by his commanding presence.

"Why would I do that? Do you not like that wine?" At this a laugh blurted out and I couldn't help it when I said,

"Well, unless it's ever been sold at Tesco on special offer then I very much doubt I have ever tried it but that's not the point."

"I sincerely doubt it at over a $1000 a bottle," Sophia said laughing.

"What!" I shouted letting a hand bang on the table and then looked around shamefully as everyone had turned to look at me. Draven shot Sophia a look and then turned to me and said,

"Keira it's..." But this time I interrupted him and put my hand out over him to try and get the waiter's attention but it wasn't working as well as when he did it.

"You have to change that order, seriously the water is fine, plus I don't have that type of money to pay my half and besides I am working tonight and shouldn't be drinking anyway...seriously, why isn't he looking, waiter! You don't think he would have opened it by now do you, maybe I should just go check," I said in a worried bombardment of words that had Vincent laughing again.

"Keira, calm yourself," Draven said also chuckling at my little outburst. He took my hand in his to pull it down from continuously trying to wave it over his head.

"Firstly, I do not expect you to pay for the wine, let alone a single dollar of the bill and secondly, drinking wine is fine as you are not working tonight and that is the end of it. Now relax," he told me releasing my hand and I could barely swallow back my shock. I looked to Sophia who just smirked because she knew all along that Draven wouldn't let me work tonight. Then I turned back to Draven and shook my head a little as if this would help in forming the right words.

"But...but I wasn't brought up like that," I said wanting to ram a breadstick up my nose to see if it would help in unscrambling my brain...well that was if there had been any! I guess fancy places didn't do breadsticks these days I thought wryly.

"Excuse me?" he said looking as though he was trying not to let on how endearing he found my little freak out.

"I was taught to pay my way and not expect others to..."

"...to what, treat you to a drink that I promised you last night or to allow my sister the pleasure of your company and thanking you by way of a meal? Surely you were also brought up and taught how to accept the kindness of others?" Draven said making me stumped for words, so all I ended up doing was saying,

"Well yes but I...I..." What I did do was stop there with one look from Draven that told me to do so. After this the waiter came and the seconds became a blur as he opened the bottle in front of us for Draven to try. Sophia had already started drinking hers and caught my eye with a smile, tilting her drink at me.

"Here you go, if you don't like it I can order you something else," Draven told me putting a fancy glass of golden coloured wine in front of me.

"Thank you," I told him and left out the part where I wanted to add that I would have drunk it if it had tasted like dishwater for how much money he'd just spent on it. I hadn't realised but he and his brother were drinking a bottle of red, so it looked like he had only ordered it for me, something that had me blushing once more.

"Keira, do you know what you would like?" Draven asked me as the waiter was obviously waiting for me to complete the order.

"Um...the soup please," I said thinking this would be the obvious cheaper choice and Draven growled low which gave me a flashback to my dream. It had been the exact same sound and I found myself questioning my sanity again as to how I would have known that sound so well. Draven released a deep sigh before speaking.

"Do you eat pasta, red meat and chocolate?" he asked me bluntly and I nodded.

"Yes, but not all together," I replied making Vincent burst out laughing and even Draven cracked a smile at me before turning to the waiter and saying,

"She will have the same as me."

"I told you she was funny." Sophia said to Draven and I had to wonder how I was going to make it through the meal without my cheeks becoming permanently inflamed.

"That you did," he replied coolly, taking a sip of his wine whilst studying me. I decided not to look at him and shifted uncomfortably under his gaze. I decided to take a sip of my own wine, thinking I would be needing that bottle if I were to survive this.

"Oh wow."

"Nice?" Sophia asked grinning.

"Oh yeah, it's lovely, here try some." I offered it out but she declined and said,

"I will take your word for it." I took another sip and then said,

"Oh, how rude of me, do either of you fancy a try?" I asked first looking to Vincent who also shook his head and passed on the offer with a handsome smirk. I then turned to Draven who was giving me a half smile, as if he wanted to say something that was on his mind but he didn't. Instead he surprisingly took me up on the offer and took the glass from me. Then amazingly I watched as he purposely turned the glass, placing his lips over where mine had just been. He took a large drink and I swear I saw him slightly lick the edge before handing it back to me.

"Mmm, sweet indeed," he said and I knew he wasn't referring to the wine. I also couldn't help but notice the way he presented it back to me was so that I would purposely have to turn it back around again if I were to choose not to do the same as he had and drink over where his lips had been.

So, I gave him a look that accepted that silent challenge and I took a sip over his lingering taste. He was right, it was sweet indeed but not thanks to the fermented grapes.

"So, what are your plans tonight Keira, now that you have the night off?" Vincent asked me kindly and looking at the two men I could barely believe there was a single strand of shared DNA between them. They were like Yin and Yang. One light and one dark. They were both incredibly handsome and the rest of the room knew it as well as I did. But neither of them even acted as such, let alone seemed to acknowledge the type of attention they were receiving. Most of the customers probably just wondered what I was doing sat with them and perhaps thought was it some kind of outreach program.

Draven coughed suddenly and frowned at Sophia as if they were having some secret exchange. She just shrugged her shoulders at him and looked sadly down at her drink.

"Keira?" Vincent called my name softly as if trying to gain my attention back away from his siblings' strange behaviour.

"Oh, well I don't know but really, I would be alright to work as it's not like I have much planned anyway," I said looking to Draven as it was obvious he was the one calling the shots on such things.

"No," he said, taking a drink of his own wine this time and that was that. I slumped in my seat and thought well there goes my night's plans. Maybe it would be a good thing, putting some space between myself and Draven. Maybe a good opportunity to get some clarity, maybe an evening walk might be a good idea.

Draven looked at me as though he had heard me thinking aloud and I was starting to wonder if they weren't a family of psychics or something because just like that, he looked away at exactly the right time.

"So, what do you usually do with your spare time?" Vincent asked kindly trying to find out about me and it was nice.

"Well, I like going for walks, although I am not great at hiking as that seems to be a favourite pastime around here...well not here but you know, Evergreen I mean." Vincent smiled at my clumsy answer and nodded.

"There are many great trails to follow. Any in particular you like?" he asked just as two waiters presented us with our first course.

"I don't know the names of them or anything but there is a good one not far from my sister's house," I told him and looked down at the yummy looking posh ravioli in front of me. There were only three pieces but they were bigger than the tins I was used having on toast as a kid.

"I hope you don't go alone, it is not safe," Draven said sternly as though what I said was pissing him off. Sophia even rolled her eyes at him.

"The track behind my sister's house is fine and I don't really go far, as knowing my luck I would probably get lost or something," I said trying to sound light-hearted before taking a bite of the most amazing pasta I had ever tasted. In fact, I couldn't help the moan that slipped out.

"And she enjoys her food clearly," Sophia said giggling.

"Oh…sorry." I said biting my lip when Draven must have taken pity on me.

"Seeing you enjoy it brings me even greater joy in buying it for you," he told me and I had to swallow my next bite slowly so that I wouldn't choke. Then I looked to Sophia and said,

"But I thought she was paying." Which made all three of them burst out laughing. I watched the three of them and realised like this our table looked right. I no longer felt like the wandering outsider looking in and I wished it could stay this way forever. I craved it and the more I was allowed a taste of his life, the harder it was to walk away. Especially when he turned to me with a smile and then took the remaining two raviolis off his own dish and placed them on mine.

"Oh no, I couldn't…no really I…" he leant closer and I froze as his lips touched my cheek and he whispered,

"Ssshh…eat." Then he kissed me there and went back to his wine and chatting with his brother about their earlier meeting. Meanwhile Sophia was smirking like a Cheshire cat at witnessing the tender moment he showed me. Half of me wanted to just sit here and bask in the sweet gesture and the other half wanted me to slam my cutlery down and demand what the hell was going on with him. Thankfully for the rest of the diners, I decided to go with the first one.

After this the rest of the evening flowed as well as the wine did and I found myself becoming more and more at ease. And I wasn't the only one if Draven's relaxed arm on the back of my seat was anything to go by. Our main dinner plates had been taken away and I found myself thankful that they did smaller portions in fancy places like this. Occasionally I would be talking, answering a question from Sophia or Vincent and would feel Draven touching me. It would be my hair, moving it to the side or a squeeze of my shoulder if I said something they all found funny.

It seemed to be his siblings who wanted to know everything about me and Draven would simply sit back and listen to my answers as if he himself had been the real one that had wanted to know.

In fact, it was when I mentioned about my old college that I knew I had to be more careful about taking about my past. Of course, it was Draven who didn't miss it.

"You went to college in England?"

"Umm...didn't I mention it...oh well, never mind...I am just going to pop to the restroom, if you will just excuse me," I said nodding for him to move knowing I needed to get out of there quickly, hoping by the time I had returned that the conversation would be forgotten. Draven gave me a look as if trying to read what was really going on behind my excuse to leave. I couldn't help it but I scratched at my gloved arms and his gaze travelled to them making me stop instantly.

"Dom," Vincent said his name and nodded, no doubt bringing him back to what I had asked of him. Draven gave him another stern look.

"I think she needs to use the bathroom," he reminded him. Draven exchanged one of those, 'I have no clue what it meant' looks and then got up out of the booth. Then he turned back to me and held his hand out for me to take. I bit my lip and placed it in his. He took care with it as it was my injured hand so gently helped me up out of the small space. Then I found myself staring up at him and for a moment I forgot where we were, as I lost myself in his dark eyes. It was only when Vincent cleared his throat that Draven took a step back and I did the same.

"Thanks," I mumbled before looking round for where the toilets could be.

"The far-left corner," Draven said nodding in the right direction and taking the advantage to get closer to me again for the moment.

"Oh, okay," I said nodding and wishing I sounded cooler than the babbling mess I felt. I walked away and looked back once, not missing the nod he gave to Sophia. I didn't catch what he said but I decided it wasn't my business anyway and I needed to get out of there to collect my thoughts.

I walked with a fast pace to the fancy bathroom barely taking in all the marble and shiny chrome. Instead I pushed open one of the cubicles, let the toilet seat bang and sat down. I then got right to scolding myself for my little slip up. I needed to be more careful, especially around Draven. He didn't seem to miss anything and the last thing I needed him knowing was what happened to me back in England. I had run from all of that for a reason and I didn't need anyone's pity because that was all telling that story would get me. And I was sick of being *that girl*.

So, before I left this cubical I needed to have my story straight. I thought back to the time frames, coming up with answers in case they had questions.

So that when I walked out of there I felt at least semi confident I could do this. I washed my hands, put my wet cold hands to my neck and looked at myself in the mirror. I swallowed hard and told myself...

"Catherine is dead Keira."

Book I

27

Finders Keepers.

NEW…

"Catherine is dead, Keira." Then I closed my eyes for a second longer, trying to rein in my emotions. This was when I heard someone clearing their throat behind me. My eyes snapped open to see Sophia leaning casually back against the wall.

"Oh, Jesus Christ, you scared me!" I said as my hand flew to my chest.

"Yes, but I doubt he had anything to do with it. Who is Catherine?" she asked after her cryptic reply about Jesus but that was still ringing in the background of me screaming 'SHIT' in my head. I turned around to face her and said the only thing I could, which amazingly turned out to be the truth.

"Someone I don't like talking about." Then I left the bathroom. She followed of course, without using the toilets telling me she was only in there to check on me.

"Hey, Keira wait." I stopped and looked straight ahead for a minute before turning to face her.

"I'm sorry, that was insensitive of me to ask like that."

"It's fine, I just don't feel comfortable talking about my past, that's all." I told her, taking a chance on trusting her.

"I get it, I really do and I know what it means to have to keep secrets but I just wanted you to know that if you ever need anyone to talk to, well then…I am here you know." I gave her a smile and then pulled her in for a hug, taking her off guard.

"Thank you, my friend," I told her sincerely. Then I stepped back to see she almost had tears in her eyes.

"I have never had a friend like you before, Keira," she told me as a way of explaining her emotions and I grabbed her hand, squeezing it once before telling her the same thing,

"Me either…now let's go back, unless you actually needed to use the bathroom?"

"No, I was just checking on you." I laughed at her honesty and said,

"I thought so." Then we walked back to the table, but just before we got within earshot she pulled me back and whispered in my ear,

"And who do you think was concerned enough to tell me to check on you?" I sucked in a startled breath before she let me go and I looked to Draven to see that he had obviously been waiting for us to get back. In fact, he scanned my face as if checking to see evidence of some girly breakdown and only seemed to relax again when he didn't see one. He then stood up and allowed me to get back in my seat but that wasn't until he stopped me with a hand at my arm and asked,

"Are you alright?" I gave him a smile, looked back at Sophia and answered,

"I have good friends." Then I looked back up at him and he took this as my answer that yes, everything was fine. He gave me a warm smile knowing I was talking about his sister and I could tell that he loved her very much…probably too much if he was only being nice to me for her benefit. But if that was the case, then wasn't he going a little over the top? Would he really go to all this effort just to make her happy? Well these were even more questions to ask myself when I was out walking later to clear my head...and it needed some major clearing with Draven around confusing the hell out of me.

I shifted over in the booth and nearly shouted with excitement to see what greeted me.

"So, when you said you liked chocolate, what you meant to say is it takes you to a happy place?" Vincent said smirking as he teased me. I just looked up at him and shook my head with a big daft grin on my face, making him laugh. Then I picked up my weapon of choice and dug my spoon in the gooey slice. Slowly, as if trying to savour the moment, I lifted it to my lips and let the first rich taste burst across my tongue in sheer ecstasy.

"Nice?" Sophia asked and I made a sound that could have been interpreted by any culture in the world.

"Oh my...this is soooo good," I said after swallowing my first bite. Meanwhile Draven had been quiet and when I finally looked at him, he was grinning down at me.

"So, are you not going to offer us a taste?" he asked and my eyes went wide. I then pulled my plate closer to my side and shook my head telling him no. He raised a surprised eyebrow at me and I bit my lip trying not to laugh.

"I don't share chocolate," I told him trying to keep my face straight. Sophia laughed and said,

"Oh no, now you have gone and done it. He now has a new challenge." I turned back to Draven to find him shaking his head, telling me his sister was right.

"You're just teasing me," I guessed but then as quick as a flash he had my plate over to his side of the table before I could blink. Jesus, he was fast!

"Oi! Give it back!" I said giggling and trying to reach for it but he put himself in my way.

"I will make you a deal, if you can get it from me, then you can have it at a simple cost," he said and I looked at him as though he was no longer my boss. Like he was no longer the stern broody man that I never believed I could have. No, right now he was simply a man I was attracted to and was having fun flirting with. He was easy going and playful. He was...well he was happy and that was when I realised that in all the times I had seen him, this was the first time I had seen it. And from the looks he was now getting off his siblings it looked like they were as surprised as I was.

"Well that's not fair," I complained.

"No, why so?" he enquired with a sexy look.

"Because you're bigger than me," I said folding my arms across my chest pretending to pout. He watched me with curiosity and then leaned closer and said,

"Then you will have to be very clever about it." I bit my lip to hold back a grin and thought about it for a moment.

"All right, I accept your challenge but in return I need something," I told him having already noticed a waiter walking past with a maraschino cherry with the stem still attached inside someone's drink.

"Very well, what is it you need?" he asked me and I was half tempted to ask for a kiss but knew I would never be brave enough, so instead I went with my first choice.

"Can you call the waiter for me." Draven gave me his usual questioning look but did as I asked without question. Meanwhile Sophia just clapped in her seat as if this was the best entertainment she had seen in ages.

"Oh, this is so exciting!" she squealed as the waiter came rushing over.

"I am sorry to bother you but I have a bet with my friend here and was wondering if I could trouble you for one of your maraschino cherries with the stem still attached please." He looked taken aback and I didn't know if it was my request or that I had asked so nicely he wasn't used to it.

"Yes of course and it is no trouble at all, Miss," he replied and quickly left to get what I asked for.

"Now I am intrigued," Vincent said and Draven nodded, agreeing,

"Yes, as am I, brother." I on the other hand was hoping I could still do it or this was going to be a lot lamer than I envisioned in my head. Well it was now or never as the waiter soon returned with a few on a small plate for me to choose from before leaving. Of course, I picked up the one with the longest stem.

"And what exactly are you planning on doing with that?" Draven asked me, turning his full attention my way, which was precisely what I was hoping for. So, I plucked the stem off the cherry and held it up.

"Simple, I am going to tie it into a knot in less than ten seconds."

"Well that doesn't sound that hard," Sophia complained making me smile, so I elaborated for her,

"With my tongue." To which she responded with,

"OOooooo now it gets interesting again." At the same time Vincent whistled. I looked to Draven who seemed to fixate on my mouth as if he was picturing it for himself.

"Okay, so if you wouldn't mind counting for me please," I asked Draven in hopes this would distract him further.

"But of course," he replied with a grin.

"Okay, here goes." I said and then popped it in and started bending it round the way I had done a hundred times before. The second I knew I was done I started to pull it from my mouth, tightening the end with my teeth before showing it to them. All the while Draven watched me like a hawk having only got to six seconds. I first showed it to Sophia as proof, then to Vincent and last of all to Draven. Then the second he focused on it I quickly grabbed the plate and had it in front of me before he knew what I had done.

"HA! She got you!" Sophia shouted clapping and I dropped the stem back on the plate with the other cherries and picked up my spoon. I had a mouthful of chocolate in my mouth before I looked at Draven again. The shock on his face was priceless and Vincent laughed, banging a hand down on the table as he mocked his brother.

Draven ignored them both, his sole focus on me as before but this time he leaned in closer and whispered,

"A skill indeed and one I would very much like to see repeated but for now, you still owe me that payment." I gulped down the piece of cake and briefly prayed his payment was a taste of me, not the dessert. I nodded, knowing that when he looked at me like that I would give him anything he asked of me. But to my great disappointment it wasn't a kiss but instead he picked up my used spoon. One still smeared with lines of sticky chocolate that I hadn't gotten around to licking off and he took a piece of my cake keeping his eyes to mine.

I was suddenly jealous of a spoon, to the point that I was half tempted to steal it so that I could take it home with me. Once finished he handed it back and it was now clean. And I wasn't ashamed to admit that I took great pleasure in finishing my dessert with something that had been in Draven's mouth.

After this came the sad part as the evening was coming to an end and I wished I could have done it all over again. Draven signed his name to the bill as Vincent and Sophia were up out of their seats, making their way to the door. However, I was still sat down next to Draven as he hadn't yet moved allowing me to follow the others.

I tried to look as though I wasn't staring at him which I too often found myself doing, so now I was looking down at my hands, nervously pulling at a thread on my bandage.

"Keira?" Draven's voice pulled me out of my own thoughts and I looked up to see him now standing, waiting for me. As before, he held a hand out for me to hold as I stood from the booth. He then turned, taking my jacket off the waiter who held it out for him and I went to take it off Draven but he didn't let go.

"Let me be a gentleman, Keira," he told me and nodded for me to turn around when I gave him a look of confusion.

"Oh...oh right," I mumbled and turned, letting him help me with my jacket by holding it out for me. He lifted the rest onto my shoulders and then gathered my loose hairs off my neck and placed them over the collar, his hands lingering on my skin. I shuddered and turned back to him quickly, hoping he didn't notice how having his touch affected my body.

He motioned for me to proceed him towards the exit and I knew this was going to be my last opportunity to thank him for tonight so I turned to face him as soon as we were through the doors. Of course, in true Keira fashion I stumbled a step and kind of half fell into him sideways.

"I swear it's not the wine," I said with my face planted in the bend of his arm from where he had caught me. He chuckled and said,

"And there is my clumsy waitress." I just hoped he didn't hear my startled breath at hearing him call me *his*. I stood up straighter, holding on to his arms for support.

"I just wanted to thank you...for tonight, the meal and the wine."

"And for the company I hope," he teased and I blushed.

"You're most welcome, Keira," he added and I nodded as the same black car that had brought me and Sophia here pulled up, but speaking of them,

"Where are Sophia and Vincent?" I asked Draven just as the roaring sound of a bike's engine could be heard.

Then flying past went Vincent on some black, sleek beast with his sister laughing behind him.

"See you two later!" Sophia shouted just as Vincent slowed enough for her to be heard, then he raced off like someone had just shot a gun in the air.

"Well they seemed to be off in a rush but wait, shouldn't she be wearing a helmet?" Draven smirked watching as they left and said,

"She will be fine, I am sure," making me frown and as if I was missing the joke. Well considering how much he cared for her it seemed a little out of character not to care about her travelling unsafely on a high-speed bike ride.

"My brother is an excellent rider, Keira," he said as if once again hearing my thoughts being voiced.

"Shall we?" Draven said nodding to the parked car.

"Oh yes, sorry I am dawdling, aren't I?" I said wondering why quickly after, Draven chuckled.

"Dawdling?"

"Oh, it means stalling for time...uh, no not stalling, I am not stalling, just taking my time...well not like that...um in that way I mean, as if I don't want to leave...of course I want to leave, but not in an 'I didn't have a great time' kind of way..." Okay shut up, shut up, shut up now, Kazzy! I wanted to slap myself and it made it even worse when Draven laughed and said,

"I know what dawdling means, I just haven't heard it said in quite some time."

"Of course, you do." I muttered turning back to the car and making a face of horror at myself. Of course, this was when I realised the car windows were practically like black mirrors so Draven could see me silently scolding myself and of course, *he was looking*. So instead I opened the car door, making Draven reach out behind me as if to do the same. He came so close to my back with his arm around me that I froze.

"Do you ever let a gentleman treat you like the lady you are?" he asked me seductively and I bit my lip.

"You're biting your lip again, Keira," he added making it pop out again just like it did last night in his bedroom. I didn't say anything but I looked up to find him looking at me in the reflection of the window. I swear I saw his eyes flash with some kind of glow but then realised it must have been a trick of light. Well at least it was a dark reflection so he couldn't see the colour of my cheeks, silver linings and all that.

I didn't know what to do next. Did he want me to move out of his way or did he want me to just continue with my first blunder in opening the door before him? Thankfully his skills in mind reading were still switched on as he gripped my waist and gently moved me to the side so that he could open the door for me.

"Thank you." I told him, reverting back to my shy ways and I stepped up, so that I could get in…something he also helped me with by giving me his hand to steady myself along with another hand at the small of my back. I drank in the feel of him touching me, knowing I would be adding that one to my next dream no doubt.

"Um…thanks again, big cars and little legs don't mix you know," I said referring to my lack of height making him grin down at me.

"I don't see the problem," he said getting in after me.

"No?"

"Not at all, any taller and I would be denied the pleasure of helping you, something I happen to enjoy," he added and my mouth dropped.

"Where too my L…"

"The usual." Draven answered quickly before the driver could finish his sentence and just like last night, he would stop his staff before they could call him what he obviously didn't want me to hear. Then he pressed a button so that a privacy screen went up and the journey became all about us being alone.

"Umm...does he need to know my address?" I asked in a croaky voice I had to clear first.

"Why would he need it?" Draven asked me as if the reason I was in the car right now wasn't for him to give me a lift home. I gave him a confused look and said,

"I uh...well Sophia said she wouldn't mind taking me home but if you are in a rush then I could just get a taxi or something." I told him really hoping I didn't have to get a taxi home. Draven turned to face me, placing his arm at the back of me, resting an elbow on the middle section of the seat. Then he grinned down at me and said,

"Do you really think for one second I would let you get in a taxi alone and make your own way home, driving an hour to get there with some stranger driving you?" Then he pushed a stray piece of hair behind my ear causing goosebumps to rise along my arms.

"I...okay so I am confused, I'm not going home?" I admitted asking the question.

"Clearly you are...let me rectify that... no Keira, you are not going home," he stated as if this should have been obvious, which it really wasn't!

"I'm not?" I asked frowning.

"No." Okay so his answer wasn't really giving me much to go on, so I took a deep breath and said,

"Can I ask where I *am* going?"

"You're coming home with me, to Afterlife," he said as though this should have been the most natural place for me to be.

"I am?!" I said getting high pitched again.

"You are," he said smirking and obviously finding these simple-minded reactions of mine amusing.

"Why?" I asked unable to help myself.

"Why not?" he answered by throwing the question back at me and looking truly curious as to what my answer may be.

"Um well the obvious one is that you don't seem to like me when I am there, so I guess, yeah that would be a good reason to ask," I said blurting out the truth of how I felt and wishing that I hadn't followed my bravery up with slapping a hand over my mouth.

"I am sorry, I shouldn't have said that...please forget I did...or ignore me, must be the wine talking," I told him, trying everything to take it back. I looked away not brave enough to witness his reaction to hearing it.

"Keira, look at me," he demanded softly and I didn't want to but when he asked me like that, then really, how could I deny him anything. So, I turned slowly from looking out at the night sky through my window and instead was granted with the darkness of his eyes. He sighed heavily before speaking.

"I am sorry if my actions have given you that impression of me, but you have to know, that is not how I feel about you."

"I get it, I do but honestly you don't need to explain. I understand and your sister's happiness is important," I told him making him frown.

"What do you mean...what has Sophia got to do with the way I feel about you?" he asked me, sincerely confused and now it was my time to frown in confusion.

"But I thought...?"

"What, what did you think Keira, that I was only being nice to you for my sister's sake?" he snapped, obviously hurt by the notion.

"Well no, I mean yes...maybe, I don't know, I just couldn't make sense of why," I said trying to make sense of any of this, and it looked as if he was trying to do also.

"Why what?" he asked, obviously trying to rein in his anger by using a somewhat calming voice.

"Why you would single me out."

"Single you out? Keira, you have this all wrong," he told me and I felt like an idiot. I wanted to slap myself this time so hard I would sleep for a week! Well I obviously couldn't do that so I tried backtracking instead.

"What I mean is singled me out by being nicer to me because I was…am, your sister's friend…I don't mean romantically or anything," I said trying to fake laugh it off as though he was the one that had it all wrong. The look he gave me said it all…and that was he wasn't buying it. He folded his arms across his chest and said,

"So, if I were to kiss you right now, you think I would be doing so out of some duty in keeping my sister happy, is that it?" he asked raising his eyebrow in question and making me gulp at the sight of his dominant nature coming into play.

"Kiss me…uh, well no…you wouldn't do that…would you?" I asked getting flustered and wondering if the heat in the car was on full blast or was it just Draven's presence.

"Man, it's warm in here…are you warm? Do you think the driver put the heat on? Can I wind down a window or something…jeez, its warm in here." I said trying to do everything possible than look directly into his eyes that were once again studying me. Suddenly the window went down without having to press a button or anything.

"How did you…" I started to say but stopped when he started to pull my jacket from me, one I hadn't yet zipped up.

"Oh, okay, yeah, good idea," I mumbled nervously, talking constantly like I sometimes did. He took my jacket off me, folding it like he had done in the restaurant and placing it next to him on the doors side so that he had the excuse to shift closer towards me. I in turn shifted closer to the door thinking he would wanted the extra space…*he didn't.*

"I think we need to get a few things straight before we continue down this road." I looked out the window, seeing the city streets whizzing by and then looked back to him,

"Are we not on the right road?"

"No. We. Are. Not," he said leaning closer to me, telling me with his serious tone that he didn't give a damn about which road we were on. It was a metaphor for where we were heading personally.

"Oh," I said deflated and readying myself for the point where he was about to tell me that any feelings I thought he had for me had all been in my head.

"Anything I do that concerns you, isn't down to my *sister's needs*." He hissed this last part so that I would take notice of what he was saying.

"Oh…well okay then I will…" This was when he placed two fingers over my lips and said,

"I haven't finished." I found myself well and truly silenced and when he was sure of this he moved his fingers, so that they trailed down the side of my cheek.

"Now just to clarify for you, the reason behind my sister's constant interference is not because *she* wants us to become romantically involved, as you put it, but because… *I want it.*" He finished and his look said he couldn't have been more serious in what he was saying. I, on the other hand, thought I would pass out from shock! Could it be true? Could he really feel that way about me? No, it just didn't seem possible! In fact, my face must have said it all.

"No, you don't believe me?" I shook my head, too afraid to speak.

"Well I will have to change that…right now in fact," he said taking my face in both his hands and kissing me before I had time to brace myself for it. My eyes widened momentarily before closing them in a blissful state of mind. It felt like one of my dreams only this time the cold air hitting my overheated skin couldn't have been conjured up. Nor could the feel of his lips over mine, or the hands in my hair, holding me to him. This time it wasn't a dream…it was real…very, very real.

I moaned, opening up to him and he took advantage, taking the kiss to deeper levels, levels that had me gripping onto him just for something to hold onto. I felt like I was falling and in a sense, I was because how was I ever to walk away after this. And like so many times before as soon as the thought entered my mind he responded to it. He gripped me tighter and growled over my lips before he captured them again.

His hands bunched the material of my top and for a moment I thought he was going to tear it off me. The idea both scared and exhilarated me. Especially when he found my bare skin and the feel of his fingertips running down my spine, well, I couldn't help but moan, arching myself back and pressing further into his chest. Once at his mercy he took the opportunity to kiss along my neck, one that was being bared to him for his lips to taste. I moaned again and again and he in turn growled, rippling his breath along my sensitive skin.

Then he sucked in my tender flesh, holding it for a time with his teeth. The small pain morphed into a pleasure of the likes I had never known and half of me was on edge, waiting for the bite I was expecting him to inflict. It was as if even he was losing control and thinking it seemed to be once more the red light he needed before he went too far. I thought this would be the end but before I had time to mourn his lips leaving my neck, my lips gained in the loss.

I don't know how long we kissed but it wasn't long enough when he pulled back, leaving me gasping. My lips felt completely abused and he placed a thumb along them, caressing them lightly. I couldn't help it but having him look at me like that, I pulled my bottom lip into my mouth.

"Tut, tut, I told you how distracting that is," he said pulling it free with the thumb he still held there. I swallowed the confused and bewildered lump down and I thought I would choke on it, it was that hard to push down. Was this even real?

"Looking at me like that isn't wise, beautiful," he warned pushing my hair back from my face. I didn't know how I was looking at him so braved speaking for the first time, even if it came out in a breathy whisper,

"Like what?"

"Like I just ravished a damsel...a clumsy one," he added with a wink, referring back to our conversation last night.

"Besides, the backseat of a car is hardly how I imagined making you mine for the first time," he said as if this was a given and I coughed on a ragged breath.

"I...you want to...make love to me?" I asked, sounding like this was my first time. This made him laugh, pull me forward and kiss my forehead as though he found me endearing.

"What, you thought all I wanted from you was a single kiss?" he asked me as if I must have been joking.

"Well, yeah." I told him honestly and he looked at me like the very thought of it was unthinkable.

"You really think one kiss is all it will take to quench the building thirst I have for you. You think one kiss will sate my needs to have you in my bed and keep you there forever?" he asked and the picture he painted was one that made me nearly weep and beg for it to happen! But surely, he couldn't be serious...although if that demanding kiss was anything to go by then, yeah, I would say he was pretty freakin' serious.

"Even thinking about those perfect lips of yours makes me want to kiss you again," he told me and I did the unthinkable and whispered,

"Then, why don't you?" Even the shy way I asked seemed to affect him. He leaned into me, pulled me at the waist so I was suddenly pressed against him, an action that made me yelp.

"Because my beauty, if I did that then no force in Heaven, Hell or Earth could stop me from thrusting myself inside you and taking you right here and now. And the first time I want to hear you screaming my name is not in the backseat of a car but in *my* bed, where you will remain…do you understand?" he said and my reaction to this was my inability to breathe. Holy shit, was he serious? Looking at his face now then there was no other way for me to take it as anything *but* serious!

I couldn't believe it. I couldn't even think a coherent thought let alone speak one, but this wasn't good enough for him.

"I asked you a question, sweetheart," he said making me realise he was still waiting for something.

"I…don't know…I…" I stumbled on my words and I had to admit, it wasn't my coolest moment.

"Tell me you understand what is going to happen when I get you back to Afterlife," he said helping me out with his early question of 'do you understand?'

"What is going to happen when we get back to Afterlife?" I asked again just to clarify, if what I had heard…well I had actually heard. He looked me up and down, still with me locked to him with a firm arm he kept behind me. With his free hand, he raised it to my face, cupping the side of it. Then he gave me a dark, short laugh before kissing my forehead softly before pulling back to look at me.

His eyes, now pools of purple fire, just like they had done in my dream last night.

This was when he issued his promise,

"I am keeping you."

AUTHORS INSIGHT.

Chapter 28
Book 1

In this next chunk of the book was another part I decided to cut because in the end I didn't want Keira to see Draven's true form for the first time, tainted by RJ's influence. I also knew that for future books I needed to have Layla stabbing Keira at some point, so decided to join the two branches of the story and entwine them. Personally, I think it worked out better this way, which meant getting rid of them completely, another heartbreaking choice to make but in the end the right one I think.

This next one starts with RJ and Keira spending time together after a shift in the VIP, weeks after receiving money for her new car, which she bought with Frank. Draven is still cold towards her after she refused to show him her arms after her run in with Layla dropping the tray. Keira is getting tired of the cold treatment from Draven and decides to finally agree to Jack asking her out making the mistake in telling Sophia.

After college, she finds out Libby is pregnant, making her five minutes late for her shift, one that Draven doesn't take lightly. I have added it from this point so that you get a sense of Keira's mood, as this chapter would have gone quite differently had I kept it in, so here it is for you to enjoy.

Oh, and FYI, after reading it, I do wonder how many of you will be googling if Kermit is married to Miss Piggy...?

I know I did

28

Cold Mistakes.

"I'm sorry I'm late, Karmun!" I said as I whizzed past him taking my first tray to my tables. When I came back for my next one he stopped me.

"Umm, sorry honey, but Mr Draven wants to see you." My heart dropped. This had been the last thing I was expecting. I couldn't help but ask,

"What about?"

"I don't know, but he wants you to go over to his table right now." He said it as if he hated being the one to tell me this. Once again, I felt like running. I had never been over to his table before and it was somewhere I never wanted to go. Not only did I have Draven to face but now I had to face a whole table of unfriendly faces! Sophia was the only one I wasn't scared of but against six others, I didn't think it was going to make much of a difference. So, I placed down my tray and took a deep breath feeling as if I was about to be thrown to the lions.

It was like walking towards the electric chair, I couldn't stop from shaking and I could feel my pulse pumping under my scars at what I was about to do. I could see them all as I got closer and their faces became clearer. But my eyes focused on the man who had requested my presence at his table.

I decided that I wasn't going to speak. I would just nod. This was because I didn't think I could have formed the words even if I tried. I walked up the steps to the same level of his table and was stopped by the biggest guy I had ever seen. It was one of Draven's bodyguards, but this guy looked like he ate other bodyguards for breakfast.

It was the same guy who I had seen briefly twice now, once when they first arrived and the second was when Draven had come to my aid in the carpark. His face was scarred and full of potholes, his eyes were small and dark but rimmed with red. His hands looked as though they could have crushed the head of a cow and he reminded me of a Viking warrior. He stood in my way with his arms folded, which looked like hard work considering how big they were.

"Ragnar, let her through!" Draven's voice ordered. I shuddered as I walked past him.

Once I was next to the table, I froze. It was like being in front of a king and his court. His sister looked up and smiled which gave me a bit of courage, but not enough to get me to move or speak. I looked at the other two, whom I had never seen fully, but I didn't hold my eyes to them long as everyone was staring at me as though I was their next meal. It was like being in a confined space with every type of deadly creature and they were all thinking the same thing...

Snack time!

"Why were you late?" Draven said without looking at me and the others raised their eyebrows at the sound of his words. I still couldn't find my voice and Sophia was about to say something to her brother but he held up his hand to stop her. She gave up and turned back around to face the front.

"So, let's have it," he said with no emotion and my heart sank at his coldness. The anger I felt from this replaced a bit of my fear, so I gritted out,

"It's personal." Which wasn't a lie but my angry voice made it sound like one. I bit down on my lip and tasted the blood as it cracked inside.

"Right, well in that case, you *will* work tomorrow night to make up for it." Sophia looked up at me, eyes full of sorrow, but my face must have got the message across that I wasn't happy because she quickly looked away. The way he had emphasised the word 'Will' was a clear indication there was no getting out of it.

"Fine! I could do with the extra shift, so that's just great, it's just dandy," I said with my angry take over in the form of sarcasm and the man next to Sophia shot me a disapproving look. He was very serious and the huge scar that went down one cheek wasn't the only thing that added to his frightening look.

All of one side of his face was covered in a strange series of tattoos which snaked around the scar and ran the full length of his face. The black ink passed through the damaged skin but the ink disappeared when it reached the injured tissue. It made it look as if there were pieces missing from the design.

Apart from this, he had a very serious but handsome face with long platinum blonde hair that fell down under the black hood he wore over his head. He was ice white and scary. He was also the first albino man I had ever seen. So, when I received this look I couldn't help but find my feet with my eyes before braving another glance. Draven shot him a glare and his eyes looked elsewhere. Then Draven spoke again.

"That will be all." And then he picked up a shot glass shaped like a claw that had been defying gravity by staying up on a single point. He shot it back and placed it back on a tray that Layla was holding out to him. Again, the claw stood up, floating as she took it away. Ragnar, the giant, motioned for me to leave and I did gladly, without looking back!

The rest of the night I worked in a red mist of anger. I couldn't believe that ten minutes of being late warranted that! Jack was right, what a stupid rich pompous ass! Who the hell did he think he was? I just didn't get him.

One minute he was acting like the most amazing guy and the next he was some scary bad ass godfather type, getting pissed off because I was all of ten minutes late! It was ridiculous.

I finished my shift and changed back into my normal clothes, as if to make some point when I walked past his table to go home. Okay, so I didn't know what type of point I was trying to make but his eyes followed me all the same. When I got downstairs, I was met by Jack and the rest of the gang. RJ had wanted to catch this band playing that was called 'The Dizzy Bandits' who were a mix of punk and rock.

"Hey, what's wrong with you, you look tense?" Jack said as he joined me at the bar. I looked back at the VIP area and glared in the direction I knew he could see me from up there.

"Yeah, tense is a good word but pissed off is a better one" I said as I ordered a coke from Mike and then changed my mind saying,

"Ah hell, give me a shot of tequila."

"Whoa, aren't you driving?"

"Yeah, but one won't hurt and trust me, I need it!" I said downing it in one without the lemon or salt.

"Wow, you're hardcore, baby!" he said, giving my chin an affectionate little squeeze. Then, I don't know why, but I did something so out of character that I shocked myself, as I went on my tiptoes and kissed Jack on the cheek, not being able to help the look towards Draven as I did this.

"Well, the band might be crap, but it was definitely worth coming tonight. But I have to ask, what was that for?" he said with the biggest smile on his face.

"For being sweet and cheering me up," I said as I ordered a more sensible coke.

"So, come on, what happened... leader of the vamp pack been throwing his weight around?" he said as we walked back to the others.

"Something like that, yeah! But hey, I'm really sorry I'm going to have to cancel our date."

"What? Well that sucks! But it's nice to see you all worked up about it. What can I say? I bring out the fighting spirit in every girl." He laughed, leaving me feeling guilty. So, I excused myself and went to the ladies toilets to compose my thoughts. Of course, it didn't help that I felt like I was being watched everywhere I went.

I looked in the mirror back at my reflection and didn't like what I saw there. I shouldn't have used Jack to get to Draven. I mean, why would it even affect him anyway? He had made it perfectly clear on his feelings for me and if not by treating me like a leper for the past couple of weeks, then most certainly tonight's humiliating torture.

It had felt like 40 lashes to my heart and I hated that I still felt the same for him. I was like a magnet for the worst type of men, they would dig their claws in and I couldn't escape their clutches. Only with Draven, he would suck me in again and again, then spit me back out whenever it suited him.

I splashed some cold water on my face and rubbed the back of my neck with my hands. What a fool I was. Here was Jack, who thought that I was angry because I couldn't go on a date with him and secretly I had been relieved. There was nowhere I would rather be than at the club. The reason I was so angry was the way Draven had spoken to me. His coldness, his disrespect and disregard for anyone else's feelings just because he was angry was excruciating and completely unacceptable!

NEW...

I decided to stay later than I had expected to, but I knew that if I had gone early I would have just spent the time in my room stewing over 'Lord Draven'. So, I decided to have some fun with my friends.

"Hey, I know, why don't you leave your car here and get a cab with us, that way you can join us in having a drink," RJ suggested and Jack joined in and said,

"Well she's already had a shot of tequila so I am guessing she deserves it tonight." I smiled and thought about it for all of five seconds before agreeing.

"Great! Now go and get the drinks in Gaston, I be having a thirst on," RJ said in a posh accent to her brother, seeming like she was half way to happy town already. Meanwhile I had already arrived at destination Misery, so really, what did I have to lose?

"Gee, thanks Sis, you're all heart letting me pay...*again.*" Jack said sarcastically.

"Actually, the next round is on me, just asked Mike if he could open a tab for me." Jack smirked down at me and asked,

"Think you will be needing one, eh?" I briefly looked up at the VIP and then turned back to him and said,

"Yes, most definitely." Making him laugh.

A short time later and I was sat laughing with my friends as they all exchanged stories they had heard about the dreaded Reed and how half of the faculty thought that he still lived with his mother! Well, at his age that was as good a reason as any to be pissed off with life, I thought drinking down the last of my Corona.

The night was coming to an end, as most of the club had emptied already and we were just working out who was travelling with whom in the taxis home.

"Well I am further out of the way than most, so why don't you just stay at mine RJ and that way we can travel together," I suggested and Jack looked disappointed but this served more than one purpose as I didn't trust myself not to do something stupid after drinking as much as I had. All right, so I was no way nearly as drunk as RJ, but to be fair she had half the night ahead of me and there was no way I could catch up in the time I had.

"Woohoo, party at Kazzy's place!" RJ said getting excited.

"What, you mean just the two of us?" I laughed and she then decided to change it to,

"Woohoo, slumber party for two at Kazzy's place!" making me laugh harder this time.

"Well, it's a good thing we got that all sorted as our cabs are outside waiting," Chaz said as he had been the one to go and check. We collected our stuff and walked outside to find that one of our booked cabs had been taken by someone else.

"Hey! Assholes! Come back here!" RJ shouted after the disappearing cab.

"Look, you girls go first and we will..." Jack started to say but I saw the faces of the other three and decided to cut them a break.

"No, you guys get this one and we can just wait inside, I'm sure they won't mind seeing as I work there," I told Jack and RJ loved this idea, getting it in her drunken head that she could have another drink. I decided not to correct her on this notion until the others had gone.

"Are you sure?" Jack asked full of concern.

"She's sure, now come on, we are freezing our asses out here," Chaz said giving me a smile in thanks before getting his 'frozen ass' in the cab. Lanie said good night to us both with a little hug and she too looked a little worse for wear on the drinking front, even though she was just better at hiding it than RJ.

"Okay, but you guys text me if you need anything or have any problems," Jack said being the one to get in the cab last. He flicked his sister on the nose, making her complain with a giggle. But he saved his hug for me and it lingered longer than friendly would have warranted.

After the cab went out of sight we looked at each other and giggled for no reason other than we'd had too much to drink.

"He has it bad for you!" RJ said and I groaned as this was the last thing I needed right now.

"We're friend's RJ, that's it," I told her making her black lips pout.

"But I want a new sister and I have my sights set on you, so please just marry my brother already so I can move into your garage and get away from my bitch of a mother," she said making me laugh and I decided it was best to let her have this drunken moment to believe it would happen one day.

"Okay, I will get right on that, but first let's get home and our asses into bed, Chaz was right, it's freezing out here."

"Hell, yeah and my fishnets do shit...seriously what was I thinking! Unicorn PJ's next time I come out...they're fleece lined," she said as if picturing them now.

"Unicorn PJ's...isn't that a little...well, colourful for you?" I joked looking at her Goth attire and thinking little cute magical ponies was the last thing that metal spikes, black makeup, skimpy netted dresses and big ass leather boots, screamed she wore behind closed doors.

"Tell anyone and I will kill you," she joked back making me laugh. I held up my hand, crossed my chest and said,

"It dies with me, cross my heart and hope never to die." She laughed and nearly fell over doing so. In fact, if I hadn't caught her then she would have.

"Right let's get back inside and...oh..." I said turning around and not realising it until now that the doors were closed and all the lights were off.

"Oh shit, well it looks like we will just have to wait for our cab out here then," I said pulling my jacket closer to my neck but then I looked to RJ and realised that she would bloody freeze dressed like that. So, I shrugged out of my jacket and wrapped it around her.

"Mmm, that's soooo nice," she said snuggling down into it. Okay, so I was freezing but with trousers, long sleeved top and my gloves on I thought I would survive…at least until our taxi arrived.

"But what about you?" she asked and I gave her a smile and said,

"Warm blood, I will be fine." But then she frowned at me and said,

"But you always wear gloves and say it's because you're cold…bad circulation or something." I inwardly cringed at that damn excuse I had to give everyone. Thankfully though, RJ was drunk and wouldn't remember any of this tomorrow so I knew I could get away with it.

"I hope that taxi comes soon, warm blood or not, it will be frozen by the time it gets here," I joked which was when RJ decided now was a good time to inform me we were waiting for nothing.

"What taxi?" I turned to face her and said,

"What do you mean, the taxi that's coming."

"Oh, you mean our cab that was stolen and never rebooked?" I turned back round to face the exit of trees that made a living tunnel to see that she was right, there was nothing…and nor would there be.

"Bollocks!" I said making her giggle.

"Alright, we will just ring another, have you got your phone on you." I asked and RJ's eyes opened wide and said,

"Good plan batman!" I smiled as she rummaged through her sugar skull bag, making a 'Tada' sound when she found it.

"Oh…shit."

"What?" I asked as she dropped it back into her bag as though it was garbage, which it might well have been for all the good it would do for us when she informed me,

"It's dead. Damn it, I knew I shouldn't have used my battery life taking all those pictures of the drummer."

"Never mind, we can use mine...what is it with you and drummers anyway?" I asked as I started going through my bag trying to find my own.

"What's the matter?" RJ asked as I started muttering.

"I can't find it," I said resorting to bending on one knee and tipping the contents of my bag onto the frozen ground.

"Any luck."

"Shit!" I said instead of answering her.

"I will take that as a refined no," she said and I looked up at her and corrected,

"You can change that to a 'Hell no' and then added 'we are screwed'!" Then I stuffed all my stuff back in my bag and said,

"I must have left it on the bar or something, shit what are we going to do."

"Maybe someone is still in there?" RJ suggested, at least sobering enough to think clearly.

"We can give it a try but I already saw the doormen leave and now thinking about it, I'm sure Mike has left as well," I said thinking back to the bar being all closed up just before they left their table...could he had left early too? Either way I needed to give it a try, so I walked up to the door and hurt my cold hands by knocking them on the door. Unsurprisingly there was no answer.

"Well shit outta luck with that one," I said turning back to RJ.

"If only we had a phone," RJ said blowing into her cupped hands to try and keep them warm enough not to lose a finger to frostbite. Okay so it wasn't that cold but it felt close enough to lose at least a toe or two.

"It's a shame they never gave you a key," she said looking around as if a window might be open or something, which was a joke in this place but then something hit me.

"Say that again," I said as my first day came flooding back to me.

"You mean about having a key."

"RJ you're a genius!" I shouted and started walking the other way, knowing she would follow.

"I am...? Well of course I am," she said running a little to catch up with me.

"So, what are we doing?" she asked as I walked around to the other side of the building.

"Oh no, tell me we are not planning on spending the night in a dumpster right...'cause you know how long it would take to get that stink out of my hair."

"Nope, not dumpster diving tonight honey, just plain old breaking and entering," I said nodding to the door as soon as it became illuminated by the security light.

"Oh, hell yeah!" she said nearly running up the steps.

"So, what's the code?" she asked rubbing her hands together as if getting ready to put in the code but needing to get some feeling back into her fingertips first.

"Ah, well this is the tricky part."

"You don't know!?" RJ screeched.

"Ssshh, someone might hear you," I said feeling guilty just thinking about what we were about to do. Then she cocked a hip and placed her tapping fingers on it.

"And that would be a bad thing because...?" she said and I wanted to smack myself.

"Okay, good point." I admitted it was a stupid comment considering that would have solved all our problems right then.

"So, what now, we gonna climb the damn ivy next?" she asked and we both looked up to the VIP balcony slowly.

"No."

"No." We both agreed at the same time.

"Let me give it a go," I said trying to think back to that night when I had felt that strange guiding hand come over me. Mike had told me the number but if I could remember it now it would be a miracle, not considering I hadn't been able to only minutes after he first told me. But then I hovered my hand over it and let my mind go blank, as if trying to replay those few strange moments over and over again in my mind.

"Oh, my God, you did it!" I heard RJ's voice and opened my eyes to see she was right.

The door was open...

We had broken into Afterlife.

29

Intruders.

NEW...

How the hell had I done that when I didn't even realise I had pressed a single button?

"Come on, what are you waiting for?" she asked running in and I followed her in there.

"Oh wait, you don't reckon there will be an alarm or anything right...?" RJ asked now looking cautiously around her as if she half expected there to be a big red flashing warning light or something.

"Again, I think if anyone turns up they should guess we aren't here to rob the place," I said this time taking her views on being found.

"True...I mean if I was going to rob somewhere I certainly wouldn't wear heels!" RJ stated and looking down at the height of hers I couldn't help but add,

"No, you wouldn't get far in them." She giggled and said,

"Yes, but then dreamy Dominic Draven could capture me", making me roll my eyes. Just the thought of him finding us and seeing us both drunk and sneaking around his club after hours had me close to bolting. I was already in his bad books after all, and that was just for being a few minutes late! So, I didn't think that I could get away with breaking and entering with just a mild warning and a small wag of his finger.

"Yes well, let's not mention him right now," I said as I let go of the door, forgetting about its heavy weight. We both jumped and shrieked when it slammed behind us, making us jump.

"Ooops...sorry," I said seeing RJ had her shoulders bunched around her neck like I did.

"Come on, let's get this over with," I said moving through the back room where we stored boxes of mixers and soft drinks that I had spent many a time having to haul to the front of the bar at the end of the night. Well at least I didn't have to do that job anymore, not with working in the VIP. For starters, I didn't think they had anything that didn't have a high alcohol content, other than water and most of the time I think that was only put there on my account. It certainly wasn't ever ordered by anyone.

We both walked gingerly around the bar area as if we were half expecting someone to jump out at us any minute. I was just surprised to see that even the VIP looked dark, and from down here, even more menacing.

"Well it looks pretty closed to me," RJ said squinting in the dark like I was.

"Yep," I muttered just to take the edge of the eerie sight of Afterlife after hours.

"Look this is stupid, we will never find anything in the dark like this...let's just hit the lights." She had a point but why did the thought have me running my sweaty palms down my trouser legs and me biting my lip with anxiety.

"I guess so," I said knowing where the control box was situated and heading tentatively towards it. I left RJ where she was as it was probably safer that way. She could barely walk straight as it was and I didn't think it was on account of the heels. Then I took one more look around and pressed on the small plastic door letting it release off the latch. There were so many switches I didn't know which ones did what and I didn't just want to light up the place like Blackpool Illuminations! Of course, RJ must have been getting impatient because the next thing I knew her hand was coming past me and flipping the master switch. This time lighting the place up like bloody Vegas!

"RJ!"

"What? We needed light didn't we and besides, not a bad thing if people coming running…right? I mean we are still rolling with that theory…yeah?" I bit my lip again and then said,

"I guess so."

"Well we have no choice now, I think the only thing we are missing in here is a bloody Christmas tree with twinkling lights," I said making RJ giggle.

"You're funny, you know that?" she said and I gave her a wink and returned,

"English wit, my dad calls it."

"Well it's fucking awesome!" RJ shouted making me want to smack my forehead for like the millionth time tonight. Well scrap that, I had also wanted to smack someone else around the head first. I thought looking up to see that even the VIP was now lit.

"All right, let's find this stupid phone."

"Oh, I know, let me ring it!" RJ said as if coming up with a brilliant idea and I gave her a pointed look until she realised what she'd just said.

"Oh yeah, I forgot." Yep, and there it was I thought silently. After all, if her phone had some battery life instead of forty pictures of a drummer she could probably stalk online anyway, then we wouldn't be in this position.

"Jesus, what happens when they close the doors, does it suck all the hot air out with it?" RJ complained and I had to agree with her…it was strangely cold in here.

"I'm going to check the booth we were sat at, you check out the bar," I said thinking it easier if RJ didn't have to go too far.

"Gotya!" she said snapping straight to her job. I walked over closer to the double staircase and shuddered as I looked up again. Well, if God was on our side then I might end up actually getting away with this without anyone knowing. Well, chance would be a fine thing I thought with irritation as I still couldn't find my phone.

I looked back to RJ hoping to see that she had it but then panicked when I couldn't find her. Maybe she had decided to look round the bar or try Jerry's office. Well, as long as nothing creepy was inside like Gary, his creepy twin brother, then it should be fine.

"RJ?" I hissed her name, not wanting to be too loud as I was still convinced that I could do a snatch and grab without anyone being the wiser. Well that was until I had gone and lost my accomplice, I thought wryly.

"RJ! Where are you?" I asked the dark space behind the bar but again, nothing. I then turned around and slammed my hand on the bar's top and cursed,

"Damn it!" Then I caught a flash of hot pink in my peripheral vision and looked up only to be left speechless...well that was unless a horrified gasp could be classed as speech. Because there was RJ walking up the last few top steps into the VIP area.

"Shit! RJ...what the Hell are you doing?" I asked myself as I legged it across the dance floor towards the staircase she had just sneaked up. I looked up at them as though half expecting them to open up into the mouth of Hell or something. Then I closed my eyes and took that first step. After I didn't fall into the fiery pits I opened my eyes and ran the rest of the way up there.

"RJ! What are you doing?!" I said on a desperate whisper at seeing RJ stood by the top table and running her fingers along Draven's chair. She didn't even seem to notice I was even there as though caught in some other

place that had captured her mind. Like Alice falling down the rabbit hole and coming out the other side not trying to get home but trying to find a way to stay in. I knew how she felt as I had been trying to do that ever since first setting foot up here.

The only problem was that Draven didn't want an Alice in his world and his red roses could shred you to pieces with just one look.

"Come on RJ, we shouldn't be up here." I told her gently this time as I understood her curiosity but the saying it could kill was probably more a promise with these people, than just a harmless saying.

"Is this where he sits?" she asked and I nodded thinking back to who had filled it less than an hour ago. I also thought back to how intimidating he had been, sat there, master of his domain and commanding the obedience, compliance and demanding answers from his servants...and well, at the time, *that servant was me.*

"What are you doing?!" I asked in a panicked voice, as she started to sit in his seat and I nearly had a heart attack just witnessing the sure disaster that would bring.

"I am just trying it out." she said innocently, yet the action was anything but.

"Come on, let's just go," I pleaded with her but she was already lost in her own fantasy. Then that disaster I predicted started to happen the second her ass touched the seat. Voices were heard from behind the big double doors at the back. I knew that was somewhere I had been warned more than once about even going near but now...well someone was coming from behind it and I didn't know what to do.

"RJ run, someone's coming!" I hissed and thinking she would follow me or leg it, I made a mad dash for the only place I thought to hide...behind the bar. I swallowed hard and waited to hear the doors opening but even preparing myself for it I knew my body would react when it happened. Because you felt their presence the second they stepped through those doors, like a wave of fog rolling over the mountain peaks.

I couldn't help but take a deep breath, hoping that it wouldn't be long before they found nothing and decided to return...well that was until one of them spoke.

"Oh look, a lost lamb...I wonder how this got in here." Someone said and I didn't recognise the voice as being one I had heard before, so at least I knew it wasn't Draven as I would know his voice from anywhere. But then I had to slap my hands over my mouth as it was obvious RJ hadn't taken notice of my warning. I knew I had to look and only hoped that their focus was solely on RJ as I did so.

"Go get our Lord." I heard the rough raspy voice that I recognised as being a growl just earlier tonight and when I looked I saw that I was right, it was the giant named Ragnar. He was talking to the pale, scary one, who looked like an albino and had a thick spikey black tattoo snaking through a wicked scar down one side of his face.

"Don't eat her." The pale one joked making Ragnar growl and the other one chuckle. Then I heard footsteps getting closer and whipped my head back round, waiting for him to pass. I didn't know what to do but my inner turmoil must have been on overdrive. I could only assume that by 'our Lord' they meant Draven and that thought terrified me even more than the massive brute who stood guard over RJ. In fact, when I finally braved another look, the giant was staring down at RJ like he was waiting for her to move, so that he could simply knock her out again. One hit from him and he would be doing it for good, Keira thought with horror. He was a beast of a man and one Keira could understand anyone using as security as you would have to be out of your ever-loving mind to want to go up against that!

"What is this?" I heard a new man's voice and sighed in relief when I knew it wasn't Draven's. I looked around and saw that wasn't entirely true as it was a Draven, just not the one I secretly wished was mine. It was Vincent, his brother.

"We found it." Ragnar stated and the pale man rolled his eyes as if what he said was obvious. The giant didn't sound like English was a comfortable language for him to use.

"She was alone?" Vincent asked and this time the Albino answered him.

"As we found her, Vince." I watched as Draven's brother looked around the room and I ducked back behind just in time before he got to the bar. He didn't look sure and I soon found out why.

"She is wearing Keira's jacket," he informed the others and my panic doubled. They knew I was involved.

"You think she is here?"

"I have no doubt that she was...but where she could have gotten to is anyone's guess." Vincent replied to his pale comrade.

"Should I inform the King?" he asked back in return and I turned back around and mouthed the word 'King' in question. Tell me they didn't class Draven as their king?

"No. Take this one with you, place her in a bed chamber. Then look for the girl. I will inform my Brother."

"Yeah, good luck with that...better you than me." The pale one joked and I bit my lip. I looked back around and saw that Vincent shrugged his shoulders and said coolly,

"Just call me shit storm delivery boy. You know what to do," he added, nodding down to the sleeping RJ who must have passed out from drink. Then Vincent started walking back to the doors when he paused, looked back and at first I thought he had 'felt my presence' or something.

"Make sure she doesn't wake...after all, we can't have two lost girls running around the place."

"It will be done," the pale one said bowing respectfully making me wonder two things, each equally as dark as the next...what the Hell were they going to do with RJ to insure she wouldn't wake and second, who the Hell were the Dravens! I watched Vincent leave and then the big one bend down to pick up RJ, which looked difficult considering his colossal size. Jesus but the guy looked close to being eight feet tall!

He picked her up as though she was just a child and given the size difference she looked it.

"I know not why don't we put outside." Ragnar said frowning down at his new burden.

"Because she would freeze to death and I think our little mortal waitress would have an issue with that...which means the King would as well," the pale one said half laughing that his large friend would even think about it. Meanwhile I was still lingering on being labelled as 'Mortal'.

"I forget, they break," Ragnar replied making the albino chuckle.

"And just when I thought the King's foul mood couldn't get any darker. Looks like Takeshi is going to be busy in the training room," he commented as they both walked through the double doors, letting them shut on an echoing slam. I took a deep breath, let my head fall back against the bar and said the only word to describe my current situation...

"Fuck!"

I then waited another minute before getting up and trying to decide what on earth I was going to do next? I guess I could follow them through the doors and try and sneak RJ back out but what then? And damn, why hadn't we thought about just using the phone downstairs behind the bar...we could have had our asses in a nice warm taxi by now heading our safe and lucky backsides back home. Oh but no, I was back here, hiding like some sneaky little burglar soon to find Mr Brute Strength, crush a man's skull with one hand and the Pale Ninja who looked like he ate kittens for breakfast, the bloodier the better!

"Shit, shit, shit! Think Kazzy!" I said to myself looking around the room and trying to decide what to do. And more importantly, what type of shit would I find myself in when Draven knew? I doubted I could talk myself out of this one, or get out of here without implicating myself so that was out of the window. No, the only thing next was trying to get RJ back to know that she was safe. Because one thing I was now certain about and that was whoever these people were, it hadn't been who I thought. So, I couldn't trust them not to hurt her and she was my main priority now, not this farce of a job!

So, with nothing else to lose I walked to the back doors ready to do something stupid and something I was warned against ever doing…

Stepping into their world.

30
Lost and Found.

NEW...

Well okay, I would have stepped into their world if the bloody doors would have let me! I didn't know how but they had seemed to have locked automatically once Mr Large and Mr Lean had walked through carrying my friend off with them.

"Great! Just great! Now what do I do?" I asked myself, looking around and wondering if there was another way in there. Then my last chance came to me and I ran towards the door I usually used when getting up here to do my shift. I pulled on the door, only to find that it too was locked so my very last shot at this was to run back downstairs and check it from the other side.

"Ha! Bingo!" I said when it opened thinking they must have been in a hurry to leave tonight because someone forgot to lock it. Well, lucky for me they did as there was only one more door between me and getting back there and I just had to pray that this one wasn't locked like the rest. I ran up the side staircase that was hidden in its enclosed room that reminded me of sneaking around in a castle. I reached the top and instead taking my usual door into the VIP, I tried the one opposite.

"Thank you, fairy Godmother," I said aloud thanking whoever was responsible for locking up around here as they had obviously forgotten this one as well. I pushed open the door and my mouth dropped. Facing me was a huge open walkway that was exposed to the elements, making me suck in a frozen breath and hug myself. Again, you think I would have learned by now not to jump when having a door slam behind me but that was what happened anyway.

I turned, tempted to try and see if it was still unlocked but decided there was no going back now anyway so what was the point. So, instead I turned and faced my two options. The long passageway went straight ahead or off to the right, which would make the most sense to take if I wanted to follow the same direction the two men had gone. It looked like some kind of open gallery, only looking down into the centre there was no ornate gardens or statue filled courtyard to admire. No instead there was just a massive golden dome that looked as if it was some sort of temple roof that must have been built deep into the ground. I frowned not understanding any of this. It wasn't exactly what you would have expected to see attached to a Gothic nightclub in a small town in Maine!

No, something wasn't right here and RJ and I had just unknowingly placed ourselves in the centre of its secrets. Secrets its Master obviously wanted to be kept under lock and key. I decided to shake my thoughts of dread back to the depths of my mind so that it wouldn't stop me from carrying on. I needed to find RJ and get us both the Hell out of here without being seen. Now if I could accomplish that then granted, it would be a freakin' miracle…but I had to try. I couldn't just let my friend go through whatever they had planned for her.

So, with this firm in my mind I walked on, trying not to let the cold seep too deeply that it could freeze my steely reserve, one that was starting to feel more like jelly the closer I got to the other side. I tried to stay as close to the wall as I could as even with the strong stone balustrades that separated me from the daunting drop below, I still couldn't look without feeling sick...and that was with a belly full of liquid courage. One that, at the moment, was more of a hindrance than a help as I stumbled a step just before I heard a sizzling pop igniting behind me.

"What the..." My voice trailed off as I watched one by one the iron cage lamps that lined the walkways start to burst into flames as if on their own. I screamed and decided to make a run for it! Nope, I didn't need that right now and looking at the demonic looking lights, I was happy with just the moon that was showing me the way.

I slammed into the door at the end just before the last lamp could blow and flung myself through it just in time. Then I slammed the door closed behind me and panted behind it, waiting for my panic to subside. I was safe. I was...in a strange room. I thought as I finally started to take in my surroundings. It resembled a drawing room from a stately home back home. We had many Manor houses, castles and rich estates back in England to choose from if anyone fancied a day walking in the steps of history. But here in Maine, I wasn't sure a country that was only a few hundred years old would have anything like this in some small town like Evergreen Falls.

Rich furnishings and exquisite carved antique furniture filled the room, along with bookshelves filled with what looked like first editions and some crumbled spines. It looked like some books had been used more than others and I was half tempted to check for names, quickly remembering I was on a mission here. History would have to wait.

The side of the room had massive sliding doors of glass so that the room could be opened up to the view of the mountains beyond. In fact, it was the only part of the room that looked to belong to the twenty first century. Currently the doors were open which would account for how cold it was in this room as well. Okay, so I understood trying to save money on your heating costs but what was with keeping all the doors and windows open? It was almost as if they had been left that way for a purpose, one I couldn't fathom for the life of me.

I decided to have a look out onto the balcony the open doors led onto and see if I could make head or tails out of this labyrinth of stone. The cold hit me even harder now that I had walked into a big open space that no longer gave me the barrier against the cutting wind. I was just about turn back and see if there was another door in the room that could lead me into the belly of the beast that was Afterlife but then something caught my eye. It looked like lights coming from some window further along and I wondered if there was a way in there.

So, I took a deep breath and hurried along the side of the building, hugging the wall as the balcony curved around towards the other side. It seemed like the whole place was connected by balconies and gallery walkways, as though it was important to have all rooms easily accessible from this point, looking out towards the national park. Well it certainly offered a lot of privacy because unless you were in a helicopter, there was no one seeing in on this side of this fortress.

I continued to follow the path round until I found another door, this one again thankfully unlocked. I walked through it and was amazed at what faced me. It was like a huge, square room that had tall arched glass windows that were the full length of the high walls. In fact, the whole two sides of the room were full of them and thanks to the open walkway that framed its length, it made it easy to see inside.

I crept around, making sure to try and keep out of view but also spy on the room below. It looked like a private party was going on, with it being some kind of ballroom. The floor wasn't level with the windows, so it gave me a good advantage point to look in and watch what was going on. The place was full and in full swing at that. Heavy rock music played from a band set up in the corner, one I hadn't seen before playing at the club. Club lights mixed with the old church pillar candles that were dotted everywhere. There was even a bar running along the length of the room like in Afterlife, and there too were candles stood in dried pools of their own wax.

I couldn't help but notice that Karmun was behind the bar and the usual waitresses were all serving the groups of people filling the spaces…all the waitresses except me that was, I thought bitterly.

It was easy to see that if Afterlife's VIP was the party, then this right here was the private After party, one that was cut off from the rest of the world. And on closer inspection I could see why. The groups below weren't just gathered close together in groups to be friendly but more like that friendliness was better described as a damn orgy!

"It's a sex club!" I uttered in my curious horror, gasping at the idea. I quickly scanned the large room for the only one I needed to see and I held my breath hoping that I wouldn't find him engaging in some sordid sexual act with anyone other than me. I knew it was sad but I just couldn't help it, the sight would have crushed me.

Thankfully this wasn't the case as, just like in Afterlife, he was situated at the centre of the room watching over his domain. He was raised up slightly, sat in some throne like seat, that was surrounded by cushions like you would have found in some ancient Persian land and coming across its King. Well, he may not have been engaging himself in any sexual acts but that wasn't to say that he still wasn't surrounded by half naked beauties. I bit my lip and looked down at my shivering self, knowing that I could never compare and to say the word compete would have just been a joke, I thought bitterly.

Girls with hair of ebony, long and flowing down to their naked bellies as they danced for his pleasure. But then where was that pleasure? No, there was none as Draven looked more pissed off with it all instead of getting in the mood for taking one of them to his bed. I even jumped when he downed what remained in his glass before crushing it in his hand, throwing the shards off to the side. This was when the dancers started to back away, obviously knowing that tonight they were not going to get lucky like they no doubt hoped.

This was just before the doors at the end opened and in walked Vincent, strolling in like he too owned the room, which being a Draven, I guess he did. Jeez but what was it with these brothers, it was like they were born with some commanding gene that demanded respect and fear all rolled into one. I watched as he walked straight up to his brother, approaching confidently, unlike the others who probably weren't brave enough to do so. I saw him lean in and whisper something in his ear, no doubt telling him about RJ and me breaking in. Well, if I thought the shit would hit the fan when hearing this, I never expected it to do so on a nuclear level.

Draven erupted out of his chair and roared in anger. I screamed unable to help myself or the shock. He looked directly at me for a split second and then the light blew, plunging the place into darkness that obviously mirroring his mood. I yelped at the sight of what Draven could do when fury hit him and I didn't want to ever be within arm's length of it. I watched the room, placing a hand on the window, trying to peer inside. Then suddenly the lights came back on and Draven was gone. I couldn't be sure if he had seen me or not but thinking about it, the lights may have gone off in there but the moonlight had stayed just where it was…shining down on me.

"Shit!" I said knowing this was my cue to get the Hell out of there. I ran back round to the door only now I couldn't believe it…it was locked.

"No, no, no!" I tried it a few more times and then knew I had no choice but to continue round the 'playroom'. So, I did, trying to hurry but unable to divert my eyes from seeing where Draven's seat had once been filled was now toppled over, where it had landed in his outrage.

"You'd better be open," I warned issuing the pointless threat to the door at the end and kissed my lucky stars when it was. I ran through it not wanting to chance if he had seen me or not. The door led down a small tunnel of steps and to another door at the bottom. I took a deep breath, put my hand on the handle and pushed down on it. The light blinded me for a moment but it only took me a second to realise my mistake.

"Oh shit." I muttered to myself as I realised what I had done. I had walked into the middle of the party…one I knew I definitely hadn't been invited to. I turned quickly to go back but a sudden draft or something ripped the handle from my hand and it slammed right in front of my face. I felt like crumbling down to the floor and hoping no one would notice me until it was all over.

But I didn't do that. No instead I sent up a prayer in thanks that at least Draven was no longer in the room, so if I kept my head down, chances were no one would notice me. After all, it wasn't like people weren't busy. No, if they weren't already occupied with taking body parts into their mouths, then they were accepting them and throwing their heads back in erotic bliss.

Well, whatever was keeping them busy, Keira thought with a blush, the temperature equivalent to the red-hot sands of Saudi Arabia. Jesus but how that woman got that thing all the way in her mouth was Guinness Book of Records worthy! My eyes opened wide and my mouth dropped but nowhere as big as hers had, that was for damn sure.

Okay so all I needed to do was make it to the doors on the other side and it meant I still had a chance, now if I could just find my legs and make them work that would be great! Yep, just dandy I thought sarcastically.

I finally pushed myself off the door I had momentarily plastered myself against. So, had this been their big secret? A sex club? If so, well then it wasn't that bad, surely. Not like there was drug ring, gun cartel living in the building. I had sudden visions of shipments coming in and someone opening one of the many smuggled crates to find them filled with condoms. I even smirked and tried to rein in a giggle making me wonder if hysteria was setting in.

Okay, time to get a grip Keira and that meant getting your ass to the door and through this sex crazed nightmare without being seen. So, with this in mind, I continued through the crowd, deciding to pull my clip out and let my hair fall down. After all no one had seen me with my hair down and it was long enough that it could help in hiding my face. I split it at the back and pulled each side forward, making sure the shorter bits fell over a good portion of my face. Okay, so it wasn't a black ski mask like I wished I had hiding in my bag somewhere but it would have to do.

"Oh sorry," I said cursing myself when I bumped into a couple dry humping to some rock song that cast its heavy base line across the room like some hypnotic sex anthem they were all addicted to. I looked quickly towards where Draven had been sat, making sure he hadn't returned and hoping to make it out of there before he did. Thankfully, it was still clear and free from the angry face that was Draven, but his brother seemed to have taken his place beside the throne and quickly covered himself with an array of willing beauties.

One started biting the tight and hard lines of his abs after she lifted up his T shirt, which obviously wasn't something he allowed. One of his hands snapped out and circled her wrist in a punishing hold. Then he dragged her up his body, whispered something in her ear, which must have been a demand. Because the next thing she did was bare her neck to him, and he took no time at all before sinking his teeth into her tensed flesh. I almost cried out in pain for her but one look at her face and it told me enough to know this was her kink because she was obviously getting off on the pain.

I turned away, feeling like I was intruding on something private which was pretty much the same as anywhere you looked in this place. I was just happy that the doors out of here weren't that far away and a few more metres and I would be free. Well, that was until I reached the doorman.

"No one leaves," he said looking down at me with a snarl.

"I'm sorry but I came in here by mistake, if you could just..."

"The King's orders. No one enters, no one leaves," he repeated telling me I was screwed!

"But I really..."

"NO!" He leaned closer down to me and shouted the one word in my face and with it, sealing my fate. I shivered, walking away rubbing my arms as the room wasn't exactly the warmest, just like the staff, I thought with annoyance, wondering what I was going to do now? I looked to my right and saw a strange wall of sheer material hanging down from the ceiling and I wondered what was behind it. It could be a door or somewhere I could at least hide until I was allowed to leave. I walked closer but then stopped in my tracks as a line of naked figures started to come closer behind them. A bright light lit them up from behind and they all started their erotic shadow dance as the next line up for tonight's entertainment.

Well, I wasn't going to get far with them in the way. Seriously, was anything on my side at the moment? The only thing I could think to do next was to try and get to Karmun, in some last-ditch attempt at someone helping me. Okay, so it was unlikely but what other choices did I have? Who knows maybe he would fear Draven's wrath when finding me so would want to help me...yeah right Kazzy. Not exactly a sure thing I thought as I changed directions, taking me into the centre of the room.

There was a lot more people...well, *enjoying themselves* should we say, in this part of the room, so it was harder to move around in. Some of the belly dancers started when the music changed to something more sexual and ancient sounding. The lights changed, dimming to a soft warm glow of sunset colours, making me feel like I had just stepped back in time. They looked at me, smirking and holding out their scarves so that they would brush along me.

I needed to get out of here. Trying to get to the bar had been an obvious mistake as I had done the last thing I had ever intended to do, which was put myself at centre stage. I looked to my side and saw that not only was the bar directly to my right but more worryingly was what was directly to my left. The raised seating area where Draven had been sat was right there and I looked that way in what seemed like slow motion. My hair whipped around showing my face to Vincent who was currently looking at me over the beauty he was sucking blood from.

I bit my lip and at least could take a breath when I saw Draven was still missing. But Vincent had seen me and his lips slowly left the girl's neck as though he were some predator with his sights on new prey. But his eyes were no longer looking at me...they were looking behind me. Suddenly the air around me started to shift. Like someone had sent a dominating current through the sound waves and I sucked in a startled breath as the room shifted. All those eyes that had once been centred on me now had a new target and by the looks of all those wide, fearful eyes, I would say it was one that was far more important than I was.

I swallowed hard as I felt a presence step closer and invade my space from behind. I knew who it was. The whole room knew who it was. And the whole room now knew how much trouble I was in.

And I knew just how much trouble I was in when a voice belonging to the man in charge spoke in my ear…

"I found you."

BOOK I

31
Am I the Frog?

NEW...

I couldn't help my next actions as my fight or flight mode kicked in and my mind chose the obvious choice...I ran. Or at least I tried to. I think I made it about three steps before I was engulfed in a pair of strong arms from behind.

"No! no...no...let me go," I told him trying to struggle out of his hold but it was pointless.

"Stop." The command was hissed close to my ear and I did as I was told. But then I looked around and hated the way everyone stared at me. I couldn't stand it and felt my breathing become laboured...I was having a panic attack and I tried to control it like the therapist taught me to but with his arms around me it was getting more and more difficult. I couldn't focus with everyone looking at me...pitying me...I was that girl again...No, no, no!

"Calm down, Keira," Draven said behind me but I was too far gone. I couldn't calm down. They were all watching me. I couldn't calm...I needed to...I couldn't breathe. I was surprised when the only desperate word that made it past my lips, using my last breath to do so was his name...

"*Draven.*"

The next thing I knew the lights all went off again and this time they stayed like that. Silence hit the room like a crashing wave of death. In fact, it was as if the only two people left standing in a sea of darkness was myself and the man at my back, *Draven.*

"Ssshh, they are gone now. You can breathe," Draven cooed in my ear and his hold on me started to ease up so that I could take in a lung full of air.

"That's it. Deep breaths for me. Good girl," he said in a hypnotic voice that was all smooth velvet, one I knew could change to deadly in a second. The room was still as dark as night and I wondered how he did it. Did he make some kind of signal to someone near the power switch? And how had he made the whole room go silent like that?

"Now are you going to try and run again?" he asked me once I had got past my panic attack. I couldn't speak, so I shook my head to indicate 'No' but then I remembered he couldn't see me. But he leaned closer to me and whispered,

"I can see you, Keira." And I frowned, mentally scolding myself as I must have spoken my thought out loud without realising.

"Are you ready?" he asked and I didn't know what he meant but he must have taken my silence for a yes because the lights, music and sound all came back on as though someone had flipped a switch on the whole room…people and all. I was just about to feel the insecurities flow back into me when Draven spun me around to face him.

"Eyes on me, sweetheart," he demanded and I bit my lip when I did as I was told, looking up at him and finding myself stunned by his masculine beauty. And of course, there was trying to make sense of the way he called me 'sweetheart' making me question my sanity. I don't know how I was looking at him, probably like some lost, big eyed

Disney princess, looking into the eyes of her saviour because the next thing he said confirmed it,

"You keep looking at me like that and we are going to have problems," he told me and I felt like an idiot, looking away quickly and feeling the rejection and humiliation of it cut me deep. But as if my face had my fears graffitied across it, he turned my face back to him.

"Not what you're thinking," he said giving me no hint to what he had meant.

"Come with me," he ordered, taking my gloved hand in his and pulling me along with him towards his fallen seat. Vincent saw him coming and shifted, moving the beauty he had been amusing himself with. He whispered something down to her and she got up, looking sullen. He slapped her bare ass as a way of goodbye before she was out of reach and then he reached down and picked up his brother's chair ready for him.

"I see you found our missing waitress," Vincent said light-heartedly nodding his greeting towards me. I gave him a small nervous smile back wondering why it felt like I was being led into a trap.

"Did you doubt I would?" Draven replied with a confidence that said he didn't even need to try.

"Not for a second, brother," Vincent replied granting me a wink. I felt like holding up my hands and saying, 'okay so what's going on?' Only minutes ago, I felt like I was being hunted and now what, I was being invited to the party? Draven didn't offer any answers, he simply let go of my hand and turned around to swiftly sit down on his throne like chair. Now, being up this close, I could see the details of it and it was the perfect combination of solid carved craftsmanship and luxurious expense. It was a massive chair that looked like one made for both comfort and importance, one that suited the body that was now sat upon it. In fact, it was the only item in the room that was black and it complimented the darkness in Draven's features...including right now, his eyes.

I didn't know what to do with myself. I was just stood opposite him waiting for my next issued command and hoping it was to sit down as I was starting to feel myself getting tired from all the running about this hidden gothic palace of his.

"Sit down, Keira," Draven said as if he too couldn't understand what I was still doing on my feet. I looked around for another chair or an available cushion, when I shrieked as Draven's hands grabbed my waist.

"Ah!" I shouted in surprise, making Vincent laugh next to us. Draven had seemingly plucked me out of my standing position and turned me round, before placing me gently on his lap.

"Oh no…no, I can't sit here…I can just go…" I started trying to excuse myself from where he had placed me, feeling my shame hit new heights.

"By the Gods woman, you are freezing!" he said sounding angry. And I jumped in his lap at the sound, flinching along with it. It was at this point that Vincent leant closer and decided to inform him,

"She gave her jacket to her friend." I heard Draven growl behind me and again I tensed at the sound. But if he noticed my discomfort at being here sat on him like this he didn't make it known. No, instead he just added to my embarrassment and started rubbing his hands up and down my arms as if trying to get me warm.

"I…I am fine," I told him after first having to clear my voice to do so.

"You gave away your jacket in this weather?" he asked as if needing to hear it confirmed by me and once again ignoring any issues I might have with him being this close. Okay, so the only issue I had with it was that everyone was watching us and my cheeks felt like they were melting because other than that, having Draven's hands on me was like living out one of my dreams.

"Ignore them and answer me." Draven told me as I shifted uncomfortably under so many scrutinising eyes looking at me. Then when I didn't comply straight away he caught my chin in his hold and turned me to face him.

"She was wearing less than me and I was worried about her when we were waiting for our taxi." I told him quickly and he frowned.

"Taxi. You have a truck Keira, is there something wrong with it?" he asked me sternly as if hating the idea.

"Oh no. It's great!" I said getting a little high pitched with my nervousness and wishing I could take it back.

"Go on," he prompted and I took a breath and told him,

"I am really sorry. We didn't mean to come back in to the club...well break in but technically not, as I knew the code to get in the side door... but then I couldn't find my phone and RJ had too much to drink so got it in her head to sneak up into the VIP...I tried to stop her I really did but..."

"Ssshh, calm yourself," Draven said trying not to grin and Vincent looked as though he could barely keep a straight face.

"Let's start from the beginning shall we...why were you waiting for a taxi?"

"I don't drink and drive," I told him as if this would explain it all and some of it did.

"Ah, I see. So, you decided to get a taxi home with your friend. Then what happened?"

"Well, someone stole it!" I told him flinging an arm out in my exuberant outrage, one that nearly hit him but he caught just in time. He gently brought it down and kept it in his grasp for now, no doubt worried I would do it again.

"Someone stole your taxi?" he questioned as if for some reason, he could picture it.

"Well someone got in the one we booked and it drove off, so it's not really stealing but it wasn't very nice." I added feeling that if I didn't shut up soon I would say something even more stupid than how that sounded.

However, Draven just gave a me a small grin and nodded for me to carry on.

"So, anyway we were stranded there outside and it was cold so…"

"You were alone?" he cut in sounding once again pissed off.

"Well…yeah but…" Again, he never let me finish.

"Didn't I tell you never, *ever* to wait outside my club alone at night," he said reprimanding me with a tone I didn't want to mess with but I had to defend myself, so I bravely placed a hand on his chest to get him to listen.

"Yes, but wait. The first taxi went without knowing we were stranded outside and we let it without knowing it too. We thought we could just wait inside the club until another one turned up but when we turned back the place was shut up tight," I told him, unknowingly patting his chest gently and we both looked to what my hand was doing. I made a 'sorry' face at him and started to pull it back when he stopped me by grabbing my hand in his.

"I see. Which is why you re-entered the club…you did…"

"Yes, I know it was wrong and I really wished we hadn't. I am so sorry but we couldn't just wait outside and wait for another taxi because RJ's phone had run out of battery by taking pictures of some drummer guy and I seemed to have lost mine or forgotten it in the club, or so I hoped but couldn't find it…but anyway… so we had no way of calling for one." I said shaking my head and trying to explain all at once so he couldn't get angry, which only made my loose hair fly around the place and land on his shoulder.

I bit my lip and slowly picked it up and mouthing the word 'Sorry' placed it down again. Damn those tequila shots I thought, feeling more drunk now than when I had running about the place. He gave me a gentle look and pushed some of the loose hair behind my ear before giving Vincent a look I didn't understand. Vincent then motioned to one of the waitresses to come forward and he said something to her in another language I didn't understand,

"Su." (means 'Water' in Turkish.)

"You did right by coming back into the club, Keira," Draven told me, shifting my focus from his brother back to him.

"You're not angry?" I asked surprised by his reaction.

"No. I would have been if I'd heard you had waited any longer in the cold, especially after so selflessly giving another your jacket," he told me and I exhaled a deep breath feeling like a weight had been lifted.

"I am, however, angry that you chose to run and hide from my men, men who would have listened to your reasons and brought you straight to me, where I could have decided what was best for you." Draven said firmly and I gulped.

"Well I...I..." I tried to tell him why and when I couldn't get it out quick enough he raised an eyebrow in question at me.

"They scared me," I told him in a small voice, looking down at my lap, ashamed to admit it. He lifted my chin up and made me look at him again. This time his gaze was soft and gentle, as if he understood.

"They would never hurt you, Keira...*no one, will ever hurt you."* The first part of this sentence was said tenderly, the last part was said in a murderous promise that said he would kill anyone who tried. Little did he know that someone already had and I had barely survived it, I thought in one of those rare moments I couldn't help. I closed my eyes a moment and pushed the cruel memory deep down in the vault I kept it locked in but Draven looked at me as if he could read my mind, plucking it back from that dark place I was trying to cram it into.

"What did you say?" he asked determinedly and I shook my head and said,

"I didn't say anything."

"Your water, my Lord" the waitress said to Vincent who took it, nodded his thanks, and handed it to Draven. But Draven wasn't looking at him. No, he was fixated on me and I shifted uncomfortably at being the focus of such an intense gaze.

"Dom." Vincent said his name in one of those, 'Snap out of it' kind of ways. Draven wasn't in a hurry to tear his eyes from me, so instead held out his hand to retrieve it without looking. Then he twisted the cap and handed it to me.

"Drink. It will help rehydrate you after all the alcohol," he told me and I did as I was told, drinking back the cool water like it was a magic elixir for how good it tasted. But then a thought entered my head and I hated myself for how long it had taken me to think of her. So, I whipped the bottle from my mouth and shouted,

"RJ!" feeling a drop of water rolling down my chin. Draven saw it and caught it with his thumb, tenderly wiping it away.

"She is fine."

"I'd better go to her," I said making a move to get off his lap, which must have been aching for how long I had been sat in it. His arms quickly enveloped me, holding me right where I was and he growled a low rumble, startling me enough to flinch in his hold.

"Easy, Dom," Vincent warned as if he knew as an outsider looking in that his brother needed to rein in his obvious heightened emotions. I didn't think that Draven would ever hurt me but scare me, well then yeah, that could easily happen and often did thanks to his dark moods. Draven obviously listened to his brother, probably more than any other person in his life, so I wasn't surprised when he took a deep breath, closing his eyes as if this would help in getting control of his temper.

"I apologise if I frighten you. I just need you to trust me when I tell you that your friend is fine and simply resting in my guest quarters." As he said this he once again took it as an opportunity to touch me, like it was his right and I couldn't say I hated the feeling. Quite the opposite in fact, so much so that I relaxed back slightly allowing him to pull me closer. Then he continued to gather my wild hair in one hand and drape it over my shoulder out of my way. Or more like his way as swiftly after doing this he started running the back of his fingers down my blushing cheek.

"She's really okay?" I asked feeling strangely vulnerable like this. He nodded with a warm reassuring smile but it still felt as though any moment I was expecting him to just stand up, let me fall and walk away from me like I was nothing to him. Hell, but I couldn't understand why he was acting like I meant something to him now, as it hadn't been long ago he had been reprimanding me for being five minutes late for my shift. Which was why before I could stop myself I stated,

"You were angry at me for being late." He tensed and took hold of his goblet of what looked like red wine before placing it to his lips and taking a drink. He didn't take his eyes off me.

"I was," he stated back and nodded for me to take a sip of his drink. I took it without question, placing the metal cup to my lips, surprised to find it was cold and made of black glass. He nodded when I hesitated to drink for a second, looking down at it like I expected it to be drugged or something. But then why would he drink from it first...was it to prove there was nothing harmful in it, I wondered? In the end, I took a sip of it, realising it was as I first thought, red wine, only cooler than I had tasted it before. I then handed it back looking at the demonic design of a twisted spine that bent back, holding the symbolic cup that had markings etched all around it.

"But why?" I asked, this time looking down at the bottle of water still nestled in my lap and playing with the cap nervously. He obviously didn't like that something else was taking my focus off him so he picked it up out of my hands and placed it down on a small table next to his wine.

"I have my reasons," he told me cryptically, making me frown.

"And those are?" I pressed.

"Private," he told me firmly.

"Right," I said deflated, knowing the reasons would have meant something to me but he kept it to himself. Suddenly sat here with him was starting to feel wrong and the realisation that I was sat in a private party I had crashed, on my boss' lap was one I wasn't comfortable with anymore.

"I'd better go," I told him softly, taking a moment before giving him my eyes.

"Why must you go, Keira?" he asked as though he didn't agree.

"Because…well because…" I tried to think of the right way to say it but stumbled on the first hurdle.

"Because you think this is wrong…because I am your boss…is that what you think?" he asked, pausing after each question that all meant the same thing. I nodded biting my lip and wishing he wouldn't look at me like that…like he wanted to study me as if I was some kind of hobby of his…like collecting butterflies and pinning their wings to a board for all eternity.

"And do you not think it possible that you are here now because I *want* you to be?" he said emphasising the *'Want'* in that sentence. I swallowed hard and tried to look anywhere but at him.

"Give me your eyes, sweetheart," he demanded softly and I did without thinking about it. Just obeying. Just like that. What did this man do to me exactly that had me bending to his will without question? What I needed to question was my sanity as this man seemed to render it useless.

"Good, now answer me."

"No, I don't think it's possible," I told him honestly. He raised an eyebrow in surprise at my honest answer.

"Tell me why...why I would not relish the feel of you here in my lap, sat with me in my home and talking to me with ease?" he asked and my mouth nearly fell open. Had he really just said all those things? It was so unbelievable that I blurted out why,

"Because you hate me." To which he laughed as if now I was the one being unbelievable. I took the reaction as most people would and tried to get off his lap as quickly as possible. And thanks to his laughter he let me slip off but the second I made it one step, he had me around the waist again. He lifted me up as though I weighed nothing at all and simply placed me back where he wanted me.

"I could never hate you, Keira...now stop struggling or I will throw you over my shoulder and take you to bed...*to sleep,*" he told me adding the last part before my overactive and obviously sexual imagination could take it as something else. It must have shown in my eyes.

"You wouldn't," I dared, looking around the room and seeing it still full of people watching us.

"No, you don't think? Do you want to try me and find out?" he teased and I shook my head quickly, knowing that he would. His eyes spoke of a man who followed through with his threats and I didn't want to be the victim of that.

"Then stay where you are and relax...let me enjoy your company as I intend to," he told me in a way that was no doubt supposed to put my fears at ease. But, in actual fact, the way he said it had me wondering if he ever intended on letting me go. Alright so if I were being honest with myself I wasn't in any rush to leave him and I was still half convinced that this was just some depths of a dream I had fallen into. The problem I had with that was...where was my body whilst all this was going on?

He decided to help me try to relax like he suggested I do. So, he gathered my legs up so that I was sat across him, then side on like I had been. Now my back was against one armrest and he propped my legs over the other. Then he frowned down at my big Doc Martins as if they shouldn't be there.

"I am sorry, I shouldn't have my feet up against your nice chair," I said trying to move them back down when his hand shot out and gripped my thigh, stopping me. I sucked in a startled breath at the feel of his strong hand gripping my leg and tried to calm my beating heart or raging hormones.

"I care little for my chair," he told me as though that thought never even entered his head.

"Oh, well I..." I started to say my excuses for my moving them anyway when he cut in.

"But what I do care for is that you have no doubt been in those boots all day and on your feet working," he said placing my foot against the wooden frame, like he said, not giving a damn about his beautiful chair. Then he pulled my trouser leg up and over the boot, before he started pulling at the laces.

"That's all right, they don't hurt or..." He gave me a look that stopped me mid-sentence and continued to take each boot off for me. Then to my horror, he took my sock covered foot in hand and started rubbing them. I almost cringed and he noticed,

"Do you not like having your feet touched?" he asked and I gave him a small smile.

"No, I do...I do but, I can't imagine they smell at their best right now," I told him, this time making him smile. Then he turned to his brother and said something that made my embarrassment levels reach new heights,

"Vin, can you smell Keira's feet?" I made some kind of weird choking noise, one they both ignored.

"Nope, sure can't," Vincent replied winking at me.

"No, me either, must be all in your head, however, I do wonder at your choice of socks," he teased and I giggled making his eyes widen as if it was the first time he heard the sound and liked it.

"I understand the Union Jack flag, on account of your heritage but I must admit, the frog I am struggling to understand," he said again, making me giggle.

"I couldn't find matching socks this morning," I told him honestly making him grin down at me.

"Oh, and the frog's name is Kermit." I told him, wondering why I felt like adding this part. He raised a quizzical eyebrow but this time more in humour at me.

"And you named him this because…?" he asked and I couldn't help my reaction. I burst out laughing no doubt making him jiggle with me thanks to where I was sat. He held on to me as if there was a possibility of me falling off him and I found the gesture sweet.

"I didn't name him. He is one of the Muppets, you know, from 'The Muppet Show'." I told him and then decided it was a great idea to start whistling the theme tune, hoping this would help him but no, in the end it just had me blushing. Draven looked highly amused by my little performance.

"You have no idea what I am talking about do you?" I asked him and he shook his head slowly.

"But maybe if you describe it to me in more detail then it might prompt a memory," he said and at first I didn't pick up on the fact that he was teasing me…that was until it was too late and after I had started going into an explanation of who they were.

"Well you have Kermit the frog, oh and Miss Piggy, who he is in love with, but she's also a bit of a hussy, so he usually has his hands full," I said making him laugh.

"A frog married to a pig, now I have heard everything," he teased and getting carried away I placed my hand to his chest again and played along by saying,

"Oh, they aren't married…at least I don't think so anyway." He smirked at me and then covered my hand, holding it where I had placed it, then he gave it a squeeze and replied,

"Ah, so they are living in sin." The way he said the word 'sin' caused me to shiver and he knew it.

"You're teasing me." I told him and he faked shock.

"You're the one spinning tales of love between frogs and pigs thanks to cute socks on even cuter feet," he told me playfully and then grabbed a foot and ran a fingertip up the centre of my sole, making me laugh as it was ticklish.

"My nan bought me them for Christmas," I told him folding my arms across my chest, faking attitude and sucking at it. He leaned back as if pretending to be affronted and playing along.

"Is that so?" he said and I nodded trying to keep the smirk from my face.

"Then please tell me that you didn't do something unthinkable..." he asked leaning forward and I froze wondering what he could mean.

"...Like lose Miss Piggy," he finished, nodding to my un-matched sock with the little flags on it. I burst out laughing, this time so hard that I couldn't help but let loose something I hated...no, not hated...more like loathed! *I snorted.*

My hands flew to my mouth as Draven's eyes went wide in shock. Unfortunately, that wasn't the look of a man that had missed it like I prayed.

"Now what was that I wonder?" he said mockingly unable to keep the bad boy grin off his face.

"It was nothing," I said shaking my head and momentarily pulling my hands from my mouth but putting them right back there, straight after.

"It didn't sound like nothing to me. In fact, it sounded just like I have found my little Miss Piggy in person." He tormented me enthusiastically and I groaned making him laugh, this time making me bounce with the action. Then just before my shame could fully sink in, he pulled me closer and took it all away by asking,

"But I wonder...*does this make me the Frog?*" He finished this question close to my ear and I didn't know how to take his question. Hadn't I said that Kermit was *in love* with Miss Piggy? Was that what he was implying? No, surely not. No, this must have been a dream, there was no possible way it wasn't. Okay so granted, talking about the Muppets' love life wasn't exactly how I would have imagined dreaming about Draven. But I guess you were never in control of your dreams, were you, which was half the point wasn't it?

Dreams were a way to process the information collected through the day, and if you were worried or concerned...or more like in my case obsessed, then didn't it give you the chance to rewrite life? Rewrite time and bend it to what you wanted it to become? So, whether it was chatting about the weather or even the Muppets, it was basically giving me what I wanted...*time with Draven.*

A waitress came close to 'our' chair and topped up Draven's drink and I wondered if this was the part of the dream that really represented me and what I really was in his life...Just a passing shadow that floats close enough to do his bidding before disappearing back out again, unseen and unheard.

I bit my lip in worry and Draven must have seen it. So, he handed me his wine once more and this time I didn't just take a sip, I gulped it down.

"Easy there sweetheart, I think that's enough," he told me taking it back off me and drinking some himself before putting it down.

"Now tell me your worries," he asked shifting me slightly so that I was even closer to him. One arm was snaked around my back and rested at my arm, whilst he draped the other across my lap where his hand held firmly onto my hip. He looked so at ease I could almost convince myself that this had been something he had wanted to do for a long time. But the trouble with believing in the unbelievable was that it always proved its true nature, and snatched your belief back with one sharp word, or scathing look. And tonight, I had received both sides from Draven and I didn't know what to believe anymore.

"I am confused," I said knowing he was still waiting and Draven wasn't a man that you kept waiting…*ever*.

"I can see that beautiful, its telling a story in those alluring eyes of yours, but what exactly is confusing you, I am yet to find," he told me, calling me both beautiful and alluring in one sentence. Could he really think so…or was he just saying this out of guilt, or to try to put me at ease? Oh, God how could I feel this confused if it was just a dream? Surely, I would just be enjoying it?

"I don't understand why I am here and if I am because it's all just the dream my mind is trying to convince me it is. And if that's the case, then why am I so confused and not just enjoying it while it lasts." I blurted out all at once and then braved a look at Draven to see he looked truly shocked.

"You think you are dreaming?" he asked as if it needed clarifying.

"Yes."

"And why do you think that?" His question threw me off guard…what could I say, because I dream of you most nights. Because my obsession of you would naturally bring me here. Because I have been practically begging my dreams to bring me into your world that now, finally it has been granted and I am here in your arms. In front of everyone in his domain as if he relished in telling the world that I was his. Oh yeah, I could tell him all those things but first I would have to be sure, as in one hundred percent certain, that this was a dream, because if there was even a single thread of a chance that it wasn't…then no. I could never tell him those things. Which left me the question what could I say now.

So, in the end I told him the truth.

"Because after the way you have treated me the last few weeks, as if I never existed...well, then the very last place I would ever expect to find myself now is sat in the middle of a sex club, on your lap, after all I have heard all night is everyone referring to you as their King." I said taking a deep breath after as if my lungs would burst if I didn't.

I don't know what reaction I was expecting from Draven but looking to his brother wasn't it. Vincent had heard everything I had said, being sat close enough to hear and the look he gave his brother was one of knowing. It was as if he had warned him of this very thing and was now proven right. He shrugged his shoulders as if to say, 'well brother, this is your mess, now it's up to you to deal with it'.

Draven released a heavy sigh and raised his hand to the bridge of his nose where he held it for a second, as if this was a habit of his when frustrated. This was when it hit me and horror started to seep in.

"This isn't a dream, is it?" I asked in a quiet voice and Draven dropped his hand and shook his head, telling me no.

"I am really here?" I said, now being the one that needed this clarifying.

"You are," he stated firmly.

"But I...I..." At this, he finally took pity on me and leant closer to me so as he could whisper,

"Your mind has been lying to you. You are here because..." He paused a second so that he could get even closer to me, leaning forward so his lips were at my ear.

He first ran his nose part way up my neck before whispering the last of his sentence,
His confession…

"…Because I want you."

31

Bitches and Bites.

NEW...

On hearing this, I froze. It was as though someone had just switched on an internal panic switch and I didn't know what to do. Had he really just said what I think he said? And if so, how could he mean it!

"Say something," he told me and I simply shook my head as though he was wrong. He couldn't want me...it...it wasn't possible. I had just been talking about the damn Muppets for Christ sake! This must be some kind of trick. Yes, that was it. He must be trying to control me somehow...maybe worried I would tell the world about what went on here. This could be done just out of panic that I would spill his secrets. What could that do to a business man, to not only be associated with a sex club but to actually own one? Well I am sure that could destroy a man's reputation in a heartbeat.

"I have to go to the toilet," I blurted out making him frown. He wasn't taking me seriously so I said,

"Please...I think...I think I am going to throw up. I don't feel well," I told him and thankfully this time he took me seriously. He simply held a hand out as if to say, 'there you go then' and I got off his lap quickly, looking down at my discarded boots. I grabbed them, knowing I would need them if I was to get out of this place, so hopped around like an idiot trying to get them on.

"Here, let me…" Draven reached out as if to help me but I took a step back.

"It's okay, I've got it," I said making him frown…he didn't look happy. Well tough shit! He was the one that had taken this too far. Maybe if he had just asked me to keep this place a secret then I could have told him that he could trust me. That I would never speak of it. That I would keep any secret he asked of me and I would do so by taking it to my grave. But no. He hadn't trusted me. Instead he had used my obvious feelings of want for him and twisted them in a way to try and gain my trust that way…a trust he never knew he already owned.

I looked around as if trying to find the toilets, trying to make it believable, even though his look said I was doing anything but. Well, I was actually searching for my escape route, but he didn't need to assume that as surely, I had given him no reason to. He sighed before he motioned a waitress over, the one named Candra who also worked in the VIP.

"Yes, my Lord?" she said sweetly.

"Keira is feeling unwell, can you escorted her to the restroom and then see that she makes her way safely back here… *to me,*" he added this last part as a threat I was sure, given that he had turned to look directly at me when saying it. I couldn't help my reaction when I bit my lip. Okay, so scrap that, he knew.

"But of course, Keira, the restroom is this way," she said sweetly and I almost felt sorry for her, after all, I doubted very much that she would be returning here with me in tow. Not if I had anything to do with it that was. I stomped my other foot into my boot, not stopping to tie up the laces as I didn't want to do that in front of him. I just needed to get out of there and clear my head. I wanted to find some hole to swallow me up in and stay there until my tears ran dry. I had been played and I knew it!

"Idiot, Keira!" I said to myself making Candra turn back to me and ask,

"Sorry, did you say something?" I shook my head and smiled. Then I continued to follow her to some hidden doors at the back of the room...the furthest point from the exit I thought with a grind of my teeth.

"I will wait here for you," she told me and I laughed trying to sound light hearted, even though it felt like it had been pumped with lead and landed in my bloody stomach.

"Oh, that's all right, I am sure I can find my way back," I told her, hoping she didn't take her job as seriously as Draven thought...I was wrong.

"I obey orders," she stated simply, telling me basically I was screwed. I laughed nervously and muttered as I walked into the restroom,

"But of course, you do." I then let the door shut behind me and I looked back to see if it had a lock, as I was half tempted to stay in here all night if it meant getting away with not seeing Draven for the rest of it! I walked to one of the fancy cubicles briefly taking in all the pale marble, carved stone and wrought iron fixtures. I shut the door behind me and sat down on the closed lid. Once in what I considered a safe place I leant forward cradling my head in my hands as I let the tears fall. I just couldn't help it. The emotional roller-coaster that was Draven was breaking my heart and he didn't even know it.

So, I cried for the taste of Draven I had been given and now lost. Because the reality of my situation was clear. I could either go out there and continue to drink in his flirtations as if I had no clue as to the reasons behind them or I could put a stop to the lies and leave. I was stupidly tempted to do the first but then I knew it wouldn't have been real and I couldn't live a lie. Not unless it had been constructed from my own fantasies and lived out through a harmless dream. But a lie? No, I couldn't live out a lie and enjoy it.

Now the question was how the Hell was I going to get out of here? I supposed I could just walk out there and scream the place down, shaming myself and him enough that I would give him no choice but to get me out of there…maybe even having me escorted by a member of his staff. It sounded good, if even the idea of doing so had me feeling sick for real this time.

A few minutes later, after a brief knock at the door from Candra I pulled myself together enough to say,

"I am coming, just give me a sec." Then I heard a muttered voice say,

"Allow me, I will see if I can help." Then I heard the door close and I jumped when I heard a bang on my door as if someone had slapped a palm to it.

"Knock, knock, piggy," said a voice I loathed. I snarled inwardly knowing that by that comment alone the bitch Layla had heard everything between me and Draven. I opened the door feeling my anger replace my hurt and saw that she was smirking, leaning against my door frame like she was relishing the sight of me upset.

"Do me a favour and crawl back to whatever hole you just crawled out of…I am not in the mood for your shit!" I snapped pushing past her and going to the sinks. I looked at myself in the mirror and saw that it was obvious that I had been crying. The whites of my eyes were now red and tear lines still stained my skin like invisible tracks of despair.

"I would be more than happy to, the only problem is you are there," she told me making me frown at her. Had she really just implied that she thought of Afterlife as a hole? If so, then why was she here?

"Well there isn't much I can do about that with Candra waiting outside the door to take me back to 'Your Lord'." I threw back at her. This is when she hissed at me and in a heartbeat had her hand at the back of my neck, pushing me against the mirror over the sinks.

"*He is no Lord of mine,*" she snarled next to my face.

"Get off me!" I warned but it felt like an empty threat as she had hold of me and there was little I could do.

"Not yet."

"If you don't then I will scream and everyone, including Draven will coming running in here," I threatened her, knowing this was probably my only hope.

"Then that will only defeat the object of your current desires," she told me in a sickly voice, which made me shudder.

"And what is that?" I gritted out.

"To get out of here without him seeing you leave," she told me and I hated that she was right. Because in this moment in time that was all I wanted.

"Oh, and you're going to help me with that, are you?" I asked sarcastically and she snapped her teeth at me twice, like some strange creepy tick. Then she released me, making me fall forward as she pushed me aside. I saved myself on the sinks before righting myself up.

"I don't help your kind, *I destroy it.*" She added this last part as though something else inside of her had said it. It was some demonic rasp, grating against the bars of reality she was keeping it locked against. I wanted to ask her what she was but I was afraid to. I took a step back, knowing now that I wasn't simply against another catty woman acting like a bitch with a grudge. She was dangerous and I…

I was in danger.

"Ah, finally you are starting to see. Well I will grant you with the sight you chose to ignore, so you can see this place for what it really is. Consider it my gift to you, that and my helping you escape," she told me calmly pulling out a tube of lipstick from her bag and reapplying the red stain to her pouting lips.

"But you said that you don't help my kind."

"Yes, but it will be done so for my gain," she answered me calmly.

"You want me out of the way." I guessed and she grinned, her lips reaching higher on one side.

"It is only a matter of time until he casts you aside anyway, I am simply speeding up the process," she threw at me, straightening her long platinum hair off to one side. I couldn't help but look at myself in the mirror in comparison. No makeup, I looked tired with sore eyes that had been self-abused with my crying. My hair lay in a mass of wavy curls the colour of straw, loose and untamed. My clothes black and plain, just like I was.

"Did you really think a man like Dominic Draven could want something like you. Look around his world and see the beauty that fills it…you certainly won't find yourself there but more like cast to the shadows where you belong." She told me playing on my insecurities like a puppet pulling strings of a doll that didn't want to hurt herself but couldn't get away. I hated her but I hated myself even more for believing…if only for a second. She was right. Why would a man like Draven ever want…

Want me.

"What about Candra?" I asked deflated but knowing that if she was the only one who could get me out of here, then I would have no choice but to take what warped help she had to offer.

"Leave her to me, all you have to concern yourself with is getting yourself gone."

"And how do I do that when the only exits are either locked or guarded?" I asked hating myself even more for it.

"There is a side door. It is hidden from sight by a red curtain. I made sure it was left unlocked. I will create a distraction and when I do, you can run for it," she told me, making it obvious she had planned this from the start.

"Where does it lead to?" This was something I needed to know if I was going to be successful as she no doubt hoped I was.

"It leads to the roof."

"Oh, and let me guess, you want me to then jump off it." I mocked sardonically. She gave me a flat lipped look as if to say, 'Funny but no'.

"Well if you would prefer then please don't let me stop you. But if falling to your death doesn't appeal, then take the staircase down. It leads around Draven's private chamber and balcony." I thought on this and hated the idea that my last few steps in Afterlife would be in the place I had dreamed of being in the most…Draven's room.

"Once there you will be able to slip through his chamber and into the main hallway. This leads directly back into the club…from there on I think you know your way out," she said, stinging me with this last piece of venom and emphasising that my station in Draven's life was always meant to lead to one place… outside his front door.

"Of course, I don't have to remind you never to set foot inside these walls once again or I cannot be held accountable for what may happen to you," she threatened, looking down at her nails as if waiting for them to change into claws so she had a weapon to back it up with.

"I don't think you have anything to worry about," I snapped.

"Well I should hope not but just in case you momentarily lose what sanity you have left, I will leave you with the gift I spoke of." This was the only warning I received before she attacked. I tried to scream out as she landed on top of me but her hand slapped down over my mouth. I tried to bite her and kick my legs from under her but it was as if she had the strength of ten men. I couldn't understand it, that was until her eyes started to glow red and I knew in a terrifying heartbeat that she wasn't human…no, she was one of my demons!

"Now you will see the horrors that no longer hide under your bed but above it, with you beneath us like the insects you are!" She growled down at me before biting into my neck to open a wound. I screamed in agony under the restraints of her hand as I felt her teeth pierce the taut skin arched back with her hand pressing hard on my forehead, holding me still. Then she released me, pulled back a bit and seemed to spit in the open wound she had created. Her sadistic mouth smiled as she looked down at me, with long strings of crimson ribbons dripping from her lips as my blood escaped her.

"Now you will see the true nature of the nightmare you dream of having in your bed," she snarled down at me just as my vision started to blur. I closed my eyes as a strange feeling started to rise up in me. I felt drugged and I shook my head feeling her hand now slip away.

It was done.

She had finished and so was I.

Visions of Draven flickered through my mind over and over as though they were being played out in some kind of flicker book my mind had created. I would see him first as a man and then he would change. A great shadow would slowly appear behind him until the images would change quicker from man to monster until pretty soon no part of the man was left. What was happening? What had she done to me?

I don't know how long I remained on the floor but at some point, I started to open my eyes and the ceiling above came into view. I raised my hand to the pain in my neck and looked back to see my fingertips painted red. I decided I needed to move. I didn't know what I was going to do next but I couldn't stay here. What if she came back or worse, what if Draven found me and what she had shown me was true. What if the secret Draven was trying to hide wasn't that he spent his time in a private sex club at all.

What if it wasn't what Draven was into but what if it was what *Draven was.* Either way I needed to get out of here and my last hope started and ended with that crazy bitch's schemes. So, I pushed my body to move, no matter how much it hurt to do so. The aches and bruises from having her land on top of me and tackle me to the ground would mean pain tomorrow no doubt but that wasn't my main concern right now. It was making sure that there was a tomorrow for me that was what I needed to ensure and getting my ass up was the start of that.

I pulled myself first to my knees and then, placing a hand on the sinks, I pulled myself to my feet. I looked in the mirror to see that my neck had been torn into and the streams of blood that trickled down it were the result. I stepped over to the shelf, falling side on into the wall thanks to the affects her bite had caused. I still felt drugged, which was why my hands were shaking as I reached for the folded black hand cloths that I guess were used to wipe your hands after washing them.

I placed it by my neck to aid in stopping the bleeding and grabbed another one for when I needed it, stuffing it in my pocket. Then I pushed open the toilet's main door a crack to see if Candra was still there...she wasn't. It looked like the bitch was keeping her end of things at least I thought with a sneer. Well it was now or never. I pushed myself through the door and looked around trying to see what her idea of a diversion was.

I squinted as my sight started to blur once more and then it would clear after I rubbed my eyes with my one free hand. My other was trying to keep the cloth in place and I could feel the blood dripping from beneath it down my side. Then just as I starting to write Layla off as the traitorous bitch she was, there came a loud noise from one of the waitresses serving a rowdy group of drinkers. It was Layla and she slapped a man before kicking him in the chest. He fell back onto another man and quickly a fight broke out. My eyes automatically went to Draven who had motioned for his men to sort it out.

This gave me my opportunity as the door she spoke of became accessible. I turned around, looking down as they passed and then back again to the door. I ran towards it at a steady pace as I didn't want to make a scene as I pushed passed people but thankfully they seemed too busy in getting in on the fight to take much notice of me.

I just reached one table and the effects of Layla's bite started to take hold again. I bent over it for a moment as my vision went and my legs with it. I managed to hold myself up using the edge of the table until it started to clear but before it did, I looked left, testing that vision and saw the unbelievable.

A girl's face changed from being beautiful to horrendous with one shake of her head. Teeth, row after row of them embedded not only in her elongated mouth, but down the line of her chin. Eyes like fire burned back into mine as if she knew I could see her for what she truly was. She snarled at me and I turned to her friend who made me want to vomit. Red flesh hung down in patches as if she had been sown together over a rotting corpse. They were terrifying and I stumbled back and would have fallen had it not been for another table behind me. I looked to its occupants and they too were monsters. It was all true. My demons were back and this time they were everywhere!

I turned and ran as fast as I could to the door and just as I pulled it open I turned to look.

I knew it was wrong.

I knew it was a mistake.

But I had to know...I just had to know.

And I was right.

Draven was a Demon.

BOOK 1

32

Bathroom Blood.

NEW…

I pushed open the door and ran to save my life as my heart had already been lost in the sight of what Draven really was. If I were to live until the grand old age of a hundred, I don't think any sickness of the mind would be strong enough to eradicate that image and cast it aside, putting it down to madness. I wished I could have believed I was simply drugged and it was all an illusion but the problem I had with this theory was that I had seen Layla for what she really was before she had bitten me.

So that, along with all other excuses for Draven sat upon his throne with dark wings and purple veins pulsating around his body, were all but spent. I had nothing left but dangerous questions. Questions I certainly wasn't stupid enough to stick around to have answered. Hell, but I wasn't even sure that if he ever did get his hands on me that he wouldn't just kill me saving himself the bother. It wasn't exactly as if he wouldn't be able to make it looked self-inflicted, not with my past and scars to go with it.

I shuddered this horrific thought away, casting it from my mind as much as my current situation would let me. Instead I ran up the stairs and like Layla had said, it led onto the roof. It was freezing up there and with the winter's chill, it had also started to rain. It felt like icy shards were cutting into my skin, whipping and lashing down at me like the Gods above were angry.

I looked behind me, my hair becoming soaked as waves clumped together and stuck to my face. But I didn't care, what I cared about was whether or not I was being followed. I released a small sigh of relief when I saw no one and I continued around the stone roof looking for a way down.

The small walls enclosing the space looked like they had been taken off a castle, with square dips in the blocks so that someone could peer over the sides. Well that wouldn't be me, that was for damn sure as I hated heights. A thought that hit me full throttle when I saw the winding staircase she had spoken about.

"Shit!" I said out loud, wondering if jumping off hadn't been a better option right now, as I was sure my nerves would never survive such a thing. The steps that wound around the turret like structure were without balustrades or anything to stop you from just falling off the edge. They were wet and slippery and being this high up in the dark it looked like a never-ending abyss below me. But what other choices did I have?

None.

I knew this when I heard an almighty bellow of rage, that was quickly followed by the shattering of what sounded like a thousand windows. I knew then.

I had been found out and…

Draven was coming for me.

So, I took a deep breath and just hoped that I didn't fall to my death.

"No time for being clumsy today, Keira," I said taking that first step. Then I took another and another before I no longer thought about it and desperation took over my fear. A greater horror over another could do that for a person, I found as I thankfully reached the bottom.

Once there, I looked to see that everything she had described was right in front of me. A large half-moon shaped balcony spread out like a marble fan in front of me. This was accessed by a large glass door that had no handle. I felt the soaked cloth by my neck and dropped it, letting it slap to the floor. Then I pulled the dry one from my pocket and placed it over my wound as I walked to the door.

I could see his life spread out in front of me. His personal space as though some Lord of the Manor lived here and I guess...well I guess that he did. But the Lord of what exactly, I didn't know. I looked across towards his bed, one that was situated opposite the doors so that no doubt he could wake to a perfect view of the sunrise over the national park. I could just imagine the sight. Being so close to it you felt as though you could almost touch it.

I reached out to the glass as if seeing it all there reflected back at me. Waking next to him. Stretching out, my fingertips being met by the warm sun kissed skin of my lover...Draven. He would grab me from behind, wrap his arms around me and together we would bask in the beauty before us. I was so close, I could almost feel it. I could almost feel the first of the sun's rays as it rose to signal the new day. I even closed my eyes as if it blinded me. His world merging with my own. I was so close now that something in my mind started to make sense of some of it. Could it be that I was...I was always meant to see?

"NO!" I shouted banging my hand against the glass door in anger. What had come over me? I wasn't part of his world! I wasn't...and that's when I felt it as the door whooshed past, opening up so close to my face I felt the cold air slap at my skin. One I had needed and it had been named *reality*.

But it wasn't just the door opening that I had felt, it had been what was coming.

Or should I say…

Who.

I heard it first above me, as if some giant force was commanding the air, the wind, all the elements that the stormy night had brought. I turned around to face my fate and looked up at the night to see the demonic figure watching me from above. I tried to swallow but it felt like a lead ball was stuck there. I tried to move back but my legs wouldn't work. It was as if my body was betraying me and my need to run.

So instead I stayed where I was. Rooted to the spot as he let his massive wings fold so that he could drop down with speed. He landed on the marble floor with such force it cracked under the one knee he had to the floor. His other leg bent with foot to the floor aiding him as he slowly rose to full height.

"Draven." His name escaped me on a frightened breath and he looked as though he had heard it.

"Going somewhere, Keira?" he asked me, the anger in his voice slipping through the cracks of control. I couldn't speak and looking at me and where I was, it was obvious he didn't need an answer. He took one step closer and again I cursed my legs and my inability to move. His movements were slow and precise, as if he didn't want to move too quickly in case he frightened me into running. But looking at him now and I think that hope was out of the window or more like cast to the brutal wind that lashed out around me.

As he walked closer he noticed something on the ground, a red, pinkish puddle around a black cloth. He frowned down at it and bent to pick it up, bringing it to his face as if to smell it. The second he knew what it was he crushed it in his hand and growled, my blood dripping down his bare arm, like crimson veins.

"You're hurt." The demonic rumble sounded deadly and he scanned over my body as if trying to find the cause of my blood that was now dripping from his hand. I momentarily moved my hand that was held by my neck and he noticed the motion, now finding the source of my injury. He took a demanding step towards me and finally my legs started to work. I took a step back and into his room out of the storm of nature but welcoming a storm of a different kind indoors.

Draven didn't stop this time, nor did he slowdown in fear of frightening me. No, now he had new focus and he was intent on getting to me and my wound. I didn't know where I was backing up to but I looked down for a second and found my back against a large post. Seeing that it was part of his bed, I tried to move to the side but a strong arm shot out and stopped me. His strong muscle pulsated with purple blood flowing in his veins and it held me in place like a demonic barricade.

I took my time in looking from his arm to the demonic being it was attached too. Turning my head so slowly I followed it along from forearm, to elbow, to bicep and then to shoulder where I finally braved looking up at the man I had been falling in love with. Once there the purple flames in his eyes died down slightly, turning his irises a darker shade like I was more used to.

He didn't say anything at first, he just reached up and took my wrist in his hold. Gently then he started to pull my hand away from my blood-soaked neck and the sting made me suck air through my teeth. Hearing my pain affected him in a way I didn't understand. His eyes flashed purple flames for a second and his grip tightened on my wrist as if it were an impulse. But he never hurt me and his actions weren't screaming the murderous kind that I would have expected to see.

"Who did this to you?" he asked me, the threat in his tone not easy to miss. But it wasn't aimed at me, I knew that. It was aimed at the one who had inflicted the injury.

"Keira answer me, *answer me now.*" His warning spoke of a man on the edge...no, make that a *demon on the edge.*

"Layla." I said the one name that he must have expected me to say. I jumped at the demonic sound that rumbled up from his chest, like some caged beast was trying to get free from the depths of where his soul had kept him locked away.

"Calm yourself, for I will not harm you...do you understand?" he told me softly and for the first time since the bathroom I took my first easy breath. So, I might now be faced with this version of Draven but at the very least it didn't seem like he was set out to kill me. Capture me and make me his prisoner, I wasn't so sure but I couldn't say that experiencing this tender side of a demon was the worst thing that had happened to me tonight.

He let go of my hand and took hold of my chin instead so that he could gently turn it to the side for a better look. I hissed in pain and he gave me a sympathetic look.

"I am sorry for the pain, but I need to see what that bitch has done to you," he explained before going back to examining it with gentle fingertips.

"She bit me," I told him, speaking for only the second time.

"As I can see. Where did this happen?" he asked, putting my head back straight before lifting it slightly so that I could look him back in the eyes.

"In the bathroom," I told him and my voice sounded so small that I felt weak when saying it. But then again, I had been bitten, drugged by some demonic spit and then bled all the way to the roof and down.

"And now you see..." His question trailed off, looking back to his side where his wings remained folded at his back. I didn't say anything, as I didn't know what to say. For starters, I didn't really know what he was, so I simply nodded, looking down.

"Don't be afraid. I won't hurt you…alright? Tell me you understand, Keira," he told me and it seemed very important to him that I comply. So, I nodded again. He must have known how difficult this was for me, so he let that be his answer and found it good enough.

"You're freezing. Come with me," he said running the back of his fingers down my cold cheek. After this he took my hand and pulled me further into his room. I let myself go with him because really, what other option did I have.

He led me over to one corner where a long tapestry hung. I didn't have time to make out the design as Draven pushed it aside with his free hand in one sweeping motion. Behind it was a hidden door, one I couldn't help but pull back from. He looked back at me, to see I wasn't following like he expected and he gave me a questioning look before finding pity on my ragged nerves.

"It is only my bathroom…see, no one, but us," he told me, holding the door open and stepping back so that I could see inside and understanding my fears for what they were…*warranted mistrust.* I nodded and followed him inside slowly, as if any minute I expected someone to jump out at us.

"See, just a bathroom," he told me gently as if scared I would bolt any second like the fearful doe I felt. But at the sight of Draven like this, then who could blame me. Even in here, a place that was none threatening, with its luxury walk in shower, beautiful gilded mirror and marble pillars framing a huge sunken bath… even then, he was intimidating. With his huge wings shadowing his every move like a dark frame cast around his large body. A wet t shirt was plastered to every muscle, and even the part of his torso that was covered, you could still see the power beating against his skin beneath it.

My dark Angel of Hell stood looking down at me as I watched him with trepidation.

"Don't be frightened of me, not even as you see me now," he asked and I closed my eyes as he confirmed my sanity was still intact and this was real. I felt his hand at my cheek and I opened my eyes up to him as we shared this silent moment of acceptance. I nodded and he seemed to relax his tensed shoulders, as if half of him had been expecting the worse...as I had done.

"Good. Now let's get you warm, starting with getting you out of those wet clothes," he stated firmly and I jumped when I heard the sound of rushing water.

"Calm yourself, it is only the bath." I looked to see he was right, as water spilled over a flat piece of stone and down into the pool that was Draven's bath.

"How did you..." I started to ask how he had made the water come on like that but then he grinned at me and said,

"I think it best not to test your limits too soon, not after all you have witnessed tonight." I nodded thinking this was probably the wisest decision and I gladly let him take that responsibility from me.

"Now let's get this off you," he said stepping up to me and gripping the material at the bottom of my top. I placed my hands on his to stop him and asked nervously...

"Wh...what are you...?" He didn't let me finish.

"What I am doing sweet girl, is getting this wet, cold and bloody material off you before you freeze to death," he told me softly but with enough force to know that I wouldn't get far if I refused. I hadn't even nodded my consent before he started to peel it from my cold pale skin and up over my head. My wet hair fell down in thick waves that had all joined together thanks to it being soaked. It was the only sound made as it hit the bare skin on my back and I shivered because of it.

I covered myself, hugging my arms over my bra and the look he gave me wasn't impressed. He raised an eyebrow in an expectant way and I bit my lip before lowering my arms down. This was what he wanted as his features smoothed and he praised me,

"Good girl." I only wished that hearing it didn't affect me the way it did as my body gave an involutory shiver. One that wasn't down to how cold I was. He acted as though it was his given right to see me this way and I couldn't help but wonder if it was down to him being the one in charge or just down to it being me. Either way my answers would have to wait as what he did next had all thoughts flying from my mind, making enough room for the insecurities that came next.

"I...I...can..." I was about to protest as he started to go for the button on my trousers but his actions stopped me mid-sentence. He gripped my waistband with his fingers dipping down against my underwear at the front. Then he gripped it tight and hauled me closer to him so that I had to arch my neck back to look up at him, placing my hands against his chest to steady myself. I ran a tongue over my dry lips at the feel of solid muscle beneath my palms. His eyes burned at the sight of what I was doing with my tongue and I heard before I felt the sound of my trousers tearing. He looked like a man on the edge, holding himself back from what he wanted to do to me and from the looks of things, that something was ravish me.

"You are mine to take care of," he told me, gritting out the statement and I simply nodded, telling him silently to continue. No matter how confused I was at hearing it. He thought of me as *his?* Maybe he meant 'his' as in 'his responsibility' because I worked for him? It was possible, well that was until he looked at me like a man starved of my touch.

He slowly let go of his demanding hold and undid the button so that he could then slide my zipper down. I swear the sound of it echoed in the room as I felt every line of teeth it unlocked, swallowing hard when it was finished. Then he lowered himself before me, getting slowly down on one knee and it was a place I could imagine he rarely found himself before anyone. His wings curved slightly at his feet, started to evaporate as their room became limited in the space given. I looked on in awe as if this was done without even needing to think about it and I found myself wondering where half of them had gone to?

Once knelt by my feet, there he looked up at me, put both hands to the side of my hips before gripping the waistband. Then as if the act itself was one to be savoured, he slowly pulled the material down, first over the soft triangle of my panties before the tops of my pale thighs came into view.

He watched as though a gift was being unwrapped and I wanted to sink to the floor to hide from the intensity of it all. I had never been looked upon so closely, as if he were studying every inch of my skin and filing it away in some private memory bank.

"You're so pale, your skin looks as though it has been bathed in milk," he told me in a tender tone and I blushed, proving it wasn't all pale. He tapped each foot, telling me to step from the last of my wet trousers and once I had done so, he rose once more to his full height. I looked away, unable to challenge his gaze as he drank in his fill of me stood here in just my underwear and gloves. I flinched when I felt the back of his fingers run up the centre of my belly until he reached the curve of my heaving breasts.

*"Beautiful...*you're so beautiful, Keira," he told me and I sucked in a startled breath...did he really think so?

"Beautiful but still cold," he said as my only warning before he picked me up in his arms and walked me towards the bath.

"Wait, what about you." I said in shock as he walked us both up the steps and down into the warm, comforting water that surrounded our bodies together. He was still dressed but he didn't seem to care as his main aim seemed to be getting me warm. I watched, utterly fascinated at the sight of his wings being submerged under water and I had the greatest urge to reach out and touch them. Would they feel wet or would they have some kind of oil protecting them against such things.

"When you look at me that way I find myself curious as to what you are thinking?" He told me tilting his head slightly as if trying to read me. He shifted me around so that I faced him and I almost shrieked out in surprise when he placed each of my knees by his thighs, either side of him. I was basically sat astride him as he gathered all my wet hair back from my face.

"Well sat like this, I think you could probably guess." I told him blurting out my first thoughts and regretting it instantly. My hands flew to cover my mouth and he laughed heartedly.

"And there she is, that spirited little waitress of mine," he said and I bit my lip at once again hearing him calling me his. But he didn't give me much time to focus on it as he said,

"Now let's see what can be done about this neck of yours." Then he reached a hand up into my hair at the back and gripped it slightly, using it to turn my head to where he wanted it. He arched my head to one side so that he could see my wound more clearly.

"The bleeding has stopped at least," he told me, softly running a finger around the crescent moon of teeth marks.

"I do not like seeing another's mark upon your body," he said surprising me enough to ask,

"Do you…do you bite people?" He looked taken aback for a moment as if trying to decide where the question had come from but then seeing his world from my point of view.

"No, I do not but others of my kind, yes sometimes," he answered truthfully and I couldn't fully explain the relief I felt on hearing that he didn't. The green snake of jealously definitely had something to do with it. I then braved asking my next question,

"And what is your kind exactly?" He gave me a look as if assessing what he should and shouldn't say next, probably seeing if I could accept it or not. The outcome was a disappointing one.

"All in good time sweetheart, but for now, I think it best not to push the limits of your mind, now hold still," he told me, smirking a little at the sight of my little pout I was unable to hold back.

"Why...what are you going to do?" I asked timidly.

"I am going to heal you," he stated as if it should have been obvious. Then with no other warning he placed his lips over my bite and started to suck, as if trying to take the poison away. Well whatever he was doing it felt amazing and it was a good job he had hold of the back of my head because it felt as if it could roll off my neck at any minute! I couldn't help the moan that escaped as I arched my neck further into him, an action he must have liked if his throaty growl was anything to go by. His hand gripped my hair in a more possessive hold as if he were afraid I would take his prize from him.

Then something strange started to happen and it wasn't a feeling that at my age, was something I didn't recognise. Oh no, I recognised it alright, only too well but this, well it seemed to be amplified by a hundred. It started to rise up from that place deep inside you where you always wondered after your sexual high where had it really come from. It felt like every nerve in your body had synced and were working as one in perfect harmony with the sole purpose of building your pleasure until you just couldn't contain it anymore.

That was what this felt like, only instead of it bursting when it usually did, something was allowing it to build up until insanity felt like the only outcome.

"Draven, Draven...Draven you have to stop...I can't..." I told him desperately trying to hold on to the last thread of self-control I had left. I gripped onto his shoulder just for something to anchor myself to and he growled at my neck before releasing me enough to say,

"Just let it go...*trust me Keira, I have you.*" The second he said this I realised that he must have known all along. He must have known what his actions would cause and as he gripped me closer towards him, it felt like he would never let me go. He sucked harder, taking in my blood and feeding on me like some wild beast. This thought alone was enough to trigger something inside of me and my body responded to the possessive act by doing as he commanded...by...

Letting go.

I suddenly threw my head back and screamed out my release into the night, my body unable to contain itself bucked and jerked in his hold. My core tensed and convulsed over and over as the rest of my body continued to shake in his arms.

"Ssshh, calm...calm now." He cooed into my hair, holding my head to his chest as I hadn't realised but he had left my neck and had shifted me, so that he could hold me close in his lap. I was panting into his wet t shirt trying to catch my breath and he took deep breaths, prompting me to do the same.

"Deep breaths, that's it, good girl," he whispered, gently stroking back my hair and I had to admit, that in all my life I had never experienced such a moment as this before.

I had never felt so safe.

So, treasured...*so...*

So, wanted.

AUTHOR'S INSIGHTS.

Chapter 33
Book 1

Now in this next part I must point out that it doesn't follow on from the first part of the chapters given to you in this book. The reason for this is that I cut a huge chunk of the book out, (twice) as I decided to change the direction as to where it was heading. So, I rewrote it from the point of where Keira is working the VIP for the first time. This means that the following chapters for you to read, lead on from the original book, the one you all have read.

This is one of those chapters that carried me away to a place in the book I was desperate to get to, which was Keira in Draven's arms sooner, rather than the later it became. But unfortunately, I decided to rewrite the chapter as I found it hard to follow on from this point the way I wanted to. I did however want Keira and Draven to have their first argument, as by this point they both needed to release the mounting tension and get out some of that frustration they both felt towards each other.

So instead, I wrote Keira leaving the club with Malphas and being followed by Vincent. This way he could issue his warning and inform her that her presence was demanded the next day by Draven.

This also meant she could still have her heart to heart with Jack, where she finds out about his 'Missing Girlfriend'. And of course, have even more to throw in

Draven's face when they finally get their explosive moment.

This version goes a little differently though but I do hope you enjoy it all the same, I know I did when writing it, wink, wink...

(Jack has just been kicked out of Afterlife and Keira is going upstairs to demand why from Draven...fuelled by a little too much liquid courage that is.)

33
Halloween Heartbreak.

"Draven wants to see me," I said with such confidence that they both looked at each other then back at me, so I continued,

"You can go and ask him if you like, but I can tell you now, he doesn't like to be kept waiting."

This was enough to achieve my goal as they parted to let me through the doors. Once inside, I took a moment to think about what I was going to do. Was I really going to walk straight up to his table and demand a reason from him as to why he would give an order for Jack to be taken away?

"Shit! Yes, I am!" I said aloud. It just didn't make any sense and there was absolutely no way I believed any of the accusations against Jack were true. No, this had to stop and it would stop tonight!

The liquid courage helped me get through the doors and walk straight over to his table. I barely noticed anything else as I could feel my blood boil, I was so angry. I was shaking at the thought. I reached the front of the table standing directly in his view and stood there fuming.

Oh, and didn't he know about it. Draven's face was controlled well but I could see the underlying surprise in his dark terrifying eyes. There was also something more there, but it was a look I had never seen before. However, this just added fuel to the fire that was scorching inside my belly. I was burning hot at the very sight of him. I walked straight up to the table but was stopped by the giant Ragnar. Even then my courage didn't fade. No, if anything it had the opposite effect. I folded my arms across my chest and looked up at the brute.

"Excuse me!" I said through my teeth when what I really wanted to say was 'Get the hell out of my way, you big oaf!'

He didn't move but he did turn his head towards Draven waiting for a command, like a dog did from his master! I, on the other hand still hadn't taken my hateful eyes from Draven's. I was standing there getting ready to be escorted downstairs, thinking how much this would make me snap. I knew how Draven would not like a scene. But what he did next surprised me.

"Let her through." At this his dog backed down letting me pass. I ran a frustrated hand through my hair as I walked by and I could swear I heard him growl at me. Draven and the rest of the table came into full view and my heart missed a beat at the sight. I tried to control the pounding in my chest but I knew that I couldn't falter now I had come this far.

Draven was wearing all black, which enhanced his terrifying beauty. The rest of the table were also dressed very grand, as though they were celebrating something of their own. My eyes scanned the table and I realised there was another man present who I had never seen before.

He had long straight hair that looked almost like ice as it was whiter than white. His face was long with a thin straight nose to match that reminded me of a crow's beak. He looked older than Draven or anyone else on the table, for that matter. This gave him a very wise and knowledgeable looking face. I scanned his frame and saw he was wearing an unusual suit that looked like half a robe with a long hood at the back and a cape that came across to one side.

He looked as if he could have been royalty or someone very important. He even had his own bodyguards, who looked equally as terrifying as Draven's men. They stood behind his chair on their guard as I approached. He must have sensed their unease as he held up one long white hand at them without turning his head. There was something strange about him as I found myself drawn to him but couldn't understand why.

I got to the edge of the table and all eyes stared at me like the intruder I was. Sophia's eyes were the only kind ones I found, but I couldn't let this influence my objective.

"You have something to say?" Draven's voice was the first to slice through the silence. Okay, so now I was here I was going to have to find the words. So, with that in mind I took a deep breath and came out with it in the strongest voice I had in me.

"Yes, I would very much like to know why you had my date removed under false accusations." The pale man to the side of me eyed me curiously and held on to his amused grin.

"Well, I think even I can answer that, my dear." The man said in a very hoarse voice, sounding more than happy about this new turn of events. I turned to face him and Draven looked beyond furious.

"With a beauty like yours, you are more fitting for a king than a mere servant boy, wouldn't you agree Dominic?" he said and I was surprised to find him calling him by his first name, as if making it clear that these two were equals in power.

"Keira is just a waitress who works for me downstairs," Draven said in the coldest manner, twisting the arrow he had once again shot into my heart. I couldn't believe the audacity of this man! This was slowly pushing me over the edge with fury.

"Really, just a waitress... umm, all right, if you say so. My dear, I am very pleased to meet you, a rare creature you are indeed," he said standing to take my hand in his, lifting it to his lips. I let him do so freely as the look in Draven's eyes filled with hate at the sight, so I happily complied as if this was my little bit of revenge.

"*Malphas!*" Draven hissed what I assumed was his name. Malphas however, didn't seem anything but happy about Draven's reaction. His eyes met mine over the hand that he still held in an icy grip.

"No...I didn't think so," he said smirking, as he finally let go of my hand.

"Keira, I think it's time for you to be getting home," Draven said, glaring at me as though I was made from dirt.

"Well, that would be a great idea but unfortunately someone unjustly kicked out my date therefore leaving me stranded and without a ride home...so you see my predicament!" I snapped folding my arms again showing him my bravery, which was now mixed with fiery passion.

"Well, I think I have seen enough to satisfy my curiosity. My Lord, I will now take my leave, but my dear please allow me to escort you home, for it would be my great pleasure." Malphas' very deep, gravelly voice offered.

"Thank you that would be very kind," I said looking at Draven, who now looked as if he wanted to shake me to death.

"That won't be necessary. Zagan, take Miss Johnson home, *now!*" He ordered to one of the men who sat at his table. He was the one who always wore the hooded jacket and had the scar and tattoos upon his face. He stood at this command but stopped when Malphas' men got closer to me. I didn't really understand what was going on but Draven's voice ended it quickly before things got out of hand.

"*Malphas*, you *DO NOT* want to push me on this!" He said his name with a clear warning behind it and in return Malphas' hand went up again as it had done before.

"But of course." He stood and came closer to me once again saying,

"It was a pleasure to meet you, my dear Keira." He stepped forward, close to my ear and whispered so no one else could hear,

"*I will be at the front of the building waiting to drive you home...meet me.*" He then kissed my cheek as if that was what he was planning to do, for everyone watching.

But I jumped back at the sound of Draven's fist going down on the stone table with such mighty power it not only shook but also cracked under his hammer-like hand. His voice roared out making everyone look on in fear, including me.

"ENOUGH! Keira, go and wait for me on the balcony! *Now girl!*" he demanded on a bellow when I hadn't moved quickly enough for him. His black eyes flickered with the same purple I had seen before, as he stared at Malphas as though he would soon rip his throat out. This was one order that I would not disobey and I left, but not before I could just hear Malphas saying,

"Fear not my Lord, I would not hurt the girl, not after what I have seen with my own eyes...After all, she is..." But his voice trailed off and I didn't hear the rest as I was heading towards the balcony.

NEW...

I found myself stood by the glass doors unable to walk through them freely. I felt the angry tears fall down my face and I swiped at them as though they burned. He said I was 'just a waitress' as though I was nothing to him but hired help. But if that were true then why did he care about Malphas speaking to me? Why would he care about him driving me home? None of it made any sense. So now, instead of being angry about Jack, it quickly morphed back into the real reason I was *extremely* angry...Draven had hurt me...*again*.

"Walk through the door, Keira." The sound of Draven's voice behind me made me flinch. I turned around to find him stood too close for comfort so I swallowed my sadness and replaced it with well-appointed fury. I sidestepped away from him and snapped,

"After you." I held my arm out for him to go first and the look he gave me told me all I needed to know...I was in trouble. But the look I gave him back told him that I no longer cared. We were both well past the point of no return. So, in the end I won the staring contest when he nodded his head and said,

"Very well." He walked past me as the doors opened granting him entrance. This also allowed me the view of Malphas being escorted through the back doors that I now knew led into Draven's manor. He turned back to look at me over his shoulder and tapped on his watch, telling me silently that he would see me soon. I shivered at the creepy smile he added to it, suddenly wondering what I had been thinking, wanting to go with that dangerous looking guy.

"I am waiting, Keira." The sound of Draven's voice brought me out of my inner turmoil and brought it all back to the frontline, one I had no choice but to step up to.

"And we can't have that now, can we?" I muttered under my breath before I turned to face him on the balcony. I walked through the doors and this time when I shivered it was from the cold. Although which affected me more, the temperature or Draven's glacial stare was yet to be answered. He stood there, all six feet four of him looking fit to burst with pent up anger. Intimidation wasn't even a strong enough word to describe how he looked right now, in his black tailored suit and dark eyes searching for answers. I knew this when he snapped,

"What you hoped to accomplish out there tonight I do not know, but you have no idea what you just started."

"I started?" I said getting high pitched and pointing at myself with obvious disbelief.

"I believe there was only one foolish girl out there tonight making demands of me." Hearing this I nearly choked on my breath.

"Yes, and I believe there was only one arrogant club owner who had my date removed under false accusations....so you see my problem with being blamed here," I said trying to keep my voice calm and not let him see how much his words affected me.

"Maybe what you see as arrogance is actually knowledge and experience of such things, so believe me when I say, that boy you call a date had no business being in my club!" Draven snapped and my hands turned into fists as my anger hit new heights. But instead of hitting back with the insult I had in mind, I responded with gritted teeth.

"That boy was *my date* and therefore his business, was being there with me!" The second I said this something further in Draven visually snapped. I could swear his eyes flashed purple for a second but even if that was just my imagination, that tick in his jaw wasn't. It looked like he was grinding his teeth in frustration.

"Yes, I think the entirety of the club saw who he was there with, thanks to the flaunted display you were obviously putting on for my benefit." Okay so there went my calm!

"How dare you! Who the Hell do you think you are anyway? You're my boss at work Draven, not my boss in life and besides, what do you care anyway...it's not like you didn't make your feelings perfectly clear the last time we were here?" I snapped back and he growled in frustration, tearing his eyes from mine.

"My personal feelings for you should not be considered at this time, when my actions are only driven by my concern in trying to keep you safe." I frowned wondering what on earth that was supposed to mean?

"Personal feelings? I'm sorry Draven but I was under the distinct impression that you didn't have any."

"Don't be foolish, Keira!" he said slicing a dismissive hand through the air.

"Oh, well I guess this means I am just on a roll tonight then, as according to you 'foolish' should become my new middle name."

"No, I think that should be reckless and stubborn," he retorted and I shook my head and said,

"Ha! Your idea of me being reckless is me standing outside a club full of people waiting for Frank."

"If I do recall the only reason those cretins left you alone was thanks to me and my men." I knew he was going to say this, in fact, I was counting on it, so I could catch him in his lie.

"Yes, and what were you doing there in the first place if you didn't care?" Draven frowned and looked as though he was caught between two lines he didn't want to cross.

"I never said I didn't care," he replied, softer this time and I swallowed hard.

"No, you just blamed my...how did you put it... young, overactive imagination twisting the truth and being foolish enough to believe you actually gave a shit!"

"Keira, please be reasonable here. Everything I have done has been to keep you from harm's way."

"Oh, and how is that going for you Draven, because ever since I met you I haven't felt safe! The second I set foot in this damn town I have been followed, seen things I can't explain, had your staff attack me and push me around and all of it seems to be centred solely around you and this bloody club!"

"That never..."

"Don't! Don't you dare lie to me! I am not crazy and I did not imagine a damn thing and you know it!" I shouted threatening him with a shaking hand pointed at him.

"I never called you crazy."

"No, I just twist the truth, eh Draven. So, tell me, should I just get my ass back on a flight now and save myself all the heartache?" I said as an empty threat, knowing I would never go home, no not when this right here was my home...*my true home*. But I needed to seize my opportunity to push him and it worked, only not in the way I had hoped for.

"Maybe that is the wisest choice." Draven said after swallowing hard himself. I gasped in a startled breath and took a step back as though this time he had just shot me in the chest. I was even sure my heart felt the impact his brutal honesty just inflicted.

"Keira, I..." I stopped him by shaking my head and holding a hand out, silently begging him not to say another word. He sighed heavily as his shoulders slumped and for the first time, I was tempted by the empty threat I just made. Should I go home? Would it just save me future heartache? After all, he was engaged to be married and who knows where that marriage would take him in the world. I didn't know but I was sure it wouldn't ever be a place I could follow. Because getting to the root of the matter was simple. I was in love with a man who wasn't in love with me. Maybe he was right and I had just twisted the truth?

Maybe all those moments shared were just a kindness shown to someone his sister cared for. Had I really manifested the whole thing? I had to know...I had to prove it once and for all.

"Can I..." I had to pause as my voice hitched and I bit my lip to stop the tears momentarily before carrying on,

"...have a moment alone please." I finally raised my eyes to Draven and his look of remorse was painful to see. He looked about ready to say something more but instead must have thought better of it, so he simply nodded. I held myself around my corseted body and shivered finally letting the cold to seep past the anger that had kept me warm until this point. Draven saw it and slipped out of his suit jacket. Then he walked up to me and I took a step back, no longer able to stand being so close to him. He looked hurt by the action but chose to ignore his inner feelings on the matter.

"I will leave you a moment but only if you wear this," he said handing it over and I took it without looking at him. It was too painful for what I knew I had to do next. He took a deep exasperated breath and after a brief pause next to me he continued to the door.

"You may not think I care Keira, pero no podrías estar más equivocado," he said before walking through the door. My mouth dropped open as he had finished his sentence off in Spanish, *a language he didn't know I could speak*. So, he didn't know he had left me wondering why he ended that sentence with '…But you couldn't be more wrong'.

"Time to prove it, Draven," I said aloud dumping his expensive jacket on the floor and walking to the edge of the balcony. I knew from seeing it so many times in the daylight that thick ivy covered all this side of the building, so just how strong was it, I had to wonder? Well there was only one way to find out. I took a deep breath and put one leg over, closest to the wall and tested the ivy's strength by pressing down on it to see if there was any give. Doing this in heels wouldn't have exactly been my first choice, but neither would climbing down some overgrown ivy bush have been …but that's where we were.

"Well, time to see if this crazy idea ends with a broken neck," I muttered to myself and added my other leg, gripping on to the balustrades. I lowered myself over and slowly used the ivy as a ladder to the bottom. I was surprised how well it worked, although when my feet finally touched the floor, I did feel like shouting

Halleluiah and high fiving myself for not doing something even stupider...like dying! I looked up and shook off the dizziness I felt.

"Now that is what you call reckless, Draven!" I said and gave the empty balcony a one finger salute before making my way round to the front of the building. I rounded the corner, looking back over my shoulder, and swiftly bumped into a hard chest. Hands shot out and grabbed me by the tops of my arms to steady me. I looked up slowly into a pair of glowing purple eyes and swallowed hard. Draven looked down at me furiously and instead of shaking me to death as it looked as though he wanted to, he simply answered my earlier comment about being reckless.

"Yes, it was Keira...*extremely.*" Then he pulled me closer and I stumbled into him placing my hands on his solid stomach. I looked up at him, too dumbstruck by his raw beauty to speak.

He looked down at me and closed the space between us so much, I thought he was going to kiss me.

I even closed my eyes ready as he whispered a dark promise...

"Now it's my turn."

AUTHOR INSIGHT

Chapter 34
Book I

Now in this next chapter we see Draven being pushed to his limits as he must choose between hurting Keira by letting her go or taking a chance that his loving her won't get her killed. I think it's a great chapter as things certainly heat up between the pair, but unfortunately another one I couldn't use in the end as it is a continuation of the last one.

So here it is, the woulda, shoulda, coulda of Chapter 34.

Enjoy.

BOOK I

34
Clifftop Confessions.

NEW...

"Uhh...mmm...your turn to do what?" I asked after stumbling to find the right words. He smirked, lifting my face up by applying slight pressure under my chin so that I couldn't look away from him.

"To be reckless." He then lowered his lips to mine and I sucked in a startled breath without releasing it again. He was close, oh so close to kissing me that I was quickly losing my grasp on reality again.

"Breathe, sweetheart," he whispered over my lips without yet making contact.

This was it. This was now. This was finally *us...*

Our time had come.

I reached up on tiptoes holding onto his hard biceps to keep myself steady. I wanted this, he wanted this and nothing was going to stop it...nothing was going to...I opened my eyes and saw he was no longer that close and worst of all, I was no longer his sole focus.

"Draven?" I braved saying his name as he was looking over his shoulder at the sound of a car driving into view. I looked around his large frame and saw it was a long black limo driving from around the other side of Afterlife. But instead of driving away as I hoped it would... *it didn't.* No instead it pulled up to the front doors and it took me a minute to register why. My breath left me all at once and Draven didn't miss it. He snapped his head around to me and his face said only one thing...*he knew.*

"What did Malphas whisper in your ear at my table?" His voice had changed from caring to cold in a heartbeat. The deep grate in his voice told me this time to be cautious but his hand held at my throat even more so. He wasn't hurting me but it was placed there as a warning, one I took seriously enough to answer him.

"He told me to meet him out the front and he would take me home," I whispered hoping my small voice would help in calming this unpredictable situation...*it didn't.* His eyes flashed purple and I shuddered wanting more than anything to ask what he was. But that fury in his eyes told me not to speak. I half expected to feel him applying pressure to my neck but strangely his thumb simply moved up and down its length in a seductive way that could have been his way of drawing secrets from me. He looked back up to his balcony as things for him started to click into place.

"And was that where you were headed when you left me?" It was a dangerous question, one I knew to answer cautiously as he looked close to the edge.

"I...I..." I couldn't answer him but that wasn't good enough for him. So, he changed his tactics, to one he knew I wouldn't have been able to resist. That or he knew how much he was frightening me. He ran the back of two fingers down my cheek and using that velvet smooth voice of his to extract what he wanted to know.

"It's all right sweetheart, you can tell me." So, I looked up at him, my eyes wide, open and honest... then I told him.

"No, I left because your words hurt me." The briefest look of pain flashed in his eyes for a second before the sound of the engine revving drew his attention back.

"He will pay," Draven said with a deadly rasp to his voice that sounded as if it came from somewhere buried deep within. Then he let go of me and was gone. I blinked once, twice, and then saw him standing in front of Malphas' car, looking as though he had the power to command it and those in it.

I couldn't understand how he had reached the car so quickly. I didn't know what he was going to do but I felt I needed to stop this before it got out of hand. So, I ran over there as fast as I could just as he calmly walked around to the passenger side door.

I reached them just as the window wound down and what I heard made me stop in my tracks.

"I know not this game you play Malphas, but if you ever touch what is mine again then that game ends with your life...am I understood?" Draven said with deadly intent lacing his words. I didn't know what not to believe first, the fact that he had threatened to kill someone for approaching me or on hearing him calling me *his.*

"I intended no harm my Lord, a simple chance to understand the fates more clearly. It is obvious who she really is and the part she must..."

"Enough!" Draven hissed slamming the window the rest of the way down with both hands. The sound of it shattering in the door frame made me jump and Draven heard it. He turned to look at me and our eyes locked for seconds that felt like a crushing eternity. I backed away a step and his focus shot to my movements.

He mouthed one word at me... 'Stay' and suddenly I wanted to do the opposite.

When he seemed assured that I would obey his order he turned back to Malphas to issue one last warning.

"You will leave this place and never return, do you understand?"

"As you wish, my Lord." I heard him reply and Draven leant closer in and I gulped as I saw him crush the bottom of the window's frame in his grasp. It was impossible!

"You mistake me *servant,* I do not *wish...* I fucking *demand!* NOW LEAVE!" I didn't hear anything from Malphas after this, just the sound of the car driving away. Draven stood there and watched it leave until he finally turned back to face me.

So, there we were, one minute closer than ever, about to share our first real kiss and the next, well the twenty feet between us could have been an infinite chasm for all it was worth.

He had lied.

"I didn't lie," he said as if hearing my thoughts and I shook my head, an action that said this wasn't happening.

"You said I was just a waitress," I reminded him. He looked away for a moment as if trying to compose himself ready for what was to come.

"I said that to Malphas yes but..." I didn't let him finish.

"You told me there were misjudged affections that do not exist." I told him repeating his very words back to him. He winced and closed his eyes for a second as if seeing it on playback for himself.

"I..."

"You said that!" I repeated hissing it at him.

"I did," he admitted. I swallowed hard and knew this was my one and only opportunity left to get answers, so I took a deep shuddering breath, hugged myself as if this would help and asked the question,

"Was that a lie?"

"Keira please..."

"Answer me, Draven. Was that a lie?" This time it was my demand to be voiced in the dark, cold night.

"I lied," he admitted again and I wanted to crumble to the ground and wallow in my own pity. How could I be in love with a man who would play with my heart this way?

So, I took a deep breath and made my decision.

"Then I am done," I said firmly before I started walking. I didn't care about the cold. I didn't care about my heels. I didn't even care how far it was I had to walk. I just knew one thing and that was how much I needed to get away from him right now.

"Keira don't be foolish, you are not walking home," he said frustrated but something in me snapped.

"You have no say over what I do, Draven," I reminded him and he had the audacity to scoff at this.

"If you think I am going to just let you walk home then you're wrong."

"And if you think I am going to keep letting you play with my heart then so are you!" I shouted back at him walking past. I must have made it about six feet before I was suddenly in his arms. I tried to struggle free but it was useless.

"I'm not letting you go," he told me sternly and I wanted to hit out at him.

"You have no choice, *I am not yours to keep,*" I told him, despite the lies he told Malphas. His arms tightened for a moment as if my words had deeply affected him.

"You have no idea just how wrong you are," he told me and I couldn't help it when the tears started to fall. My mind just kept going back to that day on the balcony and back to the beautiful redhead who walked through those doors and crushed my fragile, vulnerable heart.

"I think your fiancée would disagree," I told him and then pushed myself out of his hold. I knew he could have stopped me, I was just thankful when he didn't. I needed space and I needed to think.

"Alright Keira, have it your way. You need your space, I get that but if you think this conversation is over you are wrong."

"What, just so I can hear more of your lies?" I threw at him. He folded his arms and I hated seeing the way his shirt tightened across his muscles. I didn't want to want him the way I did but it was like a sickness. It was as if the more I saw him, the more I would fall into this spell until I couldn't ever see a way of getting out.

"Any lies I told you were..." I held my hand up to stop him and snapped,

"Save it. I'm done," I said firmly, but the next thing I knew I was back in his arms and he was whispering in my ear with even firmer intent,

"We will never be done you and I...*ever.*" I shuddered in his arms at the feel of his lips at my neck.

"Let me go," I asked him softly but this only provoked a growled promise from him.

"Never."

"Draven, please," I begged, my voice near breaking point.

"Alright Keira, I will let you go home but the only way I am allowing it is if I drive you myself." I closed my eyes, hating that I knew I had no choice in the matter and just to confirm I was right I asked,

"Do I have a choice?"

"You already know the answer to that," he told me sternly and then just like magic, a car came around the side of the building, stopping next to us. He hadn't even called anyone so how did that happen...had he planned for this? Speaking of which, how did he get down to me so quickly when leaving that balcony? Unless he knew the second he walked though those doors that I was going to run? But even then, if he knew would he really have let me climb down some stupid ivy where the chances had been high for me falling? There were just too many questions but only one left my lips.

"Who are you?" I asked on a whisper, one he heard despite the distance he had put between us. His look said it all...*there was something*.

The huge black SUV was like the one I had seen pulling up outside the campus. I bit my lip when thinking back to how I had fallen inside only to find Draven there.

Well, this time he wouldn't be sat in the back being driven, this time he was driving. A man got out from behind the wheel, one I recognised from Draven's garage who was dressed in a grey jacket and grey hat.

"My Lord," he said nodding and leaving the door open for him. Then the guy walked away.

"Keira, if you please." I tore my eyes away from the sight of the guy disappearing around the corner and saw that Draven was now holding open the passenger door for me. Before walking over to him I looked back over my shoulder longingly wishing I had my own car, so instead of going home, I could just drive…far away.

Draven cleared his throat and that was my cue. I walked over to the high vehicle and then down at the small step wondering how I was going to accomplish this in these heels. In the end, it was taken out of my hands as Draven put a hand either side of my waist and hoisted me up as though I weighed nothing at all. I sucked in a sharp breath from the feel of having his hands on my body, hating myself for wishing that they would never leave me.

"Uhh…thanks," I muttered with my head down to hide my damn blush. I didn't like how my body responded to him the way it did. It felt like it was betraying me.

"You're welcome," he said, once more leaning into me and obviously not giving a damn about personal space. Then he shut the door, the sound making me jump. He got in the other side with ease thanks to his long legs and started up the engine. I didn't know what to say, so I said nothing. Instead I looked out of my window and was greeted by my own reflection staring back at me. I looked how I felt…like a lost girl on the way to nowhere. Because I had spent the last two years trying to smile and mean it. Well, since meeting Draven I had finally had something real to put behind that smile, even if it had been done in secret. I had thought about him and that smile had been real but now… well now,

I wasn't smiling anymore.

"Wait, why are we going this way?" I asked when he turned the opposite way to my house.

"You will see," he told me cryptically and I folded my arms, releasing a heavy sigh, knowing there was no point arguing.

"Relax, I will get you home but first there is a place I want you to see." I looked at him side on and tried to judge the impossible, that being, what was going on in his mind. Half of me wanted to demand he take me home, the other half demand that he give me answers. So, the bottom of that list was having him take me somewhere I didn't know and into a situation I couldn't control.

We sat in silence for most of the drive and every now and then I would feel his eyes on me but I refused to look. Instead I continued to look out of the window, seeing the night flashing past and with it adding even more miles between me and home. He saw me holding myself as I usually did when I felt uneasy and he must have taken it for being cold because he reached for the controls and put the heater on. I wanted to say thank you but in the end, I couldn't find the words, so we continued our silence, that was until sometime later Draven broke it.

"Almost there," Draven said with a sigh and I couldn't help but get the impression that this was something he didn't want. Which then begged the question…why? He pulled the SUV off the main road and turned onto a dirt track that was surrounded by thick forest on either side. I felt my palms start to sweat under the thick gloves I wore and I fidgeted in my seat, not liking the uncertainty I felt.

"You have nothing to fear from me, Keira." I almost jumped out of my skin when Draven said this. As if once again he had been tapping into my thoughts. But it wasn't the physical type of pain I feared Draven would inflict. It was the emotional pain I knew he *could* inflict that had me terrified of getting out of this car. There was only one reason he would bring me all the way out here that I could think of. A place that not a soul for miles could play witness to what Draven wanted me to know...was it finally the truth? And if so, was it really that bad that it needed to be done somewhere totally remote to ensure this? I didn't know but I was suddenly terrified to find out.

We kept driving for a short while longer until the woodland started to become sparse and the road became wider. Then it suddenly opened up as if God had swiftly lifted a veil on a proud piece of art work of his. I couldn't help but gasp at the sight of the national park in all its dark, mysterious glory. We looked to be on top of it all and at one of the highest points of the park. A blanket of stars above and the moon casting light upon the black silhouette of thousands of trees below.

Draven pulled the car around in the wide, open space and cut the engine. Then he got out of the car and I watched as he walked around to my side to open the door.

"Come," he said holding his hand out for me to take and I looked down at it, hesitating.

"Trust me," he said softly. My eyes shot to his, and before they got there I was intending on saying something like 'Is that a joke?'. However, once they got there and I saw the depth of intensity in that dark gaze, I couldn't do it. Because for the first time I saw something in Draven I had never seen before...

Vulnerability.

So instead of throwing something cruel at him and hoping it stuck, I placed my hand in his. He pulled me closer to him and lifted me out of the car, keeping our eyes level for longer than what was needed. Then he lowered me down and took my hand in his. I let him walk me closer to the edge so that I could see the view better than when I was seeing it through a window. When I felt that we were close enough, for my own comfort, I pulled back on his hand. He looked back at me and I muttered my reason,

"I don't like heights." For some reason, this amused him and he smirked at me.

"That's interesting," he said and I frowned for a moment.

"Why is that interesting?" I asked with a raised eyebrow.

"Let's just say that heights and I, kind of walk hand in hand." This time he laughed aloud when he saw my frown.

"Never mind...do you like it?" he said changing the cryptic subject, nodding back to the view. I walked a step closer to him and told him the truth,

"It's magnificent." He looked down at me, not the view and said,

"I agree." I felt those two little words as though they were a caress across my bare shoulders and I shivered.

"I will be back," he told me before walking back to the car. I briefly looked over my shoulder at him, to see him grab something I couldn't make out. I looked back to the view after I heard the car door shut and seconds later I felt a blanket being placed over me. His hands lingered on my shoulders and he remained at my back. This time I could find the words to thank him.

"I don't like you being cold."

"Thank you," I said but had to move away, or at least try to, as the second I did his arms came around my torso from behind.

"Draven, I..."

"Ssshh, just let me hold you...just let me have this moment," he told me and I found I couldn't refuse him, even if I had wanted to which, if being honest with myself, I didn't. So, I did as he asked. I gave him that moment, taking the time to secretly relish in it myself. Until my overactive brain clicked back on and I couldn't help but ask,

"What are we doing here, Draven?"

"I come here a lot. It's my place of solitude if you like. A place to think, to reflect on the past," he said and his arms left me so that he could come and stand next to me.

"I came here that day…" He looked side on at me and he clarified when I gave him a questioning look.

"…After what I said to you on the balcony." Hearing this I bit my lip, unable to speak from fear that he would stop.

"It was the first time I had come here with feelings of regret. You see, I never intended to hurt you the way I have. To be honest I am simply not used to concerning myself with the repercussions my words may inflict, but that day I knew my words had cut you deep, just as I intended." He looked remorseful at least but that wasn't enough for me.

"But why?! Why would you…"

"Because I needed to hurt you." I shook my head and said,

"I don't understand."

"And you weren't supposed to until the time was right," he replied honestly and I turned to face him, the view no longer holding my interest.

"And now? Is the time right now, Draven?" I asked him brazenly.

"No but I find I can no longer bear the entirety of it all."

"The entirety?" I asked him, obviously confused.

"Of my feelings for you," he said raising a hand to my cheek as I sucked in a startled breath.

"But you said…"

"I know what I said, Keira," he told me softly, stepping closer. I looked up and I could barely believe this was happening. I couldn't breathe. I couldn't move. I just waited for what felt like an eternity that Draven held the key to ending.

"But now I need you to hear the truth." I swallowed hard and prayed even harder that this wasn't going to be another stab to my heart. I wouldn't be able to take it.

"And that is?" I asked in a quiet voice, one even I was unsure of hearing. He gave me a small smile and lifted my head as he had done back at the club. His fingers lifted up my chin so I had no choice but to look into his eyes. A way to read the truth. A way to read his fear.

A way to read his...*heart.*

"I'm in love with you."

AUTHOR'S INSIGHTS

Chapter 35
Book I

This next chapter it is yet another continuation of the last and one that again, unfortunately I couldn't use. I wanted an epic backdrop to Keira and Draven's first kiss but shortly after this I realised that if I wanted to write the rest of the story how I envisioned, then their beautiful first kiss would have to wait. Because in the end I wanted their first kiss not to be about beautiful scenery or to come straight after declarations of love. I wanted it to be raw. I wanted it to be because they simply had hit a point when keeping their hands off each other was no longer an option. It was too painful to bear. So, in the end I chose to cut these last few chapters out completely and come at it from a different angle, with Keira going home.

I do wonder where else the story would have taken me from this point though? Would Draven have taken her back to Afterlife with him? Would she had calmly found out about Morgan's escape in the comfort of his arms? Well I am afraid that will be one left for the imagination, but here it is anyway.

Another of Keira and Draven's first written kiss…and it is beautiful.

35

A Kiss to Remember.

NEW...

"I'm in love with you."

Hearing this I almost fell into him. I felt myself trembling, but I had to ask. I had to make sure, so I stuttered out the question I never would have believed I would find myself asking this man...this man who owned my dreams.

"You're...you're... *in love with me?*" The last part of this question escaped on a whisper. The second my words were out he stepped into me and swiftly lifted my face up to his with both hands at my cheeks. Then he lowered his lips to mine and whispered a firm promise above them.

"Yes." Then he crushed his lips to mine and something inside of me ignited. It was as though God had reached down from the stars above and touched my soul. His lips moulded to mine as if we were born for one and other. His taste intoxicating, his touch exhilarating and his scent was like a drug named euphoria. His hands kept me locked to him and I was thankful for them. Because right now they felt like the anchor keeping me rooted to this earth. Like the only thing keeping me from floating away. I wanted more of him, I was addicted to this feeling,

I knew after only moments and didn't want to think about what would happen to my fragile heart once he pulled away. In fact, I almost panicked, and only did so internally when his hands left my face. But thankfully they did so only so they could wrap around my body, so this time I wasn't just anchored, I was imprisoned.

I found that I could only hold onto him, gripping onto his shirt scared to make a single wrong move. But thinking about the way he kissed me, the way he tasted me, exploring me in a way like no other...then did I really ask myself, was it even possible *I could* make a wrong move? If anything, it seemed as though he had been waiting to do this for just as long as I had. And like him, I never wanted it to end.

But end it had to, and this time I was unable to hold in my reaction. It came out in the form a small moan of protest, one that left my lips half a second after he did. I still had my eyes closed with my head held back, waiting, praying for just one more. No, that was a lie. I didn't just want one more...*I wanted them all, forever more.*

"Open your eyes and see me," he ordered softly. I did as I was told as right then, I would have signed over my soul if he'd have asked it of me.

I was met by flaming purple eyes, which startled me enough to take a step back...or at least try to.

"Oh no, you're not going anywhere, little one," he told me pulling me back to him and securing me there with his strength. I swallowed hard and he watched my slight nervous reaction.

"Don't be afraid," he told me and it took me back to that night on the rooftop. His eyes had been the same. I took a moment to take it all in before tentatively reaching up and touching his face. He closed his eyes and suddenly I wished I didn't have my gloves on, just so that I could feel his skin under my fingertips.

"I am not afraid," I told him and in that moment, it was true. Because I knew what happened on that rooftop had really happened and if I had been as terrified as I should have been, would I have really demanded to see him the very next day. No, I didn't fear Draven as a man or whatever being he turned out to be. I only feared what he could do to me, if he walked away.

"It was all real, wasn't it?" I asked softly and he simply nodded, knowing without words what I meant.

"And you lied to protect me from what you are?" I guessed and once again, he nodded. It was a beautiful moment. His silent confession, all there in a simple action and a depth of sorrow written in his eyes.

In that moment, I made the decision to be honest myself. So, I slowly started to peel down my gloves and with it, my protection against the truth of my past. He watched silently, taking in each line as they appeared. They looked almost to be glowing under the moonlight but right then, I couldn't find myself to be ashamed. So instead I finished my statement by laying myself completely bare, once and for all.

"I don't need you to protect my body, Draven…" I took a deep breath and looked down, as I knew I couldn't have said what I wanted if I had been looking at him.

"…I need you to protect my *heart.*"

"Are you saying what I think you're saying?" he asked bending slightly to catch my eyes and I braved looking back up at him, reached up on my tiptoes, my hands creeping their way up to his neck and said,

"Protect it, because it's…*it's yours.*" I whispered this last part over his lips before this time, being the one to start the kiss. The second my lips touched his something in him snapped and it was like awakening a hungry beast, one being starved of his favourite meal. He held me to him, a hand entwined in my hair holding me, locking me to his lips as though he would never let me go.

If I thought the first kiss had been intense then the second nearly saw me finding my release from it. It was as though we couldn't get enough of each other and soon we became two desperate people trying to make a connection with not only our souls but also our bodies as well.

He gripped me from behind and hoisted me up, locking my legs around his waist. Thankfully the skirt I wore helped with this, thanks to the big slit that travelled up the front of my thigh. A place his hand thought to travel as well. I pressed myself against him, relishing in the feel of the hard length of him I found down there. He threw his head back, tearing his lips from mine and growled low.

"By the Gods, you are the most beautiful creature ever created," he told me and I couldn't help but blush at such a compliment. He ran the back of one finger down my heated cheek and said,

"And displaying your demure attribute only adds to the appeal. All of those blushes I have seen, you know not what it has done to me." At this I bit my lip quickly before asking,

"What do you mean?"

"I have been watching you long enough now to know what makes you blush, or bite that lip of yours..." he said pulling *that* lip from my teeth with his thumb before continuing,

"...and every time I have wanted to see it because of a different reason, one other than your shyness in being in my company..." He then paused holding me to him with one hand underneath me and the other, using it to explore my exposed skin.

"...I have wanted to see that beautiful blush bloom as I strip you bare for my eyes to drink in the sight of your naked skin. To have you bite your lip as I lay you down on my bed, before I kissed every inch of your body. To see you open yourself up to me, wet and ready to take me with a breathy moan escaping your bitten lips." Hearing all of this I couldn't help my reaction to his sexual desire being explained, painting a picture so vivid in my mind. I wanted it, I wanted it all!

My head fell back as his fingertips grazed along my collarbone and down to the line of my cleavage. That moan he spoke of, well it was first heard coming from me not at it happening the way he described, but just from the thought of it.

And this was what made him stop. He let me slide down the length of him as he held me steady, almost as if he knew my feet were not yet up to the task of keeping me upright. I was dazed and confused.

"Why did you…?"

"Trust me sweetheart, you know not of the strength it takes to stop what it is I really want to do to you."

"Then why?"

"Because our first time was never meant for this mountain top under the eyes of the Gods…" he said, running a hand through my hair, pushing back the stray strands that had half covered my face.

"…Our first time is meant for my eyes only and in the same bed that I have lain awake for many a sleepless night, just thinking about what having you lying next to me would feel like. To hear the sounds that you make when being woken with me making love to you again. Holding you through the night and welcoming the dawn with you still in my arms. That is how our first time was always meant to be." When he finished, I was half tempted to argue with him as my need was overriding his romantic gesture, but then when I looked deep into his eyes I knew that this wasn't just for me, it was for him also.

That was how he wanted it and for the life of me I wanted to give him that…despite my raging need for him!

"So, what happens now?" I asked, once more feeling vulnerable and stepping back.

"Well from the worried look on your face, I would say anything but what you may be thinking," he said looking amused.

"Come here," he added, grabbing my hand and pulling me back to him.

"Tell me, what worries you?"

"Honestly?" He nodded and I took a chance, no matter how silly it may have sounded.

"Waking up and finding you gone."

"I will admit that having you in my arms feels like a dream but I can assure you, it is one we will not wake from," he said reassuring me and holding me to him in a much-needed hug. It felt so natural being with him like this, I just didn't want it to end.

"Can I ask you a question, Keira?" This time I smiled up at him and replied,

"But of course."

"Do you dream of me often?" I laughed once and said,

"Occasionally, yes…why do you ask?" I thought he was joking but his face said otherwise.

"And do you always remember?" This time I raised an eyebrow in question at him. Where was all this going?

"Only the ones with you in them," I admitted blushing. He gave me a soft smile and ran a thumb across my lips, reminding me once again that I was biting them. But I knew from his eyes that he was deep in thought so, in true Keira fashion, I asked.

"What is it?" He didn't answer me but instead turned to face the world in all its natural dark glory. It was almost as if the night sky had the answer there written somewhere amongst the stars.

"Draven?" I said his name on a whisper, prompting something from him. Only in the end what I got, wasn't what I expected.

A confession that it was never a dream, it was all real…

"You weren't supposed to remember."

AUTHOR'S INSIGHT.

BOOK 2
The Two Kings

Now in book two there was always so many different ways I wanted to introduce Lucius to the world and being a mean bad ass was always going to be one of them. But this was difficult to do as I knew that in book three I would have an even greater battle on my hands in making you all fall in love with...well such a lovable rogue.

Lucius was always meant to start life in my books as a misunderstood Vampire King, as was the challenge when he first met Keira, becoming conflicted about the way he felt about her. I needed to get across a man you all expected to hate and fear, then into one that became caring and even in certain moments, showing tenderness.

But he is the complete opposite of Draven in most ways. Where Draven's confidence comes naturally in the form of being a King, Lucius' is displayed more openly with his cocky nature and harsher rule. Oh and of course let's not forget his raw desire at taking something that belongs to Draven and taking it for himself.

AUTHOR'S INSIGHT.

Chapter 18
Book 2

In this chapter, we find Keira and Draven having just spent their first night with Libby and Frank, after Keira cooked dinner. Draven gets called back as he is needed to prepare for the ritual, one that at this time, Keira knows nothing about. At the end of this chapter, Lucius comes to her in a dream but what I first wrote about in this scene would have then finished very differently. Because of this it would have made it almost impossible for Keira to have caught Draven in the temple, doing what he does best…*ruling over his world.*

So here it is for your enjoyment…Lucius' and Keira's first *real* encounter.

Book 2

18

Following Ghosts.

I grabbed my jacket and ran out of the door to find a huge black Rolls Royce in the drive waiting for me. A man in a grey coat and black hat was holding the door open for me, only it opened the opposite way compared to other conventional cars.

It looked like a deadly creature under the moonlight, with its angry square grill that looked as if it would take a bite out of the Aston Martin that was behind it, waiting to be driven by another of Draven's men. Its emblem gleamed silver and I was sure I remembered the winged figure was called the 'Spirit of Ecstasy'.

Well, that sure was fitting. I don't think I could think of a better description and I wasn't just talking about the car. I stepped forward cautiously as though it wanted to eat me and only when I saw the figure of Ecstasy himself sat there waiting, did I hurry my feet. As soon as I ducked to get in I had Draven's hand held out to help me.

This car reminded me of two different forces fused together. The inside was the complete opposite to the outside. The inside being made with pure luxury in mind and the outside had you gulping at the sight. It was a bit like Draven. Half of him you would kill just to receive his soft touch and caresses all over your willing body and the other half would kill you if you were crazy enough to go against it.

I ran my hand over the soft cream leather seat and thought it to be far too comfortable to be in a car. The back seats were more spacious than I expected and there was a clear screen between the driver and us. As always, Draven watched me like prey as I looked around at the walnut finish and cream carpets that also held foot rests.

"You seem to like this car." Draven's voice was deep and smouldering, making me jump at the sound and when the doors locked before we pulled away, I swallowed hard. Like this it was easy to see him as a King. He sat back casually as if he'd known this level of luxury all his life and I felt like Oliver or Annie being taken under his wing.

I bit my lip at just how different our lives were and prayed to God for not only opposites to attract but for them to be able to withstand anything. I needed Draven and it pained me to know my need was far greater than his. It just had to be. Anything else just wasn't plausible. I mean, he could have anything he wanted and I didn't know if I would ever understand why he would ever have wanted me but I was left thanking God daily that he did.

"It's a beautiful car, but why didn't you just drive the Aston back?" At this he cocked his head and smiled to himself.

"Because, I like to have my hands free for other things," he whispered into my hairline before tilting my chin upwards for a gentle kiss. We both sighed at the same time, when the sound of his phone vibrating brought our lips apart. I started to pull away but with supernatural speed his hands grabbed my body and pulled me in to his for a demanding kiss.

"Only when I am ready to let you go, little one," he said in a hoarse voice, clearly thick with lust. Meanwhile, the phone became a background buzz soon forgotten as Draven's lips seared mine with burning need. I could tell he was fighting himself to keep control and if the deep frustrated growl was anything to go by then I would say that his rational mind had returned.

He let me go with a deep inhale and reached into his pocket to answer his phone.

"Speak!" He demanded in one of those 'I am your Lord and Master' tones. He listened for a moment before switching to another language to reply. I got the distinct impression he didn't want me to know what he was talking about.

I decided to ignore the call and I watched the night fly by in a black haze. Only when Draven's hand reached for mine as he moved closer to me, did I realise the phone had gone. I didn't turn my head to look at him but instead I rested it on his shoulder and snuggled closer before my insecurities got the better of me. He responded to this by stroking my cheek with his other hand.

"You must be tired." I didn't know whether he was asking me or talking to himself, but at the very sound of the word I could feel my eyes closing and getting heavy. The hum of the engine was creating a rhythm that my brain responded to by drifting off and shutting down. When Draven's hand started to make circles on my palm, I couldn't fight it any longer, so when his words whispered their usual command in a velvety tone, I was totally compliant.

"Sleep now." His words were the last thing I remembered.

I woke as I felt movement under my body and I soon realised I was being carried up some stairs. As soon as Draven felt me stir, he pulled my body closer to his and leaned his head down.

"Ssshh, go back to sleep, my young beauty. You will be in our bed soon." The way he said 'our bed' made me smile under his jacket, which was pulled tightly around me. I could just hear a door open and the usual smell of old furniture filled my lungs. This room felt more like home to me than any other place on earth.

I felt him stop and the sound of the covers being pulled back made a whoosh sound in the air. I knew he was using his gifts, considering that his hands weren't free. He lowered me down and I could feel the heat escaping from my body as the distance between us grew.

I seemed to be in a semi-daze and didn't know whether this was me dreaming as I started to feel the air on my skin where my clothes were being removed. His soft hands made sure to come into contact with skin with every inch of material that he pulled away from me. I bit my lip at the feeling his undressing did to me and the craving to have him take me was nearly uncontrollable. He lifted me slightly to pull the top over my head and then expertly removed my underwear. Then he ran his fingers gently over every curve and I inhaled deeply, taking in his scent.

He gently rolled me over so that I was lying on my front and he did the same motions down my back. His palm flattened on the base of my spine and he ran it up slowly till it reached the back of my neck.

He must have thought that I was in a deep sleep, as he started to whisper things to me in a different language before letting my hair loose. He gripped it with both his hands and twisted it. Then he placed it to one side so that he could kiss my neck and continue downwards, making my spine feel like sticky dough. Every touch felt like little electric pulses that lit up my nerves and senses like fireworks on New Year's Eve.

"My Lord, everything is ready...they...they are here and are awaiting your command." An unsure voice I didn't recognise spoke and when I shifted slightly from surprise his soft hands held me still.

"Ssshh... le sommeil mon pure" ("Sleep my pure one" in French). His voice acted like a warm blanket over my mind and I tried desperately to stay awake and focus on what was happening, but it was proving impossible.

"Tell my Council I will join them soon." His authoritative voice filled the night air making it such a contrast to how moments before he was talking so sweetly to me. He wasn't yet finished with me as his hands explored my skin and I knew that if I rolled over to fully announce I was awake, his movements would stop and he would leave. I wanted to ask him what it was that would soon take him away, but I was captivated by the immense bliss that having his hands on my body created.

He smoothed back my hair so that he could see my face and the back of one finger traced my jawline. I couldn't help but bite my lip as he got closer to them and I heard him let out more air through his nose at his amusement. I felt his hands flatten on the bed either side of me and his body weight rested on them while he lowered his body closer to mine. His lips rested lightly on mine but for no more than seconds. Then he moved them to my ear and whispered,

"I love you, Keira."

And then with that, he was gone.

NEW...

I woke feeling strange. It felt as though a presence was near, so close in fact, it felt like the shadows of someone else were reaching out and touching me. I gripped onto the covers still half trapped in sleep and half aware of the reality facing me, had I only to open my eyes. But the simple matter was that I was scared. It was as though somewhere deep within myself I knew...I knew that whatever was out there, wasn't safe. Not like it was in Draven's arms. Not like it was with him beside me.

It was having this thought that made my eyes snap open to see that it was true...Draven wasn't here. But that didn't mean I was alone. I sat up slowly as if trying not to alert my presence to anyone that could be near. Then, taking a deep breath, I pulled the curtains back from around the bed, holding the sheet to my chest, hiding my naked body. I took in the empty room and released a sigh in relief, one that turned out to be premature. A figure walked through the door and I smiled softly as I saw it was Draven.

"Oh good, I was getting...*Draven?*" I started to speak to him but as he walked past me without even a look or word I frowned, letting my sentence turn into a question. At the sound of his name he didn't answer me, if anything, it looked as if I wasn't even here. But no, that wasn't right...it wasn't me that wasn't here...it was him.

Draven looked like a ghost.

I sucked in a horrified breath and shook my head a little. What was going on here...was I still asleep? Could that be it? I still questioned myself when I saw his shadowy figure walk to the glass door and straight through them as though they were already open. I shuddered watching the scene play out as though a lost memory and real life were trying to catch up with one another.

I watched him stop once on the other side of the door and he looked back over his shoulder at me. His eyes looked like purple fire as he mouthed the words,

"Come...come with me." I jumped and let out a small shriek as he may have said them out there on the balcony but they were heard as if whispered right by my ear. Then the smirk as his eyes flashed red for a second before turning his attention back to the night.

I didn't know what to do, whether to stay here or to find out what this all meant and go out there with him. What if there was something he subconsciously wanted me to see? I didn't know anything about my purpose in his world yet, other than there was one, so what if now was my only opportunity to discover the true meaning of the word...*Electus?*

The temptation was too great to pass up, which is why I reached around for something to put on and strangely found a silky black nightdress and matching robe folded at the end of the bed. I got up, shivering thanks to the middle of the night chill and with no body to warm me. Then I grabbed the black satin and pulled it down, letting it fall to the ground around me. It hugged my breasts tight in lace covered triangles just big enough to contain my flesh and flowed down from the gathered part under my bust.

I wondered if Draven had left it for me, hoping to see me in it in the morning? That seemed like the most plausible explanation. So, assuring myself of this, I pulled on the large floaty robe to match, marvelling at how the wide sleeves touched the floor like some Kimono style. I grabbed the tie and knotted it at the front, trying to give myself some protection against the cold. It was a beautiful set but not exactly practical in winter.

I looked down seeing nothing for my feet and decided I wouldn't be out there long anyway. I just needed to check on what was going on and if I was unsure, then I would come back inside. So, with this firmly in mind, I walked towards the glass doors and unlike Draven had, I placed my hand on them so that they would open. I sucked in a startled breath as the cold hit me like a blistering wave.

I decided to let my hair remain under the cover of my dressing gown as it would help in trying to keep me warm. That and it meant it wouldn't get blown around in the elements and become a mass of knots come morning.

"Draven?" I said his name in question, looking around the balcony for him but movement in the corner of my eye made me look towards the winding staircase that I knew led to the roof I remembered so well from that night. The night I ran from Draven. It was the first time I had seen him in his true form and back then I refused to believe it. Seeing Demons most of my life caused something to snap inside me and not fully understanding what he could be, I ran from him in fear of what I thought he was.

Now though I knew better and I walked up the stone steps, following him up there without fear of what I would find in him. I trusted Draven and that trust included knowing he would never hurt me. No, now the fear I had was looking down at the immense height that one wrong move could have plunged me into…an abyss of trees…but surely Draven would save me if I were to fall?

I decided to keep going and keep my eyes firmly planted on the steps in front of me, trying not to let the wind freak me out as it whipped around my body. Finally, I reached the top and this time I didn't need to look around to find him.

"Draven? Draven!" I called his name first in question when he looked back at me but kept walking. Then I shouted his name as he walked towards the door at the other side, one he had held me trapped against that night. This was when I started to run towards him and just as I was about to get to him he opened the door and walked through it.

"Draven no!" I shouted as he looked back one more time and mouthed the words,

"Goodbye, Keira." Then he shut the door on me just as I reached out. I tried the handle but it wouldn't open, so I screamed in frustration, slamming my open hand against the door.

"I don't think that will help, Pet." A voice behind me spoke and I froze to the spot. My fingers curled inward with my nails scratching against the wood panels as I made a fist. I don't know how I knew who that voice belonged to but I did and because of this I didn't want to turn around...I really didn't but what choice did I have, especially when I heard him snarl his demand,

"Time to face your fate...*now look at me."* I swallowed hard knowing he was right. It was time to face my fate and the face that had terrorised my dreams. So, I turned around slowly, dreading what I may find this time and hoping it wasn't a room full of blood like the first time. But this time we were alone and the only blood was my own that felt like it was drowning my heart as it worked overtime. Because there he was.

The Handsome face of the Devil I didn't want to know...

Lucius.
King of the Vampires.

… Book 2

19
Lucius.

NEW…

I hated the fear seeing him brought out in me, nearly as much as I hated myself for being such a fool. He had created Draven's image, manipulating it so that I would follow it up here. *Up here to him.* He had laid the trap and I had just walked straight into it.

He leant his frame against one of the corner stones that rose higher than the rest, with his feet crossed casually. He looked briefly at his hand before swiping something off his long leather jacket. One that was like some old, worn military style with a gothic element to it. Underneath this he wore a black t shirt with strapping over the chest as if he carried weapons of some sort. Dark charcoal jeans and boots, seemed to be his typical casual bad ass style and I shuddered as his killer eyes met with mine. He smirked at me, showing me the glint of a fang and I tore my gaze from his, putting an end to his game of cat and mouse.

"Ah!" I shouted in surprise as the next thing I knew he was right in front of me, gripping my chin and forcing it up to look at him.

"The game has just begun, my dear," he warned.

"What...what do you want with me?!" I demanded after first trying to find my voice. His hand slowly crept down from my chin to the column of my neck and I took a step back away from his threatening hold.

"Ah ah ah, tut, tut" he said slapping an arm tightly around the back of me and yanking me forward into his hard chest. There he held me to him and I struggled to get free.

"It's not nice not giving your guest a welcoming hug. Now be still before I bite you," he warned, snapping his teeth close to my face like a wild beast about to take a chunk out of me. His cool calm voice sounded even more deadly than one shouting down at me. As the contrast to his strength and forceful movements were made even deadlier by his controlled tone. So, because of all the warning signs this twisted dark king gave me, I instantly did as I was told and stilled in his hold.

"There you see, you can be a good girl when prompted by the idea of pain...already I can see you are going to make me an excellent play thing," he told me and I closed my eyes against the idea of being under this man's control. It was obvious what he could do to me and in truth it terrified the living shit out of me.

"Please...just let me go." He smiled down at me and there was nothing amusing about it. It was all evil and malicious intent. More about the dark things he promised and the thoughts of acting them out no doubt the forefront of his mind.

"And tell me, why would I do that, for I find your cold, quivering body fits nicely right where it is...tell me Keira girl, do I frighten you?" I bit my lip and nodded but this wasn't good enough for him.

"Speak the words little pet of mine, for I do so love to hear fear being voiced as well as felt," he told me, running his thumb up and down my throat, smiling when he felt me swallowing hard.

"Yes, I am afraid of you." I told him, hating admitting it and feeling weak, which was no doubt all part of his plan.

"Good, that means there are some brains beneath all this blonde mane of yours after all. It is smart to fear me…" He paused to grip the top part of my neck in a bruising hold for a moment as if to drive the seriousness of what he was saying home, once he saw my tears building he smiled and continued,

"…For it should do you well in keeping you alive, so long as you understand it not wise to piss me off, that is," he told me and then once he saw that I had ran out of air he released me. I choked and coughed, trying to drag precious air back into my lungs.

"That's it, calm now, deep breaths…easy does it," he cooed pulling my head to his chest and stroking back my hair as though he suddenly cared.

"But that's where you're wrong my dear…I do care…*deeply,*" he said pulling back after reading my mind again and I wanted to lash out at him but like he said, I was too afraid.

"I care…" he said again, only this time he ran a finger down along my collarbone, making me shudder.

"…Deep beneath the confines of your skin…" His finger continued along my shoulders and back again until they started to dip lower. I closed my eyes against the feeling he was awakening in me and I hated how he could manipulate that too.

"…Deeper than flesh and bone…" he added and then when his finger was where he considered his bullseye, he tapped it against my heart twice and ended it,

"...But at the very core of you, where your blood is its sweetest, oh but a taste of you...*just one.*" Then he snapped and I found myself spun around, my back held securely to his chest, one arm bound across my torso and his other hand at my head, forcing it to the side. I screamed when he sunk his teeth into my arching neck and the first break of my skin was pure agony.

I cried out in pain and he moaned into my neck as if the sound only increased his pleasure, one I could feel pressing into my back. He sucked deep and I could feel him drawing my blood from me, like a thief in the night.

"I...please...don't...*kill me.*" I moaned as I felt my legs get weak and just as I was about to crumble he held me tighter, ripping his fangs from the comfort of my flesh. He bent his head back and looked up to the sky as if he could see answers there he had been reaching for.

"What are you?" he asked and I didn't know what to tell him. He growled and just before my hand could cover my neck, as it tried to do he grabbed it and held it down.

"Now just look at the mess I made...let's clean you up, little doll of mine." Then he leant back down and started licking at the wound, cleaning it and what felt like fusing the holes he had made. It felt strange as my skin knitted itself back together under the ministrations of Lucius' tongue lapping up every drip, as if not wanting to waste a single drop.

"Mmm...*fucking nectar!*" I shuddered at the demonic growl that laced his words.

"Oh, how I do look forward to our time together."

"Never!" I hissed, finally finding my bravery. He heard this and laughed.

"What makes you think you have a choice? The board has already been set, long ago before you were even born and seen in the stars of your ancestors..." He said this as he started to run his hands over my satin covered body, his pale hands a startling contrast against the black.

"...This is a battle of Kings and men and you my dear sweet soul... *are just a pawn we added to the table,*" he told me sternly gripping at my robe's tie and pulling it free so that he could explore more freely.

"I am no pawn," I told him with gritted teeth.

"No, you don't think so...then tell me pretty girl, you really think a man, a king like Dominic Draven would freely pick you, a girl next door beauty over the entirety of the world. A man like him could have anyone...why now do you think he chose you?" Lucius said and I flinched in his hold as his words affected me.

"He loves me," I told him and I could feel his smile even though I couldn't see it. Almost as if his amusement crackled in the air.

"Because he has to...because he has been told he must by the very Gods themselves but you're a fool to believe he chose you...the Gods chose you, not his fucking heart!" he said snarling at me and I wanted to cry out at the agony.

The hurt he inflicted was no doubt done to test me, or to drive a wedge between Draven and I. Either way it hurt and I hated how much it did. Half of me knew he had said this for the reaction I couldn't help but give him.

I ripped myself out of his hold and faced him. Fists held tensed at my sides I roared back in his face with all fear long forgotten,

"YOU LIE!" At first, he looked shocked but then a small sadistic grin started to arch up one side of his mouth. Then he caught a bit of my blood from that same corner and put it into his mouth to suck. He closed his eyes briefly and moaned. When he opened them again, his blood lust looked to be back in the form of crimson fire filling the whites of his eyes.

"Maybe you're right, or maybe you taste just too damn good!" he said as my only warning to run. I started to move backwards slowly at first to get away from him, but he took this as part of the game he wanted to play. Cat and Mouse was on. He stalked towards me and I turned around and ran, hoping to make it to the wall so that I could scream for help.

Needless to say, I didn't get far.

I screamed as he flew at me and plucked me off the roof, grabbing me around the waist. I saw myself being taken higher and the roof terrace below becoming a small square as he took us both up into the night. My screaming became lost to the sound of the wind whipping around us and his grip of me tightened.

This was it. I was taken and snatched right out of Draven's world just like that. In the blink of an eye, I was lost to him. I felt the tears being forced from the corners of my eyes as the pressure of air pushed them into my hairline. I gripped onto Lucius as if my life depended on it and I hated that in this he had become my only chance at survival. I wanted to close my eyes, trapped between which fear was greater, the fear to look or not.

The sight of the national park below was faintly touched by the moon's rays, casting shadows and slithers of white as the light brought out the different rock types in the mountain peaks. The canopy of rolling trees looked like a black river of death below, that if dropped from this height then that was what they would be.

I didn't know where he was taking me, but when we started to descend I could only hope it wasn't so that he could get a closer look at how my mangled body looked like for when he dropped me. But then I knew I was too important in this 'Game of Kings' as he called it, as like he said, I was just a pawn. A means to an end...*for both for them.*

No! I couldn't think like that. I was important to Draven not because the Gods deemed it so, but because he loved me. I wasn't going to give in to Lucius and his manipulation. He was trying to cast doubt in me where there was none and now he had planted a seed that I needed to eradicate.

He started to swoop lower and every thought flew from my mind other than my fear of heights. I screamed again as he found what he was looking for and turning slightly to catch the right air current, he skilfully took us in to land at the top of a ridge. As soon as my feet touched the ground my limits burst from within me. I ran out of his hold then turned around and pushed against his chest with both hands,

"You could have fucking killed me, you asshole!" I screamed at him. My little outburst seemed to amuse him and he laughed once not taking me seriously.

"I guess you would need to be of high spirit to challenge a man like the King. I do wonder though," he said and I snapped out,

"What?!"

"How he punished you for it!" He snarled back and grabbed me. I tried to struggle out of his hold but it was no use. He grabbed the back of my hair and pulled my head back with force.

"Calm down little rabbit, before I decided you taste too good to stop...after all, we wouldn't want me to drain you dry now would we?" he said then as if to prove it he leant down and ran an elongated fang across my neck, causing pain. It made a tiny slice, as if I had been scratched by a cat's claw. It was enough to take the threat seriously as he had intended.

"Good girl. See, you can be tamed after all," he told me and felt up my body once more as if to prove his statement true. I wanted to scream and cry at the same time. His control on me was making me feel things I didn't want to and hated myself for. Like how his fingers snaked around my breasts, making my nipples harden the closer he got. I wanted to believe it was the cold and nothing more, but my body knew the truth.

"Look, see how your body reacts to my touch...maybe you will enjoy our time together after all," he mocked and I turned away, utterly ashamed.

"Did you like my gift to you?" he asked as he gathered up the long dress, exposing more and more of my quivering legs. This was when I realised he had been the one to leave this satin set for me at the end of my bed. The shadow I first felt must have been him.

"I knew it would look good on you but I must confess, you surprise me," he hummed down at me and when I didn't ask, he grinned against my neck and whispered,

"Your pale skin against the black looks like milk fighting ink produced from the dark heart of a demon," he told me running his hand up further, closer to my core and most private place. I swallowed down both my disgust and pleasure, knowing in my

mind it was my own reaction's fight against those he had planted there.

"Almost as appealing as having your pale skin bathed in blood...my crimson white doll." The way he said this sounded like a whispered promise and once more I shuddered against him.

"Ah, here at last. About fucking time, cretins." He spoke this time above my neck where he had been kissing, at the sound of a vehicle driving up the forest track. I looked around to see a large clearing that was obviously used by tourists probably because of the amazing view it offered.

The big luxury SUV cut though the enclosed forest, with lights blaring and just before I needed to shut my eyes thanks to being blinded, Lucius covered them for me. I felt him make a kill sign over his throat and thankfully it was the lights that died not me.

"My Lord, we must leave now..." A man said as he approached us and I looked to Lucius who raised his eyebrow. He looked back towards where we had just flown in from, and I guessed his eyesight saw Afterlife whereas mine couldn't.

Then he looked back at me with a grin as the man finished his sentence,

"The King...he knows...he knows you have the girl." Lucius' smile grew and he said in a knowing sadistic tone,

"And the game begins..."

Book 2

20
Washing Away Sins.

NEW...

As soon as I heard that Draven was looking for me, I knew I had to do something. Anything in fact to stall him, so in my panic and desperation that 'something' I chose was of the stupid variety. I pulled from his grasp, surprising him as his attention was on the man who informed him that Draven was looking for me. He tried to grab me but I ran towards the edge of the cliff and shouted,

"Don't come any closer!" I warned holding a hand out to him taking a small step closer to the edge. My heart was pounding as I faced my greatest fear, for the first time ranking it secondary to the fear of being taken away from Draven.

"And what do you think that will accomplish exactly?" Lucius said crossing his arms across his chest.

"Well you can't blackmail someone when you have nothing to bargain with, now can you!" I snapped making him snarl back at me.

"My Lord, he is coming." The man behind him tried to reason but Lucius' arm snapped out and gripped him by the throat. Then he dragged his body up, towards him and roared,

"THEN RUN!" Then he let go of him. He fell to his knees, coughing with his hands around his neck.

"As you can see, time is of the essence little doll and my patience has limitations...*now get your ass over here!*" he demanded with a growl.

"I will do it, I will jump and then you will have nothing...so ask yourself Lucius, what is more important? The taking of me now and risking my death or the possibility of tomorrow and my survival, it's your choice...but I tell you now..." I paused looking down for a second as if facing my death and then back at him and spoke the truth with every fibre of my being.

"I would rather die than go with you!" Lucius looked at me as I issued a threat and he knew I wasn't bluffing. In fact, the look he gave me was a mixture of respect and surprise.

"Well played my pet, well played, but you are forgetting one thing..." He told me looking down and side on at his fingertips.

"And what's that!?" I spat out the question and then shrieked as he answered me only an inch away,

"I am faster than you." I screamed in surprise as he grabbed me and spun me, so that I had nowhere else to look other than straight down. The black satin whipped around me as the wind lashed out as if angry with me.

I looked back at him with anger and then something came to mind...Draven wasn't alone in looking for me. Suddenly my anger twisted as I looked above into the night and I started laughing. Lucius raised an eyebrow in question at my outburst, one he wasn't expecting along with something else,

"You're also forgetting something Lucius..." He snarled at me and found my answer in the form of my loudest possible scream,

"DRAVEN!" Then I looked back at him and said,

"Eyes in the sky." Showing him what I had seen...*Ava.*

"That fucking bird!" he said and this was quickly followed by an almighty roar, telling us both that it was time. My king had come and Lucius was right, the game had started now the other player had arrived. I looked towards the sound of anger and power cutting through the night, like a dark avenging angel appearing ready to do battle.

Lucius saw this and knew he would only have one chance. A chance he used...*me.* He spun me back around so that I was facing the edge of the cliff, once more, this time holding me out so that I would easily fall.

"Give her to me, Lucius!" Draven demanded after quickly assessing to see if Lucius had inflicted any damage on my body.

"What, is that how royalty greets old friends these days, by issuing demands without so much as a how's life treating you?" Lucius mocked and looking at Draven in all his wrath, I couldn't help but think that Lucius must have had a death wish.

"You don't deserve a life, you traitor!" Draven roared back at him with hateful venom lacing his every word.

"And the word traitor coming from your lips is a fucking joke!" Lucius snarled back making me wonder what it was between these two, a question I would be asking Draven if I ever made it out of this scenario alive.

"You see my little doll, your dark angelic knight stole something from me and now, well now that you're finally here, I have come to collect," he told me holding with one hand at the full length of my neck and the other at my waist, his fingers being the only thing keeping me from plummeting to my death.

"And you're insane if you think you will ever get it from me." Draven informed him and I really wanted to hold my hand up at this point and say, 'Um…is that a wise choice considering he has his hand around my breakable neck?'

"No…you don't think so? Umm well I guess we will just have to wait and see how you feel when I have *your Electus kneeling at my feet, begging me for release,*" he said planting the threat of both possibilities in Draven's mind, one escape and the other… *unthinkably sexual.*

"Not if you die tonight by my hand," Draven told him but for the moment the threat was hard to imagine thanks to the situation we found ourselves in. Draven was still a small distance away, up higher than the cliff face, suspended in the night and using his powers to defy gravity as even his wings were still. Lucius was at my back, holding me captive with a possessive hold, telling Draven that he wasn't backing down either. And because of it, Draven was unable to make his move as his one big problem… at the centre of it all, *was me.*

"I look forward to see you again soon…My. Little. Keira. Girl." Lucius said into the back of my head, kissing my hair and pronouncing his new nick name for me like it would stick.

"Now. Let. Her. Go." Draven threatened and Lucius laughed once and said,

"As you wish." Then Lucius…well, he simply let go. Just like Draven had asked of him.

I watched in slow motion as I fell forward with what must have looked like some frozen death mask as I faced my deadly destination. I was sure I was screaming inside but to the world, I faced the end in silence. I plummeted to the ground looking like a fallen Angel of death as the black satin robe flared out around me like wings, as the air was forced up, catching the floaty material.

It was like reliving a moment in time and once more I was falling by the hands of another, one that like before had stolen my free will. But like before, the arms of a dark King saved me. I shrieked in shock and Draven's arms tightened around before he cooed,

"Easy there, I have got you...*I have got you now.*" I clung onto him, finally able to breath once back within the safety of his hold. He held my head to his chest and I closed my eyes, no longer needing to see where we were headed, as there was only one place Draven would take me now and that place was home...*Afterlife.*

In fact, I was so lost in the feel of Draven that I didn't know we were back until I heard his voice being spoken in my ear.

"You can open your eyes now, you're safe little one," Draven whispered gently as if afraid I would crack. I did as he said, and opened them to watch as he carried me back into his bed chamber. Once there he placed me gently on the bed, so that I was sat up and my legs were hanging off the side. Then he stood looking down at me as if trying to control some part of himself. It was almost as if he had hit his limit and now it was all over, he could finally process what might have happened.

"Draven?" I said his name in question which seemed to snap something inside of him. He then fell to his knees in front of me and pulled me closer to him.

"Draven it's..."

"Ssshh, I just need to hold you...I just need to feel you," he told me placing his forehead to my stomach and wrapping his arms around me. I decided to swallow down my concerns taking his actions for what they were…*something he needed.*

So, I ran my fingers slowly through his hair in what I hoped was a comforting way.

"I nearly lost you," he told me and I shuddered at what could have happened if Draven hadn't got to me in time. It was then that I realised the thought of losing me had brought him to his knees and I nearly choked on a sob as the powerful emotions hit me.

"I know," I agreed in a small voice that nearly broke. He brought both his strong hands up my thighs and suddenly his hands stopped their travels to fist the satin at the top of my legs. Once there the demon in him let out a low growl.

"I can still smell him on you," he said forcing the words out and if I didn't know him better I would have said it sounded threatening. But the fact was *I did know Draven* and this side of him didn't scare me anymore. No, because I knew that it was his heightened emotions and demon side that spoke now and his possessive side was out in full force.

He rose up slowly in a predatory manner, forcing my body back on the bed as he climbed up the length of me. He snaked a hand under my back and lifted me further up onto the bed joining our movements together. I knew that look and even after everything I had been through tonight, I still found myself getting wet just at the sight of the man. His raw energy had me near pulsating and begging him to make me his…to make me forget the only way his touch could. I wanted to erase the memory of Lucius' hands on my body by replacing them with the only hands that mattered.

He placed his knees either side of my thighs as he knelt above me looking down at me like I was some rare treat to be ravished, only he didn't know where to start first. Actually, scrap that, I knew where only a second after that thought as he ran a flattened hand down from my neck then in between my breasts. He stopped for a split second before grabbing a fist full of material each side and tearing a line down the centre of the nightdress as easily as if it had been made from paper.

Quickly after he had fully exposed my body for his pleasure, he took no time at all before he started to enjoy it. He shifted down my body so that he could get to tasting my skin, starting with the sensitive flesh around my nipples. I moaned aloud, arching up to him at the first feel of his tongue swiping across my erect pink bud, begging him without words to take it fully into his mouth. He didn't disappoint.

I cried out as he licked, sucked and nipped at it before adding to the pain by rolling it around in between his teeth. It was maddening to the point I begged him to join his body with mine. Shamefully asking for his cock, all the while with my head shaking back and forth as my impending orgasm was just out of reach. I needed more. I needed to be touched, penetrated, or tasted…anything to make me tip over the edge as I chased my need to come.

"I love hearing you beg for me, almost as much as I love giving you what you want," he told me in a deep rasp before proving his statement and thrusting himself deep into my core. One, two, three times feeling the length of him and I came screaming. After that, he took over by chasing his own orgasm. It was as if his own need was overwhelming him and the chance of losing me caused a fever of need deep within him. He covered me, consuming as much of me as he could with his body and he placed his forehead against my cheek, pressing himself harder and harder. He held me to him so tight, I had never in this single moment ever felt so treasured but more importantly...*needed.*

"*You're mine Keira...mine...mine...*" He spoke into my cheek, saying the word 'mine' which each thrust. His hands caught my wrists and pinned them over my head in a possessive hold of dominance.

"*Now say it...! Say you're mine...tell me!*" he demanded pressing my arms into the bed above me and adding to the sexual flames he kept ignited.

"*Yes!*" I moaned but this wasn't good enough for him. He nipped at my cheek and said,

"Don't toy with me...now say it!" He shouted down at me and the sight of his frustration and sexual drive sent me over the edge and I came screaming,

"I'm yours!" Seconds later this became the catalyst for him also and he, like me had found his euphoric bliss. He roared out with his head forced down into the bed next to mine and I felt him shuddering, both above and inside me. I couldn't explain the sexual gratification that I felt having the feel of him coating my insides with his seed, or what it did to me. I felt comforted almost to know that not all of him had left me even as he pulled himself from between my legs.

He remained on top of me only at least holding himself up so as not to crush me. He panted as did I, only thanks to his abilities, these obviously included being able to recover a lot quicker after sex than a human. I opened my eyes to see him looking down at me, as he brushed my hair back from my face with one large hand.

"You scared me," he told me honestly as if needing to get his greatest fears off his chest. I cupped his cheeks with both hands and whispered,

"*I know.*" Then I pulled his face to mine and we shared our first kiss since he got me back. We were just getting into it when he tore his lips from mine and the rumbling in his chest told me something was wrong.

"What? What's wrong?" I asked frowning up at him.

"It is no good, I can still smell him on you...his hands touched what belongs to me and I can't stand it," he told me honestly and I winced feeling terrible. Then before I could roll over and curl into a ball in hopes of hiding myself from his harsh gaze, I yelped as he gathered up my body and lifted with me in his arms.

"What are you...?"

"I am rectifying my mistake," he told me cryptically and I held on to his neck as he walked me into the bathroom. I could feel his essence dripping from me and wetting his skin as he had wrapped my legs around his back.

Once inside the bathroom I realised the shower was already on and ready for us. He walked us both in there and I released a sigh of bliss at the feel of hot water cleansing my skin. I thought he would let me down but when he didn't I couldn't help but joke,

"I think I'm safe in the shower." However, Draven wasn't in a joking mood and the events of the evening still clung to him like a sticky residue of regret. I knew this when his eyes bore into mine and he told me,

"I am not letting you go." I swallowed hard and nodded, telling him silently that I understood. Then he pressed my back against the wall along with his growing arousal into my tender flesh.

"Never Keira...*never.*" He said referring to his last promise and then he kissed me, this time contentedly so in the knowledge the water was taking away the last remains of Lucius...washing him away.

"Never," I whispered pulling back over his lips long enough to touch him with my words. After this Draven kissed me with a passion that verged on dangerous for a breakable human such as myself but just before he could go too far he would stop himself. Like his bruising hold on me and just as my last breath was running out, he would ease up allowing me to breathe more freely.

"I want you," I told him, linking my fingers behind his neck and crying out as he entered me without warning.

"Yes! Yes! Yes Draven!" I shouted as he powered into me and I screamed, shuddering in his arms as I quickly came. He moved me from the wall and stepped back, so that I could feel the water cascading down my hair, so I arched my back, pressing myself against his length.

"By the Gods, you're beautiful!" he told me as he continued to enter me, holding me up with one arm around me. His other hand ran down my wet breasts, cupping them and plucking at my nipples.

"Taste me Draven, I want to feel you drink from me…"

"Keira, I…" I turned my neck to the side interrupting him with the sight of my submission and he found his limit. He pushed me through the water and himself to the other side. Once he found something hard against my back he swooped low to my neck and sank his fangs deep, making me buck against him as I came again screaming.

Wave after wave hit me with every draw on my blood he made and I lost myself in the long moments of release. He tore his fangs from my bloody flesh and roared his own release, arching his neck until the strain looked almost too painful to take. The water cascade down his head and I had never seen anything so beautiful. He looked like some mighty God of the sea, a statue sculptured in his name and epic memory.

Slowly he lowered his head down after the last of his body's tremors had subsided. I reached up and brushed all his hair back with both hands and I bit my lip at the look he gave me.

"My little heart's keeper, what it is you do to me?" I blushed at his sweet words and looked away becoming shy. He chuckled as if this was impossible and I guess it was silly due to what we had just done together.

"Let's get you cleaned up, little love of mine," Draven said and I closed my eyes against the painful memory. Thankfully Draven didn't see my reaction to his words of the unknown past Lucius had created. He had turned to get the soap which gave me time to try and cast that mental anguish from my mind.

But no matter how I tried I couldn't, it was as if he had gotten inside my head or something. Because the next thing I knew Draven turned back to face me and he was no more. Sand coloured hair darkened by the water lay clung to his long pale neck. Crimson eyes took in my naked body with a hunger that, unlike Draven's, had yet to be sated. Perfectly shaped lips smirked, cocking up on one side as he screamed silent promises in his dark mind.

The dark mind of Lucius. And Draven's face had been replaced by a sadist with a new toy to play with...

His little Keira Girl.

AUTHOR INSIGHT.

Chapter 20
Book 2

Now after writing these chapters, where Lucius nearly takes Keira, I quickly decided that it would have made the rest of the story difficult, given Draven's nature. I think in truth, knowing Dom's personality, he would have probably turned caveman, by throwing a pissed off Keira over his shoulder and taken her somewhere no one would ever find her. This or he would have been too over protective too soon, making the rest of the book difficult to write.

The other reason was that I knew I needed to write the Temple scene, where Keira finds what really lies in the belly of Afterlife and I decided this was a missed opportunity to do so.

So with this in mind, I cut the chapter and made Lucius appear to her in a nightmare he controlled. This way it could easily lead on to her hearing the desperate screams of what she thinks is an innocent girl, one used to play on her own horrific past.

But this next part of the Temple was originally written differently as well. It started the same, with Keira walking into the Temple and finding what see soon discovers is the start of a sacrifice. But then she soon gets discovered and instead of having her running, she finds herself at Draven's mercy sooner.

Once more after writing this I realised my missed opportunity for some horror as she makes her way through the prison. I also knew that I wanted to have the chance to tell Ragnar's story, so decided this would be another good opportunity to do so.

So here is it for you to enjoy.

… Book 2

20
Temple Traitors.

I walked closer inside, where the brightly lit Temple hall hurt my eyes after becoming accustomed to the dark. I stood still, blinking franticly so as not to be taken by surprise, hoping that one of the pillars I hid behind was enough of a barrier from the droning voices that filled the room. My heart nearly stopped and my blood froze from being so scared.

The chanting wasn't like anything I had ever heard. Not only was the language strange and very unnerving, but it seemed to be passing between Demonic lips. Its loud echoing felt as though it could crack the walls and destroy cities with only a few verses. I couldn't choke down the fear that kept rising back up my body like a growing illness. It kept getting louder and louder, which proved to be too much for my fragile human ears.

I could feel the marble floor beneath me vibrate and this was the only reason I hadn't yet crumbled to it like a frightened child. Nothing could compare to this moment. I had never experienced terror like it and I had never prayed so hard for it to be just another horrible dream. But, as I felt the beads of sweat roll down my trembling face, I knew that no amount of hope in the world would make it so. My body shook so violently that I thought it would break into pieces.

Only when a great roar cut through the other voices, did it all go quiet. This finally made my senses return to me, along with my resolution. I decided to move further round, as I now knew I was still completely out of sight. I walked slowly to the next massive pillar which was like a masterpiece in its own right. Painted blood red at the bottom, turning into flames of orange and gold as it curled upwards to the painted sky on the ceiling and dome. My eyes followed the story around the room that depicted a great war between Heaven and Hell. There were Angel warriors on horseback attacking winged Demons from a flaming sky. I sought out the next scene and had to squint my eyes to make out the picture. There was a darker patch which at first I thought was a falling dark cloud, descending on the Demons below. But then after staring at it in greater length, I realised it was actually a wave of silver tipped arrows, flying down ready to pierce their targets with deadly intent.

The painting was so skilled and accurate that I almost thought them real enough to touch. I shuddered at the idea that this could actually be based on a truth. An unknown war that humans were utterly oblivious to. The shiny floor looked like liquid and the reflection of the painted heaven gave the marble a bluish tinge making it resemble a lagoon.

Finally, once I had finished looking around my magnificent surroundings, my eyes fell on the imposing figures that were stood around the room like a secret cult meeting. Each one was clothed in red robes that matched Hell's representation they stood by. My mind counted seventeen red bodies draped from head to foot in blood velvet then followed on as the next set of six bodies wore purple with thick gold symbols at the bottom.

This reminded me of a strange display of the signs of the zodiac combined with ancient runes. These weren't quite the same as the men who had taken the girl but I soon came across them. My gaze rested at the top of the circle these robed beings had created by where they stood. At the top was a huge stone slab that acted like an altar and it too was covered in carved symbols that matched the robes.

I could feel my sweaty hands slip from the smooth cold marble that I tried to keep hold of. I was far too close now and knew this was very wrong, but my will to turn away, wasn't half as strong as my will to stay. I bit down on my lip and rolled it back and to, through my teeth. If I hadn't been here witnessing this cult based nightmare, then I'm sure I would have felt the pain I was causing myself.

Instead I focused all my attention and energy onto the scene that was being played out in front of me like a sadistic opera. The group was clearly waiting for something or more likely someone and I had a sick feeling it was the girl who I had made it my mission to save from her cruel fate.

I didn't have long to wait for the crescendo as a huge, tall cloaked figure walked out through what looked like a series of guards who bowed respectfully as their Master passed. He dominated the room and like a Mexican wave at a football game, all the robed cult followed suit and fell to their knees. They started the mind numbing chant again, forcing me to place my shaky hands over my ears.

The deafening beat rattled my mind like thousands of war horses charging into battle and I could feel my courage getting beaten with every step. I looked on through a watery glaze and held on with shaky limbs. They all started to sway as the momentum increased into a powerful finish and as before, a great roar projected off the domed roof and echoed about the room, creating a deadly silence that followed. I peered round again to see the leader of this demonic choir hold up his hands as he commanded the rest to stand once more.

His imposing figure wore a black robe that draped long over his face. It was decorated by one large gold symbol, positioned over his chest. It was the same circled symbol that mirrored the stone altar he stood in front of. It reminded me of the different moon cycles all intertwined around a circle with one prominent symbol in the centre. Then it hit me where I had seen that symbol before. I looked down at my palm and saw the half-moon with a V shape attached to it, only now on the altar and robe the V was upright.

The skin had dried blood around the edges but the deep red shape could easily be seen. It was unmistakable. The same symbol was not only on my hand, thanks to that strange vine entrance, but it was also on the back of my neck, under my hairline. Hiding there like a dark secret, waiting until this moment to make its reason known. A birthmark that sealed my fate and brought me here to find my true path. That thought terrified me far more than the Demons before me. I was in no way part of this sick and twisted cult! I wouldn't allow myself to think it. Then it suddenly hit me...

What if the man in black was Lucius?!

What if this had been his plan all along, to get to me? First to control my dreams and then to play on my insecurities. Surely, if he'd had access to my mind then he would know my past. Then all that was left to do, was to make me hear the girl's cries and I would come running. Just like he said,

"I will not have long to wait and you will soon come to me". I started to shake yet again at the thought.

The man terrified me to my very core and to make it even worse, I was also a little bit fascinated with him. Lately, I had been trying to reject the idea and banish it from my mind like some law I was breaking. It felt against nature thinking about him but in some sick twisted way, I was drawn to him like bees to pollen. This forced me to be more afraid of myself and my own irresponsible actions. I didn't know what I would do when faced with the man who haunted and consumed my dreams but when I thought of him and his lips to mine, it made me quiver with both revulsion and a burning hunger.

I tried to put it all down to his powerful mind control and wished more than anything that I was strong enough to push him out and once again gain control over myself.

I started to look at the black figure a little closer and the size of his frame matched that of Lucius. He was tall, with squared shoulders but I couldn't see any of his features as most of his robe covered his body and face. My mind raced with thoughts and ways that he could have penetrated the fortress that was Draven's home.

NEW...

I shook my head at the possibility of Draven being hurt but I doubted very much that he knew what was going on down here. Which had me questioning the reasons why he would keep something like this from me? Why wouldn't he tell me but then I ended up answering my own question with one simple fact...he was protecting me from his world.

Well little good that protecting did me now I thought wryly. As I knew the smartest thing to do right now was to get the hell out of here but then...what about the girl? What if someone could have saved me but decided not to out of fear, was I really prepared to be that person now? No! I had to at least try or I would never forgive myself.

I looked around the gigantic space hoping to see something that could at least help me to fit in and I let out a sigh of relief when I found what I was looking for. So, taking one last look to check I wasn't being watched, I sneaked back the way I had come and found a row of cloaks hanging like limp ghosts. I picked one up, throwing the red material around my shoulders, cursing my small height. The robe was so long it was like a wedding train behind me and I kicked out the front so that I wouldn't trip. I then raised the hood so my face was hidden.

Creeping back up to the next pillar I spotted a hidden room off to the side but it was too close to the top altar than I wanted to be. But, I also knew that if there was one place in this huge circular room that they would keep her, then my first guess would be in there.

"I guess that's where I am heading then...stupid Keira...very stupid." I muttered under my breath, knowing that in reality this wasn't just stupid, it was closer to bloody suicidal!

Walking closer and keeping a hawk eye on the chanting bodies around the main focus of the room, I continued to make my way towards the ornate door. It had a scalloped arch that reminded me of the shape of a shell, and at each point that hung down it held a golden ball adorned with precious jewels. Ancient symbols I had no chance in this real-life Hell of deciphering were painted up the sides in their own gilded border.

The closer I got I realised that it wasn't a door at all but just an arched opening but more surprising still was to find it unguarded. But then when I checked one last time I realised they were all waiting for something to happen.

Their heads all turned to one side of the hall to an opening that at first was invisible but only when a snow white woman emerged could the entrance be seen. A bright light behind her just made her glow like a Heavenly entity but when it faded back to where it came from, the features of an old woman could clearly be seen.

She had long white hair that flowed around her as though each individual strand was controlled by an unseen force. The long dress she wore did the same as it wrapped in and out of her tired looking legs. The sleeves opened up into a V shape and the tips came down to the floor reminding me of Robin Hood's Maid Marion. Her face looked kind, despite its numerous wrinkles and her soft light eyes could even be seen from the side where I stood.

She reminded me of what Mother Earth would look like if she was in a human form. I felt connected to her through my love for all things pure and natural. This was how I knew this woman was most definitely an Angel. It was the same feeling I felt around Vincent, when I first saw him in his Angelic form.

They had a pull towards them and I could imagine that it was probably the same that evil people had towards Demons. Something in our genetic makeup was forged by the same hand. We were undoubtedly connected to these creatures and throughout history, even though our beliefs had never been proven, they had never faltered. Now, of course, I knew why.

I watched as who must have been Lucius, held one hand out towards the old lady and motioned to take her hand, which the woman looked more than delighted with. She gracefully floated over to him and placed a frail, wrinkled hand in his. He bowed to her and led her to one side of the altar.

Something in me told me this was my one and only shot at getting the girl. So, I slipped into the arched doorway unseen. This was when it became clear the reason she had no guards and unless I had some heavy-duty bolt cutters hiding down my pants, the girl and I were going nowhere together.

She wasn't just chained to a wall, she was also suspended from it and those chains weren't just attached to her wrists but were wrapped all around her body. I looked up at her with regret, not knowing where I would even start.

I thought about trying to maybe find someone to help but from the sounds of the chanting out there, I didn't think I had long. Her head lay limp and if I didn't know any better I would have said she looked dead already. But then she would slightly twitch her fingers and I knew this wasn't the case.

I looked frantically around the room for anything that may help when I could barely believe my luck. Hanging on a hook by the opening was a heavy set of keys and I muttered my thanks to anyone looking down at me now. I grabbed them and started to try every key on the many padlocks that looked as old as this place. Finally, one by one I was managing to get them open and just as the girl was coming around.

Unfortunately, it wasn't a quick process but even more unfortunate was the unexpected landing she had to fall on. I tried to catch her but we only ended up more in a pile of limbs as I became her somewhat softer landing. She moaned and tried to grab me as I pushed her body off me.

"Don't worry...I am going to get you out of here." I told her as she groaned again. Once all the chains fell away from her, clattering to the floor I knew there was a high chance of someone hearing. I didn't know what to do next, but looking down at myself covered in robes like the rest I cursed myself for not picking one up for the girl.

"I will be right back." I told her before I raced back to the doorway and looked out to make sure I wasn't just about to walk into someone. Thankfully the ceremony was still in full swing and everyone's focus was still on Lucius and the woman in white.

I looked left and right once more before taking my chances again. I picked up my long red train so as not to trip up and walked towards where the long robes hung down, intending to grab one. Then I turned quickly and a thundering voice stopped me in my tracks.

"<u>Daiva</u>!" ("Demon" in Ancient Persian) Lucius shouted as he pointed one long velvet arm out for the guards to his right, who were now on their way to retrieve the girl.

"*Shit!*" I hissed trying to think what I could do but I was running out of time as they were nearly at the door. The only thing I could think of was to cause enough of a distraction that they would chase me instead. That way maybe the girl would have a chance to get away. It was a long shot but it was the only one I had. I was just about to scream my lungs out when suddenly a hand clamped over my mouth from behind...

I had been found.

After this everything went to shit very, very quickly. The guards disappeared through the doorway and one came out again in a rush to tell his master what had happened. I watched frozen as the guard got Lucius' attention and then told him in hushed tones what he and the other one had found.

The rest of the people in robes all started whispering in hushed tones, ones that caused the man in charge to get angry. He slammed his fist down on the altar, and an almighty crack travelled down its centre as if it had been hit by lightning.

"PRODITOR!" He roared (Means 'traitor' in Latin.) and the room went deadly silent.

"Bring me the traitor!" he commanded in a booming voice and I shuddered knowing exactly who he was referring to...*me*. The person behind me let go of my mouth and gripping my arm tightly, started dragging me to the front of the altar.

"No...no, don't...don't do this." I whispered to the person at my back, whoever they maybe. But then when they stopped dead, I knew that they had recognised my voice.

"Keira?" as soon as they said my name I too recognised their voice and I prayed it was all just a bad dream.

"No...it...can't be...tell me it's not you Zagan?" I said wondering how this could have happened...when and how had he turned to the other side?

"How did you...?" he started to say, letting me go in his shock. I stumbled back a step and then another one, shaking my head in my disbelief.

"Is this the Traitor!? Bring them to me!" Lucius demanded in his demonic voice and I spun around to see others coming at me from both sides. I made a dash to one side but then got cut off with others blocking my path. I was trapped. Two men grabbed me either side, digging their fingers into the tops of my arms. This was when Zagan turned cold but not towards me.

"Get. Your. Hands. Off. Her!" His voice was like a deadly weapon, one took seriously enough by both men. They let me go and Lucius' interest was piqued the second he heard it.

"Her?" he questioned and for the split-second I thought I was hearing things...it wasn't Lucius' voice...was it?

"Yes, my Lord," Zagan said, solemnly lowering his head with regret. What was going on? I looked back at the man in charge to see that he had now swiftly jumped over the altar and was storming his way over to me. I cried out in surprise and stumbled backwards a step as I tried to put more space between us, space that he was quickly cutting down.

"I...no, I...please..." My words of protest mumbled out of me in a pathetic attempt to stop him but it was no good. The man's actions looked half controlled by a demon possessed. He reached me in no time at all and just as he was about to make a grab for me I made one last attempt to get away. I turned to face Zagan and ran towards him thinking he was the only one who seemed to still care about what happened to me. But then I saw him nod to the cloaked man behind me and knew I had made a mistake.

He grabbed me before I had time to change direction and I struggled against him.

"Let me go! You...you don't have to do this, Zagan!" I told him but then he gripped me a little harder and spun me round to face my fate. Then he lowered his lips closer to my ear and whispered his reasons, reasons that broke my heart,

"I have no choice, for he is my King."

My breath caught as realisation started to take hold and my biggest fears came to light with one simple motion,

A hood removed and a King emerged...

Dominic Draven.

Book 2

21
Hitting Demons and Understanding Angels.

NEW…

I couldn't believe it. I just couldn't! I felt Zagan pull my hood back on my robe so that now my identity could be revealed as Draven's was. His eyes widened in utter shock and for one small moment I felt like running into his arms just for a single second of comfort I needed right now. But then I remembered what role he played in all of this and I couldn't do it.

Meanwhile Draven looked as though he was fighting with himself on what to do next and like me, the rest of the room was frozen with fear on what that would be.

"Circum Vertere!" (Means 'Turn around' in Latin) Draven spoke commanding the room with an echoing boom added to his voice. I didn't know what he had said exactly but it must have been something along the lines of telling the room to give us privacy, as everybody in the room turned around all at the same time. The action made me jump as that too echoed off the wall and hit me from all angles.

Even Zagan at my back let me go and turned around, to face the other way. Which left only Draven and I facing each other with nowhere to go. Because after what I had just seen, then where would we find ourselves now?

"You woke up," he stated the obvious and I frowned up at him and answered,

"Unfortunately for you, yes I did." I was breathing heavy and he looked over me as if trying to assess if I had attained any injury in getting here. Then he asked me a question that confused me.

"Who was it, Keira?" His tone was calm but I knew it wouldn't last long, not if that bulging vein in his neck was anything to go by.

"I don't..." I was about to tell him that I didn't understand but he cut me down. He took a step closer to me and I swallowed hard.

"You will tell me who and you will do it now!" he said in a tone that was dangerously close to the edge. I was getting so angry I could feel my own rage also getting dangerously close to the edge and the two of us like this was only heading down one road, the destination...*temper town.*

"I don't know what you're talking about, Draven!" I snapped back at him and he looked ready to erupt as he must have thought I was lying.

"Keira, this is your last chance," he warned and surprisingly I was the one who lost it first.

"My last chance at what! To tell you that I don't know what the hell you're talking about!" I shouted back at him and he growled low before trying to grab me but I moved my arm from out of his reach and gave him my own warning,

"Don't touch me!" He looked taken aback by this as if it was his right to and someone was stopping

him, something he didn't like. I saw the flash of hurt burn in his eyes before he quickly hid it behind a feigned look of indifference.

"Fine, have it your way Keira," he told me and before I could utter a word of protest he grabbed me too quickly to do anything about it. I was over his shoulder slung there like a fighting piece of meat.

"Let me go! Put me down!" I demanded but he said nothing. He simply walked out of the Temple with purpose. I looked up to see that not a single person looked back at me. They all had a master to obey and I was nothing but a complication for their king. I felt small and unimportant in his world for the first time since being together. And I quickly lost the fight as he walked us into a circular room that was like a smaller temple, one more suited this time for worship than sacrifice.

This one was all white marble with a black and white diamond tiled floor. The walls were covered in black granite statues who each sat on thrones of gold in their own little alcoves. Each one was different and they all represented different forces. Wind and the Oceans both had great sapphires and pearls encrusted on their feet, while Fire and the Sun had rubies and amber, held in their hands. There were others like Earth, Night and the Moon all with various gems embedded amongst their figures.

The parts of the walls that weren't paying testament to these Godlike effigies were masterpieces in their own right. Covered with so many patterns and carvings you didn't know where to look. It was as though your eyes couldn't take in all the splendour they created. You just wanted to touch them. To run your fingers along the channels that formed integral art. The room was bright, as if the day's sun was getting at it somehow, but with no windows and the night not yet over, I couldn't understand where it came from.

Once he deemed it far enough from our compliant audience to be out of sight and for now, out of mind, he let me down. He gripped my waist and I slid the length of him until my feet touched the floor. He made sure I was steady before he let me go. I huffed and tried to move further away from him but with a taxing sigh coming from him first, he started to back me into one of the statues.

"Now you have two minutes to tell me what happened and how you gained access to my Temple before I start a manhunt." I frowned up at him and shook my head a little as if this would help me to make sense of what the hell he was talking about.

"A manhunt for who?" I asked and again this was the wrong thing to say as he growled...something that just pissed me off even more.

"Stop that!" I snapped shaking my hands in the air as my frustration mounted.

"Believe it or not, Draven I am not asking these questions out of stupidity, but because I literally have no idea what you are talking about?! No one brought me down here, I came because I heard a girl crying for help and you were nowhere to be found!" I told him despite the look of disbelief he was giving me throughout.

"You expect me to believe that you entered this place without help from another?" he asked, folding his arms and looking even larger than usual thanks to his robe.

"Well, unless I have finally found a language you *don't* understand and I am unknowingly speaking it, then yes, that is what I am telling you!" I threw at him putting a hand to my hip and matching him in the attitude he was giving me. It seemed like he was trying to stare me out and when I didn't budge, he tore his angry gaze from me as if he couldn't stand to look at me any longer.

I had to admit, it hurt.

"Why is that so hard to believe?" I asked at the sight of his actions. He whipped his head back round to face me and almost snarled his words at me,

"Because it is impossible!"

"So, you're calling me a liar, is that it?" I asked never expecting his answer to cut me deep the way it did.

"Yes, I am," he told me and that was it...I lost it. What came next was the result of a lethal cocktail of madness, fury and agony. I felt my hand fly out at him before I could stop it. I slapped him across the face so hard I felt my palm burn seconds later. His head whipped to the side and he stayed looking that way for long moments after as if in shock. Both my hands flew to cover my mouth in horror as realisation sunk in at what I had done.

Someone behind Draven cleared their throat and I felt my shame double.

"Dom, you are losing time." Vincent's voice slowly seeped into to our situation and no matter how softly those words were said, it felt like someone cutting into our time with a hot blade. Draven didn't look at me again but instead turned his back on me altogether. I wanted to cry, to shout, to say anything but just let him do what he did next. But nothing came as he walked towards his brother and voiced one last command with what sounded like icy indifference,

"Get her out of here."

Vincent simply nodded and then looked to me, being the only one to witness my tears fall. Then as Draven walked past his brother, about to go back into the Temple I tried one last time,

"Dra...Draven I..." the words came out thick and forced from my emotions, which Draven knew just hearing the tears being shed behind them. He stopped dead in the archway, put a hand to the wall as if to steady himself and lowered his head. I thought I'd reached him. I thought I'd managed to make a difference...to stop him leaving me. But then I knew all was lost when I watched his other hand turn to a fist at his side. He battled his own emotions for only a second longer but he didn't look at me.

No, instead he simply...simply... *walked away from me.*

I burst into tears and my legs crumbled but the floor never caught me, Vincent did.

"Easy now, I've got you...I've got you," he told me as he pulled me close. He heaved me up into his arms and I found myself sobbing into his shoulder as I held on to his neck.

"He...he...didn't believe me Vincent... *why didn't he believe me?*" I managed to ask pulling back from him and crying out my question. He gave me a pitying look and shook his head in a small way that told me his answer, even if he soon voiced it himself,

"I don't know, sweetheart," he said wiping away my tears with a thumb to my cheek and the sweet, tender gesture had me in tears once again.

"Come on, let's get you out of here," he said after looking back towards where his brother had left as if he could hear something I couldn't. I nodded and said in small voice,

"I'm all right now, you can put me down." He looked as though he was going to deny my request but I guess after what I had just experienced thanks to domineering men, then well, he must have thought better of it.

"Very well," he said and let my legs down first. Like his brother had done, he made sure I was steady until he stepped back and held his hand out for me to take. I was just about to put my hand in his when a blood curdling sound stopped me. The sound of a girl's scream seemed to vibrate along the walls and there was only one place it had come from... *The Temple.*

I made it about five steps towards the opening before Vincent grabbed me.

"No! We have to do something! We have to help her!" I shouted, pleaded and begged trying to get from him but he grabbed my wrists and crossed them over my breasts, holding me locked and immobile.

"He's going to kill her! We can't let that..." I started again, struggling in his hold...little good it did me.

"Keira listen to me. The girl is not who you think she is..."

"But, but..."

"She is a killer, Keira! She is the worst of our kind and she needs to be punished." Hearing this I suddenly stopped struggling against him. Could it be true?

"She's...she's really a killer?" I asked quietly and he spun me round to face him, lifted my face to his and said,

"Tell me now, did you come down here alone?" he asked me, surprising me with his question and I nodded before confirming what happened with words.

"I swear to you Vincent, I swear it. I came down here alone!" I told him, looking into his eyes so that he could read the truth in them easily.

"I believe you and in turn I ask for your trust in me when I tell you that the girl in there deserves to meet the Underworld, her body in flames for her crimes against not only my kind but also yours, Keira." Vincent said with an arm pointed towards the door, indicating the one currently screaming for her life. But now the only difference was that she did so alone. Because no longer did she have an ally in me. Because I knew without a doubt that Vincent spoke the truth... a truth I needed to hear in order to let go.

I nodded my understanding at him and this time took his offered hand without hesitation. And together we walked from this place and left Draven to his unfortunate work. But with each step further from him we took I couldn't help but wonder how our joint discovery should have gone. I looked at Vincent and couldn't help comparing the two.

How his brother had handled finding me there and instead of realising it for what it was, a massive misunderstanding on both parts, he simply refused to do what his brother had done...*believe in me.*

He had basically called me a liar and that was when something had broken me inside. I had never lied to him, where he had done so to me...on numerous occasions in fact. So, what right did he have to judge me under the same light that had first been cast on his own actions?

I looked to Vincent again, both now and in a dream world looking down at who held my hand and I knew it should have been Draven...it should have been us. Me and my boyfriend walking away from the experience together and overcoming the differences his world and mine threw at us. But it wasn't. It was someone else and my dark knight had just cast me aside, deeming me unworthy of a truth told and a truth believed.

So, I let Vincent lead me through the maze of tunnels and stone hallways like some lost lifeless doll. The only thing that felt real anymore were the tears that rolled down my cold cheeks and fell to the floor from my chin.

Was this the end? He demanded for me to leave...no, not just leave but to be *taken away*. Did it then mean what I thought it meant? Had Draven ended things with me without actually saying the words? I swallowed down a sob and just as Vincent reached a door I dropped his hand to cover my mouth.

He looked back at me and that's when he saw it....*My heart breaking.*

"Oh Keira." He uttered my name and then I was lost. I looked down and let my tears fall, this time without restraint. I don't know what happened after this, but at a guess I was being carried. And I did so all the time feeling like my world was coming to an end, *even in the arms of an Angel.*

I had no knowledge of how, but soon I found myself being taken back through a pair of familiar doors.

"Afterlife." I muttered and Vincent chuckled.

"I thought I had lost you for a moment then," he told me thinking I had fallen asleep.

"It's okay, you can just put me down now and I can find my own way home," I told him wondering where my truck was, here or at home. He raised a blonde eyebrow in question and like that, he painfully reminded me of his brother.

"Why would you need to make your way home? I brought you in here because I thought you could do with a drink," he said pulling Draven's chair out and setting me down on it. Then he left me and I watched him walk to the bar. I left him to it and turned my gaze back on the world I knew and loved. *Afterlife...* in truth it was the real start of my new life. A place that quickly became home and all it held inside this unlikely place of dreams was what would consume my heart.

I often wondered what would have happened had Frank never got me a job here. Would I be here now? Or would Draven have kept me at arm's length forever, for fear of what his world could do to me? Would I have just been like the rest of them, down there trying to get a glimpse of the shadowed world above, fantasising about the club's owner just like RJ had?

But I soon realised that I was asking myself the wrong questions, as what I should have been asking was...what happens next?

"You join me for a drink," Vincent said as I must have asked this last question aloud. He placed a bottle of tequila and two glasses down on the table as he took his usual seat next to Draven's. I took one look at the bottle and thought why the Hell not, after all, I might as well drink to my time here and bury my sorrows the only real way one can...by drowning themselves in a 38% proof bottle.

Vincent filled up his shot glass and tipped it to mine and I said a toast,

"Here's to disbelieving boyfriends and slap happy girlfriends...it was good whilst it lasted." I said miserably before shooting the clear liquid back and feeling it's burn, like a welcome friend. I looked to Vincent who just shook his head once, as ifa he didn't believe me but he drank anyway.

"Answer me something Keira, did you really think my brother is destructive and cruel enough to be the hand behind killing an innocent girl?" I placed my glass down slowly at his question and said honestly,

"No, I thought it was Lucius." He frowned on hearing my answer and then asked,

"Why would you think that?"

"Because just before I made my way down there I woke up to a dream...well a nightmare really, but it was one that had me convinced that he had somehow made it into Afterlife." I told him and he chewed on this new piece of information for a moment before asking me his next question, filling my glass again.

"And once you found out it was Dom...what then?" I shrugged my shoulders and said,

"I knew there would be a reason but one he didn't think important enough to give me...you did that, remember," I told him, giving him a look and once I received one back that told me I was right, I swigged my second shot back.

"My brother is many things, hothead being one of them but being used to handling a human heart is not something that comes naturally to him."

"And handling a Demon, Angel half breed King of the supernatural world, comes naturally to me?" I asked getting high-pitched and this time Vincent shrugged his shoulders and said,

"Point made but you have to understand that Draven has never loved this way before. He doesn't know what it means to be in a relationship that is equal. He doesn't know what it means to have to explain himself to another or be accountable for his actions. He has never known any other life, Keira and for all intents and purposes, he is still trying to rule over you, like he does his kingdom." I listened to what Vincent said and I put myself in his shoes as an outsider looking in and seeing his brother struggle like never before.

I got that, I really did but now it was time for him to see it from a different side...*a very human side.*

"And you have to understand this from my point of view, Vincent. Draven isn't alone in the world he wants me to live in but *I am.* I'm the only human in this life, *his life*...one that I chose to step into and one I gladly took out of the love I have for him but that still doesn't mean I don't get lost in it." I took a deep shuddering breath, trying to rein in my emotions so that I could carry on and carry on I did.

"Lost Vincent, and when I only have Draven to guide me...well, then, what do I do when he rips his hand from mine? Where does that leave me...I will tell you where Vincent, in a world I don't belong in, standing there alone, lost and confused, that's where." Vincent nodded as what could he really argue with.

"I don't have the all the answers Keira, only that you will have to take that up with my brother and now it seems is..." He was about to tell me something important but I cut him off getting up out of Draven's chair as my frustrations drove my actions. I placed my hands on the table in front of me, letting the robe I still wore cover them.

"Yes, well that would be too easy now wouldn't it because last time I checked Vincent, he cast me out like I was some silly little human that needed to leave his sight. 'Get her out of here' I believe was his command to you Vincent and now you want me to believe that all it will take is a little chit chat and all will be hunky dory again!" He raised an eyebrow, looked behind me once and then back to me again and said,

"So, what is the issue, you don't think he will want to talk to you after this evening?" I slumped back down into Draven's chair and told him the truth,

"What I am saying is that given the way your brother turned his back on me tonight, well I think that speaks volumes on what Draven wants and I...I think it should tell me something about how much he cares." I added this last part losing some of the fight and letting the hopelessness of the situation sink in.

"Then maybe you should be the first to turn it around." Vincent offered and I raised my head, swiped at my tears and said,

"I slapped him remember. I wouldn't be surprised if he turned his back on me because he wanted to end things between us. So how do I do that…how do I turn things around, Vincent?" I asked in a dire tone. He stood up, walked a step towards me and then bent down to whisper in my ear,

"You can start by facing him." Then he walked past me and before I could ask where he was going he spoke again, only this time it wasn't to me.

"Brother, *be gentle with her heart, for in it lies all the truth you need."* Then I heard the door close and my head snapped up to see him standing by the bar looking on.

He had heard everything.

Draven had heard my heart…

Breaking.

Book 2

22

Make up or Break up.

NEW...

Draven stood there looking at me, no longer wearing his robe but a fitted t shirt instead, one that looked as though he had put on whilst running. Had he been desperate to get to me? This question allowed that flower of hope to bloom deep inside me. The other question on the tip of my tongue was of course the one I asked.

"How long have you been stood there?" He gave me a pointed look and said,

"Long enough to have heard all I needed to hear," he told me and I nearly choked on the lump I tried to swallow. He had heard everything and that flower of hope quickly dried up and crumbled away in the wind of disappointment. Any minute now, he would simply ask me to leave and he would turn his back on me for the last time. So, what was left for me to do…beg?

Plead with him to listen to me? Tell him how sorry I was and ignore the hurt he inflicted just so that I could keep him? I knew he was worth that sacrifice to my pride but that wasn't the question that needed answering...it was, what did I really mean to him if he would so easily cast me aside?

In the end, it didn't matter. Not when the next question voiced came from him.

"You think I want to end things between us?" The way he asked this was as though he was barely keeping his anger and hurt in check. I bit my lip and tried to focus on the pain *I* inflicted, not the pain *he* inflicted with his harsh tone.

"I wouldn't blame you if you did." I told him in a small voice looking down at my hands.

"And what of you?" he asked and my gaze shot to his.

"What do you mean?"

"Do I grant you the same blame for wanting to end things with me?" His question took me off guard and I shook my head a little as if trying to make sense of what he was really saying.

"I...I..." I started to try and find the right answer to his question but his building anger wouldn't let me.

"And explain to me exactly how is it is even possible you think I could just end the feelings of my heart?" he asked after interrupting me. I gasped praying he meant what I thought he meant.

"Draven, I don't..." I tried once more to speak but he was too far gone.

"If you think I am just going to stand by and let you walk out of my life, then you are very much mistaken, Keira. There is no ending things..." He paused and suddenly he was pushing off the bar and storming his way over to me. I got up out of his chair and just as he reached me he took me in his arms, pull me close and said,

"...There is only fighting for them." Then he crushed his lips to mine in a heart stopping kiss. It was so powerful that I opened up to him, almost

praying that he would consume me whole. I knew that it wasn't goodbye, just the opposite in fact, as I knew that by the way he kissed me now, he would never let me go.

He lifted me up so that I was sat on his table and he spread my legs so he could step into the space he created. It reminded me of our first kiss in his bedchamber after placing me on his desk. And just like back then, it was as if he couldn't get enough of me.

Finally, he tore his lips from mine and before I could utter a word of protest, he pushed me back after knocking the empty glasses and almost full bottle to the floor in his haste.

The sound of smashing glass was the only other sound to be heard, other than our heavy breathing. I was about to sit back up but he growled down at me, his demon side telling me to stay where I was. I couldn't help it but his possessive actions turned me on and I let myself be pushed back down with a strong hand to my neck. Anyone else looking in would have seen the aggressive gesture as threatening. I, on the other hand, knew it for what it truly was...my demonic king dominating me and expecting my submission.

One I gave him freely.

He leaned down over me and whispered,

"I told you, you're not going anywhere, my little trouble maker." Then his hands tore down the robe, letting it fall around me, framing my body like a prize for him to play with...*and play with it he did.*

"Answer me, did you really think I would just let you leave me?" His question caught me off guard as his hand roamed down the length of my torso. I arched myself up and pressed my body into the feel of his flat hand, desperate for him to take hold of my breast and apply greater pressure. But the opposite happened as his touch left me altogether. I moaned at my loss, something he was counting on.

"I am waiting..." he told me softly, speaking over my neck and then moving slowly over my lips to finish his next command,

"...for your answer." Then he pulled away and smiled when I bit my lip, for he knew that he had me.

"I thought you would want me to leave." I told him and he raised an eyebrow in question.

"And why would you think that I wonder?" he asked in an amused tone.

"I slapped you." I told him in a way that I thought was obvious.

"And what of it, after all, I certainly deserved it...that and more for not believing you," he said picking up my hand and running his fingertips over the mark the door had inflicted on me. This was all the proof he needed and I pulled my hand from his, realising it wasn't my words that had made him trust me, it was what he had seen.

"You didn't trust me," I stated firmly, sitting up and thankfully my tone told him to let me. He sighed heavily and took his seat as he knew the time for action was over...now it was time to explain ourselves.

"That is not entirely true," he told me and I couldn't help but blurt out,

"Bullshit! You did everything short of calling me a liar," I told him crossing my arms across my chest. He closed his eyes briefly as if this would help in looking for the answers.

"You must understand Keira, that no access has ever been granted to a human and even those of my own kind that are allowed to enter, do because I deem it so."

"So, what you're saying is it seemed impossible for me to enter on my own?" I asked making him nod at me in return.

"But isn't your world also full of impossibilities...including me?" I asked making him frown.

"What do you mean?" he asked me back, doing so with obvious caution as if I was trying to trick him in some way. I almost found myself smiling had we not been talking about something so serious.

"Well you said yourself how surprised you were after I witnessed you that night in your true form, the night I was stabbed, how I came back the next day and confronted you."

"I am afraid I don't follow."

"What I am trying to say is that even someone who has shared this earth with humans as many years as you have, that one still surprised you... that a human still managed to find the courage to face you, even after all the impossible facts you first made *her* face." He obviously saw where I was going with this as his eyes went soft, and he reached out to me. I allowed myself to be pulled into his embrace and sit on his lap where he wanted me. He cupped the side of my face and said,

"You are right. You are the impossible made possible and I should have trusted in all that you have shown me...I was foolish." I bit my lip to stop my smug smile but it was like locking it behind a cage...you could still see it behind the bars.

"Getting cocky now are we, Keira?" he asked raising a brow but also trying to hide his own smile.

"Well, what can I say, you must be rubbing off on me...that and I am a girl so, enough said really," I added making him laugh.

"So, this is the battle of the sexes, is it?" I gave him a cocky grin back and shrugged my shoulders as my answer.

"Right, well time to prove the power of your sex, I think," he told me confidently and I was only left to wonder and worry about what he meant by that statement. I wasn't left to worry for long. He pushed his chair back and pulled the robe from the table in one quick motion, creating a cloud of red to one side. Then he picked me up and raised me high enough until my feet were at the table in front of him.

"Draven?" I said his name in question but he simply nodded for me to step on to his table. I did as instructed and soon found myself stood before him feeling uncomfortably 'on show'. However, this was nothing compared to what he said next.

"Now strip." My mouth dropped open comical style, something he found great pleasure in.

"What's wrong, Keira?" he asked with a feigned concern as he knew exactly what was wrong.

"I can't strip...not here." I said in hushed tones making him laugh once.

"Why not?"

"Because someone might see." I told him sternly but it went over his head as he was clearly enjoying himself too much.

"Now you know I would never allow that," he said clicking his fingers so that the double doors at the back slammed closed and the distinct sound of a lock turning could be heard swiftly after. Then my head followed the echoing sound of all doors around Afterlife locked one by one. I looked back to Draven who sat back down and once comfortable, he held out a hand to indicate I could now start.

I nervously played with the cuff of my sleeve and bit my lip looking down wondering how I ended up here so quickly. Being cocky, that was how I thought scolding myself.

"Another problem, Keira?" he asked making me jump a little.

"Well I...um..." He could see I was struggling so decided to take pity on me.

"How about this, we will play a little game...you ask me a question and in return for an answer, I get a piece of your clothing."

"Like strip poker without the poker?" I asked making him smirk and nod. I thought about all the things I could ask him and smiled back but then I wanted to be sure.

"I can ask you anything?"

"I think it's only fair." he replied softly.

"Alright...I can do that," I told him making him smile his bad boy grin before saying,

"Excellent." Then he clapped once making the light dim lower which I wasn't going to complain about as it would only make it easier for me...well that was until he turned on the stage spotlights so that they were now directed solely on me. Purples and pinks lit me up and I blinked a few times to adjust to the lights. This wasn't the only change in our sexy setting as he also brought life to the speakers downstairs. So now some rhythmic beat created the perfect background noise to what was starting to look more like the beginning of some private striptease. I looked down at myself and swallowed hard knowing I would soon be standing there naked.

"What is your first question?" he asked making me jolt out of my internal panic.

"How did you get here so quickly?" I asked, blurting out the question quickly.

"I flew half the way and ran the rest," he answered quickly.

"But why?" I asked but he shook his finger at me,

"Tut, tut sweetheart, that's not how we are playing this game, now is it?" he reminded me and I blushed. Then I smirked as I lifted up a foot and tore off one running shoe and threw it to him. He caught it one handed and I nearly laughed when I saw him squeeze it hard enough that he was close to breaking it in two. Then he let it fall from his hand and nodded for me to continue.

"Why did you run?" I asked, repeating my earlier question.

"I was concerned."

"That I would leave?" I asked and before he could demand another item I threw him the other shoe making him smirk.

"Yes."

"And you thought I would leave because…?" I let my last question hang in the air, waiting for him to fill in the blanks. Draven could see where my questioning was going. He had an elbow propped against his armrest and his chin held in his hand as he watched me like a hawk.

"I turned my back on you," he answered honestly so I lifted my leg ready to pull off a sock and he cleared his throat.

"I think I have had enough footwear, time for something bigger," he said nodding to my top and I rolled my eyes once before unzipping my sweater and throwing it towards him, which again he caught one handed before letting it fall from his hand like he had done my shoe.

"Why did you turn your back on me?" I asked and he frowned, folding his arms across his chest. Then he motioned with his hand an order, voicing it at the same time.

"Ask me something else." I rolled my lips to stop from smiling as I put both my hands to my waistband, popped open the top button of my jeans and pulled it open, showing him a tiny hint of my black, lace panties. Then I stopped suddenly and looked up at him with feigned innocence.

"Oh, what a pity," I said biting my lip and giving him my best seductive look. He narrowed his eyes, zoning in on my underwear and the usual rumble of a slight growl rose from his chest.

"How often do you…how should I put it, conduct your business in the Temple?" I asked instead, knowing I would get the answer I wanted eventually…well that was if he wanted to see me with my pants off.

"Usually when the moon is full," he answered with ease and I thought back to how many times, since I had known him, he had been down there playing at judge, jury and executioner. He nodded to prompt an item from me in return and I nearly laughed when I saw his face, after I pulled the clip from my hair and threw it to him.

"I hardly think that counts," he complained.

"Well you had your chance at something bigger…" I said shrugging my shoulders and letting my hair fall all around me as I pulled it from its twist. It flowed down in waves and framed my body that was still mostly clothed…much to Draven's disapproval.

"When you first met me…"

"In the forest." Draven butted in and this time I was the one to make a 'Tut, tut' sound.

"Easy there, tiger, that wasn't my question." I told him laughing, making him try to hide a grin.

"No, my question was how often did you come to me at night when I was sleeping?" At first, he looked uncomfortable as if he wouldn't answer that one as well, so I took pity on him and lifted the bottom of my top, letting him know his reward. Oh, this worked, I thought with my own grin.

"Every night...next," he said firmly and my mouth dropped. *Every night?*

"I am waiting, Sweetheart," he told me, no doubt liking my reaction. I bit my lip once and lifted my top up, throwing it to his awaiting hand. My hair fell down around my now nearly naked torso and he lifted the material to his nose and inhaled deeply.

"Mmm...*so fucking sweet,*" he rumbled out the compliment as if he was close to forgetting this game and just taking me without another word uttered. I was just glad I was wearing matching underwear and one of the nicer sets I owned.

"Why every night?" I asked feeling the intensity of this game reach a new level thanks to the way he was looking at me. It reminded me of a wild, caged beast that wanted to devour its captor the second it got close enough.

"Because I was addicted," he told me and I sucked in a startled breath. He had been addicted to me...even then?

"Addicted?"

"Yes...now you owe me two pieces," he told me and I was about to argue when he said,

"You know the rules, Pet." Then he tapped his fingers across his lips in waiting. I smiled and said,

"Fine, you wanna play, I can play." Then I bent each leg and pulled each sock off before throwing them at him. He chuckled, nodded his head in respect and said,

"Touché."

"Did you ever see me naked?" I braved asking and I saw his lips twitch once before he looked at his fingertips as he answered me,

"I might have."

"Draven!" I shouted his name in horror, then added,

"So, you stalked me!?" He just shrugged his shoulders as if it was nothing and then said,

"You were always mine to stalk…that's another two," he said nodding to my body and I decided to get him back by pulling down my gloves and throwing them at him as I had done with my socks.

"I think you will find you are quickly running out of accessories, Keira." And he was right, I was. All I had left was a bra, knickers and my trousers, which he wasn't getting until he answered me my previous question…or at least that was the plan.

"Three questions left…which will you choose next I wonder?"

"Did you ever…" I was just about to chicken out on my question and he arched one dark brow in question.

"Did I ever what…? Ask me, Keira," he said seductively leaning forward, this time with an elbow to his knee and a chin resting on his clenched fist.

"…Fantasise about me…*sexually?*" His eyes widened as it was clear I had shocked him with my brazen question. He licked his lips as if they had gone dry before granting me a bad boy grin. Then he answered me with only one word,

"Often." I swallowed hard and then reached behind my back to unclip my bra. I then reached up and slowly pulled each strap down my arm, feeling the sensual action heat my blood and I gave the slightest of moans…one Draven heard, if the growl was anything to go by. The second growl however was due to me bringing my hair forward and covering my breasts with golden waves that looked pink in the spot lights.

"What…what happened in them?" I asked feeling the flush bloom in my cheeks, one he noticed.

"I had many..." He paused a second and he tapped his cheek as if giving it thought and then a bad boy grin was back and crossed his lips again. That's when I knew he had found one from his memory.

"...but do you want to hear my favourite? Is that what you're asking me for Keira, to hear what naughty thoughts would keep me up at night and leave me hard and wanting you?" This time my mouth went dry at the thought of him lay in that bed of his late at night, touching himself to the thought of everything he wanted to do to me. In the end, I couldn't find my voice so kept it simple and nodded, or I feared any sound I made right now would only come out as a high-pitched squeak.

"You would be asked to work late and one by one my people would be asked to leave the VIP, until before long I had you all to myself...A little like now in fact," he told me, pausing to look around the empty room.

"And?" I asked in a small voice.

"And I would demand your presence and knowing how difficult it is for you to deny your boss, you naturally obeyed."

"Obeyed?" I asked with a laugh.

"Yes, obeyed Keira, it is after all *my* fantasy, and you do so *love to obey me in them,*" he teased leaning closer now and lacing the last of his sentence with sexual context thanks to a velvet soft voice.

"I would then stand," he continued, standing himself.

"Then I would offer you my hand and simply ask you to step up onto my table," he told me holding out his hand to the pretend version of me, playing out his role just as he had done.

"You're teasing me," I told him giggling but then the look he gave me told me I was wrong.

"Am I? Then ask yourself, who started this game, Beautiful?" I bit my lip as I asked myself the question...had he done this because it was always a fantasy of his?

"Then I would demand you strip for me and I would sit back and admire your body as you presented it to me bit by bit...I practically recall the same blush that would heat not only your cheeks but also the rest of your body... as it does now," he said nodding to where a blush had appeared.

Of course, it didn't help as I tried to think back and wonder how far and fast would I have run away if he had made such a demand...shy wouldn't have been a strong enough word for it!

"And...and then?" I asked in hushed tones.

"And then, well once naked and ready for the picking, I would throw you over my shoulder, take you to my bed and tie you to it so that you could never get away..." He came closer towards me and I asked,

"And um...after that?" He nodded to my jeans and I forgot my past question, caring little for it now he had suckered me into his fantasy. So, I pushed them down passed my bum and down my legs, kicking them off to the side. His eyes flashed purple and I knew he liked what he saw. I was naked other than my panties and he looked close to tearing them from me with his teeth.

"It is simple, once I had you at my mercy then I wouldn't stop torturing your delicious body until I had you screaming and begging me to cease...After that...well I would just take what I wanted from you, begging or no begging...I would consume you! Now come here," he ordered and I decided to see how far I could push him. I crossed my arms over my naked breasts and looked down at the last piece of clothing I had on then back up at him.

"Nope, sorry no can do," I told him throwing him some sass.

"No? Are you denying me, little Vixen?" he asked in a dangerously low tone that had me close to caving first.

"You know the rules Draven and we can't break the…Ahhh!" I ended up finishing my sentence with a scream as suddenly the table rocked towards Draven thanks to the legs snapping like twigs. Draven caught me as I slid towards him.

"Oh, look what I caught…You were saying something, sweetheart?" he said in a cocky tone before righting the table and making the heavy carved legs reform with a crack.

"You don't play fair." I told him and he laughed and replied,

"I never said that I did." Then sat me on the table and once there, he took his rightful place, stepping in between my legs. He took hold of my wrists in both hands to place them behind my back.

"What…what are you doing?" I asked in a tentative voice.

"Playing by my rules," he said taking back his control over me. Then he transferred both my wrists into one grip, easily holding them thanks to his large hands. This allowed one hand free to run his fingers up through my hair line before pulling my lips to his roughly. Once there he finally got his opportunity to devour me.

He kissed me with such fever I was panting by the time he tore his lips from mine. My heaving chest must have taken his fancy next as he growled low before pulling at my wrists at the same time gripping my hair so that he could pull all of my body back in sync. It made me arch up and he didn't waste a second before feasting on my breasts.

"Ahhh...Draven." I moaned his name as the erotic sensations shot through me and straight down to my soaked core. But none of it was enough for Draven as his tastes for me lay elsewhere. He released my hands and pushed me down so my back was flat against the table. Once there, he issued his next demand for me to *obey*.

"Raise your hands above you and leave them there," he ordered and I did it without question, well that was until he sat down, spread my legs and yanked me to the edge of the table.

"Draven no! Umm...can't we just...I mean, I..." I started to make excuses as my embarrassment was nearly making my cheeks melt. He chuckled and pushed me back down with a hand to my chest, rising from his seat momentarily.

"Easy sweetheart, I won't hurt you. I just want a taste of what is rightfully mine. Now relax and do as you're told," he told me and I swallowed down the shy lump, before giving in to his commands. He once more pried open my shaky legs, smirking down at me as if he enjoyed seeing me squirm and that was all part of the fun.

Oh yes, he was enjoying himself alright, especially when he ran a knuckle down the seam of my panties, brushing along my clit and making my legs jerk as if I had been touched by a cattle prod.

"Hands, Keira" he reminded me and I looked down to see that they were currently trying to stop him from doing that again. He nodded above me and I did as I was told, trying this time to keep them there.

"You're so wet for me," he murmured, this time running a fingertip down the centre and I bit my lip, as my shame doubled. He was taking his time, making me suffer as he began by feeling the length of my inner thighs but stopping before he reached the black lace that still covered me.

"Draven I..." I started to protest again when he dipped lower and this time to my horror he ran his nose up my panties and inhaled deep.

"Your scent is intoxicating, like forbidden fruit spilling its nectar...just begging to be tasted," he told me and I shrieked a little when he suddenly caught the side of my underwear and snapped it. Then, ever so softly he touched me where most of my arousal was gathered and I sucked in a quick breath when he placed it to his lips and sucked in two fingers glistening with my 'nectar'. He let his head fall back as he closed his eyes and muttered,

"By the gods," to himself. It was almost like being allowed to try the wine before the waiter poured you a glass from the bottle.

"Breathe, sweetheart," he told me and up until that point I hadn't realised I had been holding my breath. The second I filled my lungs all the air quickly left me once again as he dived in, taking my most private place into his mouth. I cried out and arched my back, forming peaks with my breasts.

This was when he didn't just devour me there...no, instead he made a meal out of me. He sucked and licked and nipped out at my tender flesh. He lapped me up like he couldn't get enough, like a man who had found the fountain of youth or the secret to immortality. Of course, Draven didn't need these things but that didn't take away from what he obviously wanted...or was it more like *needed?*

He was acting like a man possessed, and with the onslaught of what his mouth was doing to me and my impending orgasm approaching, the intensity became too much to bear. I tried to shift from him but he growled over my clit, making it vibrate. Then he secured his hold on me, with his arms under my legs and hands gripping the tops of my thighs, yanking me up and anchoring me to his ravenous mouth.

I could barely take the pleasure as he refused to let up on my over sensitive bundle of nerves and even when I felt close to bursting, he simply fought harder against me trying to get away. Then he pulled his lips from me and cruelly asked me the question,

"You want to come...you want to come for me to taste, Vixen of mine?" I could barely form the words and he knew it but I would have agreed to anything he asked if he just let me fall into the abyss of euphoria.

"Yes...oh please, yes, yes," I said and then ended up crying out quickly after, when he penetrated me with two strong fingers. His mouth went back to my clit and both worked in perfect rhythm, dancing on my nerves.

"Draven...Draven...DRAVEN AHHHH!" I screamed his name as I felt it explode from me in wave after wave of shuddering bliss. I even felt the tears force their way from my closed lids it was so powerful.

"Please...please, I beg of you, no more...no more." I begged over and over until finally he turned my pleas into actions of mercy. He finally let up on my most sensitive, abused and no doubt swollen part of me. No, now instead he took great pleasure in leisurely licking me clean until all evidence of my release had been consumed. He was just making me moan as he pulled his fingers from me and I could still feel my inner muscles pulsating and clinging to them as if trying to hang on that moment longer. These too he licked clean.

"Mmm, fantasy just can't compare to the exquisite taste of reality," Draven said making me cover my face with both hands and moan again, this time out of shame, making him laugh. He took hold of my hands and pulled me up to sitting so that he could see the embarrassment there for himself.

"I believe I owe you an answer as payment for that one, darling," he told me kissing me softly on my lips and I couldn't say that I hated being able to detect my womanly taste hiding there. I bit my lip and pushed my hair behind one ear, wondering if asking what I really wanted to know would be considered as bad timing.

"Ask me sweetheart," he told me as if he knew from my sheepish look what I wanted to know.

"Why did you turn your back on me?" I asked, looking down at my joined hands and playing with my fingers so that I wouldn't have to look at him when I asked this. I felt his bent finger under my chin before he applied pressure making me look up at him.

"Because I knew I was wrong." I frowned and shook my head a little, telling him silently that I didn't understand.

"I should have believed you and when I didn't, I let you down. That slap made me realise my mistake but more than that, it made me realise how much I had hurt you...after that, I couldn't face it..." he told me honestly and my mouth dropped to free a gasp, one that never made a sound.

"What couldn't you face, Draven?" I whispered my question and he took my face in both his hands and placed his forehead to mine and whispered his deepest regrets down at me.

And it was beautiful...

"Disappointing the woman, I love."

AUTHOR'S INSIGHTS.

BOOK 3
The Triple Goddess

Now comes the third instalment of Lost Chapters and this time they are from Book 3. As you can imagine there were a lot of chapters I wanted to write that included our lovely but misunderstood Lucius. But in the end, I found it took away from the main part of the story or became too complicated for our Keira. After all, many of the chapters I wrote would only have you falling even deeper in love for our rogue hero and this wasn't something I was prepared to do. Yes, there are elements of a love triangle but in the end, I simply wanted Keira's love for Draven to be everything to her, no matter how she felt about Lucius in secret.

I hope you all feel like this has continued throughout the saga. With of course, the exception to them both nearly taking things too far in Germany. But I like to think that considering what Keira had been put through, that she was certainly entitled to a little Vampire comforting. Once again and like most things in this saga there was a reason behind this and one you will no doubt secretly curse me for as my lips remain sealed. But thankfully, most people these days don't have pitch forks and angry mobs are usually only seen on the Simpsons, so I feel safe for now ;)

So, without further ado and anymore waffling from me, here they are for you to enjoy...the very, very forbidden Chapters of Book 3...The Triple Goddess.

AUTHOR'S INSIGHTS

Chapter 21
Book 3

Okay so I might have lied about the 'Finished waffling' part but I swear this will only take a minute. Okay, so we start with our first chapter which begins after Keira learns who Draven's father is for the first time thanks to our lovely and adorable Pip. They are in the middle of their Gothic tea party and Pip has just told Keira about her little 'Black Death' mishap and being punished in Hell, were she met the Demon part of her husband.

Now when writing this I always intended to write about how Pip found Adam but thought it would be further down the line. However, it never worked out this way and I knew there was only one natural place to write it in.

Which meant this chapter had to go and with it, another one with Lucius and Keira finding themselves in each other's arms once again.

So, for your enjoyment, here it is…

Lucius saving Keira from a very bloody mess, once again.

BOOK 3

21
Bloody Vampire Massacre.

NEW…

"King Asmodeus is… Draven's father!"

"Well of course he is you silly Goose Pillow!" Pip said, giggling at my reaction to it.

His Dad? Was it possible? Well of course it was, I mean he had to come from somewhere and he did tell me about him and his siblings being a product of an Angel and Demon naughty get together. So why was I finding it so difficult to comprehend? I think it was probably down to the fact that now I knew of at least one man who had a say in Draven's life and no-one likes to piss off their Daddy!

"The King of Lust…you're sure?" Okay so it sounded stupid asking it now, considering what Draven was like in the bedroom.

"Things starting to make sense now…eh?" Pip asked with a wag of her eyebrows.

"You can't hear my thoughts, can you?" I asked making her double up laughing, rocking like a child cross legged.

"You're so funny! And not just like haha, Charlie Chaplin style, but like a whole bag full of funnies!

Like those cartoon crispy guys from the cereal, those guys just crack me up!" she said slapping her leg and I found myself asking yet another unimportant question around her. And in a time, where there were oh so many others that should have come before,

"You mean Snap, Crackle and Pop?"

"Yeah! Those guys! You know Rice Krispies are also known in Australia as Rice Bubbles...what's with that! Oh, and did you know that they are gnomic elves and were originally designed by illustrator Vernon Grant in the early 1930s," she informed me and I shook my head in wonder at where on earth she kept this type of information. But more importantly, what was that file labelled in her head, 'Useless crap I might need one day'?

"Which reminds me, damn it all to the Bermuda worm hole! I forgot the snickerdoodles!" Pip shouted throwing up her hands dramatically.

"The what now?" I asked with a smirk, looking down at all the food I had consumed and not sure how I would fit anything else in my belly.

"The freakin' snickerdoodles, dudette! Wait, hold up a few heartbeats and back the fuggle up...are you telling me you have never had a snickerdoodle?" she asked...I think.

"Uhh...that would be a no," I told her and she screamed, as in full out slasher movie style! I held my hands over my ears for a second until she stopped.

"Feel better?" I asked and she smirked at me.

"Hell yeah, love a good fucking scream! Right, I will be back...Terminator style but armed with awesome cookies not guns, man I would so jump those guns, Arnie has got it going on!" she said laughing and bouncing up in a way that only looked achievable if you were a contortionist!

"Well, I will be here," I told her and she stopped in her tracks. She then looked around and sucked in her lip ring as if torn. I held up my hands and said,

"Pip, come on, where am I going to go?" I asked laughing because unless I had a 'freezing my ass off death wish', then really, where was I going to run to? She laughed it off and said,

"Yeah and anyway, Luc would just hunt your fine ass down and drool like a hungry ass wolf whilst doing it…silly me," she said walking off and laughing to herself. Although, the thought she left me with wasn't exactly what I would call 'laugh worthy'. Anyway, I think she was forgetting one small factor in all this and that was I didn't have bloody wings so where she expected me to go exactly I had no clue.

I decided to put my gloves back on and get up to have a look around. It was a stunning open space with a haunting beauty thanks to the startling white snow that lay upon every surface like a blanket. Even the air looked white, if that was possible. It wasn't like fog but more like a cloud bed that surrounded the crumbling walled garden like a protective barrier. It even rolled over the stone like the ground was drawing it in and it flowed like a waterfall of white mist down the sides.

I decided to be brave and look over the sides to see if there were any lower levels that could be seen. Although I would be surprised in this weather but it was worth a shot. I buttoned my jacket back up and walked closer to the edge, the only sound was the eerie crunch of crisp snow under my feet. The whole place felt as if you were in some ethereal dream or even approaching the gates of Heaven…it just didn't feel real.

It made you want to gather up balls of snow and throw them, so that you could prove it wasn't magical and could show the result by a little destruction. But

I didn't do that, instead I simply ran my fingertips through the snow that lay perfectly moulded to the top of a half-broken balustrade. It was deep enough that I would have lost my hand in it if I had applied more pressure.

I clapped the snow off my glove and continued towards the side when I started to hear a strange noise. It was only very faint but in this deathly still place, you would have heard a pin drop. It sounded like scratching against stone and it was coming from where I was walking to. I moved a little closer, this time more cautious as to what I may find. Suddenly a strange thought entered my mind and I had no control over it, as I wished for Lucius to be here.

I think that it was down to fear of the unknown and in this place, he seemed to be my only anchor to safety. It was messed up. I knew that. But I couldn't help but feel as though he would never let anything happen to me. That he would even...*kill for me.*

I shook the feeling off and decided I was being silly and just letting the creepy surroundings get to me. When Pip had been here it had been fine. There was laughter and chatting and getting to learn the history of who I considered was becoming a great friend. But now...alone in this silent, winter garden. Well, it looked like the place that lost souls came to walk eternity in peace.

I looked back over my shoulder once more before making the last two steps to the edge. I placed both my hands on the stone wall, this time pressing down and creating dips in the snow. Then I took a deep breath and looked over the edge into an abyss of endless white. I couldn't see anything thanks to the heavy cloud, so thankfully my fear of heights didn't come into play. I released a sigh and shook my head, cursing my own imagination. I was just about to turn around, with one hand still left on the wall when I screamed,

"AHHH!" I looked back at my hand that was now covered by someone else's! Someone was reaching over the wall as if they had just climbed up the side. I scrambled backwards, righting myself on the balustrade just before I fell. Then I started to back away from the wall as a body started to emerge over the side. I knew with what followed in his other hand he was an enemy of both myself and Lucius, thanks to the glint of his lethal looking blade.

"A knife." A whisper left my lips and I began running. I knew there were only two options left to me and if this being was a demon then one of them would be useless. So instead of running for the way out, knowing he would no doubt easily catch up with me, I went for option two. I ran back to the tree and grabbed the wicked looking butcher's knife that was still sticking out of the cake. I turned back and held it out in front of me, threatening anyone that came close.

My eyes homed in on the figure emerging from the cloud of fog that had rolled in with him. He wore all black and he was easily double my size. He cracked his neck to the side and his evil smirk told me that my knife did nothing but make this interesting for him. I gripped it tighter, my leather glove creaking against the handle.

"What do you want with me?!" I demanded backing away from the tree and knowing eventually he would have me trapped.

"What *I want* with you is to rip your flesh from your bones but I doubt the Master will let us play with you before you die," he told me, snarling and licking out his tongue which was long enough to cover his chin. He was rough looking, and I'd bet my lifesavings that he was a demon of some kind.

However, his human host looked to be in his mid-fifties, and one that had seen every bar fight this side of Germany, because he looked as though his nose had been broken at least ten times. Even his skin looked as if it had been shaved with a rusty hatchet.

Dirty hair, small dark eyes and yellowing teeth completed the hillbilly hick look.

"Well, what can you do but call your union rep?" I said masking fear with humour. He chuckled once and said,

"They told me you had spunk...all the better to..."

"Wait, I have heard this one...will it help if I lose the red jacket?" I asked interrupting him making him growl.

"It's not the wolf in front of you, you should be worrying about but the wolf at your back!" A voice from behind me said making me scream. I backed off to the side wondering where this other person had come from. That was when the cloud started to lift slightly and I realised that the silent garden wasn't as private as I first thought.

I moved away from the two men and followed the stone wall that arched up, looking briefly at the framed picture of the mountains around us. From here you could see the lake and the natural walls that surrounded it, sheer cliff faces that dropped straight down without so much as an incline, drops that would kill given one wrong step. I don't know why but this added to its raw beauty and to the dangerous situation I now found myself in.

I sucked in an icy breath when the wind picked up and I wondered how I was going to make it out of this one. That's when I finally had a good look around, trying in vain to see where I could run to. I found myself further than I should be and with another shadow closing in, I knew there were too many of them.

I turned around and saw I had passed the walls to the circular courtyard and I slowly managed to walk down some broken steps without falling. My shaking hand still held out in front of me, clutching on to my only hope.

The steps went further down and when I looked to where they might lead I saw a dead looking forest looming back at me. My eyes followed it round and noticed that it surrounded the courtyard like an army of dead, straight soldiers all waiting to be commanded forward. Shadows could barely be seen for lack of light. It was as though day never saw this part of the earth and it was forever to live in the darkness of night.

A fitting place to die, without ever being found. But no, these men didn't want to kill me...not yet anyway. However, the man they worked for, then yes, there was little doubt of what he had in store for me. And speaking of hired demon goons, one by one they all started to close in on me until my back was against the wall with nowhere left to go.

The last one to have spoken came into view and unlike the other brute, he looked deadlier in a sleek, thief of the night kind of way. His hair style however, left me wondering what he was going for exactly, 80's porn star? I think even Tom Selleck would have been envious of that slug shaped moustache!

"Come with me little girl, time to face your fate!" Mr Porn Star cheese said just before he tried to grab me. I swiped out at him with my knife, catching him in the forearm and making him growl, as I sneaked passed him after my attack.

"You bitch!" he snarled and I would have replied with a snappy come back if I hadn't been trying to keep my eye on all four bodies slowly advancing on me.

"Enough of this, get her!" The one in the shadows commanded and I gathered that he was the Beavis in charge of all the rest of the Buttheads. The big one got angry and charged at me like a bull and just before he could make impact, I sidestepped and ducked, finding myself back at the tree. He crashed into one of the walls and a large chunk of it crumbled into the abyss below.

He turned his head and roared at me, making me shrug my shoulders at him before running to the other side of the tree. I was quickly grabbed from behind, making me drop my knife. Thankfully I just managed to grab a green glass teapot, and as I was pulled backwards I swung it round and smashed it across someone's face. They howled in pain and I looked down as the handle was still in my bloody hand. A shard of glass had managed to slice me good right through the thin leather and near the thumb but the pain didn't yet register. Thank the Heavens for adrenaline.

The guy covered his eyes and I now realised it had been the 'Arsenic' teapot with vodka in…yep, that stuff would sting like a mother! I threw the handle at him and decided it worked once, so what the Hell. I reached inside and grabbed the one labelled 'Toxic' and hoped what it held was referring to the liquid inside.

"Someone fucking get that girl!" The Beavis said again, this time in a clear rage. Good, bastards thought it easy, maybe if I could keep this up for a time longer then maybe Lucius would hear…which was when I wanted to bloody kick myself!

So, just as another made a grab for me, I finally did something I should have done when Mr Charge and Grab had showed up over the wall. I filled my lungs and screamed loud enough Pip would have been proud.

"AHHHHH! LUCIUS! HELP ME!!!!" Then I was grabbed, turned around and swiftly punched across the face, losing my unconventional weapon in the process. I swear I saw stars as pain exploded around one eye and all down one cheek. I slumped forward and was slung up over the shoulder of the biggest brute.

"Let's get the fuck out of here before the King turns up," Mr Porn Star said, and I could briefly make out him shaking the blood off his hand that was running down his fingers in little streams thanks to my attack.

"You think he heard?" The guy carrying me asked in a panicked tone. Good, I hope he shits himself at the thought!

"Wait, what the fuck was that?!" One of them said when hearing something in the shadows. I managed to open one eye and lift my head enough to see a blurred motion behind one of the men, before the furthest one away suddenly screamed and was torn back into the mist.

"Shit!" The injured one said looking around with his weapon drawn.

"Let's get the fuck out of here!" Another said and came closer, no doubt thinking strength in numbers. He had been the one I had hit in the face, and I was happy to see the teapot had done me proud. He was cut up bad and still dripping with vodka...ouch, I bet that stung I thought with a bitter grin.

They all started to back up towards the wall where the first one had come over and the closer to the edge he took me the more I lost it. I needed to do something to buy me time, so I started going crazy. Screaming, pounding my fists against his back and kicking at his bollocks, which I was happy to report I manage to get twice.

"Fuck this!" he said and dumped me down on the ground with a bruising fall so I landed on the frozen snow. I groaned but knew I had to move out of the way to safety. I turned just in time to watch as the big guy grabbed the edge of the wall and jumped over trying to get away.

He didn't get far.

The next I knew his body was being dragged upwards and disappeared into the thick white sky above. His screams could be heard echoing all around us until they stopped and deadly silence quickly followed. The next thing I knew I was screaming as a bloody severed arm that looked to have been ripped from the socket landed by my feet with a splat.

"SHIT!" I screamed again as I saw a figure moving above us all. Next the men all jumped back as the rest of the mangled body landed in an explosion of blood. It looked like a crimson star had smashed into the snow, as it cast a circular pattern all around the twisted torso and broken limbs at its centre.

I thought I was going to throw up but managed to swallow it down and just in time as the culprit to the bloody carnage appeared. He dropped from the sky, landing hard enough to crack the stone floor around him, the snow melted and steamed as if he had just arrived from Hell itself.

He had his back to me but his hands were covered in blood, like the body on the floor had been ripped apart bare handed. The two men left standing pretty much pissed themselves and each ran in a different direction to get away from him. Unfortunately for me, one came my way.

The one drenched in vodka ran down the steps trying in vain to make it to the dark forest, looming ahead. The killer looked side on slightly as if this amused him and he raised his head slightly and shifted the air.

I could just see the hint of a sadistic grin before he clicked his fingers and I sucked in a startled breath as I saw a tiny flame flicker in between his thumb and finger. At first I didn't know what he hoped to achieve by it...well that was until I heard the screaming in agony.

I looked to my left and saw the flames racing towards the forest. It took me a second to realise the horror behind those flames as the man's face was now on fire, thanks to my adding the accelerant. I looked back to the vicious hunter and saw him crack his bloody knuckles once before he was off after him. He moved too quick for my eyes to track and the only thing I saw was a flash of red mist coming from the body that was running before it too disappeared with the flames.

"Holy shit," I said but this was before I realised I had my own problems. The last man standing, the one I had slashed with my knife, now decided that he needed some leverage if he had any chance at surviving this. I saw him coming for me so I turned and was once again running. Needless to say, I didn't get far.

He grabbed me from behind and quickly placed a blade at my neck reminding me of painful past events. It felt like Morgan all over again and slowly but surely my mind started to lose its sense of reality.

"Get off me!" I shouted which must have alerted a demon to my new problem. I next thing I saw was a bloody figure emerging from the fog like the devil himself.

Of course it was,

"Lucius." I muttered his name as a plea for help as now I knew who my brutal saviour was. He

walked like a man with purpose and the striking contrast of blood that covered his pale skin was like looking at the snow-covered ground. One that he had painted red with the blood of his enemies.

The man holding me captive started moving us backwards, holding both my arms behind my back in a painful grip. Lucius didn't even move like a man covered in blood and I shuddered at how comfortable he wore it as it looked as though half of him had taken a bath in it!

Blood stained clothes, arm covered past his elbow as if he had reached inside someone's chest and ripped out their beating heart with his bare hands. Even his face was half covered and on one side of his cheek was the sickening evidence of his butchery. A bloody hand print remained there as a horrifying sign of someone's last attempt to get him off them.

It was by far the most terrifying thing I had ever seen.

"I believe you have something that belongs to me," Lucius said calmly, his crimson gaze taking in the length of me, no doubt trying to assess the damage. He homed in on my cut glove and bleeding hand beneath. Then moved on to my bruised face, snarling after seeing it. Blood dripped from his exposed fangs and the guy behind me dug his blade further into my neck, breaking the skin and making me cry out.

"Don't come any closer or I will kill her!" he threatened...a threat Lucius didn't take kindly to.

"Close your eyes, Pet." This was my only warning and not one I had time to act upon before he made his move. One second he was stood in front of us and the next he was beside us. Suddenly the blade disappeared, and was no longer cutting into my tender flesh. I heard the bellow of pain behind me and I looked to the side to see the man's arm was bent back opposite to the way the elbow bends. Then with one gentle hand Lucius reached out and took my arm, whilst keeping a firm grip on the screaming man. Once he felt me in his hold he calmly moved me back behind him, so that I was out of danger.

I swallow hard at the raw power behind this man's touch. It was like two ends of the spectrum and I was just thanking every God out there that I was on the cool, calm collected side. Not the demonic psycho, cold blooded killer that was firmly on the other end...the one that held his prey ready for dishing out his flavour of carnage. He looked back over his shoulder at me and with eyes of crimson wrath, he warned,

"Close. Your. Fucking. Eyes." He growled in a lethal tone. I snapped them closed, too afraid to disobey him. Then I felt him clasp the back of my neck so that he could pull me forward and place a bloody kiss on my forehead.

"There's my good girl," he muttered against my skin before stepping away from me. I did as he asked and kept my eyes closed so tight that it made me feel dizzy.

"Please! Please I was only following orders!" The man begged for his life but from the sounds of the injury and pain that followed, I would say that Lucius wasn't in the mood for begging.

"Do you know the price someone pays when they try and take what's mine?" Lucius asked and I swallowed down the bile that rose when I heard what sounded like bones breaking.

"AHHH!" The man's screams left little to the imagination to conjure.

"He...he...said..." The man tried again but a gurgling sound quickly followed as if his throat had been ripped out.

"Malphas was wrong…the girl is MINE!" Lucius roared out his wrath in a voice only reserved for those of Hell and I couldn't stop myself from shaking with fear. Of course, it didn't help that all I could hear was what sounded like someone being torn apart. I don't know how long I waited for it to end but once the deathly silence swept once more through the silent garden I knew it was done.

But this didn't mean I was ready for it to be *over*.

I felt a slight touch on my arm and instinct took hold. My clenched fist went flying forward before I could stop it. Thankfully, another hand caught it head on and wrapped strong fingers around it, making their own fist. My eyes snapped open and I whispered his name through unshed tears.

"Lucius?" He nodded and still holding my fist he pulled me into him. He wrapped his arms around me and for the first time since this all began, I felt safe…*safe in the arms of a monster.* But I didn't care. He had saved me and even now, stood in the evidence of his demonic chaos, *I still didn't care.* He was *my monster* and if that meant condemning me under the same title, then so be it.

"Y…you…you saved me?" I stammered out, now letting the tears fall freely. He breathed deep as if letting the beast free and whispered down into the top of my hair,

"I will always save you." I swallowed down the sob that wanted to escape and found myself asking,

"But…but why?" This was when he gave me my beautiful, heart wrenching answer…

"Because, you're my little Keira girl."

Book 3

22

Clean Captive.

NEW...

After this Lucius took charge of my frail body and even frailer mind. He lifted me into his arms and carried me from this red and white nightmare back into the safety of his home. We were just walking through the archway when Pip came running back through the door carrying a black tray of cookies. Her face dropped and the look of worry made her eyes water.

"Oh no! No, no, no...Toots...? Is she...?" Lucius walked towards her and stopped long enough to growl down at her,

"You failed me, Imp!" Then he continued past and I reached a bloody hand out to her as she was left to stand in the archway, with the scene of bloody devastation in front of her, framed by stone.

"Pip." I whispered her name but she didn't turn to face me. No, instead her shoulders slumped, her head fell forward and the tray of cookies fell from her hands, clattering into the snow. I wanted to cry out to her but I only managed to cough back a sob for my guilty looking friend. It wasn't her fault and I wanted

to tell Lucius this but right now and the way he held me, well I knew he was on the edge.

So, I would wait until the time was right. Until he had calmed enough for me to be able to speak freely. It wasn't easy, especially when watching my friend being left alone to hurt. I wished right then there was some way of getting Adam as she didn't deserve to suffer. So instead of making my excuses for her, I reached up and touched Lucius' cheek, softly running my fingertip down the side of his face. He stopped and looked down at me in question, shocked no doubt at my unexpected but affectionate touch. In the end, all I needed to say was one thing for him to understand my meaning.

"Adam." His eyes narrowed for a moment but he didn't argue. In fact, he didn't say anything but instead changed direction and took a doorway we had originally passed. After only a short time, we saw Adam in the hallway speaking with someone I didn't recognise. He saw us coming and his eyes widened as he took in the sight of us both. Obviously, we looked as if we had been to Hell and back.

"My Lord?" He started but Lucius gave him no explanation, just simply stopped next to him long enough to say one thing,

"Go to your wife, old friend." Then he continued on. I looked back over Lucius' shoulder to see Adam running and I released a deep sigh, happy at least knowing that my friend wouldn't be alone much longer. Lucius looked down at me, taking note of my actions but again, he didn't comment. It was clear that he was taking this time to calm his demonic outburst of rage as it wasn't exactly something I needed right then.

Instead, he walked us both back to the only safe haven I had in this place...*my room*. Once there I thought he would leave me but I was wrong. No, instead he simply walked us both into the bathroom and placed me on the counter as though I was a dirty child, not the scared shitless woman who was currently covered in blood. If anything, I looked more like an extra out of a slasher movie and the victim of an overzealous makeup artist gone wild with a super soaker full of fake blood.

Then he placed both hands on the counter next to me and leant forward for a few moments. I was about to ask him if he was all right but then he swiped a hand out to the side as if he was touching something I couldn't see. I jolted as the tap over the bathtub came on and the sound of rushing water killed the painful silence between us.

"You fought them," Lucius stated and I was taken back by his observation. I wouldn't have thought he would have been in any state of mind to notice a detail like that. When I didn't reply, he looked sideways at me. His hair had fallen in front of his face, with streaks of red now added to the honey colour. I swallow hard and said,

"I tried to," I told him quietly.

"Tell me what happened," he said after releasing a big sigh of frustration.

"Well...I...um... they came for me!" I ended up blurting out this last part. He gave me a soft look and pushed off the countertop. Then he came over to me and placed his hands either side of my hips. This put us at almost the same height, which I had to say was better than having to look up at everyone as I usually did. Seriously though, did they only make these bad ass supernatural kings in one size?!

"I know they did, sweetheart," he replied granting me a small smile that told me of his regret that it had ever happened.

"I am sorry you had to witness the slaughter," he said and right then and there, I saw it. It was that same level of care and protection that Draven had over me but with one startling difference; Lucius was at his scariest when he was silent. As though he was quietly plotting murder in the shadows waiting to strike like a deadly viper. Unlike Draven whose rage was so close to the surface it could barely be contained. His Demon would let loose it's wrath upon the world and the aftermath was a destruction he walked away from with little thought.

But not Lucius. He was telling me he was sorry for what I had been forced to see just so that he could keep me safe. Which was when it hit me.

"You attacked them in a way to try and spare me the violence...didn't you?" I asked him, thinking back to the way he fought behind the cover of the clouds. Even at the end when he demanded I close my eyes, knowing what I would see if I didn't. It was important to him, but why? Did he really care about me that much? Had I suddenly become more than just an asset and something to bargain with?

He didn't answer me but instead looked down at my hands, in my lap. Then he picked up the one that I didn't realise I had been cradling in the other hand as it was hurting me.

"Lucius?" I said his name in question but he just looked up at me long enough to whisper a soft command,

"Ssshh."

I soon hissed in pain as he gently pulled the bloodied, torn leather from my hand. His next move had me inhaling a deep breath as he lowered himself to one knee in front of me. This put his head slightly higher than my lap so made it easier for him to lift my hand to his lips. I don't know what I was shocked at more. The fact that a man like Lucius was on his knees in front of me. Or that he was now licking my wound as though I was some injured animal being looked after by a mate.

He looked up at me as if trying to judge my reaction and when his eyes turned crimson with blood lust, I tried to pull myself free. However, he snarled up at me, showing me his fangs in warning before yanking my hand back for him to finish. After that I knew not to get in the way of a Vampire and his meal again. So instead, I just waited for the inevitable, tensing my shoulders, ready for it. But it never came. He didn't bite into me as I expected but instead just continued to lick away the blood and in doing so, making it start healing quicker.

Once he was clearly satisfied, he stood back up and pushed my hair behind my ears so he could take a closer look at my face. It was starting to swell, as I could feel the skin getting tighter above my cheekbone. Thankfully though both eyes were still open so I think it was safe to say that my cheek got the worse end of that bastard's fist.

"Not sure there is much you can do about that one," I told him light-heartedly. He gave me a small grin before he started to lift my face up. That's when the slice at my neck startled me and I sucked air through clenched teeth. Lucius made an unhappy noise and then told me sternly,

"Hold still." He then leant his face towards the cut I had received thanks to the knife held at my throat.

"Wait...what are you...?" I started to protest, once again making him growl and I stilled instantly, like he told me. He gave me no explanation but just went back to work cleaning my second wound...

Vampire style.

"Ahh" I moaned at the first lick of both pain and his tongue. However, his own moan was all pleasure as he tasted my blood for the second time today. He gripped the side of the counter harder, to the point where I heard it crack under the pressure of his strength. I knew it was probably some kind of torture, letting him lick me clean without actually doing what he wanted to do...which was sink his fangs into me and drink straight from the vein.

It felt different than before, as then it felt more like being patched up by some quirky doctor but now? Well, now it felt much more intimate. Being this close to one another with his lips at my neck. There was only one word for it and that was dangerous.

He growled low when I tried to pull back and one of his hands shot to the back of my neck so he could secure me to his mouth. I also felt his teeth hold me still and any minute now I knew that he would lose control. So, I did the only thing I could do to stop this. The only thing I had left in my arsenal against someone as powerful as the Vampire at my neck.

I raised my shaky hand to his cheek and the second I touched him he released his hold on me. Then I raised his face to mine and when he started to become compliant, I took a shuddering breath before placing my lips softly to his.

He inhaled deeply the second I touched him and the tender seconds ticked by like time had stopped all around us. I was just about to pull back after achieving my goal, but as if he knew my next move he counteracted it. In a quick move, he positioned himself closer into me and lifted my face up to his so that he could deepen the kiss.

So, I did what I knew was wrong. I opened up to him, getting caught in the moment, one in the arms of my saviour. The second I did this, the room once again filled with light. I didn't understand why this happened but it was as if every time we kissed, the Gods would show him the sun. It was as though they were blessing us in some way and I felt torn, like my body was being pulled in two different directions. Either cast to the shadows or thrown into the light.

But in the end, I decided to give us both this one moment and call it what it was, a gift that I was still alive because of him. So, as he commanded the kiss, and dominated it, I lost myself in all that Lucius had to give and boy...in that one kiss, he sure knew how to give a lot.

Surprisingly, he seemed to know when to be gentle. He handled my injured side with such a soft and light touch. Then with the other side, he would grip me more firmly, telling me without words that he owned me in this moment.

But it was this tender side that really blew me away and after all the ferocity I had witnessed, I didn't think it possible. And just like his hands, he himself was a contradiction of character. One side hard and unyielding and the other, well that was now the part of him that scared me the most.

It was the most dangerous.

This sobering thought was what made me place a hand to his chest and we both pulled ourselves apart at the same time. Lucius didn't put up any resistance to me pulling back or silently asking him to do the same. Instead he kissed me softly on the forehead and whispered down at me,

"Your kiss maybe powerful but... *you hit like a girl.*" And that was it, my teasing, cocky captor was back. He then winked at me and turned towards the tub as it was now nearly full. This time he turned off the tap the good, old fashioned human way.

"What are you doing?" I asked as he started to pull his t-shirt off and my mouth went dry at the sight of all those pale muscles on show.

"What does it look like, Pet?" he said undoing his trousers with a snap of his buttons. He turned to face the shower and made it come on with a nod of his head. Then he pushed the denim down his legs and what do you know...Lucius wasn't a fan of underpants. Oh my...my, my, my...wow, that was one perfectly shaped Vampire ass!

I actually giggled and he looked back over his shoulder at me and raised an eyebrow. My hands flew to my mouth and I shook my head making him smirk. Then he nodded to the tub and said,

"Bath's for you, sweetheart," before opening the shower door and stepping inside. I think I stood staring for a whole minute before I started to move, first looking at the bath and then back to the shower. He was stood facing the tiles with a hand on the wall as he leant his head under the downpour. I looked down at his feet and saw the crimson water pooling around them before circling the drain.

Suddenly my head shot back up when I heard a tapping on the glass. Lucius had caught me staring at him and was currently smirking at me. I coughed and cleared my throat as if this would help being caught gawping at the Adonis in my shower. Then he pointed to the side and mouth the words 'Bath' and 'Now' which finally pulled me from my carnal thoughts. I shook my head in vain as it still didn't rid me of the image of that hard-naked body all wet. But I knew there must have been something wrong with me, because even the sight of all that blood washing away didn't put me off.

I walked closer to the bath and ran my fingers in the water testing the temperature. It was slightly on the hotter side than I usually liked, but I knew after being out in the cold for so long, it wouldn't be a bad thing. Well, at least this was what I told myself as I didn't exactly want to admit that I was already feeling a little too warm after seeing Lucius naked.

No! Bad Keira! Bad! Just shut off your brain and get your ass in the water...you never know, it might help, I told myself. So, I unbuttoned my jacket and placed it gently on the side. Then after a quick look to check Lucius wasn't looking I started to peel off the rest of my clothes. Then I stepped into the water and sucked in a breath at how hot it was. Well looking to the steam coming from the top of the shower door, I guess someone liked it hot, I thought blushing.

I stood in the water, waiting to get used to it and for the usual itching skin to calm before getting the rest of the way in. Finally, I leant back and let myself relax. I thought back to how close I had come to being taken from Lucius and I frowned wondering when I had turned to the dark side? After all, I was technically still his captive but then I guess it was better the Devil you knew, than one you didn't.

Yes, Lucius had taken me from Draven and that factor still pissed me off, but so far he hadn't treated me badly and even at times shown me care and kindness. Was that why I was so confused?

"That looks like some heavy thinking, even for you Pet." Lucius' voice brought me back with a start and my eyes snapped open, and at the same time I covered my breasts. He chuckled, leant closer with a hand to the rim of the bath and said,

"I have seen them before...remember kitten?" Then he winked at me before pushing himself off the bath and back to rubbing his hair dry. I swallowed hard thinking back to the mud and the bath he had given me. I wanted to slap myself and shout 'Get a hold on yourself, you silly girl' but then that in itself would have been embarrassing.

He smirked as if he could read my inner turmoil as clear as day. I hated myself for looking at him the way I was but come on, the man was not playing fair!

Stood there in just a towel, hung low on his hips and rubbing the back of his head with another towel around his neck, making his biceps bulge with the action. Jesus, I didn't need a hot bath, I needed a freakin' cold shower...make that ice cold!

"You're staring again, Keira," Lucius said and I bit my lip and looked away, flapping my hands and saying,

"No, I wasn't! But...bloody hell, can you like...do that somewhere else?" I heard him chuckling and I looked back to finding him now staring down at me and I quickly re-covered my nakedness, making him laugh harder this time. Something that made his stomach muscles harden further and I hated how I just wanted to touch them to see if they were in fact as solid as they looked. Damn him!

"And why would I do that when I am enjoying myself right where I am?" he asked and I growled, making him chuckle.

"That's adorable you know," he told me and this time I grabbed a sponge, dunked it under the water and threw it at him. It splat on his stomach before doing the same as it dropped to the floor. He looked down to where it hit him and then back up at me with mischief clear in his steel coloured eyes.

"You wanna play, little girl?" he asked me with a bad ass grin that told me he wasn't bluffing. I bit my smiling lips and shook my head telling him no. His eyes homed in on my teeth torturing my bottom lip and he smirked before licking at one fang. I gulped at the sight and then heard to my horror the sound of the water escaping the bath. The bastard had pulled the plug!

"Wait! I haven't even washed yet!" He raised an eyebrow as if to say, was that the best I could come up with.

"I think you're clean enough for me, sweetheart," he teased, laughing when he saw my panic as the water level lowered to my stomach. I was already using my arms to hide my breasts but what was I going to use to hide my girly parts I had no clue. Oh yes, he was enjoying this.

But then his next move surprised me as he walked closer, all humour removed from his features. No, now he was giving me a softer look and Lucius once again surprised me. He bent closer to me and whispered,

"Worth it for that blush alone." Then he kissed my forehead gently before pulling back and whipping off his towel.

"Wh...what are... you...?" I stammered out before he laid his towel across the bath so that my naked body was now covered. Of course, this also left him completely naked and I swallowed hard at the sight. I quickly closed my eyes but it was no good, I had already imprinted that image in my memory bank, very large man package in all its glory.

"You can open your eyes now, it's safe," he told me and when I fell for it I was granted with a view of him from behind as he had walked towards the door. I made an over exaggerated groan and this time he laughed harder...oh yes, he was certainly enjoying himself.

"Just remember, you started it darlin'," he told me in a tone that was clearly amused and entertained as he walked through the door. I scoffed and shouted back,

"I threw a bloody sponge at you...I didn't start a sex war!" I heard the cocky bugger chuckling from inside the room. I shook my head, unable to remove the grin from my face. Damn him and his flirting making me smile this way I thought, cursing him as I got up out of the bath, holding his towel to my body. Oh hell, but it even smelled like him!

As soon as I was out I grabbed a new towel, one dry and didn't smell like a hunky, sexy Vampire that made me want to drool when naked. No, Keira, get that image out of your mind right now! I was still telling myself off as I stormed back into the room and I bumped straight into the man himself.

"You're dressed!" I blurted out and a grin played at the edges of his lips before he asked,

"Are you disappointed?" and what did I do...I bloody snorted. Snorted! Seriously did I have a single cool bone in my body!? His eyes widened which told me that unfortunately he hadn't missed it.

"Well, isn't that a delightful sound, tell me Keira, what animal was that again?" I growled pushing past him and he laughed once and said,

"Nope, that wasn't it, try again." I rolled my eyes and tightened my towel as I walked into the closet. There I grabbed the unfortunate lacy underwear, wondering what it was with this guy and lace!

Thankfully, I found a pair of jeans, a stretchy vest top in a burgundy colour and a big chunky woollen cardigan with a huge baggy hood that hung around the front as well as half way down the back. It was a deep navy colour and went well with the stonewash denim I was currently pulling up my legs after donning the underwear. I think finding these was on purpose as when I walked back out, Lucius was trying to hide a smirk behind his fingers.

"Thank you for the clothes." I told him making him nod and say,

"You're welcome, Pet." Holy Hell on a stick but was there anything this man said that didn't come out in some sexual purr? Christ but it felt like he was undressing me with his words and that wasn't even taking into account what he looked like right now.

Dark grey denim encased his long legs and a slim fitted, light grey sweater covered his torso and square shoulders. He had the sleeves pushed up showing his forearms, which seemed to be a habit of his. A black leather band was wrapped around one wrist, and I had to wonder where he had gotten his clothes from, as I was pretty sure there was nothing that belonged to a man back in the closet.

Well, at least he had lost the look of a mass murderer and now decided the Gucci model was a better choice of style. I thought that now was as good as time as any to approach the delicate subject I was planning on.

"You have something to say?" he asked first as if he knew I was struggling with the right way to start.

"It wasn't Pip's fault." The words tumbled out. He gave me a pointed look and I added,

"No, seriously. If anything, I was just glad she wasn't there."

"Why?" he asked surprised and I nearly choked as I swallowed. Was he serious?

"Because she would have been hurt! I couldn't have that, I would have never forgiven myself," I said pulling my cardigan closer together with a shiver just thinking about it. However, when Lucius burst out laughing I ended up frowning down at him angrily.

"Lucius!" I snapped his name and he finally told me why he found what I said so amusing.

"Trust me sweetheart, if my little faithful Imp had been there you would have seen far more carnage than that I created, of that I can assure you." He laughed again when my mouth dropped open. Was he being serious?!

"But…but she's so little and nice," I said making him chuckle once and shake his head like he was recalling a previous bloody memory.

"Well, as we both know, vicious tempers can come in the cutest of packages, now can't they?" he asked looking me up and down as if seeing for himself me fighting back. I didn't answer him but then I guess I didn't need to, as I knew my temper had both got me *in* and *out* of some tough places.

"If it helps ease your worried, little mind, then I will right your new friend's hurt," he said and then placed two fingers to his temple and looked to concentrate a moment. It took him ten second tops.

"What? That's it?" I said making him raise an eyebrow.

"What did you expect, sky writing and a singing gondola boy with a boat full of flowers…I know I am good sweetheart, but I'm not that good." I never got chance to answer as the next thing it was a 'Speaking of the Devil' moment. I was just about to sit down when suddenly the door burst open and I heard Lucius groan as if he knew what was coming. However, I only saw a flash of colour before Pip was flinging herself into me.

"OH, MY TOOTIE PIE! I am so, so, so, so, so, sorry, sorry, sorry, sorry!" she shouted making me lose track of the amount of 'so's and 'sorry's' she said. The next thing I saw was Adam quickly run to the door, skidding around the frame as if he had been chasing her. I saw his relief when finding her in my arms, legs wrapped around my waist and all.

"It's fine. Hey, come on now, don't cry, Pip," I told her as she started sobbing in my arms.

"I am a terrible friend! They hurt you and I wasn't there to kill them for you!" she said. I looked to Lucius to see him mouth the words 'told you' and bat out a hand in a typical 'told you so' gesture.

"Pip, no! You're an awesome friend! Don't be so hard on yourself, you weren't to know that some insane assholes with an obvious death wish were going to come and crash our party," I told her making her sniffle and rub at her nose almost using the full length of her arm.

"No, I didn't," she said shaking her head like a child.

"I mean come on! That would be like me knocking on Dracula's door with a slit vein and asking to use the phone to call an ambulance," I told her making her giggle and Lucius roll his eyes and muttered,

"Humans."

I then winked at her.

"But there is one thing," I added and she gave me a wide-eyed puppy dog look and I knew if I said the wrong thing right then, I would have crushed her big BBF heart. Thankfully though it was something as innocent as,

"You're kind of getting heavy." Lucius snorted a laugh and we both looked at each other.

"Oh, yeah, I forgot about your puny human arms...my bad."

"Hey!" I complained as she jumped down.

"Don't worry Toots, I still luv ya!" Then she jumped up and kissed my cheek. At this point, Lucius stood up and she took a cautious step back as if she half expected his wrath. He rolled his eyes again and approached her. Then he patted her on top of the head and said,

"All is forgiven, little squeak..." Then he leaned down and whispered in her ear,

"...you're still my favourite little Imp." The look on her face was priceless and as if expecting another outburst, he caught her as she jumped up and into

him sideways so that she was being held with an arm around the waist, half-cocked on the side of his hip.

"YEY!" She squealed and Lucius simply walked with her still attached to him towards Adam.

"I believe this belongs to you," Lucius said to Adam making him smile down at his now, once again, happy wife.

"I believe it does, my Lord," he replied softly taking her off his hands and walking out of the door with her clinging on to him like a monkey. Before he left he nodded to me and said,

"Keira." As a way of thanks. I gave him a smile back letting him know it was my pleasure.

Once again, it was just myself and Lucius. And when he nodded for me to follow him, I frowned before asking,

"Why, where are we going?" He didn't answer my question but instead said something in return that had me dreading where it could be…

"Like I said, Sweetheart…*you hit like a girl.*"

Book 3

23

Hitting like a Girl and Biting like a Kitten.

NEW...

After following Lucius like the obedient little 'Pet' he kept calling me, I soon found out exactly what he meant about me hitting like a girl.

"A training room? Seriously though, is there like a special supernatural realtor out there that finds you guys your homes?" I asked making him roll his eyes as we walked further into the massive room.

"Ah here's one you might be interested in Sir, we have a lovely hideaway castle with not only a spectacular view of the mountains but its situated inside your very own! And might I say, just the perfect deterrent for all those pesky battle sieges and Avon callers!" Lucius stopped to look at me as I continued with my joke, leaning back on one of the wooden beams, a grin twitching at the corners of his lips. He was about to speak but I held a hand up for him to stop and continued,

"But wait, there's more, because nothing screams castle without your very own Man Cave, complete with killer, death mud room and for those dirty, blood and mud covered, damsels in distress...too many bathrooms to count," I said trying not to laugh at my own humour but looking back at him with a wink.

"Oh, and look no further as here comes the deal breaker and a must have for every demonic king out there, you have your very own training room, complete with all manner of weaponry seen throughout the ages, ready and waiting for all your battling needs," I said putting on a posh voice, making Lucius chuckle and shake his head as if I was nuts.

"Thank you, thank you, I am here all week," I said taking an over exaggerated bow with one arm out straight to one side. Lucius started clapping and said,

"I think we just found your career choice pet, I know I was sold...but prey tell me..." he said pausing to push himself from the pillar and make his way over to me in seconds. He then pushed back the hair from one side of my neck so he could lean down and whisper,

"Do you come with the property?" I laughed nervously and tried to act like his sexual tone didn't affect me.

"Sorry but I suck at cleaning," I said before I could stop myself from setting up his next come back, which quickly followed,

"No matter, I could just *suck* the *cleaner* instead." I groaned making him laugh at me before he took my hand and led me further into the room.

It was a massive open space that had been cut into the mountain, but whereas the rest of his home showed smoothed walls, this didn't. There were massive jagged pieces of rock that jutted out all over the place and it gave it a demonically barbaric feel.

Like any minute, you half expected Hell's demons to break through the walls and join in the fight.

In fact, there was only one smooth wall in the whole room and that was situated at the far end. But it too was simply covered in a history of deadly weapons that extended all the way up the twenty-foot wall, reaching to the stalactite covered ceiling. Long dagger shaped rock formations hung down like boobytraps waiting to be triggered. It was, in itself, a terrifying room and not one I would ever like to find myself in without the man currently holding my hand.

I think the only normal thing in the room was that the floor looked modern and was made from thick woven mats that were obviously used for training. That and one section of the room held an array of bars and other metal structures for this devil only knew what. I mean crikey, I couldn't even remember the last time I stepped into a gym, so what did I know.

"So, what exactly am I doing in here, 'cause you know my idea of working out is...?"

"Yes, My Keira?" Lucius said cutting me off and his look said it all. I rolled my eyes first and said,

"Hiking or going for a walk...jeez, is sex all you think about?" I said after a groan, making him chuckle.

"And how do you know I was thinking about *sex?* Obviously, I am not the only one with that problem, now am I?" he stated cockily, purring the word and this time I growled at him.

"You're like a child, what's next, you gonna type 5318008 into a calculator?" I asked and the look he gave me was almost comical. It was clear he had no idea what I was talking about and I chuckled to myself.

"Sorry sweetheart, you lost me with that one," he told me and I laughed louder this time, telling him,

"Ask Pip, she will know what I am talking about," I informed him giggling again and hoping that I was around when he did.

"Or I could just *make* you tell me," he threatened making me almost choke on that giggle. I cleared my throat and said,

"Um...so, what are we doing here again?" Changing the subject and this time making him laugh.

"Isn't it obvious, I am going to train you how to fight," he stated walking over to a section of what looked like locker doors. I choked again and said firmly,

"Oh, I don't think so!" But Lucius wasn't listening. Instead he just threw me what looked like a karate suit all wrapped up and tied with its own belt.

"Uh...what's this?" I asked wondering, what the Hell I had got myself into this time.

"It's a Judogi, now put it on," he told me before turning back to the locker doors and tearing his sweater off over his head with both hands. I swallowed hard and looked down at the thick white material in my hands. Of course, the gulping continued when I looked back up to see Lucius pulling his pants down...of course he would have to catch me looking. I quickly turned around, giving him privacy and muttered a feeble,

"Oh...uh...shit, sorry." Yep, the bastard chuckled. Meanwhile I was still stood with my back to him, holding onto my bundle having no clue what to do next. Then I jumped letting out a yell as I felt his hands on my shoulders.

"Easy Darlin', I haven't even thrown you to the floor yet," he whispered seductively making me shiver and once again it became obvious, he was having way too much fun teasing me...at least I bloody hoped he was teasing me!

"What are you...you doing?" I asked nervously, having to clear my throat half way through speaking. He had started to remove my cardigan, pulling it slowly from my shoulders with his fingertips touching every inch of bare skin he could get at. This left me in just my burgundy stretchy vest top, that was far too low in the boobie department than I would have liked.

"More than you, *clearly,*" he told me in an amused tone and I looked down and to the side to see him casually toss aside the chunky wool. Okay, okay, get a grip Keira, this is the only bit he would need to take off...

"Hey!" I shouted, suddenly startled as his arms came around me from behind and with one swift move, he had the top button of my jeans open. But he ignored my mortified protest as he unzipped them. Then with a few fingers in my waist band either side of my hips, he bent down quickly taking my jeans with him, my nearly bare ass right in his face.

"What are you doing!" I shouted, dropping my fighting gear so that I could try and bring my jeans back up. I was just reaching for them when he snarled and nipped at my fingers stopping me for fear of getting bitten.

"Foot," he ordered, tapping at my heel. But when I didn't move quickly enough for him, he just grabbed my ankle and lifted it. I would have fallen over had he not had a firm hand on my now naked waist. He whipped off my shoes and then the denim from me. Soon I found myself stood in just lace briefs and a vest top. In fact, I was just waiting for the cocky look or smarmy comment and as predicted, I didn't have to wait long.

He stood back up and faced me. Oh, Holy Hell on a stick, could the man look any sexier! Seriously, Lucius dressed in every day casual wear was handsome, dressed smart in trousers and a waistcoat, was damn hot and now this…well this was taking that hotness to an unfair level. He now wore a Judogi, like the one he had given me only his was all black. It made his torso look even bigger and more powerful, with just the hint of pale strong rippling muscles underneath.

"Now you can get dressed or fight like that, the choice is yours, doll…I know which look I prefer," he added with a wink and I nearly scrambled along the floor to grab the Judogi. Of course, he laughed at me.

I don't think I could have got the trousers on any quicker, as I nearly toppled over getting them on. I pulled at the ties, trying to make them smaller wondering exactly how much weight I had lost since being here? What had I been eating, like once a day? Well one thing I was sure about and that was when Draven finally got his hands on me he wasn't going to be happy! I shuddered and decided to rid those thoughts from my mind as I'd already decided the things he wouldn't like to know were stacking up against me.

I grabbed the jacket off the floor and put it on, looking down at my sleeves and wondering where my hands went. Well, surely if I couldn't find my hands then this little exercise of his was pointless…right? I pulled my arms up enough so the material fell back up my arms and looked around the floor to see where the belt went.

Lucius cleared his throat before saying,

"Over here, sweetheart." I turned to see that he had the white belt in his hands, wrapped around each of his fists and as he pulled it tight between them, I visibly gulped.

"Come here," he ordered and with the look he was giving me I didn't know whether he wanted to put it on me or use it to tie me up. Damn those sexy thoughts! In the end, he gave me an 'I am waiting' look and I walked over to him with a roll of my eyes, faking the 'cool' attitude.

"Turn around," he told me and I did as I was told, not breaking tradition, I thought bitterly. Then letting one side of the belt unravel from his fist, he closed the distance between us.

Stepping into my back, he looked down at me over my shoulder so that he could see what he was doing. Actually, scrap that. He totally knew what he was doing, but I just think he used this as an excuse to get closer to me as I could feel his eyes on my face not my body. Was he trying to judge my reaction to him being this close to me?

In the end, I shut my eyes as he closed the jacket around me and I inhaled sharply when his knuckles brushed against my breast. I became like a statue, too afraid to move as he folded the other side over before wrapping the belt around me. Then he tied it once and knotted it, pulling hard at the ends making me yelp and my eyes snap open. I felt him smile at my neck before moving away and finally giving me the space I needed in order to breathe freely again.

"Now let me look at you," he said turning me around and I stumbled a step, tripping over myself. Thankfully, he still had hold of the top of my arms so I didn't just fall on my ass. Once he was sure I was steady, he took a few steps back. He raised his hand to his lips and tapped a single finger there as he looked me over. His eyes raked over me making me feel as though I was as naked as I felt underneath it all and I actually looked down at myself to check that it wasn't in fact, see-through.

"It's a little big," I said quietly, kicking out my feet trying to find them under the reams of white material.

"Umm..." he hummed and then stepped back into me, grabbing my arm.

"I think there is one in here, ah yes, here it is," he joked winking at me when he lifted my arm up to go in search of my hand inside the long sleeves. He yanked on my fingers playfully making me giggle and just as I thought he was going to fold up the cuffs, he grabbed them in his fists and tore them off in a long strip. He did the same with the other one, so that now they were the same length and my hands could be seen.

"Tada! And for my next trick..." he said before dropping to his knees so he could do the same down around my ankles. Then he rose back up with the grace of a jungle cat and said,

"That will do, little one." Then he tapped my nose twice. I was in awe at seeing him this way, so carefree yet with still that edge of commanding nature. He seemed...well, he seemed happy and this playful side of him I had to admit, was infectious.

"Now come over here and hit me," he told me and I shrugged my shoulders and said in my own cocky tone,

"Oh well, if you do insist." I walked over to face him, pulled my fist back and let it swing at him.

"Whoa!" He made a noise as he grabbed my swinging arm by the forearm and pushed me around into the motion, so that I had nowhere else to go, but round with it. I ended up with my back against his and him leaning down by my ear so that he could whisper,

"Little girl, surely, you can do better than that." I growled in response and pushed off him to turn and face him once more.

"Now again, only this time hit me here," he said holding up his palm, ready for my little fist. So, I pulled back and gave it all I had, punching his large hand. He didn't even flinch.

"Gods woman, have you any power in that arm?" I frowned at him and said,

"I don't know, wanna give me a hammer and we can find out when I am hitting you around the head with it!" His lips twitched as he tried not to smile at what I said and he gave me a look that just told me he found me more adorable than vicious.

"I think for now we will leave all blunt or pointed objects out of the mix...now take a better stance...like this, see," he instructed and I mimicked his legs.

"Now this time when you hit, step into it, bringing this leg forward," he said tapping on my leg.

"Okay, I can do that," I told him and when he nodded for me to go, I giggled making him frown.

"Keira." He said my name in exasperation but I laughed again and then tried to shake it off. I don't know why but situations where people expected me to do things always made me laugh.

"Okay, okay, right I will do it this time," I said jumping once like I was shaking off my humour. He rolled his eyes but I could see again he was fighting off a grin at my silly behaviour.

"Now remember, step into the punch and keep your arm straight," he told me before holding his hand out again for me to hit. So, I did as he said and stepped into my punch.

"No, that is no good. Again!" he snapped and this time I rolled my eyes and muttered,

"Sugar coat it for me why don't ya?" Then I did it again, this time trying harder than before.

"You need to stop twisting your hips as you punch, come at me square," he told me and I shook my head a little, looking down at myself.

"Square? I don't know..." I was just about to complain when he gripped my hips for himself and turned them to face him, then he placed a palm over my belly and pelvis. I sucked in a sharp breath at the feel of him and what his touch was doing to my insides, just beneath his hand. However, he ignored my reaction as he was obviously too busy in 'Trainer' mode.

"Square, like this. It gives you more power behind your punch so as not to get knocked down. Now hit me again and this time, remember your hips stay forward and square...don't twist into it," he told me sternly. I bit my lip and nodded seeing this serious side of him. So, I did what he asked and punched out, keeping my hips in the right place and stepping into it, trying for my hardest one yet.

"Good. Now again," he said nodding and I did it again like he asked.

"That's better," he told me and I couldn't help but smile up at him. I liked it when he praised me and I didn't know why.

"Now, here is the block," he said, nodding for me to hit at him, without his palm in the way this time. So, I did as he said and he rolled his arm out, moving my punch before it connected with his chest. The move was so quick that I actually fell forward into him and he caught me before I could face plant into his stomach.

"I will do it slower."

"Umm, yes, that might be wise," I told him making him look sheepish. So, I straightened myself back up and hit him again. This time he showed me in slow motion the way he rolled his arm, so that it not only blocked the hit, but it also rolled my arm out to the side.

"Okay, I think I got it," I told him forgetting the next part...him trying to hit me. The second he did I jumped back with my arms held up in a typical 'Don't shoot' fashion. His eyes widened in question.

"I freaked, sorry." I said and he raised a brow at me.

"Oh, come on, I am like 5'3" and 110lbs ringing wet and you are what 6"4 and over 200lbs?" I said making him smirk.

"And when you were slicing some guy with a knife and then smashing the other in the face with a glass teapot full of vodka...what was that exactly, because last I checked when I was dismembering them, they weren't hobbits, Keira," he told me folding his arms across his chest. I grimaced just thinking about it.

"You knew about that?" I asked wondering how he had taken notice of all that in the seconds before he had unleashed his own slice of revenge upon the gang. He slowly nodded and I released a sigh.

"Would you believe terror induced adrenaline rush?" I said and he gave me a soft look.

"I am not here to hurt you, only to help stop anyone else doing so," he told me gently and I knew he was right.

"Okay, let's try again."

"Good girl...ready?" I gave him a nod and he punched into me. At first, I just flinched and tried to knock his hand away but thankfully he kept his comments to himself and just gave me a look I now knew meant 'Again'. Now feeling ready for him, I did as he had shown me and tried to catch his arm by blocking it with a roll of my own arm. He shook his head and took hold of my fist and did the motion for himself. Then once he felt I understood, he hit out and this time, I finally got it.

"Good. Again," he said and when I did it better this time I gave him a massive grin, one he tried hard not to respond to…he failed, granting me a small smile in return.

"Okay so what next, Yoda?" I said making him laugh.

"Not my best compliment there, Keira."

"Okay, what's next 'Handsome Martial arts dude'…better for you Han Solo?" I asked him in a sarcastic tone making him smirk before he said,

"Hit me." So, I did as he had taught me and stepped into my punch. Then he blocked it, in that circular motion but then as my arm went off to the side, he caught it and pulled me forward. Then he swung me round, making me trip on his outstretched foot and just as I was about to land hard on my back, he grabbed a fist full of my jacket. That way he could then lower me slowly to the floor and he followed his actions by twisting his body so that his knee landed next to me. I was left panting looking up at him with wide eyes.

"You did that on purpose," I told him and he grinned down at me showing me a hint of fang. Then he lifted me up a little, still with a fist full of my jacket so that I was inches away from his face. At first, I was so close, I thought he was going to kiss me. But no, instead he ran his nose down the side of mine, breathed me in and then said in true Han Solo style,

"I know." Then he dropped me with a not so ladylike 'Humpf' sound. He walked away and told me,

"Get up and let's try it again." I grumbled to myself as I got back on my feet.

"You don't exactly play fair," I told him.

"I never said I did, Kitten," he responded and this time I decided to play him at his own game...well that was if I could actually achieve what I was planning.

"Oh, you wanna see a Kitten...I will show you a kitten, claws and all!" I said only his face said he wasn't taking me seriously, well that was until I started running at him.

"Keira...? What are you...? Humpf!" He made the same noise I made when I landed with all my body weight into his chest as I ran into him. I took him completely off guard, jumping at the last minute and locking my legs around his waist. Then I grabbed his neck and hoisted myself up, moving around to his back and basically climbing him like a damn cat.

"Keira!" he shouted my name and spun around trying to get at me but I just laughed. Then I grabbed him by the hair and yanked his head to the side. Once there I lunged into his neck with my mouth and bit him without breaking the skin. He froze in shock by my actions and I smiled around the flesh I held. After a few seconds, I let go but I couldn't help but whisper a cocky comment in his ear,

"See, even small kittens can bite." The deep rumbling sound coming up from his chest was my only warning of revenge. He reached up so fast my arm was in his grasp before I knew it. Then he yanked me forward, so I rolled over his shoulder as he moved to one of the locker doors. Suddenly I found myself pressed up with my back against it. My legs were firmly around his waist, just so I could hold on to something.

Then he snarled down at me before he grabbed a fist full of my hair, yanked me to the side and now it was *his* teeth I quickly found at *my* neck. He growled low with my flesh still captive in his fangs and I held so still, being too scared to move from fear of him piercing me with one of them.

We both seemed locked into the position and I could feel his chest beating against my own. His with the thrill of it, mine with the fear of it. Then after long moments he let go of my tender flesh and licked at it once, twice, three times as if soothing away any hurt he caused. After this he put his lips softly to my ear and issued both a promise and a warning for the future...

"Yes, little kitten, *but big cats bite harder.*"

AUTHOR'S INSIGHTS

Chapter 26
Book 3

Now it is time for our last few chapters from book 3 that didn't make it. This next chapter was written as an alternative reaction to Keira's utter devastation when seeing the footage of Draven and Aurora in Draven's bed together. Now we all know that this was just a ploy of Layla's to get Lucius to believe that the king no longer wanted Keira. But if she stupidly thought that this would end Lucius' own obsession with his 'Little Keira girl' then she was very much mistaken.

However, after Keira's refusal to believe it's true, she asks her favourite little Imp to take her back to face the man in question. Of course, she sees something she wasn't bargaining for and now believes it is true. I have added the previous chapter as a recap so that you can get a sense of why Keira is so utterly heartbroken. But if you wish to skip it, then as usual I labelled the NEW part for you.

So, in this next chapter it simply shows how deeply Lucius' feelings for Keira really are as he tries to deal with heartache the only way he knows how…found at the bottom of a liquor bottle.

So here it is…Lucius' tender side to Heartbreak.

Book 3

26
Heartbreak.

I woke the next morning after one of the most mind-boggling nights full of emotional rollercoasters, most of which I didn't want to think about. I had learnt so much in one night but none of it had done me any good, if anything I just felt even more vulnerable than I did before. I lay on my back and found myself just staring at the ceiling trying to make some sense of the last thing that had happened. The last name on my lips I whispered again and my heart started pounding like a jack hammer.

"Lucius!" Just the name made me bolt upright with the memory of last night's mistake. I realised I was still naked and couldn't help but groan as more images of the man flooded into every corner of my mind. It was as though I could still feel his hands on me, those confident fingers gripping the material of my dress and ripping it away from my skin. I felt my cheeks get hot and I started shaking my head in shame. I had pleasured myself to the thought of Lucius touching me and I didn't know what was worse, that I felt like I had somehow betrayed Draven or that Lucius had stood there the entire time and witnessed everything.

"Oh shit!" I groaned into the covers after pulling my knees up and cradling my fragile head with my hands.

"If I'm not mistaken, I would say that sounds like regret. That or your brain itches." I groaned louder before looking up to find Pip sat on the end of my bed. I hadn't even heard her come in let alone felt her sit down next to me.

"Let's put it this way, I wish it was my brain that was itching, then I could try and scratch away certain memories." I noted Pip's half smile and couldn't tell if it was one of understanding or tamed delight at my predicament.

"I take it things went well with Luc last night then?" When I groaned again and hid under the covers she laughed and said,

"Maybe not," and then pulled the covers off my face.

"Well there is some good news," she said ignoring my whiney moan.

"What's that?" I said with a muffled voice from my hands still covering my face.

"Venger the bitch is gone and is no more," she said winking at me and I smiled when I saw her crazy make-up that was painted over her eyelids. One was an open green eye painted like a Disney princess, impossibly wide and innocent looking. And the other, the one she had used to wink at me was another winking eye with exaggerated long lashes. Only Pip knew how to work craziness and get away with it, she still looked incredibly cute and pretty.

"Venger?" I asked not understanding who on earth she was talking about.

"Oh come on, please tell me you watched Dungeons & Dragons…you know, big bad pissed off guy, flies an even more pissed off looking black horse, one horn and wearing a very gay looking skirt, that if you ask me kinda spoils the whole bad ass dude thing but each to their own." I shook my head and thought it was too damn early and my head was too damn fragile to be deciphering Pip's wacky code.

"Please explain, Pip," I said no longer holding my head in my hands but now holding the bridge of my nose in my fingers, trying in vain to ease the pounding drum headache I had building.

"Layla!" She said the name causing my head to shoot round as I scanned the room for my arch nemesis, the murderous bitch Layla.

"Not here, man someone needs a vacation at rancho relaxo. I was referring to Layla as being the baddie from Dungeons & Dragons but you ruined that bit of genius for me, so moving swiftly on…Layla has been made to leave so ding dong…"

"The witch is dead!" I finished and she gave me a face splitting smile.

"Now you got it! I mean, she isn't dead but she might as well be, 'cause being cast out by Lucius pretty much means bad things for her from now on."

"What do you mean?" Pip leaned back on one out-stretched arm behind her back on the bed and looked at her nails before answering me, this time I think they were different retro sweets…was that a coke bottle she was picking at?

"I mean sister Toots, that Layla is a Vamp no longer to be." She said this like she was reciting some Shakespeare play and waved her hand in the air like Hamlet without the skull.

"She is a Vamp?" I said in shock.

"She is and soon to be a 'was'. You see dumpling, all Vamps are made by Lucius, he is like their father but he has the power to take back his gift if he chooses, which means all amplified gifts that he created get…well uncreated. All Vamps need to be around Lucius at some point each year to maintain a part of his essence, his mumbo juice if you like. But now she has been cast aside like a wet chamois when all a car needs is a good hot wax! She will soon find herself weak and that my dear is a fate worse than damnation to one of our kind." She gave me one last look when she finished and started licking her cola bottle which had white glitter to represent the bubbles. Her pierced tongue flashed out and she ran it between her teeth, displaying the pink metal ball.

Well, what she had told me certainly gave me food for thought. I now at least understood why she had looked so distraught last night and I couldn't help that the image made me smile. I mean, she did try and kill me and would no doubt try again given half the chance.

"Okay, so are you ready for flight on Pip 'o' Vision airways?" At this my head whipped up and Pip laughed at my enthusiasm.

"Now?" I said feeling both excited and wary at what I might find.

"Go shower and change Toots and I will wait for you, unless you want to be seen naked?" She nodded to the sheet barely covering my breasts and I flushed bright pink.

"Don't worry Toots, I told ya before, you don't have the right equipment to tempt me but if my tastes ever change from muscle to moobs then I might jump you."

"Oi, you saying my breasts look like flabby man breasts?" I said trying not to smile at her obvious teasing.

"Me? Never! You have lovely breasts that look nothing like a man's extra bits but if I ever fancy dressing Adam in drag then I would so go with the size of your beasties. Now go dress, you temptress you!" I got up and flicked her little nose after wrapping my body in the sheet. I could still hear her giggling when I walked into the bathroom.

After the quickest shower, I nearly fell out of the glass door to get ready quicker. I was still putting clothes on when my skin was damp and trying to get tight jeans on when water was still dripping down my hair to my legs was not the easiest task. I heard Pip call out when I slipped and managed to catch hold of the sink before falling hard on my butt.

"I'm fine!" I shouted before she came in here and found me tugging my waistband up with one hand and the other, half way sticking out of the arm of the sleeve of a soft light grey t-shirt. I looked like a failed contortionist getting dressed.

I pulled the top over my wet head and finished pulling up the jeans over the other side of my hip. I then pulled on a pair of full length leather gloves that went right up and over my elbows to my poor excuse for biceps. These were also soft and had finger holes so that half my fingers weren't covered in the black leather.

I added a chunky soft knit cardigan in cream with grey flecks that matched the t-shirt and stonewash jeans I was wearing. I brushed through the knots in my hair as best I could and tied it up without having the time to dry it fully. I couldn't find any socks so I walked back into the living space barefoot trying to ignore the cold under my feet.

"Wow, that was quick!" Pip commented as I sat down opposite her in the same chair I had been in the first time I had taken a transatlantic flight on Pip Airways and what a mind trip it had been.

"You ready, Toots?" I thought about her question and answered honestly.

"No, but go for it anyway," I said taking a deep breath. I knew this was what I needed to do to find the truth but that didn't mean I was sure of the outcome. I wanted to believe it was all lies but with the image of Draven up against Aurora in the same bed where we had first shared our bodies with each other was playing in my mind like a recurring nightmare.

Pip slapped her hands to the arm rests with her elbows sticking up in the air and heaved herself up. It was only now that I really took in today's outfit as I was so used to waking up to see a living rainbow sat on my bed it was becoming less of a shock.

She now wore a see-through hooped skirt that was covered in rows of fluffy pompoms in electric, luminous colours but I was happy to see that she at least tried to cover up her female goodies with a pair of black latex hot pants. This she topped off with a bright turquoise bustier with a pretty butterfly print that pushed up her little breasts. It also had some 3D wings that looked to be made from glass like you would find in a window catching the sun. This would have been quite a normal top for Pip to wear if not for the added four inch, wide ribbon in hot pink that was wound round her torso in random angles that slashed across her bare shoulders and arms only to finish hanging loosely on her wrists like large cuffs.

I was almost afraid to look down but found myself glad I did when I burst out laughing at the knee-high socks that were made to look like a wonder woman costume, complete with cape. This she added wonder woman converse shoes to match... which was something she rarely ever did.

"At least I'm wearing shoes," she said pouting.

"I'm laughing because I think they're great," I said honestly, never having the guts to wear them myself personally but still admiring the diversity in the design.

"Oh, well that's alright then...Right time to say bye, bye my pretty," she said in a witchy voice before jumping on my lap like last time.

"You know you could warn me before just launching yourself at me like that."

"Oh, Tootie cake, you're no fun. Good luck honey." She gave me what I could only assume was a gangster sign before slapping her hands to the side of my head and plunging me into a world six hours away.

I opened my eyes to find myself in the very familiar club Afterlife's VIP. It was dark, quiet and empty, something that only ever happened very early into the wee hours of the morning. I wondered why I would have ended up here with no one around but then I saw Sophia come storming into the room with Vincent hard on her heels. I don't know why but I decided to step further into the shadows near the bar to hear this out.

"Sophia, he will handle it, calm yourself." Vincent said in his usual soothing tone.

"I will not! Keira has been gone less than a week and this is the behaviour that is being tolerated! Why are you not as outraged as I, brother?" Sophia whipped round and folded her arms at Vincent in nothing short of an accusing manner. He just frowned and folded his own arms, making the sleeves on his long sleeved black t-shirt strain and tighten around his impressive biceps. The material moulded to his upper body as if it was trying to be another layer of skin, which showcased his fine physique beautifully. This was combined with black dress trousers and it had to be said, the man sure knew how to wear clothes that created a drool worthy effect! I shook my head to get myself back in the game and remembered why I was here and from the sounds of things it might not be the happy, optimistic answers that I had hoped for.

"Because when Dom tells me he will do something, then I have no other option than to place my trust in those words as should you."

"Bullshit! This goes deeper than Dom's word! I am surprised, as you of all people should be more outraged on Keira's behalf, considering how you feel." I couldn't believe it when Vincent actually growled.

"You go too far, Sophia! Back down and just leave it be or Dom will no doubt find out about your interference and as you know, my anger compared to his is quite different."

"As you know I am not afraid of our brother's temper and besides, don't you think he has more pressing matters on his hands than my personal feelings on what he is doing?" She really looked upset and it didn't sound like the reasons were going to fare well for me. Was it possible... was Draven with her right now? Was this what Sophia meant? I felt like praying to every God in the Heavens for it not to be true.

"Be careful, Sophia!" Vincent warned in a low gravelly voice that sounded threatening. Sophia looked like she was going to say more but in the end she lost all the heat of her argument and deflated into a nearby chair like a wilting flower. As usual, her appearance was flawless and her floor length dress floated around her where she sat. Surrounded in midnight coloured silk that made her hair look like it shimmered for the same reason, its softness hard matched, she looked like a queen goddess and it made me feel like praying to her instead.

"I miss her, Vincent," she said dejectedly making Vincent's scowl fade and my heart break. I wanted to pop up and shout 'I'm here' like a live jack-in-the-box but I didn't think they would like a supernatural heart attack!

Vincent walked to her chair and knelt down on one knee to get to her face level. He tilted her head up with a soft grip on her chin and wiped away a stray tear that rolled down her ivory skin.

"As do I Sophia, much more than anyone truly knows and much more than I ever should," he said and I couldn't help but shove my fist in my mouth to prevent the gasp that wanted to escape my tactless brain.

"If we feel like this, then Dom should be feeling it tenfold..." He nodded in agreement so she carried on.

"Then tell me why he is now in the room he shares with the girl he loves with one he never did?" This time I couldn't stop my reaction. Nothing could have stopped me.

I saw Vincent look up and take in the sight of me stood there, no longer in the shadows but now very visible, right down to my fisted hands and my body that was wracked with a disbelieving tremble. No, it couldn't be true...it just couldn't...could it?

"Keira?" Vincent said my name with the same disbelief my body was displaying and now Sophia had turned to witness it as well.

"Oh, my Heavens...Keira...it's you!" She got up and for a long moment we were all frozen like actors in a play who had all forgotten the next set of words that were meant to be heard by an invisible audience. Silence...just bitter, air slicing silence.

A silence so thick it would soon crack the skin stretched across my knuckles, my fingers were fisted to my palm that tight, until finally I could no longer stand it.

"Where is he?" I asked still shaking with a rage that I foolishly still hoped unnecessary.

"Keira, I don't think..." I cut Vincent off with an action I didn't even know I had done until I heard my fist bang down on the table top in front of me.

"DON'T!" The one word came out like the cracking of ice under a heavy foot, dangerous and fatal.

Vincent looked like he was debating whether to run to me and scoop me into his arms or not. In the end, I took that choice away from him by turning away from them both. I found the door that would give me the answers I needed to see and found myself running towards it before either one of them acted. I was actually surprised at how fast I was running. I knew they were making chase but I was faster...faster than I had ever been in my whole life. Was this because I wasn't really here and my soul was faster than my body or was it the side effects of being with Draven. Was this what it was like being supernatural?

I started to think it was, when I could hear his voice before I ever should. So, it wasn't just my speed then, it was also some other senses.

"I am not afraid of speaking my feelings Aurora, not when those feelings are of love."

"Oh, Draven." I heard Aurora say as if close to swooning.

"I am not finished my dear, as I said earlier, I do not regret our time together as it has brought us to this point but I refuse to hide the way I feel any longer. You must know of what I speak, I have presented you with enough evidence."

"The physical evidence that night was enough for me to understand your feelings, my Lord. I know what you want and I can only be happy in the knowledge that I can finally give you what you want, what you need...from me." I almost crumpled to the floor when hearing this, for I had found my answer. Layla hadn't been lying and I was the fool.

I felt myself start to waver back to my body as no doubt Pip could feel my distress but I had one last thing left to do and I had to summon all my courage to follow the truth through to the bitter, twisted end. I locked my legs and placed my fading hand on the door, ignoring the desperate pleas of my name being called by Vincent and Sophia.

The door opened and there in our sacred place was the most beautiful woman I had ever known in the arms of the most beautiful man I had ever known.

They were utterly perfect together. Two flawless beings entwined in an embrace so deep and meaningful my presence wasn't even known. I couldn't even penetrate their senses enough to become another heartbeat in the room.

A heart that at that moment had started to replace a beating muscle with cold hard stone that didn't even know what it meant to beat.

A heart that Draven had stolen in a meadow of beauty and destroyed in a grand room of ugly truth. A heart he no longer wanted and a heart...

I no longer needed.

Book 3

27
Vampire Date.

Pip released me and fell backwards when I screamed out in my grief. I didn't even look back as I ran into the bathroom and threw up an already empty stomach. The painful retching pulled at my stomach muscles in a pain I welcomed.

He didn't want me. Plain and simple. But how could something so plain and simple be so confusingly agonizing to comprehend. I knew I should have stuck with my instincts and trusted my insecurities the way I did around Draven but to witness the truth in my fears was too much to bear. I had wanted to be wrong! I had wanted my fears to be spun from not believing myself good enough and all those times that his arms held me so close to him had said otherwise. But it had all been lies.

And what hurt the most…I had foolishly let myself trust in the first man to take my heart and make it beat solely for him. No matter all the problems we had run into, the one thing we had was an unstoppable love that should had stood the test of all that Heaven or Hell threw at us but in the end…

It hadn't even stood the test of time. Not even a week.

My stomach clenched again and I spat out the remains of my disgust. I then felt a little hand at my back and without a second to hold it back I threw myself into Pip's arms and broke the dam on my heartbreak. I sobbed into her bare shoulder and she softly uttered words of ease in a different language. Gone was the energetic Pip that couldn't ever hold back the avalanche of words she usually used to describe things and in its place was a friend's comforting security. And I couldn't have needed it more.

After a time, when my eyes were too sore to even close let alone produce tears, I found myself sat outside on the balcony wrapped up in a soft woollen throw. I looked out to the white world and I found myself wanting to join it. To become lost in winter's nature, one so cold that it would steal my breath and with it, the excruciating pain. I just wanted to be numb.

Pip had left me alone as I had asked, although I could tell she hadn't wanted to but what could she do…send me back for more proof on how Draven didn't need me. Didn't…didn't want me. I swallowed that thought with a thick lump of cold hard reality. Hell, I wished I was one of those girls that could find the anger in it all. Find the guy and bitch slap the hell out of him for cheating on her but there was one solid reason why I couldn't find it…

I still loved him.

And it burned me to think that I loved him enough to want him to be happy and if I wasn't enough to give him that then…well…

Well then, here I was now. Alone and forgotten.

NEW…

I couldn't help but wonder what was next for me? Because no matter what love I still held for Draven, it didn't change the fact that I was still stuck in this place. I was here held captive by a man who needed me to bargain with but I couldn't help question just how much of that bargaining power he had left.

Would Draven simply try and get me back out of some royal duty or even worse…out of guilt? I had no answers to anything, only painfully empty questions like 'what do I do now?' or even worse, if I finally made it out of this alive, then 'what would I do when I made it back home?'

Home.

The single word even hurt, as I had once considered Afterlife to be my home but even that had been taken from me. I wanted to be angry at so many people. I wanted to lash out and blame those that had made this happen. Like Lucius. But to be honest, what had he done, other than open my eyes to an unfaithful love. No, there was only one person I was really angry with, and that was myself.

I should have known.

"I should have known," I said aloud this time before letting my head fall back on the seat feeling the tears rolling down my cold cheeks once again. In the end, I don't know how long I had been sat out there but it was after the sun went down when someone interrupted my private misery. I didn't even turn my head to see who it was, because truthfully, I just didn't care anymore.

But the person that entered my room *didn't care* for my winter misery and simply plucked me out of my seat. He lifted me into his arms and carried me back inside, making the door slam shut. I didn't even flinch with the noise or when flames erupted from the fireplace.

"Gods Keira, you're freezing," Lucius said after placing me down on the sofa and running the back of his fingers down my cold cheek. I said the only thing I felt about his statement in that moment, shocking him.

"Fuck the Gods!"

"I very much doubt you mean that, Pet," he told me softly and this just pissed me off. I didn't need someone being so nice to me now! So, I got up and pushed past him, nearly tripping but righting myself just in time.

"And what if I do! It's not as if the assholes ever did anything for me!" I shouted looking up as if I could see them for myself. I raised my arms out to my sides, the throw still around me like a cloak and I shouted,

"CAN YOU HEAR ME YOU BASTARDS!" I shouted with even greater rage this time.

"So, this was your plan all along was it!? To torture my young soul into seeing living nightmares and for what? For what exactly?! So that I would know the insane reasons behind a mad man I had to slit my wrists to get away from?" I saw Lucius flinch as I lowered my head and looked to him. His grip on the arm of the chair was all but destroying it. But I didn't care. I was too far gone in my rage, my pain, my...*my loss*.

"I died that night you know. I saw it all happening before me and I made my peace in life just as I hit the stone-cold floor. I looked down at my blood and I knew I would die in that shit hole...that prison and for what? I hadn't even lived...*I hadn't even loved yet.*" I told him, saying the words of my past I had never uttered this way to another living soul.

"And now the Gods were getting ready to take me away unless I fought for it. So, I did and look where it got me. They threw me to the wolves and I gave my heart and soul to one. And do you know what he did with it...he stepped all over it the moment he took *her* to his bed."

Lucius moved and looked ready to contain me but I stepped back, holding my hand out to him.

"Oh no! I don't need your comfort or your pity!" I told him making him think twice.

"I tell you this now because I have hit my limit on life Lucius, and I have hit my limit on all this Supernatural, Chosen One bullshit! I am done, do you hear me...*done!* So, do with me what you wish Lucius, because I no longer give a fuck! Sell me to the highest bidder for all I care but I am telling you now, there is no way that ...that *man* is going to give you shit for me...do you understand what I am telling you! He won! And we...well...we..."

"What Keira, what are we?" he asked me once my outburst had started to die. I deflated into the seat behind me and answered him,

"...We are just the losers, Lucius."

Lucius took a deep breath and slapped his hands to his thighs before getting up. Then he looked down at me and said the last thing I ever expected.

"You have five minutes." I frowned as I wiped away my tears.

"Five minutes for what?" I asked shaking my head a little.

"To get your shoes on and your shit together."

"Why...where are we going?" If I lived to be a hundred and guessed each day of my life I still wouldn't have guessed right.

"I'm taking you out."

"Out? As in outside?" I questioned further and just before he walked out the door, he turned back to me and said,

"Yes Keira, outside..." And then he left me with the biggest bombshell of all when he finished that sentence before leaving the room,

"*...on a date.*"

I soon found myself in the last place I ever thought I would on this cold winter's evening. Sat on a bar stool in a German pub, with a roaring fire behind us, on a date with the very man who kidnapped me...oh and not forgetting that he was a Vampire King. No, we couldn't forget that. Although I had to say, looking the way he did, he didn't exactly scream the Dracula type. Not unless the King of Darkness liked to wear stonewash jeans, long sleeved dark grey t shirt and a fitted leather jacket on his days off. Oh, and let's not forget the heavy biker boots.

"Zwei Biere, Krombacher dunkel für mich und ein Hefeweizen für die Dame." (Means 'Two beers, Krombacher dark' for me and a Hefeweizen for the lady'). Lucius ordered our drinks in perfectly fluent German and the sexy bastard even made that sound erotic. The lady at the bar, who wasn't dressed like a Bavarian barmaid as I expected, nodded kindly and went to pour our drinks. After of course, giving Lucius the once over and obviously liking what she saw.

"Okay so as much as I am glad to be out of your demonic mountain home...no offence..." I added making him give me a sideways smirk.

"...What are we really doing here?" I asked as everyone was out of earshot. Lucius looked at me and knew what I was doing so said,

"You're fine sweetheart, no one here can speak English."

"Oh...okay, well good but that still doesn't answer my question." I said as the barmaid came back with two pints...two very *large* pints I might add.

"I told you, we are on a date...so, cheers," Lucius said clinking his glass to mine before taking his first swig. Damn he even made drinking look hot. Well I guess there were worse places to be I thought looking around the quaint, old fashioned pub that was mainly all decorated with carved wood panelling and exposed, old brick walls.

"So, in other words, you thought it better to get me shit faced drunk rather than let me wallow in my own self-pity...is that it?" I asked making him nod.

"Yep, in a nut shell," he agreed.

"Oh, well in that case, good plan...cheers," I said clinking my glass to his and taking my first sip. Of course, when I did it I had to use two hands like a child, not like giant man hands over there, I thought frowning. He made it look as if he had spent half his life as a Viking and had been born holding a massive tankard the size of a bucket!

But then I had my first sip and wow. Now I wasn't much of a beer drinker but this stuff was, well, it was the bomb! Germans certainly knew how to brew the good stuff.

"So, what are you going to do now?" I asked Lucius, shifting in my stool to face him. Lucius continued to look head on at the mirror behind the row of bottles and glasses.

"About what?" he asked taking another swig.

"About what? About all this cold weather we've been having...what do you mean 'About what?' about me, about Draven, about the whole bloody reason I am in this mess to begin with." I said sarcastically. He gave me a sideways glance and said,

"Nothing has changed." I snorted at this, yes actually snorted and I didn't give a damn if he did look amused or raised a questioning brow at me.

"Oh, I think you will find that it has and in a big way."

"How so?" he asked and I wanted to ask in an outraged voice, was he serious?

"Well you get that Draven cheated on me." I told him wondering why he hadn't asked me about it considering it was only last night that I was denying that the footage I had seen was even real.

"I may not be the 'in touch with my feelings' type of guy, Pet, but I am not blind. I'm observant enough to know that your meltdown wasn't about your hair, hissy fit over some shoes you want or the fact you're getting your period," Lucius said making my mouth drop. Yes, actually drop open.

"Seriously, how have you ever managed to have a girlfriend and *not* have her kill you in your sleep?" I asked making him smirk again.

"Some girls are all about the body and what a man can do with it," he replied smoothly making me put my finger in my mouth and pretend to gag. Thankfully it made him laugh.

"Yes, and some girls are just bat shit crazy, knife wielding lunatics named Layla." I reminded him. He clinked his glass to mine and agreed,

"Touché, Kitten."

"Well, now even she can't have him so maybe she will finally stop trying to kill me, so silver lining there I guess." I said this time taking a big drink and trying to drown my sorrows in the light amber liquid. Finally, this was when Lucius turned to me.

"What do you mean, can't have him?" he asked making me frown.

"You know, Draven... tall, dark and handsome dude that also happens to be a two-timing bastard that likes to shout a lot...that Draven. Unless you know of another enemy of yours that just so happens to..." this is where he cut me off.

"Layla isn't in love with Dom," he said confusing me.

"But if not him then...oh." That's when it finally hit me and I felt like a freakin' idiot!

"She's in love with you," I said making him groan and he grabbed his drink, this time taking bigger gulps.

"That's why she hates me so much. it all makes sense now. You send her away to play the spy on a girl that she knows you will kidnap. So, she gets jealous and tries to kill me before you even get the chance," I said and this time he snapped dryly,

"Yes, thank you for the recap, little Miss Sherlock." I couldn't help but laugh and when he shot me a look, I placed my hand on his arm and told him,

"It wasn't one of your brightest ideas, now was it?" He growled low at me but I didn't care and I didn't take it seriously because I just started laughing again before picking up my drink.

"Well, I am glad to see you enjoying yourself at my expense," he muttered making me giggle before making a witty comeback.

"Well if I had a penny to my name I would buy you a drink to say thanks but nope, you kinda kidnapped me without my purse, so it's all on you tonight, matey." I joked and this time I could see the twitching of a grin that wanted to appear at the corners of his perfect lips.

"We'll call it an I.O.U...and have no doubts Pet, I will be collecting," he said leaning into me and placing a hand on the top of my thigh. Then he laughed when he felt me tense under his hold and gave me a squeeze there before letting my leg go. After this we sat in a comfortable silence for long minutes, which surprisingly, was broken first by Lucius.

"What you said back there, about making your peace before you died...was that true, did you make your peace with God?" At first, I was taken back by Lucius' abrupt question but in the end, I knew this was Lucius we were talking about. He wasn't exactly the 'beat around the bush' type of guy.

So, I thought back to that horrific time in my life, looking down into my beer as if the amber liquid held all the answers. Then I picked it up, took a long drink before putting it down again and turning to Lucius to give him my answer.

"Yeah, I did. My last thoughts were of the love I had for my family and I smiled knowing now they were safe, that..." I paused for a breath as my voice wavered but I carried on and I didn't know why.

"...that I could go in peace." When I finished, Lucius nodded his head once as if he had decided something. Then he too, took a long drink and simply...

Confessed.

"I looked everywhere for you," he said looking straight ahead into the mirrored wall as if the memory of himself was playing out behind it. But my own reaction to this was mirrored back at me showing me the sight of utter shock.

"Ever since you were found that day, I had been able to feel your presence in the world...*that was until you were taken,*" he told me as if it pained him to remember.

"You never saw me yourself?" I asked bewildered by the fact.

"No," he said simply and then he finally turned to look at me.

"I wouldn't allow myself. I had you watched from afar and I would receive regular updates on your life but I never intervened. It wasn't my place," he told me making me frown. I was about to speak my mind when his next statement stopped me.

"That was until I found out you were gone. Missing my men said. The fools! You were never missing, *you had been stolen, Keira.*" I swallowed hard as the memory of the day I was taken assaulted me. But what surprised me was not my own pain upon thinking it, it was the pain Lucius was also displaying in remembering it.

"It was the only time I got involved myself and by the time I had discovered the truth of who could be behind it, well by then you had been discovered too," he said taking another long swig of his drink as though he needed it to wash away the memory.

"It was the first time I ever saw you…in person that is."

"What?" I uttered this in a secret whisper, one he heard.

"When I heard that you had been found I had to see. I had to see for myself what he had done to you." Hearing this brought tears to my eyes. I wondered what would have happened had I see him. This handsome stranger watching over me, trying to protect me?

"You were having a nightmare at the time."

"I was?" I asked thinking back to my silent time in the hospital and apart from screaming bloody murder the second I got past those emergency doors, after that…I didn't speak again for days.

"You looked so lost, even in sleep. So, I placed my hand on your cheek, cooled your heated skin and entered your mind to ease your suffering," he told me and before I could stop my actions my hand shot out and covered his on the table.

"I remember," I whispered, seeing the nightmare so clearly now in my mind's eye. I had been locked down back in the dungeon. I was crying,

screaming in fact to get out but no one heard me…no one ever heard me. But then I felt a cooling hand touch my body. Even dreaming I knew it meant I was safe. I leant into his palm and the next thing I knew the walls cracked all around me and finally I could see the sun. It blinded me at first, after being without it for so long. Then it all burst around me, as if an explosion had destroyed the walls, pulling them outwards in a mighty blast of power I couldn't see.

"You carried me out of there." I said making him nod as he knew what he had done to ease my suffering as he put it.

"But why? I don't understand Lucius, why would you care? Your plan was always to kidnap me and at first to scare me and…" He raised a hand to stop me and then turned on his stool to face me. His face looked so stern and it didn't match his caring actions as he raised a hand to my cheek, just like he had done that night. He took a deep breath and said,

"I cannot explain it all now sweetheart, for there is much you still don't know and it is not my place to tell you but…" He frowned for a second so I prompted the rest from him.

"But?"

"But, you have to know that everything I did, I did so under my belief in the Fates, after all, we all have our part to play in them but no part is as important, as that of yours."

"And these fates…they planned on breaking my heart, they planned for me to fall in love with a man and then shadow that love in bitterness… in deceit, in…*unfaithfulness?* Tell me Lucius, for I am just dying to know…what the hell have they got planned for me next, because I will tell ya, I don't know how much more I can take!" I told him getting emotional and swiping angrily at my tears.

"I wish I knew sweetheart...*I wish I knew,*" he said before wiping away the rest of my tears then pulling me into him and kissing the top of my head as he held me to him. I cried out my pain, my agony, forgetting everything. Who he was, where we were and most of all who I was supposed to love and who I was expected to hate. It simply faded away and nothing but the hurt I felt mattered. There were no lines drawn in the sand for me to step over. There was nothing left for me to run towards. There was only the arms that held me now, arms that had kept me safe a lot longer than I ever realised.

I raised my head up once all my tears were spent and saw that the room was full of people but no one moved. Startled I moved back from his chest and Lucius chuckled at my reaction.

"I didn't think you would want everyone to witness your..."

"Meltdown?" I said finishing that statement for him. He cocked his head a bit and said,

"Emotional outburst. But now, I think it's time for another drink..." Then he clicked his fingers and every still person came back to life all at once. I jumped and couldn't help but marvel at the sight of so much power. It made me wonder, had it been like that the night he first saw me. Had his powerful presence stilled the world in the emergency ward and he had simply walked through the living statues and into my room with purpose.

I could almost see it now for myself. This powerful being there to check how broke and lost a human monster like Morgan had left me. His face, what would it have been like? Would he have looked upon me with his soft, grey eyes in the caring way I knew he could or the blood-filled rage that made him want to rip a man limb from limb? If I had opened my eyes right then which side of Lucius would I have seen first?

"Does it hurt?" Lucius' question pulled me from my thoughts.

"What?

"Having a head that full of questions?" he teased making me laugh and just like that, the tension fled me.

"Come on little doll, let's have another drink," he said before calling the waitress over and ordering something more dangerous this time.

He held up two fingers he said only one word,

"Jägermeister."

BOOK 3

28
Dirty Dancing.

The rest of night went as follows. I drank far too much beer, that looked more like glass buckets in my hands, and then consumed too many Jägermeister shots to count. But we laughed, we were loud and we were happy as we sat and acted like old friends that hadn't seen each other in years.

Lucius was a pretty funny guy and even though I knew the alcohol wasn't affecting him like it did me, he was still the most relaxed I had seen him yet. Was this what it would have been like being with him. Shedding the burden of what he was or more importantly *who* he was in his world? Because like this, it was hard to picture him as anything else, even if I had witnessed the Vampire King first-hand.

Oh yeah, lines were getting blurry alright, right along with my vision. Which brought us to now and the reason Lucius was carrying me back to my room after a car ride I had obviously fallen asleep during.

"I am fine!" I said overly loud and then realised my mistake, correcting it...not like it mattered now.

"Ssshh, I mean I am fine," I whispered making him laugh.

"Why are you whispering?" he asked mimicking me.

"Because I don't want to wake anyone up…jeez, loud feet much, don't you know how to tip toe?" I asked making him laugh harder this time.

"Well firstly, I don't tip toe…*ever*," he said making me giggle and then he added a very good point,

"And considering we are Vampires and sleep in the day, I doubt we will be waking anyone up and besides, who are they going to complain to…their volatile, bad tempered king?"

"HA! So you admit it, you *are* grouchy!" I teased making him groan,

"Grouchy? Really, what am I, a damn cartoon character?" I giggled this time making him roll his eyes at me but the grin he couldn't hide kind of ruined his whole 'Bad ass' persona.

We soon came to my door and he was just about to make it open without touching it when I slapped him on his chest in little motions.

"Wait! Before you do it, I always wanted to do something…" He gave me a questioning look and nodded, obviously curious as to what on earth the little human was up to this time.

"Okay, OPEN SESAME!" I shouted in an over dramatic way that made Lucius groan aloud,

"By the God's, woman." But I wasn't listening, no instead I was holding my hands out towards the door and waving my fingers as if I could do magic. Of course, when he didn't open the door quick enough I had to give him a nudge.

"Come on, you big brute, don't leave me hanging." I told him speaking out of the corner of my mouth, like you do when you didn't want the audience to see.

"Now that would be a shame, wouldn't it?" he commented dryly as he made the door swing open and I laughed once, clapped and said,

"Tada!" as he walked us both into the room. Then he placed me down on my feet, holding me steady as I swayed a little.

"I'm good, stop fussing!" I told him slapping his hands away playfully.

"Drink!" I shouted and then ran over to the little kitchenette. Then I reached up into the top cupboard, stretching up on tiptoe and trying to find the bottle I knew was in there. Lucius sighed once and muttered something in another language, only I was sure the last word was in English.

"Zu ficken cute." (Means 'Too fucking cute' in German.)

"What did you...oh?" I turned to say but found him stepping up behind me. He dwarfed me in size and easily reached over my head and grabbed the bottle I was struggling to retrieve.

"Oh goodie." I said but then he leaned down closer to my ear and said,

"Coffee for you my little drunkard...this bottle is for me." I made a whiney complaining noise, one he chuckled at.

"You know I hate coffee! And why is there no tea in this place, I am addicted to tea you know and I've been having withdrawal symptoms all week!" I complained following him into the sitting area, where he now carried a bottle and only one glass.

"Is that so?" he asked smirking. I nodded and he replied teasing me,

"I don't know how you have survived such torture, I really don't."

"It was touch and go there for a while," I told him playing along, making him grin.

"If you wanted tea sweetheart, then you only needed to ask," he said, pulling his jacket off and taking his phone from the pocket before throwing it to one of the single chairs. Then with a single tap he placed his phone to his ear.

"Hat Liessa Tee getrunken?" He said speaking German once more and I had no clue. (Means 'Does Liessa drink tea?) After this I switched off as I couldn't follow what he was saying. A minute later and he hung up.

"Dating line?" I asked teasing him again and biting my lip whilst doing it. He poured himself a drink, held it to his lips and said

"No, I have help on speed dial for all those pesky little human captive needs, they are also bringing a ball gag and chains," he replied then downed the drink, making me laugh.

"Yeah, good luck with that one!" I said before plonking myself down on the seat opposite. Then I looked around trying to find something, making Lucius mutter,

*"I dread to think...*but what, pray may I ask, are you looking for?" he said slipping into a far-gone era.

"You know that makes you sound old as dirt, right?"

"Well I am as old as dirt, as you so eloquently put it, so answer the question before I get any older," he said trying to sound stern but I knew he was just being sarcastic and besides, it was funny so I just giggled before getting up.

"Don't you have a stereo or something in here?"

"Oh, dear god Lucifer, please don't tell me you want to sing?" he said rubbing the top of his nose as if he was getting a migraine.

"Ha, ha, that would be a no...but I do want to dance." I said walking around the room and pressing on the walls.

"What in the God's name are you doing now, little girl?" he said in utter astonishment.

"Well I know you rich, old, gadgetry types, you keep things hidden, like some Bond villain or something," I said patting higher up this time. Well you never knew, I mean these guys were much taller than me.

"Will you please stop calling me 'old'." He asked coming up behind me, making me jump and taking hold of my wrists to pull my arms down.

"And will you stop feeling up my walls like some crazy woman," he added making me snort.

"Me crazy? This coming from the man who lives in a mountain and has a sex club in his living room…jeez what did you do, take a class at the Hugh Hefner convention?" This made him laugh and the motion of it made me jiggle. Then he raised a hand above me and pressed a hidden compartment, which housed a panel for the stereo.

"HA! See, I knew it! I knew it, you big, fibber you!" I told him turning around to face him and poking him in the stomach. Needless to say, it was like poking a rock. He looked down at me and what I was doing as if I was the first person in history ever to do so. A smirk emerged and a fang extended. Did he even know that had happened?

"Well you know us rich, gadgetry types, we can't be trusted," he teased making me laugh and push him back a bit so that I could extend my arms and crack my knuckles.

"Give me some room big boy, I am gonna work my DJ genius." This made him laugh and shake his head at me.

"So, what do we have here…umm…oh…"

"Problem already my little DJ genius?" he asked popping his head next to me and looking at what I was doing.

"Alright, so I am stumped, bloody Nora but don't you guys just have anything normal around this place!?"

"Not that I know much about this unfortunate 'Bloody Nora' of which you speak, but I believe if you press this button here...ah, yes, well would you look at that, a CD player," he said as a tray came from the box. He was making fun of me and I rolled my eyes even if he was being funny when he did it.

"And CD's?"

"I don't know, is there not one in there?" he asked, waving his hand around as he retook his seat, not sounding like he cared. I tried to see what was written on it and in the end the writing was too small so I gave up and pressed the button to get it to go back in. Then I found the play button and pressed it.

"Oh, my God!" I uttered totally shocked, putting my hands to cover my open mouth as I looked accusingly towards Lucius. His eyes widened in a comical way and he said affronted,

"What, it's not mine!"

"It totally is...this is yours!" I told him making him grunt once and say,

"Then you *are* crazy, doll!" he told me sternly making me laugh as the first song continued to play.

"I don't even know what this shit is!" he argued making me laugh so hard, I had tears in my eyes. Of course, I knew this album, Christ, every girl that ever had a crush on the delicious Patrick Swayze's epic dance moves knew *this album.*

"It's not shit! Its Dirty Dancing!" I told him crossing my arms over my chest and stomping my foot. He raised an interested eyebrow and said,

"Oh really? Well okay then, you may continue to dance *dirty* for me," he said leaning back and putting his hands behind his head, making his muscles bulge in a 'tongue hanging down past my chin' kind of way.

Thankfully though I had a little sense left so as not to do this and look like a dog in heat.

"Yeah right, in your dreams!" I said thinking that if he actually saw it, the only boner my sexy dancing would raise up was his funny bone!

"Frequently." He hummed the word making me blush. So, I quickly turned around to try and hide it but his damn chuckle told me that was too late. So instead I busied myself and pressed the forward button trying to find the song I liked called 'Overload'.

"Oh, I love this bit," I told him and he commented dryly,

"I am afraid to ask."

"It's the bit in the movie when he locked his keys in the car and has to smash the window." I told him making him roll his eyes.

"Is that all it takes, a bit of destructive force to get a girl all hot and ..."

"Don't say it!" I said holding a hand out to stop him.

"Now don't be rude, I will have you know that Patrick Swayze has Sex God status in this movie."

"Why, because he breaks a fucking window?" he asked crossing his arms across his chest, as if he was affronted I could think this way about another man. So, I turned around and pressed it to another song, then I slowly walked over to him.

"No, *because he can dance,"* I told him softly and I took his hand and pulled him up. I was surprised at seeing him look suddenly vulnerable as he rose to his feet. It was the slow dancing song 'Hungry Eyes', which was precisely what I was giving him now.

I decided to place his hand at my side and the other I entwined my fingers with. Then I looked up at him with those pleading wide eyes and told him softly,

"Now it's my turn to lead." Then I stepped into him and started to sway our bodies gently from side to side. I felt the slight rumbling from being so close to his chest but he didn't say anything. He simply held me closer and allowed me to move us as one.

It wasn't like his version of dancing, leading me around a dance floor to some classical piece. But what it was, was two people sharing an intimate moment and listening to a song that was about how much you wanted someone. So, as the song was just coming to an end, I looked up at him to see that it couldn't have been more fitting...as he too gave me his *hungry eyes*.

"*Keira.*" He whispered my name like it was plea and as he was just lowering his lips to mine another song saved us, making me mutter,

"*No one puts baby in the corner.*" Lucius stopped, opened his eyes and said,

"What did you say?" Then I pulled back and shouted,

"This is my favourite one! Come on..." I pulled him further into the room and started to dance again.

"This is the bit at the end that proves he loves her. He comes back and tells her dad 'that no one puts baby in the corner' and then he takes her hand and they do this amazing dance routine he taught her." I told him making him laugh,

"Seriously?" he asked me and I nodded as we danced.

"Keira, this sounds like a terrible movie." I laughed once and then smacked his arm.

"It is not! Oh its nearly at the bit where he does the famous 'lift'." I told him like it was a secret and he mocked me by pretending to be interested, saying,

"Oh, the lift...well that makes all the difference."

"Alright fine, shut up and I will show you." I told him grabbing his hand and pulling this massive man behind me as though he was my willing man slave. I giggled at the idea.

"Right, you stand there and get ready." I told him positioning him in front of the bed, just in case he needed a soft landing.

"Get ready for what exactly?" he asked raising an eyebrow.

"I am going to jump on you and you're going to lift me up, ready?"

"Keira, I hardly think this is...Humpf!" He didn't have much of a chance to back out as the part in the music started and I ran at him, launching myself up in the air last minute. I caught him off guard and he might have caught me, yes, but thankfully we both had a bed to fall back on.

I burst out laughing in a fit of giggles and placed my head on his chest as I let it all come out of me. He held me there with his hands still holding my waist from where he had no choice but to catch me. Then just as the next song came on, 'She's like the wind' sang by the Sex God himself, everything suddenly turned serious.

I lifted my head up and looked down at him, still panting and trying to catch my breath. Then he pushed all my hair back from my face and whispered,

"Breath-taking." I blushed at such a compliment and I knew that with the way he was looking at me right now, I needed to move.

But I couldn't.

I didn't want to. I didn't want to think about all of the reasons why this was a bad idea. I only wanted to think about the one reason I didn't want to move.

"Lucius." And that reason left me on a breath just before I placed my lips to his and kissed him so softly. It was as though he knew in that moment to

let me have my way with him before taking over. So, I moved back a hairsbreadth away and whispered,

"Thank you." Then just as we were about to join our lips once more there was a knock at the door. For long moments, neither of us moved as we seemed to be locked in each other's eyes.

"I have your tea, my Lord." I heard a voice say behind the door and it sounded like Liessa. Lucius groaned and then shifted me gently to the side as I was still lay on top of him. Then he looked down at me and kissed my nose, before saying,

"Don't go anywhere, Sweetheart." I nodded with a breathy sigh, one he smiled at hearing. Then I closed my eyes and began to replay the night's events, all starting with Lucius. I felt myself give in to my dreams and soon with every ounce of energy zapped from me. I quickly fell asleep. The last thing my foggy mind heard was voices by the door,

"I don't think you will be needing the tea, my Lord." I heard Lucius groan and thank her before closing the door. Then I felt myself being lifted and tucked into the bed. The back of his fingertips caressing down my cheek before he placed a whisper soft kiss there before uttering his goodbye, the last words of the night…

"Good night, my little dirty dancer."

AUTHOR'S INSIGHTS.

To be Continued…

Well there we have it lovely people, I hope you enjoyed reading these chapters as much as I enjoyed writing them back in the day.
Of course, there are many more from other books in the saga, that include not only our usual suspects like Draven, Vincent and Lucius but also our other loveable rogues, like Sigurd, Jared and even Seth.

So, keep an eye out for part 2 of
Afterlife's Forbidden Chapters.

My thanks once again to all your wonderful fans out there that made all of this possible!

I class you not just as fans of the saga but as always, treasured friends of my heart.

My devoted love is yours always.
Stephanie x

Keep updated with all Afterlife News...

Check out my ALL NEW website for everything Afterlife Saga at... www.afterlifesaga.com
(Including exciting Official Afterlife Merchandise!)

And for keeping updated on all Afterlife related news and upcoming events, please join my mailing list on the website to receive regular Newsletters.

Or you can follow me on Afterlife saga on
Twitter: @afterlifesaga
Facebook: Afterlife saga page

Also, please feel free to join myself and other Dravenites on any of the groups below...

The Official private fan groups (Afterlife's Crave the Drave & Afterlife Saga Official Fan page) on Facebook to interact with me and other fans. Can't wait to see you there!

Or feel free to email me with any questions or comments you may have about the Afterlife saga at stephaniehudson@afterlifesaga.com

Printed in Great Britain
by Amazon